Their destinies were entwined by passion, greed, and

A PROMISE OF GOLD

THE ACTRESS

As tough underneath as she was soft on the outside, Harriet Gray fast-talked her way onto Jake Dexter's ship, double-talked his crew into joining the rush to California, and sweet-talked her way into the captain's arms—before she knew that was where she wanted to be.

THE CAPTAIN

Spurned by a young wife who left him for another, Jahaziel Dexter turned to the sea. Now all he wanted from his rough-and-tumble life was to stay alive long enough to strike it rich . . . or so he thought, until he met an enticing waif with spun-gold hair and a restless heart.

THE ROTTER

Like a phantom dogging Harriet's trail, Frank Sefton is polished, charming—and utterly ruthless. Once, he had abandoned Harriet on the far-flung shores of New Zealand. Now he was back in her life—full of schemes to steal what was rightfully hers.

A
PROMISE
of
GOLD

JOAN DRUETT

BANTAM BOOKS
NEW YORK • TORONTO • LONDON • SYDNEY • AUCKLAND

A PROMISE OF GOLD

A Bantam Book / November 1990

ISBN 0-553-28197-6

Published simultaneously in the United States and Canada

Bantam Books are published by Bantam Books, a division of Bantam Doubleday Dell Publishing Group, Inc. Its trademark, consisting of the words "Bantam Books" and the portrayal of a rooster, is Registered in U.S. Patent and Trademark Office and in other countries. Marca Registrada. Bantam Books, 666 Fifth Avenue, New York, New York 10103.

PRINTED IN THE UNITED STATES OF AMERICA

OPM   0 9 8 7 6 5 4 3 2 1

1 ❧ It was the quiet hour after dog-watch. The ebbing tide muttered about the coppered hull of the brig *Hakluyt* as she bobbed at the end of her chain. Captain Dexter stood in the waist of his almost deserted brig, gazing contemplatively about. A dark arm and fist of land projected from the island which lay before him, and curled about the brig in her tranquil anchorage. It enfolded, too, the whaleship that lay a half mile away. Dexter tilted back the brim of his hat, taking in the afternoon breeze. The sharpness of salt mingled with the smell of dry dirt from the island. The weather was calm, but not for much longer, he mused. It would change soon, in the next forty hours if not in the next fourteen. It was high time to give up on the island and devise other means of gaining a fortune, just time enough to transship one hundred barrels of oil. Dexter turned slightly and stared at the whaleship again.

The whaler had come cruising by the head of the bay in the late afternoon, a sturdy bluff-bowed vessel with stout sticks

1

and slung boats and short sails. She was low in the water, full
to the bunghole with oil, judging by the way she moved. Oil
fetched 225 cents per gallon in the Valparaíso market, and the
captain of the whaleship would be lucky to get 90 cents for the
same in New Bedford. The holds of the brig were more than
half-empty, and Dexter had traded, and that most profitably, in
oil before. It had taken but a moment's deliberation to send up
a signal, and dispatch his first officer to start negotiations when
the whaleship cooperatively lay aback.

The first officer's boat had been gone two hours. Dexter felt
a twinge of conscience: He really should have gone himself.
The trouble, he mused, was that he was a deal too lazy. He'd
wanted to avoid the society of a doubtless crusty New Bedford
captain, and for more than the usual reasons: he could imagine
the questioning all too well. The spouter master must be feeling
uncommon curiosity, to know what the brig was a-doing in
such an unlikely corner of the world; he must be wondering
greatly what attractions the barren little island held. Dexter had
not felt in the slightest like providing plausible answers; his
first mate Charlie Martin was a sociable soul and could make
up answers just as well as Dexter could himself. Dexter
shrugged then, pushing slight misgivings away, turned and,
whistling, strode below to the cabin.

The main cabin of the brig was empty, the mess table bare.
The brig was quiet, nearly deserted; six of the men were
camping on shore. Dexter skirted the table and poked his head
into the little pantry room. It, too, was empty, and quite clean,
as scrubbed and neat as any farmhouse kitchen. It smelled like
home too: the steward had left a pot of beans simmering over
a spirit lamp. No doubt they were intended for Mr. Martin, but
Charlie was gone a long time. Dexter whistled as he filled a
plate, and then he carried the plate to his place at the head of
the table. He sat down in his armchair and began to eat with
relish. He ate with his hat on.

The hat, like his armchair, was made of worn and comfortable leather and suited Dexter to perfection. The hat was a very
old friend, and Dexter liked to wear it with eloquence, to match
the mood that he felt. Now, as he heard familiar boots
clumping on the companionway stairs, he tipped it back in a
gesture of optimistic inquiry.

The door opened to reveal the round and flushed face of
Dexter's first mate. Mr. Martin looked animated. He had
recently cultivated a huge lot of curly adolescent beard, which

he tugged when excited. Now he looked set to haul it out by the roots. Dexter quenched a grin and said, "Well?"

"First-rate fun," said Charlie, and guffawed. "They suspicioned we was pirates, when they fust raised us."

"They did?" Dexter was very amused. It took a shrewd New Bedford mariner, he thought, to recognize the dangerous privateer lines of his brig.

"They had old muskets, a-ready to shove in our chests if we made the wrong noise, and the old cook informed us in a quavery voice that he had two kittles o' water a-b'ilin' on the galley stove and we would be exceedin' surprised if we tried bad business. They was all so reassured to find us innocent sailor lads that the reception were extreme 'ospitable."

The brig chose that moment to roll a little at her anchors. Charlie stumbled in time to it and had some little bother regaining his balance, Dexter observed. Now that he knew about it he could smell Charlie's aura of brandy. He said solemnly, "The cook treated you to hospitality?"

"No, no, sir—the cap'n! Cap'n Smith, whaleship *Humpback*, forty days out of Auckland, New Zealand, last port of call Capricorn Island, after recruits, left there this mornin'. A bald-headed old customer, he, a short old man, nobbut half as long again as the seaboots he wore." Charlie was beaming, lost in what seemed to Dexter to be unstoppable intoxicated eloquence. "Mrs. Smith were there, 'ospitable too, twice as wide, twice as tall, three times as forebodin', but a first-rate brandy, and generous at that—"

"And he agreed to the bargain?" Dexter interrupted as he watched another complacent and jovial hauling of beard.

"That he did, sir, that he did."

"And at our price?"

"Yep."

"Jehovah," said Dexter, delighted. "You have done well."

"Thank you, sir." Then to Dexter's surprise, Charlie Martin lost a deal of his smug red look. He looked about him and lowered his voice, saying in an almost mutter, "He's agreed to the sale of one hundred barrels, sir, and that of spermaceti, his best . . . but he asked a favor in return."

"A favor?" Dexter echoed, puzzled, then the companionway door opened, and a young female came into the room.

She was tall, blond, and had careful blue eyes. She looked about, sighted Dexter, and said, "Oh, I am so pleased to meet you, sir!"

Dexter, confounded, rose slowly and heavily to his feet. Even with his easy height, this girl was merely three or four inches shorter than he; she was formidable too, for a voluminous drab cloak did little to hide a most unfortunate figure. But still she did not seem like some prim and proper New England whaling wife, for her face was so remarkably lovely. This girl had golden hair in abundance, thick and disordered, most disgracefully, and her face was pale, fine-skinned, never weathered, so fine-boned that her cheeks seemed hollowed with hunger. She was also extremely young to be married. Dexter said blankly, "Mrs. Smith?"

"Mrs. Smith?" The wide eyes blinked, and then the girl grimaced. "My God, never," she said. "I'm a passenger in the whaleship, sir. My name is Miss Harriet Gray!"

Then she paused, smiling expectantly, almost as if she assumed he would know her name. He did not: all he felt was puzzlement and rapidly growing misgiving. He shot a hard glance at Charlie, and the first mate shuffled and looked more abashed than ever. Dexter said sharply, "And the reason for this call, Miss Gray?"

"Oh, I've come to beg you to carry me to Valparaíso, Captain Dexter! And I'm persuaded—indeed, certain!—that once you hear me out you will conclude to do the favor." She smiled brilliantly, while Dexter sucked in a breath of disbelief and fury, and said in the most confiding tone possible, "I bought passage in the *Humpback* in Auckland, New Zealand, and I paid Captain Smith more than the market rate for a voyage to Valparaíso, more than I could really afford, Captain Dexter, but my errand in Valparaíso is so urgent I had little choice. It's absolutely essential that I get there by the end of June, and I relied absolutely on Captain Smith's assurances. But now I find he has changed his mind! He doesn't want to stop at that port at all. He provisioned his ship at Capricorn Island yesterday, and now he's off to Cape Horn. Sir, this has placed me in a most terrible predicament, and when your first officer came on board with your offer for some oil, well, Captain Smith decided then that this was a capital chance to get quit of his bargain to take me to Chile: he declared that you could do it instead. He's coming soon in his boat to speak with you, but I was soon convinced to come on ahead with Mr. Martin so I could lend my persuasions before Captain Smith arrived."

Dexter snapped, "So this is the favor." Miss Gray opened

her mouth but he ignored her, swinging round and transferring his glare to his wincing first mate, and said icily, "And what did you say, sir, that gave Captain Smith the impression that I would be party to such an arrangement?"

Charlie shuffled and went red, but the girl forestalled him, saying quickly, "Oh, please, if Captain Smith won't give you any money for my passage I will certainly pay you myself; you won't be out-of-pocket in the slightest, and I shan't be any trouble, that I do promise. I'm never seasick, and—and if you decide you don't want to put into Valparaíso after all, then any other port on that coast would do, just as long as I can get to Valparaíso by the end of the month, and—and I wouldn't ask, I truly would not, but Mrs. Smith assured me that you have a faultless reputation, that you are respected far and wide as a most obliging man, and . . . and . . ."

Dexter shouted, "Whatever my reputation, madam, I do not run a packet; I do not carry passengers, and Mr. Martin should have told you that!"

She cried, "Oh, please do not blame Mr. Martin! Captain Smith and his wife overruled everything he said; they were most insistent that you would listen with sympathy to my request."

Charlie was more beet-red than ever, the look on his face one of bashful adoration. Never had Dexter seen calf love writ so plain. He took one infuriated glance at the shuffling young man and shouted, "I don't buy oil when a condition is strung to the sale, Miss Gray; in fact I don't make bargains with strings attached at all! And I most particularly don't make bargains with shifty Yankee merchants who think to use me as a means to get quit of their obligations!"

Faultless reputation, he thought angrily, *respected as an obliging man*. He wondered if this intrusive waif thought him the most easily gammoned and flattered of fools, and his own breathing was heavy in his ears. He bit down on rage and turned to Charlie Martin and snapped, "Oblige me, sir, by returning Miss Gray to the whaleship."

"But sir—"

"And please inform Captain Smith that I no longer wish to buy any of his oil."

"But Captain Dexter!"

This cry was from the girl. He ignored the desperation in her voice, saying curtly, "Mr. Martin, please do it." There was a tap on the door. Dexter shouted, "What is it?" and swung round again, fully expecting to see the presumptuous and shifty whaleship captain himself. However, instead of a short, bald spouter master, Bill the steerage boy of the brig stepped in.

The boy had a knowing smirk, and Dexter glared at him repressively. He'd taken on the twelve-year-old nigh on two years before; the urchin was the misbegotten product of a Yankee beachcomber and a nameless, toothless Pacific island woman, both of whom had deserted him. An aging missionary couple had tried to bring the boy up decent and had then begged Dexter to rid them of the thankless burden. He'd done the favor, had been kind and obliging, had even taught the boy his ropes and his tables, and now he shouted, "Well, what is it?"

Bill's smirk became more sly than ever. "Nobbut this," said he, and pointed, directing Dexter's glare to what lay by his grubby bare feet.

Those feet and the bare ankles above them protruded from patched dungarees that had grown of a sudden far too short, and by those feet rested two light wicker baskets, the kind of baskets that were commonly used for carrying champagne. Dexter said impatiently, "Well?"

"These be the lady's duds, sir," said Bill, who had the sauce to leer. "A boat from the whaler come and left 'em, put 'em in my care, sir, and I dunno wot ter do wiv 'em."

Dexter said blankly, "I beg your pardon?" But before the boy could answer, Miss Gray's voice said in the most agitated of tones, "Oh, dear God, surely they haven't gammoned me again?" Then, while he was still trying to comprehend this, she pushed frantically past him and made a lunge up the stairs.

He swerved and followed her up the steep narrow space. Her feet and ankles flew ahead of him, and some detached part of his mind admired them, neatly shod in slippers, neatly hosed in white cotton stockings, slim and elegant and surely wasted on that clumsy form. Then, with a rush, he joined her on deck. She dashed for the starboard rail and then leaned far outward, so unsteadily far that his hands went out of their own accord to hold her.

She cried, "Oh, goddammit!" His hands dropped. For an instant he felt shocked, for he'd never heard a young, pretty girl speak thus before.

Then his stare shot over the starlit sea, to where the whaler had been lying so still, and he shouted, "What the hell?" For the whaleship was no longer there. Where he'd expected to see a whaleboat returning to a ship still laid aback, there was naught but secret rippling. Then he saw the vessel, a good two miles off, sails filling for the horizon with every evidence of haste. He couldn't believe it, that the *Humpback* should have got so far in so short a time, but then he heard Charlie say furiously, "I'll kill him."

"What?"

Dexter's word was blank, and Charlie said again, "I'll slaughter that boy, I swear I will; they dropped those baskets and told him to keep shut about it until they were safely off, I'm certain."

Dexter was certain he was right but made no comment. He was shaking with fury that he'd been made such a blatant fool. Six of his men were on the island; it was perfectly impossible to make sail and weigh anchor and sail in pursuit. Guilt nudged him. He should have gone to the *Humpback* himself, he thought; he was partly to blame for this predicament because of his laziness. The guilt merely made him angrier. Then, as he watched, Miss Harriet Gray moved, dropping inboard again. She turned and looked up at him and said very calmly, "Well, Captain, it seems that you have no choice; you have a passenger, like it or not."

"Is that so?" said he with savage irony. Then, with bitter flamboyance, he swept off his hat, took her slender hand, bowed mockingly low, and kissed it. He felt it tremble, but she did not snatch it away. He let go then, straightened, propped his finto on his belt, and waited.

His stare was forbidding, but Miss Harriet Gray did not seem intimidated. In fact, for an instant Dexter could have sworn he saw her lips twitch. The fine dark blue eyes seemed to dance, most definitely . . . and in that moment he was in grave danger of finding her interesting. He almost began to wonder who she was, and why he should have known her name, what she had been a-doing in New Zealand, and why she needed so urgently to get to the Chilean coast, but it was the effect of the starlight, was all, that and the silver of the moon. She moved a little so that her face was in shadow again, and the moment of danger was over.

She said, "I'm as sorry about this as you are, Captain. Captain Smith and his wife made fools of the both of us."

Fools. He didn't like the word; it made him angrier than ever. He didn't need reminding that a shifty old mariner had gammoned him, that he now had this haughty young minx in his care. Dexter contemplated the implications sourly; at best her presence would distract his men from their luckless business on the island. He snapped, "You should never have consented to accompany Mr. Martin to the brig."

"But the Smiths assured me that it was safe: surely they did not deceive me about that, as well? And after all, Captain, 'tis for only a week, just the few days passage to Valparaíso."

He shouted, "It will be less than that, Miss Gray! Why should I steer for that port, eh? For where is the oil that made the bulk of the bargain? Captain Smith has sailed away with that, as you can see for yourself. And as for you, madam, you'll be put on the first vessel I speak, be it barge, scow, or guano carrier, for I refuse to be made a fool of for long!"

She cried, "You can't do that!"

"And why not, pray?"

"I can't board a vessel where the master might be a notorious rogue!"

Dexter took a deep breath, bereft of words at that moment, and the wry humor of the situation almost seized him, he almost laughed at himself. Not a notorious rogue? How little Miss Harriet Gray knew, he thought in that unguarded instant, and she must have seen it in his face, or perhaps it was the moon again. Her eyes seemed to dance. Fury filled him anew and he shouted, "And when you concluded—for some unguessable reason—that I am not a rogue, madam, did it not occur to you that it was most unwise, that it was imprudent and indecent, to come unaccompanied as a single, unescorted female on my ship?"

She said blankly, "I beg your pardon?" Then, to his complete exasperation, she laughed. The laugh was mocking, her tone, when she spoke, teasing. "Oh, don't be such a prig, Captain Dexter," said she. "Of course I knew there was no impropriety."

"You did? And what, pray, gave you that strange notion?"

"Well, I believed—then, and that most surely, that Captain Smith was following close on my heels. After all, I knew that it had to be he who negotiated the deal. How was I to know that he was set on gammoning the both of us? Even then I thought him honest. I assure you that I had to be persuaded to accompany your first officer, and only consented when Mrs. Smith reassured me about your married state."

"My *what*?"

"She declared that you are well known to be in the habit of carrying your wife, Captain."

He stared, thunderstruck first, and then incredulous that she should be so taken in. He said flatly, "My God," and set himself in motion, heading impatiently for the companionway door. He heard the busy rustle of her skirts as she pursued him, and Charlie Martin's shouts as he pursued Bill the boy about the decks forward. He ignored both, but Miss Gray caught him up on the stairs and stopped him with a hand on his arm.

The stairway was almost dark, the space narrow and warm. She said, pausing to catch her breath, "Captain Dexter, what do you mean?"

"That you were gammoned yet again, madam."

"What!" He turned, pulling his arm out of her grip, and she hurried after him. The light, when he opened the cabin door, fell fully on the pallor of her face.

The shadows accentuated the hungry hollows in the smooth cheeks. She really was beautiful, he thought reluctantly, and thought again that such looks—and the ankles—were wasted on the clumsy form. She met his hard stare unwaveringly, and said in a low voice, "Mrs. Smith told me much of you, Captain Benjamin Dexter, much that was reassuring. Was it not true?"

"Benjamin?" he said, and laughed without humor. "And who, pray, is Benjamin Dexter? I've never heard of him, or any Dexter who carries a wife. I doubt if such a man exists."

For an instant he thought she might faint. She whispered, "Oh, dear God," and put a finger distractedly to her lips. As he watched she nibbled the tip of it in a nervous gesture . . . and for the first time he felt sorry for her, as if he truly were the gallant and kindly man the Smiths had described. She said, almost wildly, "Then who the devil are you?"

The involuntary pity made him angrier than ever. "I am Jahaziel Dexter, madam," he said curtly, and he sat down as if the whole irritating episode were over, and devoted himself to eating his beans.

Let Charlie Martin deal with it, he thought, but Charlie was still on deck, hunting down the little devil Bill. Bill, however, was out of sight and out of reach, perched like an imp on the spanker gaff, sitting still.

Finally Mr. Martin gave up and, muttering, trudged below, and Bill, at last, moved. He took a silver Chilean dollar out of his pocket, looked at it, and kissed it—such easy earnings!—

and spat on it and rubbed it. Then, smirking slyly to himself,
he hid it in his clothes.

The red-faced and furious first mate gave Harriet his room
for the night. It seemed to give Captain Dexter a nasty kind
of satisfaction to bid Mr. Martin to be thus hospitable. So
Harriet, most furiously, mused; she would stop there until the
brig spoke . . . what? barge, scow, or guano carrier, she
remembered, and looked at Captain Dexter's obstinately turned
back with more angry resentment than ever. How rude, how
uncouth . . . and those beans smelled so delicious. Her
stomach grumbled wistfully, and she clapped her hand over her
waist to hide the shameful sound. She had had no supper, and
dinner on the whaleship had been the usual pea soup with
weevils. Those beans, those beans . . . and she could smell
the brandy Mr. Martin had drunk as well, that liquor supplied
so plentifully by the usually parsimonious Smiths. It had all
been part of the plot to gull her, Harriet brooded.

Captain Dexter did not seem to comprehend that she had
been gulled as well as he. Jahaziel. It was one of those quaint
New England names that Englishmen found so amusing. She
wondered what his friends called him but was certain at that
moment that he did not have any. Then the perspiring Mr.
Martin backed out with his things and headed off God knew
where for the night, and Harriet, mercifully, was left alone to
gather what shreds of dignity she had left.

And, furthermore, to dress—or, more accurately—to un-
dress.

The voluminous cloak came off first. She folded it neatly
and laid it on the end of the bunk. Under the cloak she wore
three shawls. She took all three off and put them with the cloak:
there was nowhere else to put her things, for while there was
a little table at the head of the berth, it was taken up already
with a tall blue logbook and pens and many papers.

She picked up the book and opened it without the slightest
qualm. "Comes in fine weather," she read, and "Light winds
from the north." It was the brig's logbook, she knew then, and
doubtless very boring, but she read on, fascinated, wanting to
find out just what kind of life that *Jahaziel* Dexter led.

While she read she kept on undressing. She was wearing
three skirts, so she took two of them off, and then she began to
discard petticoats. It was a childhood habit, this wearing of

most of her wardrobe; it had made hurried departures from various lodging places a deal easier. The fact that she'd worn so much on this call to the brig showed, she mused, how little she had trusted the Smiths. Captain Smith and lady, such nasty, unreliable people. She remembered how she'd scrimped and suffered to save the price of passage . . . and she'd been reduced to asking for the charity of a miserly American skipper.

She read the logbook to take her mind off righteous anger. As she removed excess garments she read exotic names like Feegee, and the names of marvelous cargoes, too: beche-de-mer, pearl-shell, and lacquer. Then she was down to one waist, one skirt, one petticoat, shift and drawers, and she sat down to brush her hair.

Two hours later her reading stopped; she'd read the last entry. It was for the eighth of June, ten days before. The creaking quiet of the brig surrounded her. The night was warm, but Harriet was filled with a formless sense of unease. She folded her arms tightly, rubbing at the gooseflesh on her forearms. The logbook, there was something wrong with the logbook, that logbook that covered more than two years.

Then, abruptly, she realized: at no time in the account had the brig returned home. She wondered if that was unusual and stood up abruptly. The hems of her skirt brushed the floor, and the rustle seemed very loud.

Mr. Martin had mentioned a washroom at the head of the stairs. She picked up a towel and opened the door. She peered cautiously around the empty cabin, inhabited only by the homelike smell of baked beans.

Strange, she thought, and tried to shake off a dreamlike sense of delusion, for the air in the cabin was so domestic. The brig did not feel like a ship. The whaleship had been a vessel unmistakably, with all the damp and stink and discomfort that the word implied; Harriet had never lost consciousness of the fact that on the *Humpback* there had been but a few planks between her and a watery eternity. What, she wondered, made the difference? It was the domesticity, she thought then, and yet there was no sign of a woman's touch. Jahaziel Dexter did not carry his wife. She thought, *Oh God*, and moved abruptly to the companionway door.

The stairs were dark. She bumped her bare arm against the wall as she cautiously ascended. Then, when she opened the door at the top, she was momentarily unsighted. She was on the after deck, and the helm was lit by a binnacle lamp. There was a man at the wheel: a stubbled face leered suggestively out of the shadows. She had never seen him before. And why was he there, when the brig was at anchor? He did not look surprised to see her but pouted whiskery lips in a travesty of a kiss. She quickly backed away to the door that Mr. Martin had described. To her fervent relief the handle gave, and she stepped into the room and shut the door.

The washroom was tiny, indeed, and was lit by a single, small lamp. Bulky sacks used up half the limited space, and there was an overwhelming smell of onions, but the room and fixings were clean. She washed quickly, with nervous speed, and then braced herself to open the door.

Again she was unsighted; she stumbled and fell against a hard warm frame. She thought it was the helmsman and gasped and jerked away and almost fell. Then large hands steadied her and held her firm. She stilled, utterly bewildered: surely there were two men here in this space? Then she felt the long hands shift and felt rather than heard the man's swift intake of breath.

She could feel his surprise, and she froze, abruptly too scared to speak. Her chest felt tight, as if her heart had stopped; it was almost impossible to breathe. Then, all at once, the hands shifted upward on her body. The grip was tight, the fingers almost meeting at her waist, and then spreading over her ribcage until they halted at the beginning swell of her breasts. A slow heavy pulse of time, and if she moved . . . if she moved . . .

The binnacle lamp swung as the brig rocked softly, and the light fell across the intent frown of the man who held her. It was Jahaziel Dexter. She saw him blink, slowly, and then he blinked again and grinned. It was as if he had been asleep and had just woken up. He grinned and said, "Take care, Miss Gray."

She thought, *Yes*, but said nothing; her throat was too tight. Then she felt the intimate grip slacken and become casual. Dexter almost—but not quite—let her go. Another heartbeat of stillness, and then one hand left her, as Jahaziel Dexter reached for the handle of the companionway door.

He said, "Good night," and even bowed a little, sardonically, as he held the door open for her. She kept her silence but nodded as she passed onto the stairs. To her fervent relief he did not come down with her.

But it took a long time to fall asleep.

2 ◈ Harriet was wakened by busy sounds on the decks above her head. She lay still, feeling groggy, wondering where she was, beset with a sense of formless misgiving, listening to footsteps and the bumping of heavy things. Then came the sounds of the lowering of a boat, and a splash, and she remembered what had happened. She heard the sploshing sounds of oars nearby, and she wriggled round to peer through the little sidelight that illuminated the side of her bed.

A boat bobbed into view, a "half boat," made by cutting a whaleboat in half and patching on a blunt transom to make a kind of dinghy. She recognized Mr. Martin's hunched back as he sat working the tiller. There were two oarsmen who stared, and she became uneasily aware that her face must seem disembodied, floating in the porthole like a goldfish in a tank. One of the oarsmen was a crab-faced fellow she hadn't seen before; his expression was sniffish, drawn long with patent contempt. The other was the oaf who had been at the wheel the

night before, the one who had pouted his mouth so lewdly.
Now his leer was more restrained, no doubt because the first
mate could see him, but the suggestiveness of his look was
perfectly plain. Harriet's misgivings became near despair, and
she hurriedly withdrew and dressed.

She wondered how many men lived on the brig, and what
they were saying about her presence on the ship, and she
wondered, most intensely, how she would manage. It had been
bad enough in New Zealand, but this could be worse than the
worst she could imagine . . . and all because Captain Dexter
had chosen to act so ungallantly. He'd accused her of imprudent, indecent behavior, she thought angrily; he would rid
himself of her improper presence first chance. She brushed her
hair with furious energy—and a rooster crowed, a rooster!

Then she heard the clucking of hens. Did Captain Dexter
have eggs? and pigs? She heard them grunting, unmistakeably.
Did the brig have bacon? Her stomach rumbled in unladylike
fashion, and she thought of those succulent beans that Captain
Dexter had so callously eaten, and she wondered if he would be
rude enough, too, to deny her breakfast. She was horridly sure
that he would, but then she smelled coffee. Coffee! Before she
could finish brushing her hair, her feet carried her pellmell into
the cabin.

Too late she realized that the cabin already had occupants.
She halted, staring at them, nervously aware that a quiet babble
of talking had stopped abruptly when she'd opened the door,
and they all stared just as raptly. Two were by the table; the rest
were all in an attentive bunch, clustered in the doorway of what
she recognized as the steerage, the part of the ship where the
cook and steward and carpenter lived. One old man was
frowning at her: it was plain what he thought of a woman on
board of this ship. Another was a bucolic boy who gaped as if
she were an exhibit of a sideshow. That was bad enough, she
thought; even worse were the meaningful leers on many of the
young faces. Even Bill the cabin boy had the sauce to wink. A
South American man batted his lashes and pouted. Harriet
wanted to shut her eyes at the very least, or dash back into the
safety of her room, but she couldn't do that. So she smiled with
perfect brilliant poise, and cried, "Good morning!"

No one answered. They all gaped. It was awful. The two
boys at the table stared as blankly as the rest, but not a single
one of them looked shy. One of the boys in the cabin had a mop
of lint-white curls, while the other had long black ringlets.

Neither of these boys was more than nineteen, she was prepared to swear it, but no, they were most certainly not bashful.

So Harriet stood still, meeting the battery of stares with that bright false smile; she was afraid even to blink, lest they all think her intimidated. Then she was saved by the sudden opening of the pantry door. A tall thin man came out and looked around. "Do I hear no politeness?" he demanded. "None of our far-famed courtesy?"

And the faces in the steerage doorway disappeared like magic with a click as the door shut, and the boys in the cabin stood awkward, their grins at last becoming diffident. They rolled their eyes at each other, and the newcomer said, "Ma'am, I am much obliged."

And so was she, thought Harriet, as she gazed up at him with interest. He beamed down at her. He had luxuriant, gray sheeplike whiskers but was mostly bald on top, so that his face seemed upsidedown. He sniffed and said, "We on the brig *Hakluyt* are generally known for our hospitality and manners, but these boys, I fear, Miss Gray, have let us down."

Harriet smiled and nodded, still grateful despite some growing impatience that they all knew her name, but she knew none of theirs. Then the old man started, crying, "Introductions! This, Miss Gray, is Valentine Fish, second mate, and this—" indicating the tow-headed lad who blushed "he Crotchet."

Crotchet? "I'm a Massachusetts lad," quoth Valentine, "and Crotchet hails from ol' Virginny."

"And I," said the third man testily, "if I may make so bold as to introduce myself, am Bodfish. Steward," he said. Harriet, bemused, could think of nothing to say: Bodfish and Fish, Fish, Bodfish and Crotchet. It sounded like a musical turn, she thought semihysterically. She found herself shaking a long bony palm, and then the steward said, "Coffee?"

"Oh, yes," said Harriet fervently. She wondered where Captain Dexter might be, and hoped he would not turn up until she'd safely breakfasted. "Oh, please."

"Then please be seated." A rag appeared like magic in the bony hand and was swept over a bench. Harriet sat down, and Mr. Fish and Mr. Crotchet sat on the bench opposite. Mr. Fish winked; Harriet ignored him. It was much more pleasant to watch a battered coffeepot, produced as dexterously as the rag and then tipped lavishly over enormous mugs.

The aroma was ambrosial. "You may be surprised," said Mr. Bodfish indulgently, "to find a steward in such a person as myself. And why not, for I'm a deal amazed too! I shipped in Lahaina in December," he said. "As a foremast hand, imagine that!" Harriet found it hard, indeed, to picture, and Mr. Fish let out a muffled snort, which earned him another severe look.

"I have done better in the past, and I don't mind admitting it," said Bodfish with dignity. "Clerk at times, purser at others. Commerce, most surely, is more in my line. However, when the opportunity came to ship with Cap'n Dexter, no matter how lowly the berth, I grasped the chance. Men apply in the dozens to ship with Cap'n Dexter!"

"They do?" said Harriet politely. She did not believe him for an instant. Even in her most landbound innocence she knew that captains and agents had to stoop to connivery and crime to fill the berths of their ships.

" 'Tis a-cause of the quality of the grub," said Mr. Fish slyly. Bodfish had disappeared into the pantry again. Harriet said nothing, satisfying herself with one quelling glance, and Bodfish reappeared with a platter of warm, soft bread.

Fresh, soft bread! Harriet forgot the second mate's insolence on the instant. There was butter too, good butter that was as astounding on a ship as the good sugar in the bowl. Harriet closed her eyes as her teeth sank into the deliciousness, luxuriating in taste and smell and texture. When she opened them again, still blissfully chewing, the old steward was watching her with most benevolent aspect.

"Good?"

"Oh—excellent!"

"I did have my qualms about bein' steward," he said bashfully, "and I don't mind admitting it. But no sooner had I learned to furl the main royal all by myself, and no sooner had I worked off my share in the company, than Cap'n Dexter held a meeting, on account of the steward not wishing to be steward anymore. He wanted to shift to the foc'sle, Miss Gray, so Cap'n Dexter called for volunteers. It was a challenge indeed, for if the cap'n's high standards not be met, then it is squally times and no mistake. But I said to myself, I said 'Bodfish, live and learn, live and learn,' and before I knew it my feet had stepped me forward."

Harriet involuntarily looked at those feet. They were very long and thin, no doubt as bony as his hands, encased in elastic-sided boots. Then, equally involuntarily, she said, "Share? in the company?"

"Yes. You find my bread acceptable?"

"Oh, yes!" She looked about for another slice, but Fish and Crotchet had demolished the lot.

"Bread needs a routine, I've found," mused Bodfish. His long face was tilted ruminatively, while one hand whisked his rag about as if of its own volition. The rag swept up the mast and about the leaves of a potted plant that twined there, and he said, "Like any growing thing, yeast needs its sameness. Every night I go to bed betimes, and the flour, ready sieved, and the yeast, ready mixed, do the same. I rise early in the morning, and so does the bread. We have soft bread twice a day and hard biscuit every meal, all hands the same, coffee twice, tea twice. Cookie and I pride ourselves on our culinary expertise, Miss Gray, and Cap'n Dexter commends us, so surely that ain't self-praise?"

"Oh, surely not! 'Tis little wonder," said she warmly, "that men line up to ship on the brig." Bodfish beamed, quite red with gratification. She watched him disappear into the pantry, feeling much soothed but aware nevertheless of Mr. Valentine Fish's overfamiliar regard and the fact that he was no doubt hatching some more teasing.

She turned to him, smiled primly, and said in the sweetest of accents, "And where did you ship on the brig, Mr. Fish?"

He did not look discountenanced in the slightest: his smile was more melting than ever. "In Charleston, nigh on a year back," he said.

"And . . . Crotchet?"

"Crotchet," he said, "be from ol' Virginny, and I—"

"Yes, yes, but surely Crotchet is a most unusual name?"

"Crozet," said Crotchet, and smiled bewitchingly.

"We boys call 'im Crotchet, and Crotchet shipped in the same port place, in Charleston naught but five months after me. Only," quoth the unquenchable Mr. Fish seraphically, "I dunno but we can call him *shipped* for he joined us by accident. We were four hours out and then we found 'im, curled up and snorin' drunk in a coil of rope on the amidships deck, wearing nothing but his drawers and a gold Harland watch—"

"Mr. Fish!" ejaculated Bodfish, coming out of the pantry. He sounded as affronted as any society matron, and then Harriet forgot it, for she scented what the steward was carrying.

Fish, freshly caught, freshly fried fish. Despite the bread she

was immediately ravenously hungry again. There had been fish
served at times on the *Humpback*, salt fish, boiled fish,
fishheads staring from chipped and dirty plates. This fish was
moist and fragrant, cooked by the lightest of hands. Bodfish,
his manner again indulgent, heaped her plate and then gave the
rest to the men. Valentine and Crotchet fell to instantly, eating
with adolescent appetite, and Harriet ate heartily herself, with
excellent relish, for who knew when—and where—she would
eat again? The food on any barge, scow, or guano carrier was
certain to be suspect, she thought uneasily, and then, for the
first time, she wondered why the brig lay at anchor off this
island. According to the logbook, she remembered, the brig
had made the island June the eighth, quite ten days ago: surely
it did not take so long to take on wood and water and provisions?

She said tentatively to the boys, "When will the brig make
sail?"

"Oh, today, I should imagine," said Mr. Fish in his
confident way.

She thought, *Oh dear*; for as long as the brig did not leave
this place, no barges, scows, or guano carriers could be
spoken. She said, "Are you certain?"

"No, we ain't, ma'am," said Crotchet in his soft southern
voice. She looked at him attentively, much preferring him to
his comrade. Crotchet no doubt was capable of equal boyish
mischief, but his smile was a deal more shy than Mr. Fish's.
"The company has to discuss the matter yet," said he earnestly.
"But I'd wager, ma'am, if you cared to put a bet on it, that we
will set sail this very day, for even the most hopeful of the men
are of a mind to give it up."

Give up? Give up what? Harriet said cautiously, "They do
business here?"

"Yes, ma'am!" he said, and filled his mouth again.

Harriet watched him, frowning and nibbling at a pensive
fingertip. She had looked a long time at the island as the whaler
sailed along its shores the previous day. It was a small island,
strangely intimidating, with black massive cliffs that rose
vertiginously from the sea. Despite its forbidding appearance
people lived there, she'd observed; she'd seen chimney tops
and tiled roofs, domesticated trees and even the spire of a
church. Men had been working near the edge of the cliffs,
tilling the soil at the top of the rock, laboring to make the dirt
produce.

Perhaps other men made a living fishing off the rocks; this very fish might have been bought from the inhabitants, but what were the *Hakluyt* men doing on the island?

She said tentatively, "I saw a boat leave for the island this morning."

"That was Mr. Martin," said Mr. Fish, and guffawed. "Miserable, he be this morn, like the last three days of a dissipated life. He'll bother them boys into some action; they'll get a tongue-lashin' they didn't expect. I'll go myself soon," said he, and grinned.

"But I wager, yes, we'll be away by sunset, ma'am," said the southern boy. His shy smile was coaxing. "Would you not care to put some money on it . . . hmm?"

"I certainly would not," said Harriet as the companionway door opened, and Jahaziel Dexter came in.

The two boys quit the table; she had never seen young men move so fast. One moment they were there and the next they were not, and she was left alone with their skipper. Harriet watched that skipper warily, but he merely grinned at her and sat down in his armchair. When he smiled his brown cheeks creased up, somehow faunlike in a face that had a natural lopsided elvish humor. He was freshly shaved, and the sun through the skylight emphasized his a-kilter eyebrows in an expression that she reluctantly found attractive. He knew she was studying him, she saw, for he suddenly turned his head, flicked one of those eyebrows at her, and said sardonically, "Please don't leave the table on my account, Miss Gray." She stared back with simmering resentment, finding no trouble at all in hating him, for she had had no intention at all of leaving the table.

Or not, at any rate, until she was more certain of her immediate future. Now that he had delivered his first broadside, however, Jahaziel Dexter seemed set to ignore her, concentrating on eating instead. The steward brought in more fish, more coffee, and more bread, and Harriet watched Captain Dexter eat. She was determined not to speak until he did.

It did not seem to embarrass him in the slightest that she watched him so intently; in fact, Harriet had the distinct impression that he was enjoying it. He cut up his fish with a fork and then piled the glistening flakes onto bread. Then he ate with his fingers, with the neat swift movements of a cat. Those hands were strong, with businesslike palms and long fingers, the flat clean nails sunk into the skin with the years of grappling with wet rope and canvas. She wondered how old he was: twenty-five, perhaps? He had a wonderfully youthful appetite, but years had gone into the creasing of his face, and the set of his shoulders was broad with experience. He was wearing a soft striped shirt and buckskin pants tucked into rawhide boots, and he had a soft, thin leather weskit, unbuttoned, and he smelled of leather too, a clean smell of leather and soap.

Then she heard bumps, up on deck. Mr. Fish was lowering his boat, she thought, and she tilted her head to look at the skylight. When she looked back at Captain Dexter he had finished eating, and was watching her.

He smiled and said, "Did you enjoy your breakfast?"

She scowled at him, certain that he begrudged her the food. Then she said reticently, "It was excellent, thank you."

"We do ourselves well here."

"I believe," she said pertly, "that the quality of the grub is far-famed." If the men of the brig ate as well as they had done this morning, she thought, then Captain Dexter was no doubt robbing the owners blind, but she kept that thought to herself. She said, "Captain Dexter—"

"A good appetite," he mused aloud, "is, in my opinion, a virtue."

She had eaten rather a lot, she thought uneasily. "Yes, but—"

"Even in an uninvited guest."

She stared at him with simmering dislike, and snapped, "As you know, I intend to pay for my passage."

"What passage?" he inquired gently, and grinned.

"Captain Dexter, I am as anxious to quit your brig as you are to be rid of me," she snapped heatedly. "But that seems impossible as long as your brig remains at anchor in these waters. Barges, scows, and guano carriers do not call here very often, of that I am fully persuaded!"

"That's true," he admitted, and his eyes glinted so that she almost believed him on the verge of laughter, and for the first time she registered the fact that his eyes were green. His hair was an unremarkable brown color, but his eyes were a bright hazel green.

She waited, but he merely glinted at her, so she said very cautiously, "You're still determined to put me on the first vessel you raise?"

To her surprise he laughed then, a full-bodied laugh of genuine amusement. "No, no," said he, chuckling. "I wouldn't do that, even to such an inconvenient waif as you. I was in a fully warranted passion when I said that last night, but now in the light of day I've repented, for how could I leave you in the care of some notorious rogue of a barge, scow, or guano-carrier master? My conscience might be tattered, but it still forbids me that."

Harriet gazed at him pensively indeed. He did not look in the least repentant, and she did not trust him an inch, but his wit was even more charming than his laughter. She said very carefully, "So what will you do?"

"Ah . . ." he said, and paused thoughtfully while she simmered with suspense. He watched her face; he looked up at the skylight; he sipped his coffee, and all the time she wished she could shake him. Then he said idly, "I'll steer for Capricorn, that's what I'll do."

She echoed, "Capricorn," most blankly. She had seen the island the previous day from the decks of the whaler, but had not been invited on shore. Capricorn was a small island like the one where this brig lay anchored, but in contrast it was lushly tropical, and Captain Smith had bought much fruit along with wood and water, all of which had been lightered out to the whaleship.

She said, "But what will you do there?"

"I have a half cargo of wood in my holds; perhaps I'll buy more and fill the brig . . . and then perhaps I'll take my cargo to Auckland."

"Auckland?" She stared at him, aghast, thinking she'd scrimped and saved and suffered, had been mortified and ill-treated, just to arrive back at the place she had so willingly left. She cried, "You can't do that to me, sir!"

"To you?" He frowned, and then the eyebrows flew up. "But you will not be on the brig, Miss Gray."

"Then where the devil will I be, pray?"

"Who knows, Miss Gray? Surely not still on Capricorn; I'm fully persuaded that a pretty young girl of your undoubted resources will have no trouble at all in persuading some old salt to carry you to the Chilean coast. Plenty of vessels call at Capricorn; you'll have a-plenty of choice."

"Oh, my God!" She was on her feet, trembling with rage. "You can't do that to me, Captain Dexter! You can't put me on shore at Capricorn and live with your conscience! What if I don't agree?"

"Oh, dear." He ruminated then, with what she was furiously certain was a mere pretense at serious thought. "Ah well, then," he said, and shrugged, "you will have to come with us . . . to Auckland."

"But I can't! I—I won't!"

He said lazily, "As an uninvited guest you have very little choice, my dear."

"Do I not?" she cried. "Don't be so sure of that, Captain! The reins of my fate are still firmly in my hands! Your brig has proved a most uncomfortable refuge—despite the excellence of the rations!—and I insist that my choice is my own, to stay here or not! I might be but—what was it? an inconvenient waif from the night? and one, furthermore, with a most inconvenient appetite—but I coped alone in New Zealand, Captain Dexter, and I can cope here!"

She was shouting with her passion. Bodfish popped out of his pantry, the very picture of alarm at her noise, but Captain Dexter, to her utter exasperation, merely looked the picture of a most diverted man. "Tut tut," he murmured, and tipped back his chair in entertained fashion. "Such temper . . . and what the devil do you mean, Miss Gray?"

"I mean that you can leave me here, sir! Why put up with my unwanted company all the way to Capricorn! I am willing to go ashore on this island, sir, and in fact I insist upon it!"

"Tarnation," said he, sounding most astounded. Then, to the further detriment of her temper, he chuckled. "Such eloquence," he said, "such a tirade." And in that moment she was truly afraid she would lose the last shreds of control, and hit him.

He discerned as much, she saw, for his grin widened even further, and he unfolded his arms and began to duck. She stamped her foot and left the cabin in a furious rush of skirts, dashing headlong onto the deck and informed the astonished Mr. Fish that he was taking her on shore.

Mr. Fish's boat was another halfboat. She sat tensely in the stern by Mr. Fish at the tiller, watching the island as the gawping oarsmen pulled toward it. She was wearing most of her wardrobe again and her two baskets bumped by her knee, but the heat of her temper was cooling fast, its vigor quenched with foreboding. The island looked . . . menacing, and she had just remembered its name.

Judas Island. It was impossible to believe that the same creator who had made the lush, fertile peaks of Capricorn Island had formed these black and barren cliffs. There were fleeing mares' tails of clouds crossing the sun, causing shadow and light, but Judas Island seemed shadowed all of the time. There was no reef and no lagoon; the island rose precipitously from the sea, and the water at the base of the cliffs was dark and secret, full of serpentlike writhings of kelp.

The boat crunched against the rocks. Great rusty chains hung down from iron rings set into the granite. Harriet reached up to grasp one to steady herself as she stood, and the metal crumbled into a gritty handful of rust. Horizontal shadows in the cliff face marked rough terraces that unknown people had cut in the past, and there were shallow caves and piles of discarded shells to show past feasts. The boat bobbed up and down wildly, but she disdained to accept the oarsmen's reluctantly courteous help. She did allow Mr. Fish, however, to carry her baskets. Then she picked up her skirts and trudged determinedly up the terraced track to the top. They were heading, she thought, to the place where the islanders had been tilling the soil. She wondered what language they spoke and thought it must be Spanish, but Spanish hospitality was famous. And there would be women in the village, she was certain. The thought was wonderfully bracing and restored the most of her courage. Then, all at once, she arrived at the top.

Below her: the brig, floating unexpectedly beautiful in the blue-green of the bay. The vessel was as lean as a greyhound, and the white streak and black gunports painted on her sides gave her a businesslike look. Her prow was sharply raked, and a boat was pulling out from her. Captain Dexter was coming in pursuit, she thought with a lurch, and she quickly turned and looked at the men who were working on the land.

Before her: the top of the island, made of rolling grassy hillocks that undulated inland toward the trees and the rooftops she had seen from the whaler, and, in the foreground, clusters of men who had been digging. For a long black moment she couldn't understand their appearance of familiarity, but then she recognized Mr. Martin, the first officer, the lewd fellow who had been at the helm the previous night; the sniffish old man who had stared at her window so primly, and the rest, the rest were indubitably, unmistakeably seamen, employed in work that was not maritime in the slightest. All kinds of holes pocketed the ground hither and about, all joined by strings that were stretched from stakes, as if to mark out some weird playing ground.

She found her voice. She said blankly, "What the devil is going on?"

Charlie Martin arrived in front of her just at that moment, so that he was the butt of her question. He did not look at all the amiable soul who had drunk so much liquor on the whaleship and then blithely carried her on board of the brig. He rubbed a forehead that patently hurt, and said in aggrieved tones, "I can't tell you that, Miss Gray, for I ain't at liberty, but what I want to know is why you're here, and why Mr. Fish brought you."

Harriet opened her mouth, but Mr. Fish spoke first. "She insisted, sir," he said, sounding smugly righteous. "And Cap'n Dexter did not interfere."

"You mean to say you didn't ask 'im?"

Mr. Martin's voice was taking on a note of thunder, and Harriet snapped, "Mr. Fish did not ask permission, for it was my decision, Mr. Martin. I asked Mr. Fish to bring me on this island, and he did it."

She glared, and Mr. Martin rolled his eyes up as if appealing to Providence, all the time hauling at his beard in patent desperation, and she heard a peevish voice say, "She enticed our second mate, that's what. She seduced him with her female wiles, she give out unseemly orders to an officer of our own vessel, and she but a passenger and female, at that, who ain't but got no right to make requests."

She swung about, and met the rheumy stare of the old man who had pulled an oar in Mr. Martin's boat. She snapped, "I am not a passenger. I have resigned the position, so whine on, do, for your whining means naught to me."

It was almost soothing to see the old man's mouth gape open, and see the oafish suggestive grins of the other men all sag with surprise. Then she heard Charlie Martin say, in tones of utmost consternation, "But what are you goin' to do, Miss Gray?"

Harriet paused, her pose consciously melodramatic. She looked about, at the holes, the strings, the attentive men, the rolling hills and the distant rooftops—and all at once the sun came out. The grim dark cliffs were abruptly friendly, singing with seabirds, and the short crisp grass was a kindly green. She said, "When Captain Dexter arrives—which I see will be soon—kindly inform him I have gone to the village."

Charlie Martin squawked, "But you can't do that!"

"Why not? Are there snakes?"

She saw him blink and blankly shake his head. He winced, putting his hand to his forehead, and mumbled, "I can't say I ever seen one."

"Well, then," she said loftily, "there seems to be no problem." Then she nodded haughtily at her gauping audience, hefted her baskets, and set off. No one tried to stop her.

By the time Captain Dexter arrived at the top of the cliff, Charlie was about to cry mutiny. His mood and his headache were awful. It was impossible to believe, he thought dourly, that these were the very same *Hakluyt* men who'd begun their digging with such exuberant optimism ten days before. Ten days of failure had rendered them lazy, and this morn' when he'd arrived with Abner and Abijah, the men who'd encamped the night were not digging at all. Instead they were still about the breakfast campfire, and—even worse than that—they were telling each other their dirty dreams. "I dreamp of Maria," Dan Kemp was saying. "I dreamp she fell on top of me, and I dreamp she were a-slippin', so I put me hand on her *applicobation*, and I tell you boys, I hauled, and you know what, she gave right in."

The men were all guffawing and hooting, unaware at that moment that their moody first mate had arrived. Tib Greene was laughing the loudest and rudest, for he and Dan were desperate comrades. They were fond of saying they'd shipped together and would go to hell together, and now Tib hollered, "And what happened, huh, what happened?"

"Why, an interferin' bastard name of Tib Greene waked me up, that he did," was the cheerful retort. "If it 'adn't bin fer 'im, the Lord only knows what would've happened to Maria!"

Then Charlie made his bad-tempered presence known. The men all saucily explained that they were only carrying on with the favorite morning game of the fo'c'sle, that the telling of salacious dreams was the rage of the moment; but that did them no good at all, for Charlie shouted sharp that they were to look lively and lay to their shovels. They shambled then toward the diggings, but within five minutes Abner and Abijah had let out the news of the passenger on the brig, and that had been the end of the shoveling.

Ten days on dry land with naught but digging and measuring for occupation had rendered the men like oat-fed colts; they were a deal too lively altogether. Now they refused to do anything more than ask more details and express all kinds of opinions. The general mood was saucily irreverent. Dan and Tib had an abundance of salacious tales of women and their doings, and they had a most rowdy audience.

Dan had shipped once on a whaler, he told them, a whaler out of Mystic where the skipper dropped his hypocritical primness the instant they doubled Cape Horn, and looked not for whales but for the nearest island where he could purchase a triplet or two of island beauties. He was a thrifty soul and generous to boot, for when he tired of the seductive pretties he handed them on to his men. The females moved by stages through the cabin and the steerage, arriving finally at the fo'c'sle, where they were guaranteed a manly welcome. A lot of ribald laughter greeted this, and Charlie had to shout to make himself heard, but that did no good either, for the men took little notice.

Miss Gray was a decent young female, a lady in distress, he snapped, and he was most heartily ashamed of every single one of them. Goddammit, she was English, he cried, but that did no good either, for Tib Greene had a riveting tale about an Englishwoman in similar situation. Why, she had been a female convict, runaway from a penal settlement in New South Wales, certainly a lady in distress! Tib was on a trader then, a trader out of New York, and the captain of that trader certainly *helped* that English lady, oh, good Lord he did! Then when he finished a-helping her he'd handed her on in traditional style, from cabin to steerage to fo'c'sle.

That convict woman had had a fair old temper, though, he remarked in ruminative style, good Lord, she were a shrew. When the crew of the trader had gotten a-tired of her, they'd handed her on to the natives of the next Pacific island they touched. The last anyone had heard of her, Tib ghoulishly related, the natives had tired of her temper too, and had killed her, and eaten her, and then been glad of the peace. Then, while the men roared at this hilarious denouement, Miss Gray had made her appearance. That had shut up the salacious ones—though it was a deal unfortunate, Charlie uneasily thought, that she had displayed her own touchy temper—but when she'd gone, the disapproving ones had given voice.

The talk was rude and indecent, Chips the carpenter averred. Charlie agreed with him. Abijah Roe sniffed in his peevish way and said it was a scandal. "She were brought on board with no consultation from either cap'n or company directors," the querulous fellow complained. "And I do suspect," he added nastily, with a sideways look at poor Charlie, "that she were brought on board through the dire effects of ardent spirits." Evidently he was smarting from Miss Gray's sharp rejoinder to his whining, but knowing the reason did not make Charlie feel any better.

Old Sails the Swede had a different criticism: he declared "dat der womans on der ship, dey be plumb unlucky." Old Chips had agreed, and he told them all in his pompous way that he'd hoped Cap'n Dexter would take more note of the first rule of sagacious captains: Ship no sodomites and carry no women. Both, he declared, were shocking bad for the temper of a voyage. Then, just when the salacious ones were in voice again, talking of making up a party to go after Miss Gray, the captain made his appearance.

Charlie thought that never before had he been so glad to see his skipper. He told Dexter all about it, at great length and in the most injured manner. Dexter listened patiently. Miss Gray, he remembered wryly, had declared she would be no trouble, no trouble in the slightest: she was never even seasick, she'd said. Well, he thought, the seasickness was yet to be tested, but the other assertion had proved vastly wrong. Here were his men in various kinds of turmoil, discipline almost in a state of collapse, and the digging quite neglected.

Charlie was certainly angry about it. Miss Gray's effect, he averred, had been disastrous, and the randy gossip shameful. Never, Dexter mused, had he seen calf love wilt and die so quickly. If Charlie had gone on the whaleship today, he would have spurned Miss Gray's pleas without the slightest qualm.

"And," said Charlie moodily, "she has a fair old temper."

"You noticed?"

"Aye, sir. In fact, I wonder if she be about crazy."

"She seems coherent enough."

"But to storm off to the village like that, sir, surely that ain't the act of a balanced temperament?"

"Perhaps she thought she had good reason," Dexter said neutrally. He shifted and sighed, feeling more exasperated with Harriet Gray than ever. Crazy? Melodramatic was more like it. He said, "We'd better send a man along after her, to fetch her back and keep her out of trouble. She's likely to turn an ankle in a hole at the very least. Who can we trust with such a delicate errand?"

"Jonathan?" hazarded Charlie, and Dexter sighed again, for hayseed Jonathan was such an unlikely proposition. However, he agreed, for every choice was a bad one. Jonathan was called and told off to perform the errand, and then the oafish lad set off, muttering, with a wake of catcalling and whistling and lighthearted advice behind him. Then, when his rebellious, embarrassed shambling shape had disappeared over the crest of the first rolling slope, Chips, the chairman of the *Hakluyt* Company, called an extraordinary meeting.

It was no less than Dexter had expected. Ten days of fruitless digging had discouraged them all, and they were all set to give up and make sail. But the company being what the company was, none of them would allow that to happen without a proper meeting and without a proper formal vote-taking.

Bodfish was secretary, and because of this Dexter had brought him out on his boat. There were only three souls left on the brig: Bill because he was too young to be a proper company member, Cookie the Irishman because he had a most rooted and religious objection to the English invention of voting, and the nameless ex-slave they all called Davy Jones Locker, because no one yet had managed to persuade Davy that a black man was capable of influencing a white man's decision-making.

Bodfish perched on a rock with a book on his knee and pencil poised in his hand. Everyone shuffled about, and gradually the muttering and commotion died down. Chips said gruffly, "I declare this meeting in order and open. The matter a-fore us—"

Abijah cried, "But what about the minutes?"

"Is that necessary, for an extraordinary meeting?"

"Of cuss it is, of cuss! How can we do things proper if we don't start proper, huh? If you can't do it right, then I move we get a new secretary and chairman."

Everyone shifted, and Dan and Tib called out rude comments. Chips turned his pipe over and puffed great clouds of offended upside-down smoke. Bodfish rattled papers, radiating martyrdom, and then recited crossly: "Minutes of the meeting of the *Hakluyt* Company Friday June the eight, 1848, commenced with gales from east nor'east, heading sou'east for Judas Island, called a meeting of the company at six P.M. to act on various suggestions recommended by the board of directors, namely that we send parties on shore to dig for treasure. After discussion the matter was put to the vote . . ."

Dexter stopped listening and set his mind to brooding about Harriet Gray instead. Then, when the minutes were finally finished, it seemed that most of his men had been doing the same, for Abijah immediately called out, "And now we can discuss what to do about our passenger!"

"Aye," said the rest; some laughed and some sniffed.

" 'Tis a grave responsibility," Abijah hooted.

Indeed, thought Dexter, wondering what Miss Harriet Gray had made of the island village.

3 ❧ Within ten minutes the strange diggings were out of sight. Harriet trudged head down, her baskets bumping, her cloak about her. The thin clouds had left the face of the sun, and the day was growing warm; the sky was blue and full of birds, but despite all this Harriet's mood was becoming apprehensive. It was all, she thought, so unreal . . . it was an unsettlingly empty landscape, with no sounds of people . . . and why had the men been digging those holes, and for what? There was something very wrong, she thought. Harriet was growing hot, perspiring under her layers of clothes, but nevertheless she shivered.

Empty, it was all so empty. Nothing cried out except the birds. When a gull cawed cruelly right over her head she startled and flinched. The trees were right ahead; she quickened her step.

Then the trees were all around her. Their shade was welcome, but she did not feel reassured. They were fruit trees

in rows—mango, avocado, fig, and grape—but their branches
were neglected and tangled. The mango fruit lay all about, and
Harriet could smell the hot scent of their spicy running juice.
She wondered then why the *Hakluyt* men had not gathered
them up. Surely mangoes were a treat, even on the well-
provisioned *Hakluyt*, and after all there was no one here to stop
the men from helping themselves to the harvest.

And that was what was so uncannily unsettling: there were
no humans in this place. No human voices. The trees had no
caretakers, and the village ahead was just as silent. *No human
voices.* Harriet was suddenly very afraid and even more
frightened when she understood that she was scared. She had
to force herself to leave the shelter of the trees and venture into
the village.

The village: nothing more than a handful of cracked adobe
houses. They were built about a dusty plaza in the old South
American style, all crouched in the sun, in the shadow of the
jagged church spire. Nothing moved; no one came out to
inquire her business. Even the birds were quiet. The houses
waited, empty ruins, populated by ancient ghosts, angry
ghosts, for the buildings had been half destroyed with a
ferocity that was human and not just that of time. Something
dreadful had happened here; the sun shone inside the ruined
walls, but the sun outside seemed cleaner.

Something moved. Harriet's heart leaped into her throat. She
stood in the middle of the plaza by a broken-down well, and
her throat was too dry to scream. A stealthy rustle, a rattle of
footsteps. She cried out hoarsely, "Who goes there?" and a
yellow dog came slinking out from behind a cracked wall. Its
chests was furrowed cruelly with prominent ribs. It ran in the
other direction, away from her. Harriet's trembling fingers let
go of her baskets and grasped the parapet of the well. Her grip
was convulsive. Shivering, she turned a little and looked down
the well . . . down.

Down to a far-off gleam of secret water, and a pale round
reflection within. It was like looking down an endless wet
tunnel. The effect was eerie, and for a terrible instant she felt
as if she were falling. The round pale shape beckoned her, and
she fancied at that moment that it was a skull. Then, dryly
swallowing, she thought it must be the reflection of the sun on
the water. A lizard flickered by her hand, and she bit back a
frightened yell. Then, behind her, she heard a bootstep.

This time she did scream, whirling round as the sound was

jerked out of her. There was a young man there, scowling at her. He was one of the fellows who had gauped at her that morning from the steerage doorway, the one who had stared so stupidly as if she were a circus performer.

He said, "Did I a-fear you, miss?"

She took a deep breath to still the trembling. "You most certainly did."

"Ah," said he, and looked gratified at the accuracy of his guess. "I be Jonathan. Cap'n Dexter and Mr. Martin, they sent me off, told me off to fetch you."

She said, "I see," biting down the words, *thank God*, trying to gather some shred of dignity about her and hide the fact that she'd been so very scared. When he picked up her baskets and set off, her feet betrayed her, however, for they kept pace with him so eagerly.

He seemed very silent, and when she smiled politely he kept up his scowl. In fact, she thought, this whole manner seemed much aggrieved, and she wondered why. He wore overalls, and he shambled as he walked, and his freckled, sun-reddened brow was heavily furrowed.

Then, as they passed through the trees, he suddenly said, "Say sommat, ma'am."

"What?" She almost laughed. "But why?"

"Nobbut, miss, but to hear your voice. You come from th'Old Country, they tell me."

"If *they* mean England," she said stiffly, very aware that 'they' meant the ill-mannered crew of the brig, "then *they* are right."

"But you been livin' sommat else, they all say." He paused, and then said with heavy and mysterious disapproval, "You been livin' in New South Wales."

"What?" She stared at him, utterly bemused. Then she said coldly, "I've been living in New Zealand, if that holds any interest."

"That's what they said, and a long time too, for you had to be summat where they speak true English, for we all can understand what you say, ma'am, and they do tell me that be plumb unusual, in folks that hail from Lunnon. In Lunnon, they tell me," he carried on while Harriet listened with incredulous amazement, "they hardly speak to each other at all, their speech bein' so sundered that they be at their wits' end to understand what each other says."

She paused, unsure whether to be insulted or amused. Then

she said merely, "New Zealand is not in New South Wales,
Jonathan."

"Is it not? Wa-al, I guess it makes no mite of diff'rence, for
I be certain sure, ma'am, that New Zealand be a barbaric place.
You have to come to Americky now, to see some real sights."

"I do?" Then she snapped, "It amazes me that you left your
land and chose to be a seaman."

"But I ain't no seaman, miss!"

"You're not?"

"I be a Massachusetts man, and right proud to say so. My
gran'pappy fought on Bunker Hill, a true-blue son of American
liberty, jes' like my pappy and myself, and we can say we're
true-blue sons without any argument, for true-blue men all
fight with guns."

"Well," said Harriet, the amusement winning, "I must take
care then to avoid any battle of words, Jonathan. I trust if I ask
you what brought you to sea, it won't lead to violent argument?" This statement foxed the boy completely, she saw, for
he furrowed his brow with a mighty effort. Then, taking pity
on him, she amended: "Why, Jonathan, did you come to sea?"

"To make my fortune, of course!"

"What else?" she agreed, diverted. Then she looked about at
the rolling slopes and the short brown grass, and she lowered
her voice and said, "Jonathan, do the men hope to find a
fortune in their diggings?"

He bridled: to her amusement he bridled like an offended
dowager. Then he said in most reproving tones, "About that,
ma'am, I am not at liberty to say."

"You're not? Tell me about Captain Dexter, then: did you
come from Massachusetts in his brig?"

"With Cap'n Dexter? In the brig *Hakluyt*?" His eyes bulged,
and then he snorted in most pitying fashion. "You must be
jestin', Miss Gray! Cap'n Dexter dassent show his face in New
England."

"*What*?"

"He'd be arrested, and that plumb certain."

"My God!" She stopped short, staring at him, remembering
her tirade about notorious rogues. "Oh, dear Lord," she said
then, rather faintly. "What in heaven's name was his crime?"

"And about that, ma'am, I'm not at liberty to say neither."

"Not at liberty?" she cried, at the end of her tether. "You
don't seem to be at liberty to say anything much to me,

Jonathan, and yet not four minutes ago you assured me sincere that you're a real true-blue son of American liberty! What more liberty do you need, pray?"

If he had a gun, she saw then, that would have been the end of things, for he was positively snorting with bucolic rage. "Ma'am," he said in preaching tones, "I won't tell you what you're so plumb intent on knowin', and you may as well put your mind to that, for I ain't susceptible, I ain't."

"What?"

"They all told me when I were given this job to watch out for your female wiles. They told me you would tease me, ma'am, and told me too that if you tried your tricks, I were to tell you straight I'm as good as married."

"They did?" she said dangerously.

"Aye, and it's thus. Mary-Jane at home be my intended, and I promised her faithful to be true."

"And may the best of connubial bliss be yours!" she snapped.

"Thankee, ma'am, but that won't alter my disposition."

"And I am not accustomed, sir, to being the subject of sniggering talk!" But she was, she mourned furiously, she was, and familiar shame and helpless frustration threatened to rise inside her. Then like an accompaniment to her black, angry thoughts a volley of shots sounded ahead, from the diggings. She cried out, shocked, "What's that?"

Jonathan began to run in great shambling strides. She ran beside him, clutching her cloak with convulsive fingers. "They want us back, and fast," the boy gasped. A thick ominous cloud was moving over the face of the sun. A sharp gust of wind jerked at her skirts and her cloak, and then they crested the hill. The diggings lay ahead.

The first man she saw was Jahaziel Dexter. She recognized him instantly by his height and his hat, and unthinkingly ran over to him. He put out a hand to stop her but did not turn; like the other men he was staring downward into one of the holes they had dug. Then, at once, men cried out from the depths.

Harriet gripped the tossing edges of her cloak. A man came into view, bursting frantically out of the hole, followed closely by another. The men at the top all lurched back, scattering away from the leaking edge of the excavation. More dirt fell and disappeared as the edge collapsed, and Harriet saw what the digging had revealed.

Inside the hole it was very dark; it was lit only slightly to one

side by a glimpse of light from the bottom. It was as if there
had been a cliffside entrance to the pit, which at some time in
the past had been filled in. One man remained at the bottom of
the hole. Harriet saw him bend and then straighten with
something long and pale in his fist.

He thrust it upward; someone took it. It was a bone, a long
bone, a human bone, a femur. Thunder rumbled, almost
drowning out the babble as the men around all talked at once.
They milled about, their faces shiny with ghoulish fascination.
Lightning flickered silently on the horizon.

Harriet looked at Captain Dexter, instinctively moving
closer to him. He had his fists propped on his hips and his hat
tilted back. Like all of his men, he seemed unaware of her.
Lightning pulsed again, and his silhouette was framed with
silent blue fire. Then he spoke. She did not hear the words, but
rope was produced, and two men were lowered into the pit.
Other men took up shovels and began to hack at the edges of
the hole to make the gap bigger. The dirt resisted and then
flopped out of sight with loud pattering sounds of earth and
stones. A fist appeared above the edge of the hole, handing up
something round . . . and pale. Lightning flicked again, and
Harriet saw that the round object was a human skull.

Someone took it, and it was handed around quickly and
nervously. She could hear men trying to make feeble jokes.
Some—like the skull—were grinning. Jahaziel Dexter said
something again, and a bundle of rope yarn was produced and
lit to make a lamp, then lowered into the hole. Abruptly Harriet
could see the entire excavation, as the darkness gave way to the
flickering light.

The men had dug—on purpose?—into the roof of a cave.
She could see the remains of the passage that had led into this
cave from the side of the cliff. The floor of the cavern was
heaped with the dirt that the men had disturbed . . . and with
bones. The cave was filled with dirt and sprawled disjointed
skeletons.

Some had arms still outstretched to the passage, while others
hugged the floor of the cave, as if in a last frantic struggle for
air. When had they been buried thus? Long ago, she thought,
but still she shivered. It was impossible to look away.

There were four men down in the cave with the bones. They
were walking back and forth, holding the torch high, raking
back the dirt, searching. One man straightened and held up a
dark object like a snake, and one of the men by her crouched

to take it. Then she saw it was a rotting leather belt. Other objects came up then: fragments of black coarse gabardine, a few horn buttons, a rough wooden crucifix. Thunder grumbled, closer.

Then, a louder clap, deafening. She startled with fright. Lightning fizzed and the wind gusted, flapping Harriet's loose hair about her face. She released her clutch, and her cloak and skirts flapped wildly. She saw Captain Dexter turn and look down at her. The sky slammed again as thunder bellowed right above their heads; she saw his mouth move but could hear nothing. Then he took her arm. She flinched, still lost in a kind of nightmare.

Men began to run like birds over the edge of the cliff and down the terraces, disturbed by the gathering storm. Down in the bay the brig was pitching wildly at her anchors. The men in the cave were scrambling up the rope, and then they passed her. She flinched again, and Jahaziel Dexter shouted, "For God's sake, Harriet, will you tumble—for God's sake come on!" and, like an automaton, she numbly obeyed.

Within moments she was installed in a boat. The wind had veered, blowing in whirling gusts so that the sea was becoming rugged. Harriet shut her eyes and gripped the sides as the breakers took them. She heard an oarsman curse in a high, frightened voice. Her eyes flew open then, but she was more scared than ever.

It was the large boat, a whaleboat, and Jahaziel Dexter was steering with a long steering oar. He stood just behind her in the stern of the boat, and she could feel the tension in his braced legs and hear his grunts as he thrust the big sweep into the tumult. Her hair, like the rain, was streaming down her face. The boat pitched; she thought they were lost; her grip became convulsive. Then the oar seized the wave, bending like newly cut willow, and the boat was through the breakers and safe. Jahaziel was shouting. She could make no sense of what he shouted, but the oarsmen seemed to understand. They set their shoulders into their pulling, and the boat surged jerkily for the brig.

Harriet stopped in the boat while it was hoisted up in the davits, and Dexter stopped with her to work the falls. The instant they were level with the deck he bent and scooped her up in his arms, hauling her out of the boat and dumping her on the deck with no ceremony whatsoever.

Then he roared, "Tumble for your lives!" but Harriet saw, foggily, that men were already tumbling, dashing to the shrouds and springing up the masts, tumbling to loose the top-sails. The brig was bucking at her anchor, tautening the chain ready for release while other men sweated at the windlass. More men still were working at the davits, swinging in the boat, freeing the ropes as another boat arrived. Then all the men were safely on the brig.

And the brig came round, coming sharp on the wind as the sails fell loose and men ran to grip the flapping sheets. The noise was terrific, of wind and rain and dashing sea, and the rattle and clang of activity on deck. Two men were struggling to set their shoulders to the wheel. The rapidly darkening day was a cacaphony of shouting, of the thump of canvas and thrumming of tortured rigging, syncopated with the clap of thunder. Harriet stood still, held by the drama of the scene before her. The great sails billowed and then came taut, and the wind on deck gusted in different directions as the canvas rose against the sky and the racing thick clouds. Lightning spat and flickered again, and the *Hakluyt* bucked like a horse.

Then all at once the brig jerked free, and there was a ruckus of yelling as the anchor came up. The sails that were not sheeted home slatted with a deafening roar. The brig pitched and Harriet stumbled, hitting the wall of the deckhouse and bouncing before coming up against a large body rather hard.

It was Jahaziel Dexter. He steadied her and bellowed, "Get below!" Harriet merely stared; the last place she wanted to be was down in the cabin of this brig; she wanted to stop right here, where she could check that these variously unpleasant men were doing something about saving their brig and her life. Dexter reached past her and slammed the companionway door open with one hand. Then he gave her an obdurate little push, and that, along with the motion of his brig, set her on her wobbling path down the stairs. Above her head the door slammed again, and Harriet found herself alone, in this most uncomfortable of situations.

The noise was deafening. Harriet hung onto the edge of the table, her drenched garments clinging to her. Somehow in all the fuss she had lost her cloak; perhaps it had been whipped away in a gust, so briskly that she hadn't noticed. Skirts and waist and shawls all gripped her in a cold, clammy grasp, and the brig rose and rose as a huge wave lifted her and then pitched down with a crash. There was a tremendous thud of something fetching loose above on deck. "Are we wrecked?" shrieked Harriet, and as if the very heavens answered, a monstrous wave pooped the brig.

Countless gallons of salt water came hurtling through the skylight and fell directly on Harriet's head. She tried to scream, her mouth filled, she spluttered and tried again. She managed a shriek at the top of her voice, and the door above at the head of the stairs slammed open, and urgent bootsteps clattered.

Her eyes were shut. She shook herself violently, sending scatters of water all over the cabin. When she flapped her drenched hair away from her face Jahaziel Dexter was there, peering down at her, and to her incredulous rage he was grinning.

"What?" he said. "Afraid of a little squall and a cold bath?" She glared at him, speechless with hatred, and his face creased up with impish humor. "Take comfort," he urged. "The wind bears fair for Capricorn."

She shouted, "You—!" He stepped back hastily, surefooted while the brig pitched as wildly as ever. "This?" she shrieked. "A little squall?" and with a crash like doom, a thunderbolt struck the mainmast. Jahaziel whirled and ran, and Harriet pursued him, terrified at the very notion of being left alone below.

On deck it was like a scene from hell, all black and gray and flickering orange-and-yellow with flames. The top of the mainmast was on fire, and sparks spat and reached for the rigging. Captain Dexter had run forward, shouting, but Harriet stopped under the deckhouse, rigid with fright. The wind gusted and the flames curled and danced and the rain had stopped. Oh, God, she thought, the rain had stopped.

Men were racing up into the rigging, and more men were climbing over the bow with tubs in their hands, risking life to bring up water. Others ran in small circles on the deck, hauling at clewlines as they tried to save the topsails. The brig was pitching wildly, digging in her bow as she tried to shake free of the water in her scuppers, and another wave came in and crashed through the skylight and landed with a foaming splash below. Harriet watched and listened in dreadful apprehension, unable to move, aware only of the struggle to save the brig. Thunder growled again, more distant, and the horizon flickered with eerie blue light, as if mocking the flames that rose high from the hamper.

Another wave: the brig crashed down her prow and shuddered, creaking in every tortured plank. And then, as Harriet watched in utter uncomprehending horror, the futtock shrouds that braced the maintop broke, and the fore-topmast backstays vibrated with a high whining noise. Then, with the scream of sundering rope, they parted. In ghastly progression, like a string of dominoes falling, the fore-topmast hamper and then the main-topmast rigging went, slowly, slowly, in a tangle of spars, collapsing inch by inch over the slackened web of the jib. First one man who had been aloft there, and then another, cried out and fell, dropping from spar to stay and from yard to deck, in a grotesque moment-to-moment slowness.

Harriet lurched out of her mesmerized state and began to run toward them. Her skirts flapped wildly, and her wet hair tossed too, blinding her vision. As she arrived one of the men miraculously stood. His mouth was agape, and one of his arms hung like a broken wing. The other man lay still. Harriet fell to her knees beside the prone form, certain the man was dead, but as she started to turn him over, the man roused and groaned. Then she crammed a shocked hand over her mouth. The man moaned, and each time he shook his head great coins of blood sprung out and spattered in the water on the deck. Then by some strange miracle his face was abruptly washed of the blood, and Harriet could see his wound.

She swallowed. His right cheek had been almost entirely severed, caught by some projection as he fell. It flapped grotesquely, revealing shiny white teeth, the blood constantly washed away by a watery stream.

Water. Harriet shook her head in bewilderment. Then, belatedly, she realized that the heavens had opened and it was raining again. There was a gap in the sky where the heavy clouds were torn apart, and as she watched a rainbow sprang up in the murk. She listened to the flames hiss in the wreckage of the upper hamper. Within moments the flames had gone out.

4 ❧ Half an hour later it was still blowing great guns, and the seas were so rugged that with each roll the brig put her lee scuppers under water. However, the squall had lost its immediate force. The rain had stopped, and there were blue patches enough in the sky to dress a whole navy of sailors. The wind gusted fair for Capricorn, but the brig, mused Dexter, was not going anywhere much for some time yet. The decks were a mess of rope and timbers; the *Hakluyt* in the meantime had her wings clipped. He strode about organizing repairs, and then he braced himself for his next job and strode below to his cabin in the transom.

A tarpaulin had been tossed over the sofa that ran the length of the stern. The wounded sailor was Abner, the man who had been at the helm to keep the brig up to her anchors the night before. Now he lay on top of the tarpaulin, his eyes turned up in grotesque fashion, quite senseless. Harriet Gray knelt beside him, catching up the blood that welled from the awful wound.

She did the gruesome job quite casually, Dexter noted with eyebrow-high surprise; most of her mind seemed to be occupied with arguing with old Chips. Tib Greene, the man who had broken his arm, and Tib's comrade in mischief, Dan Kemp, were there too. Old Chips was whittling away at a splint for that arm, and Bodfish, too, was hovering about, mopping up water, sweeping up broken glass from the skylight.

There were too many people in the transom altogether, decided Dexter. There was scarcely room to get through the door, and everyone ignored him, including Miss Gray. She was too busy scolding old Chips. "I do assure you that I am right," she averred as she absentmindedly mopped at that flapping, bleeding cheek, "and any medical book will confirm it. I'm certain Captain Dexter himself would tell you, too, that men do *not* smoke by a sick bed."

"But I ain't nivver a-heared of such," the old man stubbornly said. "And folks with you would not agree, back home. In fact," he added, aggrieved in tone, "my own father, he *died* with a pipe atwixt his jaws, and we was all there a-smokin' too, keeping him company in his extremity." His lower lip stuck out as he whittled at his piece of stick, and he blew clouds of offending smoke as he fitted his stick to Tib Green's arm. It was time, Dexter thought, to make his presence known: he snapped at Bodfish to take himself out along with his mop, snapped at old Chips to hurry up with the splint, and hunkered down to look at Abner's cheek.

The wound was even more ghastly than he remembered. Each time Harriet mopped, the near-severed cheek lifted and then flapped back. Each flap revealed a row of white teeth and a swollen, bitten tongue. Abner's unconscious body rolled with each pitch of the brig, and Harriet held him in place with the side of one arm as she dabbed. Dexter said nothing. Instead he busied himself in fetching out his medical chest and some instruments for surgery.

One of the instruments was a bottle of potato whiskey. It had been given him several months before by a Russian beaver trapper. Dexter poured out four tots. He gave one to Chips, who immediately looked less affronted, gave one to Tib, and a third to Dan Kemp. Both men grinned widely despite the broken arm, and Dexter noticed for the first time then that they both had their whiskery gimlet-eyed attention firmly fixed on Harriet's face.

Dexter thought, *Oh, Jehovah*, and drained the fourth tot

himself. Harriet said, "Captain Dexter!" in exactly the tone she'd used to berate old Chips. Dexter ignored her. He hunkered down again by Abner's head and sorted out a new sail needle and some sewing silk. Then he refilled his glass and soaked both silk and needle in it. A hunk of cotton waste was soaked there too, liberally, before it was popped, dripping, right on top of the wound.

The effect was instantaneous and dramatic. Abner came to his senses with a most bloodcurdling shriek. He reared to a sitting posture like a corpse revived, and the cheek flapped down and blood spurted out from around the white teeth. Harriet said crossly, "Captain!" and with a mighty crash Dan Kemp fainted.

A blank voice said, "Well, good Lord, eh—wha'd'yer reckon?" The tone, Dexter noted with disbelief, was almost admiring. When he looked at Tib Greene the speaker was sitting like an open-mouthed statue, his broken arm held out unheeded. Old Chips was equally frozen, and Dan Kemp's form lay in an untidy muddle. Harriet was merely grimacing, while all the time Abner heedlessly thrashed in fear and pain. Dexter thought again, *Jehovah*, and snapped at Bodfish beyond the door to haul the unconscious body out, and then he tersely instructed old Chips to hold the patient's feet.

Chips did not move. Dexter sucked in a breath of exasperation and silently let it out. Harriet Gray was doing the job already, firmly holding the boy's legs down with an arm wrapped round the struggling knees. Her expression was as matter-of-fact as ever. Dexter only just stopped his head from bemusedly shaking, and he heard Tib Greene say in blankly unctuous tones, "Good Lord, what d'yer reckon, sir, and her but a scrap of a gal . . . how old?"

Yes, thought Dexter, and looked at Harriet himself. She met all three stares with hauteur, and said distantly, "Nineteen."

It was even worse than Dexter had thought. He said incredulously, "*Nineteen*?" and to his further bemusement she flushed.

"Well," she said reluctantly, "almost nineteen."

Eighteen, thought Dexter, and, *Oh, Jehovah*, "and not married," he said involuntarily.

"Would it make any difference if I were?" she flashed, and he was forced to shake his head.

"No," he admitted. Of course it would make no difference— except, perhaps, to the husband of this flamboyant waif, he thought, but had the sense this time to keep the thought to himself. He concentrated instead on his patient, catching Abner's head with his arm, and feeding the boy more brandy with the other hand.

The boy threatened to choke for a bit, and then managed to keep some down. The loud whines of pain became whimpers of terror. Dexter let him go and stood and looked at Chips, and the old man, at last, had finished with the persnickety whittling of the splint. Dexter bound it onto Tib's extended arm with rapid expertise, and then he grinned at the old carpenter and bid him hold the wounded boy's head.

"Tight," he said, and never did snail move as slow, he thought, as the old man did to the head of the couch. However, finally he was there, and holding Abner the way Dexter wanted. The boy was sobbing, tears running down from his tightly shut eyes, half of them running into the wound, the rest into the wide frightened mouth. And this, thought Dexter grimly, was the self-same seaman who had boasted the most in the fo'c'sle of his manly prowess. Dexter shut one eye and aimed, then pushed in the needle.

Abner exploded with an agonized yell, rearing upright again. Harriet gasped and old Chips winced, and Dexter paused to give the boy more brandy. Abner's hollering faded slowly, and Dexter finished the stitch.

He worked in a neat herringbone pattern, as in a well-mended sail. The boy, he mused as he worked, would have something new to show the girls; it might even fetch him all the pretties he boasted of fetching in port; it would be a scar to be proud of indeed. Then, just as he was getting nicely set into the rhythm of the job, he heard the carpenter clear his gruff voice. "Cap'n . . ."

The sound was strained, and Dexter paused to look up at him. The old man was pasty-faced and shiny about the forehead. Dexter straightened, wondering how many of his men were thus prone to feeble nerves. Harriet, by contrast, seemed perfectly calm, and no more pale than usual. Dexter sighed and said, "Yes, Chips, yes. Consider yourself relieved. Send in Bodfish; he should be just outside that door."

Bodfish lasted exactly two stitches. Then he asked in a shamed gasp to be relieved himself, for his constitution, he confessed, was not equal.

Dexter nodded and watched Bodfish's hasty withdrawal and wondered who to send for next. Then to his disbelief he heard

Harriet say crossly, "Oh, for heaven's sake, Captain Dexter, let me hold the boy's head, or the entire crew will fetch the vapors. All we need is one stout soul to sit on Abner's feet, and I can hold the head end."

That was easy: even with a broken arm Tib could sit on Abner. "Fancy that," he kept on saying as he settled. "And naught but eighteen, sir, think on that, on that."

Indeed, thought Dexter, but did not voice it. Instead he waited for Harriet to adjust her grip, and then he concentrated on finishing the operation.

Dexter spent the two hours of dogwatch tidying up in his stateroom and then in the transom cabin, wiping down his books and replacing them carefully. He whistled as he got his accommodations the way he liked them and sipped at times from a glass of good French brandy. Then eight bells was struck, and the brig was quiet, snugged down for the calm, warm night. Dexter lit the lamps in the transom and poured another drink. Then he settled in the chair by his chart table with an old journal set on his knee, his feet propped up on the sofa.

There was a knock on the door. He did not stand, but called out. Then, to his surprise and exasperation, Harriet Gray came in: she had not bothered to grace the supper table with her presence, and he'd thought her safely bedded down in the first mate's stateroom for the night.

Then she moved a little, and the lamp light limned her profile, and Dexter, even more irritatingly, felt little muscles of awareness shift and tug inside him. She was wearing a pale shirt and a plain slim skirt; the clothes clung to the slim lissome form and the sweet pert swell of her breasts. How could he have guessed when she first came on board that her breasts swelled so seductively, that her waist was thus long and slender, with a hollow in the small of her back that made his hand ache to touch and stroke . . . ?

A most inconvenient, enticing beauty, he thought wryly, and dared not guess what the men thought of this intrusion into his private quarters. He said in a deliberately businesslike tone, "And how is our patient?"

Abner Weeks, sewn up so his face hung together the way he'd been born, was tucked up in Valentine Fish's berth: all three mates now managed, somehow, in the lesser comforts of the steerage. Harriet had been contemplating the cabin, a slight frown on her face, and now she sat down without asking permission and said in reproving tones, "He's asleep, and I have great hopes that rot won't set in."

Rot? He said curtly, "It won't."

"Despite the use of alcohol in the surgery. Alcohol stimulates the flow of blood, Captain, and the effects can be disastrous!"

He couldn't believe it for a moment, that she should lecture him like this, that a minx of less than nineteen years could speak to him like the primmest dowager. Then he barked with laughter and said, "Perhaps you're right, but I've never known alcohol to stimulate the brain; I assure you I've seen effects a-plenty of the dulling quality of ardent spirits. Whiskey makes an admirable disinfectant. Would you have preferred tobacco juice, madam?"

"*What*?"

"Several captains of my acquaintance swear by a well-chewed tobacco cud bound to the wound."

Harriet, to his amusement, looked more scandalized than ever. She said in distant tones, "Do you do all the surgery on this brig, Captain?"

"That is American practice, Miss Gray."

"But surely other American captains carry a surgeon? There was certainly a doctor on the whaleship *Humpback*."

Dexter leaned back in his chair, tipping it on two legs and contemplating the pale oval face with more enjoyment than he'd ever expected. He said in milder tones, "And did he do any doctoring?"

"Well, no, as a matter of fact, he appeared to be fully employed in doing the cooking—" Dexter couldn't help it; he exploded into laughter. His chair rocked with his gale of mirth, and Harriet gazed at him with a reticent air. Then she said, "I presume I've made a blunder?"

"The *doctor* is a term of endearment for the ship's cook."

His words were dry, and he fully expected a sniff in reply, but to his surprise she laughed. It was a warm laugh, a young lighthearted laugh, so infectious that he laughed again himself. The light from the lamps gleamed on the disordered thickness of her hair, now dried and like gold again . . . and how would it feel in his hands, so soft and weighty?

He looked away from her, reaching instead for his *Captain's Medical Guide*, a fat volume on the shelf above his head. "I can prove it," he said. "Both alcohol and tobacco juice are recommended here."

"Perhaps even tobacco juice would have been preferable to *varnish*, Captain."

He remembered her face when she'd watched him annoint Abner's sewn cheek with good carriage varnish, and grinned again. "But it, too, is recommended practice, madam! See here: 'The remedy for cuts and burns is carriage varnish or glue or mucilage. It closes up a cut nicely, and the patient will experience no inconvenience thereafter.'"

Her expression was so incredulous and horrified that he enjoyed it for quite one moment. Then she said, "Oh, give me that book," and reached forward, and because of that enjoyment he gave it over, with no hesitation at all. Then he leaned back and relished her eloquent expressions again, watching her face as she turned the pages.

She looked so young, heartbreakingly young. Why had she seemed so much older when she first came into his life just one day before? It was the look in her eyes, he thought suddenly then; her eyes had been so cautious, so cynical, as if she'd learned to expect the worst of life. For a moment conscience touched him, and then she said, "What are these numbers?"

He leaned forward to look and then leaned back. "They match the numbers on the bottles in the medicine chest. The book informs us poor ignorant American commanders which bottles to use, and how to mix them, and when."

"Oh! So number eight is . . . ?"

"Opium."

"To be taken for . . . cholera, vomiting, and horrors after rum . . . every two hours. Opium! Every two hours!"

"Is that what it says?"

"It does, sir. A most intemperate book, Captain Dexter!"

"Number eight," said he, reciting solemnly, "is best mixed with number 12 . . ."

"Oh, yes, camphor! Merciful heavens," she said, flipping pages, "and I see that camphor, mixed with water, is recommended for concussion . . ."

"Dr. Winslow in Valparaíso is a stricter surgeon," said Dexter. "Where the book says water, he uses alcohol."

"And how many souls does he murder each year with such incontinent practice?"

"Who knows? He," said Dexter with relish, "was once a surgeon on an English vessel."

"And discharged for incompetence, no doubt," said Harriet smartly, and Dexter chuckled again. Harriet lifted an arched brow at him, and then he watched her face become preoccupied as she went back to perusing the book. He watched her with that unexpected pleasure, almost forgetting the men and the inevitable gossip, and then he heard her murmur, "Number eight . . . opium . . . is, I see, often mixed with number thirty-five, which is . . . ah, spirits of lead—of lead!—and recommended in the treatment of . . . bruising, the bruising . . . of . . . testicles . . ."

The murmur stopped short. Dexter said nothing; he was in prime danger of exploding. Harriet Gray, it was obvious, was not going to laugh away this blunder. She had, in fact, gone a most fetching shade of scarlet and looked no more than twelve. Finally she said in a stifled voice, "I apologize. That was most improper."

Dexter paused. Then he managed, "Think nothing of it."

Harriet Gray was eyeing him, as if she was aware of his hidden mirth. Then she said tartly, "And I presume that . . . graveyard on Judas Island is a memorial to the surgery of American captains?"

So this was why she'd come to his transom cabin, he thought; she had forgotten propriety in a rush of incurable inquisitiveness. "No," he said mildly. "And neither is it a memorial to American savagery. One of your own country-folk was responsible, a Welshman to be exact, a pirate by the name of Morgan." Harriet's face became lit with amazement, and then, as he contemplated her, she rearranged herself.

It was almost eerie to see the way she disposed herself for listening. Even the lamps seemed to dim as she gazed with complete attention at his face. She leaned a little forward and to one side and propped her elbow on the end of the couch and put her chin on her fist, and even her plain unadorned garments took on the essence of drapery, and when she whispered, "Who were those people who were murdered on that island?" it was as if she whispered, *Tell me a story, fascinate and enthrall me . . .*

And it was oddly flattering to have a listener who watched and listened with every fiber of her slim elegant form. The pale gold of her hair shimmered in the lamplight; it was as if she wore a halo . . . the shadows of long lashes were mysterious . . . and why not tell her all about it? After more than two years of restless wondering and fruitless hunting, Dexter wanted to talk.

He sipped brandy, thinking, and then he said, "You have heard of the pirate Morgan?"

"Of course. He raided the Spanish main until we English rewarded and tamed him, by turning him into a knight."

Harriet's wry wit was irresistible too. Dexter grinned appreciately and then said, "Morgan heard of the treasures of the Pacific coasts too and led a gang of desperate men across the Isthmus of Darien, on a quest to seize the gold of Panama."

Gold. He paused. The brig was very quiet, as if he and Harriet were the only souls awake. On impulse Dexter opened the old journal that still lay on his knee. He turned pages, searching for his place, conscious all the time of Harriet's eyes upon him. When he found the page he reached over and gave her the book, indicating a line with the tip of one long finger. She looked at the book and then back at his face and said, "What is this?"

"Never mind. Just read that entry." He wanted to hear the familiar words read aloud, in her clear English accent.

"*I saw such things which were brought from Panama,*" she read. The words were soft and wondering. "*A sun entirely of gold, a moon entirely of silver, likewise sundry curiosities, all of which were fairer to see than many marvels. . . . I have never seen in all my days what rejoiced my heart as did this gold . . .* What is this, Captain Dexter?"

"Don't call me that . . . and don't ask."

"But I insist! 'Tis most ungallant, sir, to tempt and then provoke." He chuckled at that and watched her face dip as she frowned at the book again. Then she said, "There's a map."

"Yes." If he tilted his head a little he could see the map, but instead he watched her face. Her expression was engrossed; she was deciphering scribbles and curlicues that he knew by heart. It was a most elaborate map, drawn by a man who enjoyed decoration, adorned with rivers and dragons and bears and serpents in abundance—all this to frame the wavering shape of something circular in the middle. At the top the page was frayed and salt-stained, so only the letters *I*, *A*, *S* were decipherable.

She said, "Is this the map of a lake?"

"Perhaps. The Indians had tales of a lake of gold, and a race of women who lived there, who ate off gold, lived off gold,

wore gold clothing, and had a queen called Calafia, who
named her territory California."

"But this is not a map of California, surely?"

"Nor of any Mexican territory," he agreed. "For if it is a
map of Calafia's lake, then it must be a map of some place in
South America, where the Spanish conquistadors found unbelievable treasuries of gold."

She was watching him, nibbling the tip of one finger in
thought. Then she murmured, "And the pirate Morgan? He
lusted after this gold as well?"

"Indeed he did. Whether Calafia and her lake existed or not,
'tis indubitable fact that South America was full of gold, and in
the year 1670 much of that treasure was in Panama City. A
prime temptation, for a pirate."

"So he assembled his gang of desperadoes?"

"He did, and a bloodthirsty lot of villains they were. They
set out from Portobelo on the Caribbean coast, and then they
battled across the Isthmus of Darien, intent on reaching
Panama, looting and murdering as they went, battling up the
Chagres River in dugout canoes, fighting their way through the
jungle. They fought the Indians too: one of the pirates was shot
with a poisoned arrow, so they seized a village, murdered all
the inhabitants, and rendered the corpses down for fat, to
grease the rotting wound. As the poets say," he continued,
"death ate into their ranks, and when at last they knocked on
the gates of Panama City, all the gold had been rescued or
hidden. The arduous crossing had been for nothing. Oh, yes,
the great gold altar in the cathedral was still there, but the
people had hidden it by painting it to look like wood, and that
fooled Morgan and his men entirely. Perhaps they were too
busy taking revenge on the people to conduct a proper search;
maybe they were all just too stupid."

Harriet was gazing at him; he stopped and nodded at the
enthralled expression, and then he sipped his brandy.

She said slowly, "You said some of the gold had been
rescued."

"Yes, along with the nuns of the cathedral. Word had got
ahead of the pillaging and raping, the murders that Morgan and
his men had committed, so the nuns were all put on board a
vessel, which happened to be in port, and sent away along with
most of the gold."

"And where did they go?"

"Who knows?" said he wryly. "They were never heard of again."

She was frowning. Then she said slowly, "But you do think you know."

He was amazed at her perspicacity. He sipped again, saying nothing.

"And that island—Judas Island. That was why you were digging."

"How did you guess?"

"The chains. I felt something . . . some past terror. That village . . . the well, and the ruined church . . . the skeletons in that pit. You think the ship arrived at Judas Island, that the nuns settled there, or were given refuge by the inhabitants, that Morgan pursued them, that he and his men killed them all . . . that he and his men herded them into the cave and then filled the entrance in."

He was surprised again: she had traced his ponderings and conclusions very accurately indeed. Then she said, "Perhaps the nuns' ship was wrecked, and that was why they were forced to stop on the island . . . and perhaps that is why you found no treasure."

Then, to his amazement, she began to recite: "*Methought I saw a thousand fearful wrecks, a thousand men that fishes gnawed upon, wedges of gold, great anchors, heaps of pearl, inestimable stones, unvalu'd jewels* . . . Or, perhaps, Morgan and his men did find the treasure, and merely killed all those who lived on the island so there would be no witnesses. But why did you choose that certain island to do your digging, Captain Dexter?"

He blinked, having to rouse himself from thought. The effect of her normal, clear voice after the soft mesmeric effect of the recitation had been oddly disorientating. Then he shrugged and said, "The map."

"This map of California?"

"It's a map of Judas Island. The rivers and monsters are put there to hide the fact that it is the map of an island."

"What!" The word was blank. Then as he watched she bent her head and studied the book again. Then she said, "Yes! And how ingenious! Why, there are even positions, hidden in these animals. What are they . . . llamas?"

"The sheep of the Andes. Rochester wrote down all the gold yarns as he heard them or read them in the books he studied. He was obsessed with gold, and all the fables. He wrote that the Golden Fleece of Greek legend was possibly a sheep fleece used to trap particles of gold out of streams, and he wondered if the llama fleeces were used in the same way."

"Rochester?"

"Captain Rochester, the man who kept that journal. A long time ago, he commanded this brig. When I took the brig over I found the book behind a locker when I was taking down the locker for repair. It was in a secret, hidden compartment."

He silenced then, watching her as she turned to the front page of the book. It was as decorated as the map, with curlicues and drawings to embellish the four words *Brig Hakluyt, Her Logbook*. Then she looked up at him again, her brows arched high.

"This Rochester—was he a trader, like you?"

"He was a pirate," he said tersely and enjoyed her expression. Then he relented and qualified it, saying, "He was a privateer, with a letter of marque from the American government. He wreaked what damage he could on British shipping in the Atlantic, and then one day in 1813 he took on too many English men-of-war at once, and fled into the Indian Ocean. Then he kept on going, for by that time he was fascinated by the lost Panamanian treasure."

"How did he get the map?"

She was looking at the treasure map again. Dexter shrugged, draining his glass, and then he said, "It seems he obtained it in Spain, bought it from a drunken seaman, copied it into that book, and disguised it as the map of a lake."

"Then he knew all the time it was of Judas Island. Do you think he found the treasure?"

"If he found it," Dexter said deliberately, "he left it where he found it or hid it in another place and marked it on that map, for he was certainly poor when he died."

"And how long have you—Captain Dexter—known that the map was of the island?"

"Don't call me that," he said, and sighed, thinking grimly of that cave and the bare tragic skeletons. The place had fascinated him as much as it had Captain Rochester; he had returned every four months or so, each time to try out another idea . . . and what had he gained? Dismal memories, and a few sad mementoes. "Two years," he said. "Two years."

Harriet had shifted, leaning back in her seat so that her face was in shadow. She said, "What a shame, to have such a romantic quest end like this, but perhaps the gold is there yet.

Why else would Rochester keep on noting down gold stories as he found them?"

"Because he was obsessed."

"Yes," she said, and laughed a little, ruefully. Then she began to read aloud again. She read in French.

Vers ce beau ciel ou Dieu vous accompagne
Parlez joyeux, ne prenez aucun soin
Dans ce pays, vrai pays de cocagne
L'or du Peron tiendrait un petit coin . . .

She laughed again and said, "A cultured old fox, your Captain Rochester, Jahaziel! *Quel d'or*, he writes, *such awe*—such a dreadful pun! Here's another: *Could the golden goose have been Peruvian, that golden goose that barked like a dog, barking oeuf, oeuf, oeuf*! Jahaziel," said she severely as he chuckled, "not only did he have a most unbalanced obsession with the Panamanian treasure, but he had a most awful sense of humor!" Then she put her finger to her lips, smiling bewitchingly, and said, "No, Captain, I insist that the treasure is still there, and that the map tells us where it is hidden."

"I wish you were right," said he ruefully.

"I insist that I am, sir! Tell me, what do these letters mean, this *I A S*?"

"I don't know; I've often wondered. Perhaps the *I* is the downstroke of a *D*, and in full it reads JUDAS ISLAND."

"But why then take such pains to make the map look like a lake? Captain Rochester was determined to carry the secret to his deathbed. Tell me, how did he die?"

Dexter quenched the twitch of his lips and said solemnly, "A man fell on him from aloft."

"What!" Then, childlike, she clapped her hand to her mouth, but the guffaw was unmistakable. Then she said penitently, "I apologize."

"Think nothing of it."

"I was expecting a . . . much more romantic ending."

"No doubt he was even more surprised than you are."

"And you, Captain Dexter, are you a pirate or privateer too?"

"What?" Then he barked with laughter, surprised into enjoyment once again. "I don't think so."

"You don't go in for rape and pillage?"

"Seldom or never."

"I thought not," said she with every lively appearance of satisfaction. "Jahaziel, I think you merit a good reputation more than you pretend. Do you always trade in the Pacific?"

"I do whatever I like."

"What?" Another bewitching grin, and then, mock-scolding. "Jahaziel, I do believe you're a romantic at heart, a true adventurer. And what do the owners of the brig say about it?"

He was instantly furious, and all the more so because he had been so helplessly charmed. "The brig is mine!" he shouted, and slammed his fist on the little chart table. "The *Hakuyt* is mine by right, the brig belongs to me!"

Harriet said swiftly, "Captain Dexter—" but he ignored her, shouting.

"Every plank and every trunnel and every piece of rope stuff on the brig is mine by right—"

Then she shouted, "Captain Dexter, I believe you!"

He silenced, breathing heavily, muttering, "Don't call me that." And she, with utterly infuriating saccharine soothing, said, "You are perfectly justified in your pride of ownership, Captain Dexter. You own and run a most remarkably happy ship. I am no expert," said she thoughtfully, "but the domestic aura of your brig seems to me to be of the most unusual. I hear that men line up to ship with you, partly because—I'm told—of the quality of the grub. Furthermore, I hear that you have a most unusual method of managing your crew, that they make up a company and hold meetings and have a democratic say in the brig's affairs; a pioneering plan indeed, most praiseworthy, and any likeness to the way that pirate vessels were managed is, I'm sure, a mere coincidence."

Dexter said nothing, staring at her, wondering how much soft soap one girl could produce in one sentence, and she smiled ravishingly and said, "And, sir—if you are the owner—there is no real reason why you can't alter your mind and steer for Valparaíso."

"I don't need a reason," he snapped, furious at this blatant attempt at manipulation. "Why should I make up for Captain Smith's lapse in honor? He concluded to carry you no further, and must have had good reason to play such a shifty trick!"

Harriet went white, like a struck child, and for a moment guilt touched him, making him angrier than ever. Then she said in a low furious voice, "Captain Smith was even more dishonorable than you think, Captain! And it was his wife who

had the reason—and—it was not my fault! My God, sir, you
don't know what it was like; I shipped with Captain Smith as
passenger on purpose, because of the impropriety of a young
woman traveling unescorted; I thought I should be safe on
board of a ship that carried the master's wife. But the presence
of his wife did not deter Captain Smith in the slightest from
acting the randy goat, sir; my God, my great-aunt Diana once
had a curiosity, a wooden god from some eastern land, and that
god had ten or more arms with just as many sets of fingers, and
Captain Smith reminded me often of that many-handed god!"

"Jehovah," said Dexter blankly. He didn't know if he was
amused or shocked. He could certainly imagine that the
salacious old dog would become bewitched by this pretty
young thing, and the commotion when Mrs. Smith scented it.
Then all at once, he thought, *Eighteen*, Harriet was just
eighteen, and he felt angry, almost protective.

He felt guilty again and almost decided to withdraw his
decision. However, she'd be safe enough on Capricorn; the
trader there might have been a rogue in his youth, but now he
was old and garrulous and creaky, with a native wife and
sixteen brats. The girl would be a damn sight safer there than
at the mercy of the gossip of his lusty-blooded crew, he
thought, and then he forgot it, for he heard a little rumble.

It came from Harriet's sweet little lap, and he recognized the
source immediately. He exclaimed, hugely diverted, "You're
hungry!"

She paused; then her tone was icy. "I beg your pardon?"

"You failed to arrive at the supper table, and," he added
with enormous relish, "the grub, as you call it, was exception-
able good. There was soft bread and butter, and ham, cake and
coffee, fruit, all nice; why, I think old Bodfish was putting it all
on a-special for you!" He could have sworn he heard another
wistful gurgle at that, and he said derisively, "My God,
Harriet, you were making another melodramatic gesture."

"Well, how can I accept the grudging hospitality of a man
who—"

"Jehovah," said he, and laughed. "We'll be a few hours
a-puddling about here mending the brig, you know; 'tis
thirty-six hours at best afore we raise Capricorn. Do you think
your pride will keep its backbone that long?"

"Captain Dexter, sir—"

"And don't call me that," he instructed, and grinned most
wickedly. "And don't call me Jahaziel, either. My friends call

me Jake." Then he stood in one impatient movement and threw open the door.

He nearly felled Bodfish, who hopped and rubbed his ear and looked pained; the old fellow, Jake mused, had been eavesdropping, surely. He grinned again, hugely entertained by this play. "Fix this obstinate female a tray," he instructed. "And give her coffee and make sure she learns the time to arrive at breakfast." Then he turned to Harriet and swept a low bow, but it was a wasted piece of theater, for she merely swished past him with her head held high.

She was also carrying old Rochester's journal, but in the meantime he was content to let her borrow it.

5 ❧ Next morning the sea and sky were brightly rain-washed, full of promise for a fine brig-mending day. The watch sang out as they heaved up tubs of salt water to wash down the decks, and Jake Dexter whistled as he shaved. Even his reflection made him cheerful: that face was all he had, and he did not consider it particularly beautiful, but he'd come to terms with his a-kilter expressions long since.

He even broke into song as he strode into the big mess-cabin. "Has a love of adventure, a promise of gold," he musically inquired,

E'er tempted ye to roam where wide billows roll
Where cloud-crowned coasts and green islands call
As large as the word, and free to ye all . . . ?

Then his song broke off, as he lifted an eyebrow at Harriet, sitting fresh and washed herself, eating breakfast at the table.

She was also talking to Bodfish, and ignored him, but this did not trouble Jake a whit. He began whistling again as he went to attend to Abner.

Abner was sitting up in the second mate's berth and merely scowled in reply to the tune. Miss Gray, Abner informed Jake in a grumpy mumble, had already come and tidied his bed. She had fed him beef broth with a spoon. Abner was feeling sorry for himself, for his cheek was swollen and the eye on that side was shut and he didn't want his captain: he wanted Miss Gray back. A woman's hand at the sickbed, his manner made plain, was unmatchable.

Jake listened out the sorry complaint with no comment, and then he administered a teaspoon of laudanum, according to the medical guide. The book also recommended a mustard plaster on the back of the neck and wetting the sheets with vinegar, but Jake decided against that advice. Abner, he thought, was sufficient uncomfortable already. However, Abner did not look grateful; as Jake took his leave the boy looked even more aggrieved and peered one-eyed past Jake's shoulder as the door to the mess cabin opened, in the patent hope that he'd see Miss Gray. However, it was only Bodfish, with gruel, and Abner's disappointment was equally obvious. Charlie Martin might have fallen in and out of love with Harriet with the speed of lightning, Jake mused cynically, but Abner's sheepish devotion had taken his place. The sooner he dropped the minx at Capricorn the better, he further mused, but when he finally arrived on deck Harriet was leaning over the starboard rail as if she owned the brig.

And the men, every one of them, were watching her. They were working about decks and in the rigging with their usual hearty humor, but everything was done with unusual daring and flamboyance, and eyes rolled constant sideways to see if the girl was looking. Jake stood still in the shadow of the afterdeck, his hat tipped back, his thumbs in his belt loops, and he wondered if Harriet knew that the men were showing off for her benefit.

There was old Cookie, chopping kindling at his chopping block as if he were removing a host of English gentry heads, filling the air with flying chips. And there, in the rigging, was Crotchet, sliding breakneck down a backstay, twirling over and over like a monkey on a stick. Bill, the boy, not to be outdone, was upside down in the maintop, and Old Sails was mending a sail as if he'd entered a quilting competition. Abijah Roe

minced sideways along a footrope like a superannuated acro-
bat, and Pablo the Chilean strutted along with his bum stuck
out in self-made man-of-war pants whose hems brushed full on
the decks.

Such a crew of ruffians, some accidental, others selected.
Pablo had arrived one night in Valparaíso in a gloriously
embroidered suit with foot-long spurs and jangles, extremely
dusty and tattered, with a gang of vigilantes hot on the trail
behind him; ringletted Valentine had begged a hasty berth to
avoid the consequences of saying too much to the latest lady
love; oafish Jonathan, in the foredeck heaving up timbers to
show his manly strength, had presented himself to Jake in
Honolulu, all attired out like a cartoon figure, in a claw-
hammer coat, a tall, chimney-pot beaver hat, and a standup
collar to his shirt that had sagged with much salt. Tib Greene
and Dan Kemp had shipped with Jake in Talcahuano in the
more usual manner, erstwhile liberty men who had missed their
ship and no doubt that on purpose, but even they swaggered.
Tib's arm was now in a sling, of course, but he was doing his
full share of work, and that matter-of-factly, in the manner of
seamen world over. Tib and Dan were seasoned salts indeed,
but they, too, had a nonchalant air calculated to hide their
preoccupation with the passenger.

Harriet did not seem to notice; she leaned over the rail
gazing at the sea as if the depths enthralled her. She'd declared
she was never seasick, Jake thought suddenly, and in that
moment he believed her, for she looked so uncommonly at
ease, in this, a world that belonged to men. The brig rolled
uneasily with no sails set to counter the current, but this did not
seem to trouble her at all. Her posture pulled up the back of her
skirt so that pretty feet in pretty slippers were revealed, and
those feet were set as confidently as if she were on land.

Her posture also accentuated the long narrow curve of her
waist. Harriet was wearing an apron, a white apron tied with a
bow that nestled in that curve—and Jake realized all at once
that the attention of every man above decks was focused raptly
on that bow.

He moved abruptly and arrived beside her, but before he
could speak she turned and smiled, and said. "Why did you
give Davy that name?"

"What?" He blinked and frowned, turning involuntarily to
see Davy Jones Locker. The tall, silent black was working
quietly, weaving new coops for the hens. As Jake watched,

Davy's eyes slid sideways to meet his, and he turned back to Harriet and said curtly, "Why do you want to know?"

Her smile did not flinch. "Because your brig interests me so extremely, Captain, because of the quality of your men. They've been telling me how the company works, how they each buy shares and then become interested owners, how they make motions, and second them, and then vote, and in that way help run the brig. I've never heard of such a system before, and think it most enlightened. It has captured my imagination entirely—and can you blame me for being intrigued?"

Jake stared down at her for a long moment without replying, every suspicion alert. She was up to something, he could scent it, but in the meantime he said shortly, "There's not much of a story to Davy's name. He swam on board one night when we were anchored off Guiana, a runaway slave with men and dogs after him. He grabbed the chains as the current took him past us, and the sharks would've got him if the watch hadn't heard his cries."

"So you rescued him from Davy Jones Locker and named him to suit? But that's wonderful, Captain!" said she vivaciously.

He said curtly, "Harriet, I would prefer it if you remained below."

Her eyes widened, and her smile faded. "But why?"

The reasons were obvious; he said nothing.

"But—but on the ship to the Cape Colony, from England, and then on the ship from thence to New Zealand . . . why, I walked the after deck quite freely."

He said involuntarily, "Cape Colony?"

"Yes! And I do assure you, Captain, that the ladies were given the freedom to walk to take the air. Why, without exercise we would all have grown most uncommon fleshy, and how bored we would have been. We recited to each other, Captain, and staged small dramas, and the crew enjoyed the action, too, and put on concerts to entertain us."

Jake's eyebrows were hoisting higher and higher. Then he said with heavy meaning, "You said ladies. In the plural."

"I did," she agreed, and dimpled. "That, sir, was the reason we steered for the Cape. There were jealousies, you see. The captain had to put into the Cape, for reasons of diplomacy: no fewer than four duels had been arranged, the captain himself being one of the principals."

Jake said blankly, "Oh, Jehovah." Then, equally involuntarily, he barked with laughter.

"Yes, indeed, it was dreadful exciting, Captain, for the master of that vessel was indubitably mad. He used to mutter and take fearful rages, and once he took all the weapons from the armory into his stateroom and locked himself in with them for quite five days. My father kept on leading delegations to reason with him, especially when the captain kept up a press of canvas in most threatening weather. However—" and she sighed—"my father's good counsel did not prevail. Then two of the sails split in a squall, and one of the ladies swooned, and the captain was so delighted with her abject terror that he reduced canvas for the first time in the voyage."

Again she smiled. Jake stared down at her narrowly, perfectly aware of what she was doing: she was entertaining him with her lively story, to help him forget his decision to send her below. He said, "I think I can safely wager, Harriet, that the lady who swooned was not you."

"No," she said, and laughed. "I wasn't frightened at all, not then . . . however a few nights later the captain ran the ship on a rock, just outside of the harbor."

"And . . . ?"

"And my father organized a contingent of passengers, and they all manned the pumps, and we limped into port. The captain had shut himself up in his room again, but luckily one of the passengers was a mariner himself, and he, in the meantime, commanded the ship."

Jehovah, he thought, and wondered whether to believe her. "Harriet," he said firmly, "go below," and casting him an inimical look, she mutinously departed. Jake stood still, his hat tipped back, watching her form as she went, and when he looked back at the men they were all watching that slender form too.

They set back to work smartly when they caught his eye, and seemed to work with the same goodwill, but somehow the decks had lost a jaunty air. The men missed that source of prime entertainment, Jake mused, and, perhaps like him, they brooded. He was not really surprised in the late afternoon, when Charlie informed him that the men had requested a company meeting. It was obvious that they would want another turn at discussing the problem of the passenger.

However Jake did not anticipate any trouble. The men assembled in the usual way, and old Chips declared the meeting open in the usual words. Bodfish droned the notes of the minutes. Then the steward said, "Would someone please move that the minutes be accepted as correct?" But nobody answered, for the companionway door opened, and Harriet stepped lightly onto deck.

She smiled most beautifully at all the watching faces, and Crotchet fetched her a chair. Then Jake said sharply, "What is this, Miss Gray?"

"But I told you, Captain," said she with the most innocent air. "I've already declared myself fascinated with your democracy. Won't you allow me to observe it at work?"

"I'm sorry," he said tersely, "but you'll have to declare yourself disappointed. The meetings are open only to members."

"Yes, I know," she said and smiled. "And that is why I want to join."

"You . . . what!"

"I want to become a member of the *Hakluyt* Company, and I've brought the price of a share with me." She held out her hand, palm upward. There lay a small velvet bag, which clinked. Harriet drew open the tie, slowly, and then, slowly, shook the contents into her other hand. Small gold coins fell out, English sovereigns. Harriet counted them out loud, from one to ten, and then, smiling modestly, she held them out to Dexter. "The equivalent, I know, of fifty dollars American," she murmured. "And fifty dollars—I know—is the price of one share in your group."

Jake couldn't believe her sauce; he drew in a breath and did not know if he would snap or laugh. Then, increduously, he heard Abijah Roe say thoughtfully, "You can buy more'n one share if you want, miss."

"One share, Mr. Roe," said she demurely, "will be sufficient."

"Even one share," Jake said curtly, seizing the silence, "is impossible, Miss Gray; joining our company is not that simple."

"Is it not?" said she with every lively appearance of interest. "But why, sir, not put the idea to the vote?"

Jake sucked in another breath, but all the men were nodding. Surely, he thought, the vote would end this farce, and he watched them narrowly as old Chips put the motion. "Affirmative?" said Chips, and . . .

Abijah Roe, thought Jake, watching the querulous face, Abijah wouldn't agree; Abijah disapproved of womenfolks on principle . . . but the old man raised his hand, his eyes fixed firmly on the small gleaming sovereigns in Harriet's out-stretched palm. Crotchet and Valentine, yes, would vote for Harriet simply for the sake of devilment; and Jake was right, for their arms shot up like signals. Jonathan, now; Jonathan grunted and disapproved all the time of Miss Harriet's flirta-tious ways, but Jonathan put up his arm to feel what voting was like. Davy . . . Davy never voted, for he did not understand it; but for the first time ever Davy put up his hand, for Davy's mistress on the Guiana plantation had been a white-haired elderly woman, so Davy put up his hand, for in his secret silent depths he had a vast respect for women with white hair.

Jake's was the only dissenting vote; he couldn't believe it, but perforce, fuming, he had to watch as Harriet was enrolled in the *Hakluyt* Company. As was the custom, Bodfish read her the rules. All the men watched Harriet avidly as she listened. ". . . that the stock of the Company . . ." droned Bodfish in the familiar words that few of them understood, and ". . . shares be each worth fifty dollars, or its equivalent in work done for the brig . . . that all decisions be faithfully followed when voted in favor by at least three-fourths of the Company . . . that each share of whatever value be entitled to but one vote . . . that the members faithfully labor to advance the interest of all . . ." and at last he monotoned to a stop. Harriet leaned forward and neatly signed the document, adding her name to the list of members.

All the men, unconsciously, leaned forward too as they watched her. Most of them were smiling. Even Abijah Roe smiled, as he observed in conversational tones, "You won't have a vote, o' cuss, Miss Gray, no matter how many shares you buy."

Harriet sat up straight and stared at him. Jake couldn't hold back a righteous grin; this, he thought with angry enjoyment, was where Miss Gray met her just desserts.

She said sweetly, "Whyever not, Mr. Roe?"

"Womenfolks can't vote! It ain't proper, it ain't right, no matter what them women's rightists that plague the country say. There ain't no country in the world what allows women that unnatural right, and it don't happen in our company neither."

Harriet said nothing. Jake watched her with his arms folded, more relaxed than he'd been in half an hour, relishing this moment. Then he saw her shrug. She looked about all the men, waved a nonchalant hand, and said, "Very well then."

Jake blinked, confounded, but Abijah merely looked grudgingly mollified. Then Harriet's prim smile widened, and she said in off-hand tones, "However, I would like to propose a motion: I wish to propose that we steer the brig for Valparaíso, where I can put a most profitable bit of business our way."

And that was no more or less than Dexter had expected; Harriet's motives had become plain the moment she'd stated she wanted to join the company. He tipped back his hat in readiness for argument, and then he heard Abijah cry, "Business, Miss Gray? But that ain't right! Womenfolks can't put men in the way of business; it rates the same as asking for a vote!"

Harriet snapped, "You think so? I don't understand your logic, Mr. Roe. You were glad enough to take my money for the company share."

"That don't signify. There ain't one legal act what a mere female can perform, and it jest ain't right for a woman to presume in men's business."

"Women pay taxes, do they not?"

"That don't signify neither," said he doggedly. "Womenfolks jest ain't formed to take responsibilities, and that is a Biblical truth. Why, for a start, for one whole fourth of the most of their lives they're unclean, that's what, they ain't even in control of their minds—"

To Dexter's utter stupefaction Harriet surged to her feet and shouted, "Throw that man overboard!"

The silence was stunned. Harriet had one arm extended, one doom-laden finger pointed straight at Abijah's bulging eyeballs, and all the men gauped like felled sheep.

And then she cried, "Do you think to condemn me and shackle me on account of my sex? But why, sir, why be so unfair? Are women so weak and despicable? Do they not have the same appetites, the same inspirations, the same disappointments as men? If I am a woman, then am I not allowed to dream, feel emotion, respond to the search for riches, respond to a promise of gold?

"I am a woman," she cried, "a woman!" My God, thought Dexter, utterly benumbed, the minx had the whole crew bewitched by nothing more than a melodramatic tantrum. The men all gauped like spellbound rams as she cried, "Is a woman not allowed dimensions, passions, senses, affections, ambitions? Is a woman not hurt when wounded, sick when afflicted? The same sun warms her, the same wind chills her, and if she is poisoned, does she not die?"

And at that she stopped, and the silence throbbed and seemed to go on forever. Then old Chips said gruffly, "She do have some rights that go with a share."

"I do," agreed Harriet. She smiled exactly as if the remarkable tirade had not taken place, an ineffable smile that was just a little smug. "Anyway," she said in the most practical of accents, "once we drop anchor in the harbor of Valparaíso you can forget my part in the business entirely if your man's brain cannot encompass the notion, Mr. Roe, for my brother is in control of the scheme, and the company can deal exclusively with him."

Dexter snapped, "Brother? what brother?"

"My brother, Royal Gray," and again, oddly, she looked at him expectantly, as if she thought he'd know the name.

Jake had never heard of the man. He barked, "And what the devil is your brother doing in South America, madam?"

"Oh, he's been there more than a year, Captain Dexter, on a secret mission, sir, a mission on behalf of the British government and the merchants who own the mills at Bradford."

And once again Jake was utterly confounded. Harriet smiled at him demurely, and all he could do was tip back his hat, while the words, *secret, secret mission*, were passed excitedly around the young bloods of the men on deck.

Then, at last, he found his voice. "And what, pray, is this business, Miss Gray?"

"Alpaca," said she, "alpaca" and that word was passed back and forth too. Alpaca—what the devil were they? Then Jake remembered: a kind of South American camel. With wool.

Harriet was watching him just as if she read his thoughts. She murmured, "My brother has accumulated a flock of three hundred of the beasts, Captain, and his brief from the government is to smuggle them out. My instructions were to find a vessel which could be fitted out to carry the flock to New South Wales in Australia—and, if we get them there, and break the South American monopoly by establishing a breeding stock, why, then the British government, through the generosity of the Bradford merchants, will give us one hundred thousand pounds in gold—the equal to half a million dollars."

6 ❧ The roaring forties and the current took them, and the passage to Valparaíso was swift and brief, but at times Jake thought the voyage would never end. Harriet had told nothing but the truth when she'd declared she was never seasick. On the second day the current became heavy, but she was up and about and lively as before. Perhaps, Jake brooded, a less critical captain would have found her little trouble too, but she certainly troubled him, because he never had a chance to forget that she was there.

The problem, he thought at times, was that she was just too much at home on his brig, a deal by far too comfortable. She stopped in the first mate's stateroom, apparently forever, so Jake tersely bid old Chips put a latch string on her door.

There was a latch already on the inside of the door, and Chips put a hole in the door beside it. A string then led from the latch to the outside, so that Harriet could close the door when she was not in the room, and then open it by the simple act of pulling on the string. When the string was drawn so it hung on the inside, Harriet was safe from unseemly intrusion.

"What intrusion?" she demanded and seemed most irritatingly amused. She made Jake feel three times his twenty-six years, and a prim old Puritan at that. "Who would want to sneak up on me?" she demanded, and he did not want to admit it, but she was right. Charlie Martin still acted distant when she was in the cabin, for he still smarted from being made such a fool by the Smiths. He might have voted for her, but, he declared, he had done it to make her situation on the brig "more regular." Valentine and Crotchet had voted for her out of plain old mischief, but they were a deal too busy to bother Miss Gray, being fully occupied with dandying up for an all-out assault on the Valparaíso wenches.

On deck it was different, for the men still watched her avidly. For quite five days Jake conducted a running battle with Harriet, sending her below whenever he saw her. "But I must take the air," she insisted, while the men all furtively grinned. "It's not healthy," said she virtuously, "to have no fresh air. It's bad for the complexion."

Her complexion was radiant; Jake thought it always had been. However, he was forced to admit that the voyage was doing her good. The good grub of the *Hakluyt* was smoothing out the hollows in her cheeks, and every day she looked less waiflike than ever. She had not lived well in New Zealand, and the thought made him feel uncomfortable.

"Anyway," she argued, "I have to hang out my washing." Her petticoats and waists, indeed, were flapping in the rigging, and Jake noted that they got a great deal of attention as well. Harriet had demurely offered to do the captain's washing too, which had scandalized Bodfish extremely. "On the ship to the Cape Colony," she said, in the start to a sentence that Jake knew by heart, "we ladies—"

"—hung out the washing," said he for her, but his sarcasm did not deter her in the slightest.

"Yes!" she said in the most vivacious tones. "Once a flock of unmentionables lost their stops and took flight, and the men hauled back the main yard and lowered a boat and rescued them all."

"And how did the captain feel about that, pray?"

"Oh, that was the source of one of his rages. He threatened to make a spread eagle of all of those men; he took old muskets out of the armory; he fired one into the air, and shot off a rope;

he went into his cabin and muttered. And," she said, and sighed, "that meant my father had to form yet another delegation."

Most irritatingly, Jake had to quench amusement. "Trading brigs, Harriet, are not passenger-carrying packets."

"Indeed they are not, Jahaziel!"

"And what else did your father do, while you and the ladies were reciting and play-acting and hanging out the washing?"

"But he was reciting and acting as well! And," she added ingenuously, "he taught himself to play the clarinet. And then, on the passage to New Zealand from the Cape, there were, of course, the horses."

She was back to her old trick of distracting him from ordering her off to the cabin, but Jake was utterly unable to hold back a thunderstruck echo of, "Horses? What horses?"

"Why, the horses that my father bought at the Cape! We spent quite four months in the colony, and my father did well, most profitably. So he invested in horses, two stallions and four mares. Such fine thoroughbreds, you have not a notion how beautiful. That, of course," said she off-handedly, "is why we went to New Zealand instead of stopping on at the Cape. My father heard that thoroughbred horses fetched great prices in New Zealand, for the new Zealand colonists are extreme fond of the sport of racing, so he took the chance to make a fortune."

So it seemed, Jake mused as he brooded down at her from the shadow of his hat, that the Gray family had a facility for carting beasts about on ships. "And what did the captain say when these horses were produced—or did the ship have stables?"

"No, it did not, and there was such an angry commotion. The captain was every bit as surly as the other, and he was perfect beside himself with rage. However," she said airily, "the matter was easily remedied. My father, remember, had made much profit in the Cape, and for once was flush. Money makes such a difference, you know. My father simply bought the tickets for the deck cabins from the people who had them, and he installed the horses in those cabins."

Jake winced and said, "My God." Then he added tartly, "I trust you don't plan to keep alpaca in your stateroom."

To his exasperation she laughed at that, her eyes dancing in the speckled shadow of the straw hat that one of the men had made her. "We'd build stalls, of course," she said, and waved a nonchalant arm. "You told me yourself that you have wood on board, Jahaziel! And I would work, most willingly, for all that being a groom is not pleasant. I know that," she elaborated, "because my father made me help as groom for those horses! Have you ever seen a seasick stallion, sir?"

She was back to her trick of trying distraction, Jake thought acidly. He had never seen a horse in such condition and did not want the experience either. He snapped, "Why don't the Bradford merchants buy alpaca wool from the Indians, if that wool is so very valuable?"

"Because of its length. The Indians refuse to shear the alpaca more often than every second year; it's a religion with them, and because of this the wool grows too long, and the mill machines can't handle it. They've tried to talk to the Indians, but even the most careful persuasion has not succeeded, so," she said and heaved a sigh, "the only expedient is to grow alpaca for themselves . . . and the grasslands of New South Wales would be ideal. However, the Indians worship the animals and refuse to let them out of the country, so what can the British do, apart from hiring men who are willing to smuggle them out?"

Put like that, the scheme was logical—and half a million dollars a most adequate inducement. Once the alpaca were safely at sea no laws would be broken. Jake was fully aware that like schemes abounded: why, the English merchants were advertising openly for men to smuggle rubber-tree seeds out of Brazil. As a trader Jake abhorred local laws and regulations that made free trade impossible, but yet he felt uneasy.

The oval face under the straw hat looked too innocent for such schemes. He said, "Where is your father, Harriet?"

She paused, and in that space Jake saw those wide eyes become cynical again. She said evenly, "He's dead."

"He died in New Zealand?" She nodded. "And your brother, does he know?"

"Probably not. He was on his way to South America when it happened."

Jake frowned. So here was the reason for the waiflike, hungry look, he thought; times had been hard for Miss Harriet Gray. He said abruptly, "Was it sudden?"

"Yes," she said and turned away and left him. For the first time she left the deck of her volition.

Two days after that the lookout raised the land. It was dawn. Harriet came on deck and there was a ghostly streak of mountain tops in the eastern sky, a pattern of disembodied brush strokes with no apparent connection to land.

Then after breakfast the brown hills of Chile were there on the horizon, a shadowy fringe of crags and peaks where fragile mists wafted out to sea. At noon the yards were braced about and a land breeze took them, and there was Valparaíso, a clutter of houses and towers, pastel colors and red brick and whitewash, all brilliant in the afternoon sun.

There were more than seventy vessels anchored in the bay: a British steam-bark-of-war and an American frigate bobbed ponderously in the midst of rows of shipping . . . schooners, whalers, sloops all brightly painted . . . barges, scows, and guano-carriers . . . Harriet leaned her elbows on the warm wood of the port rail, her chin set on her fists, gazing entranced at the pretty scene. She had never visited Valparaíso before and found it perfectly charming. The houses were built in the unlikeliest places, in rows along crags and up and down terraces. The foreshore, too, was picturesque, a strand where strings of donkeys and mules moved slowly in laden procession. Men rode about, hollering and waving wide hats, and other men had painted wagons, from which they apparently sold grog, for they pushed them into the water's edge in a race to meet the boatloads of sailors that pulled out from all the ships.

Then Jake's voice said dryly, "I see no alpaca."

"No," she admitted. She looked at the horses and donkeys and mules and wondered what alpaca looked like.

"And now that we've arrived, how do you expect to find your brother?"

"I thought I'd ask at the customs house." Then she thought, uneasily, that the customs house boat had not come out to them yet, despite the fact that the brig had sent up a signal.

There was plenty of other small craft, gaily colored little boats plying the bay like water bugs. Many of these, Harriet saw then, were heading with intention for the brig, and as they neared their intention became plain, for the oarsmen stood up precariously on thwarts and did their utmost to sell the crew of the brig a multitude of things.

These entrepreneurs wore big straw hats like the one that Harriet wore, and they had brightly colored ragged clothes. They hung onto the straking of the brig, all shouting out in a competition to sell. In both English and Spanish they called out varying allurements, of wine and *aguardiente* and women, offering beans and bananas, potatoes and yams, little pigs and skinny chickens.

Then three of the sellers sighted Harriet and propelled themselves nearer to where she leaned over the rail, vying to sell her needles or perfume, ribbons or laces. To her surprise Jake haggled and then bought her some light and dark blue ribbons. "For your hat," he said, slightly smiling, and she sparkled, delighted, and took off her hat on the instant to tie the ribbons about the crown. Then the sudden hush of the horde of raucous boatmen got through to her.

When she looked up the sellers were pushing their craft away from the brig's hull. Even the *Hakluyt* men roaring about in the rigging were quiet. Jake was frowning, his hat pulled low over his eyes, and then she saw the reason. The British bark-of-war had lowered a boat, and that boat was pulling for the brig.

Then with a thump of her heart she remembered that not only was her quest an illegal one here, but the captain beside her was some kind of fugitive from justice. However, the two young officers who scrambled on the deck of the brig were full of smiles and seemed empty of suspicions. One was a second lieutenant and the other was a midshipman, and their vessel, they said, was the British steam-bark-of-war *Nympha*, in the Pacific and Indian oceans on a three-year mission. They had come, they said in their clear young English voices, because there had been a report about a *lady* on the brig *Hakluyt*.

Then they executed gallant little bows over Harriet's extended hand. "Captain Mara sends his compliments," said the midshipman. "He feels some concern that you might be frightened. A brig-of-war of the Peruvian fleet is expected hourly, and there will be the usual salute of guns. So he bid us come with a word to the wise."

"Most necessary, madam!" said the second lieutenant in his turn. "There will be nine guns to each man-of-war, including the American frigate *Savannah*, and then twenty-one guns each in respect to the Chilean fort. The good Lord alone knows," said he with candor, "how many guns the fort will fire in return. There will be much noise and a little smoke. Hence Captain Mara's concern."

"A true English gentleman," Harriet murmured. She was very aware of Jake Dexter's ill-hidden amusement at this folderol. There was a sudden awkward little silence, broken by a clearing of tactful English throats.

"Captain Mara," murmured the second lieutenant, "is— h'm!—an Irishman, ma'am."

"He also," said the midshipman, "requests the pleasure of your company to dinner tonight, and the pleasure of the company of Captain Dexter and his officers and crew as well. Dinner, on English vessels," said he with ponderous tact in Jake's direction, "is a meal that is served at eight. In the evening."

"Is that so?" said Jake merely, but Harriet could feel his sardonic mirth. However, to her surprise, he assented, and the two young officers took their leave.

Captain Mara sent a boat, which arrived an hour after sunset. Harriet was waiting at the rail, and the crewmen who had been selected to go on board the *Nympha* were milling about forward, talking in a gruff happy babble. Harriet was wearing a watered blue taffeta gown, with a silk shawl wound about her hips in the Spanish style, and the blue ribbons Jake had given her wound up into her hair. Then, as the *Nympha* boat touched the side of the brig, she heard a footstep and turned, and there was Jake.

He was wearing black broadcloth and snowy white stock and looked most unexpectedly splendid. His eyes were on her but he said nothing, turning instead to give last instructions to Mr. Martin, who was remaining behind in his role of first officer, looking after the brig.

Then Jake offered her his arm, to help her into the boat. The boat was a gig, with eight oarsmen and seats, and was, furthermore, draped in red satin. Harriet's dancing eyes met Jake's incredulous ones, and then she didn't dare meet his eyes again, lest she explode into unseemly mirth. Jake seated himself as fastidiously as any cat, and then they pulled away. The *Hakluyt* men were to follow them, in one of the *Hakluyt* boats.

The bay at night looked magical. The darkness glowed with yellow lamps set on all the ships, and water dripped phosphorescently from the blades of the sweeps as the eight oarsmen slowly pulled. The *Hakluyt* boat was off to Harriet's left, and she dreamily watched them as they pulled in time. But then all at once, she noted with startlement that the *Hakluyt* boat was coming closer, that it was, in fact, overhauling them.

The grins all over stubbled mischievous faces were sly, and Valentine Fish at the steering oar was exhorting the oarsmen in clearly audible whispers. Merciful heavens, Harriet thought with silent disbelieving amusement, the *Hakluyt* men were surreptitiously racing the *Nympha* men for the bark. It was the War of 1812 all over again, she thought semi-hysterically; the

Yankee fellows in the *Hakluyt* boat were set to show these limey sailors how to move! Then all at once the limey sailors saw what was up, it seemed, for with a lurch of the gig that forced Harriet to grab Jake's arm for balance, they suddenly set up a spurt.

Neck and neck they raced, while the huge stern of the bark-of-war loomed nearer. The gig arrived at the gangway with a reverberating clunk that unbalanced Harriet yet again, but the *Hakluyt* boat was there, and the *Hakluyt* grins were victorious. Captain Dexter's face was bland, but when he assisted Harriet onto the deck she could feel him shaking with his own secret mirth.

Marines saluted and a whistle piped, and the *Hakluyt* men shied like colts as they clambered onto deck. They recovered in an instant, however, Harriet observed, and swaggered perceptibly as they were ushered forward to whatever food and entertainment awaited in that lowly part of the ship.

Captain Dexter and Harriet were to be entertained aft, in the sailing master's sitting room. The second lieutenant and the midshipman waited to escort them there, standing poker-stiff in the most formal of receptions. Two Americans were already aboard, they informed Harriet as they all walked aft and below. One was Captain Mervine and the other was Lieutenant Bartlett, and they were from the frigate *Savannah*.

"I notice," Captain Dexter said in his drawl, "that the Peruvian brig has not yet come."

"Perhaps tonight, sir," said the second lieutenant, and beamed. "They are expected hourly, their business being urgent."

Harriet frowned. Then she heard Jake say, "Urgent?"

"Aye, sir." That was the midshipman; Harriet was beginning to tell the clear young English voices apart, for the midshipman's tones were that much more ingenuous. " 'Tis a desperado," he confided. "A villain of the most audacious kind who has managed to evade Peruvian justice. He has offended the Indians in some drastic way, sir, and is reported to be in flight to this port. Hence the brig-of-war! Our assistance has been asked," he said.

"And, of course, will be given," importantly continued the second lieutenant. "One foot in Valparaíso, and the rogue will be brought to justice!" With that he stopped and knocked on a door, and the door was opened at once by a portly man in a vast blue suit.

This, Harriet deduced at once, was no less than Captain

Mara; his Irish aura and affable whiskey breath were immediately palpable. "Right welcome, right welcome!" he boomed.
"Come right in, Mrs. Dexter!"

She should have expected it, she confusedly thought, but she
had been distracted, and now her cheeks were as hot as fire.
She glanced quickly at Jahaziel in her confusion, and then as
quickly away again, before she even saw his expression. Then
she heard his even tones, saying, "Please allow me to introduce our passenger . . . a part-owner of our brig. This lady,
sir, is Miss Harriet Gray."

"Not Mrs. Dexter?" inquired Captain Mara. He appeared
thunderstruck, and not very intelligent either. "A supercargo,
you say?"

"Miss Gray is from London," murmured Jake. His sideways
glance at Harriet was brooding, she thought. "She has voyaged
on the brig just a short while, a part of her passage from New
Zealand to this port."

"London?" echoed the Irishman; he seemed amazed at this
non sequitur and waggled his brows extremely. "Well, well,"
he said and grumbled to himself, and then he roused himself
from profound puzzlement and introduced the two officers
from the *Savannah*. They were large and noble fellows too.
Harriet shook their hands sedately, gathering her wits.

Then Captain Mara barked, "You say from London, Captain
Dexter?"

"Miss Gray has been living in New Zealand . . . and Cape
Colony."

"Ah, then, she can't be the actress gal, the one that I did hear
of, the daughter of that Charles Gray that all Britain do
revere!"

"But I am," said Harriet rather tartly. She was angry at being
spoken of as if she were not there. "My father is—was Charles
Gray, and my mother, Mary Sissons Gray, sir."

The effect was all that she could have wished for; she smiled
prettily at four startled expressions.

"You're from that playacting lot?" Captain Mara demanded.
"I am."

"That family of the London stage?"

"And the provinces, yes."

"By thunder," said Captain Mara, who shook his head and
drained his glass and looked about for another. "But confound
it," he said, "this be a true compliment, surely. I do swear it,
truly, I saw her father thrice—no, stump it, four times at

least!—in 1806, or was it seven? It don't really matter but by God the experience was tremendous inspiring, and her mother, sir, her mother . . ." Then his voice faded away, and he clapped himself on his bright red forehead and he cried, "But I must beg a favor of Miss Gray!"

"You must?" echoed Jake.

"But of course! In the matter of playacting, sir, and recitation!"

"Playacting, sir?" Jahaziel murmured. His sideways glance at Harriet was wicked. "I'm certain Miss Gray will oblige, for on the ship to Cape Colony, she tells me, she and the other lady passengers recited and playacted with enthusiasm!"

If Captain Mara was surprised at this, he certainly did not show it; he was patently lost in an enthusiasm all his own. "But I mean more than that, sir!" he cried. "We have a band of Thespians on this ship, a playactin' group what is this very night about to stage a portion of Shakespeare for our entertainment, and amateur jugglers and songsters and acrobats, too. They plan a right feast for a concert! Tell me, Miss Gray, are you amazed, amazed?"

She wasn't amazed at all, but had no chance to voice it; no sooner had she opened her mouth then the door was opened, and more guests were announced. A babble of dignitaries from on shore had arrived, the women like flowers and the men like peacocks, and Harriet found herself alone with Jake.

She lifted her glass and sipped champagne to fill the enigmatic silence. He was watching her face, but she could not read his expression. He had a glass in his hand but was not drinking; instead he was studying her with his eyebrows a-kilter.

Then he said musingly, "And are you amazed?"

"No, of course I'm not." She kept her voice light. " 'Tis a remarkable fact, Captain Dexter, but wherever British troops are stationed in a far-off place, they set to and form a playacting company, and it's remarkable, too, how they always turn to Shakespeare when choosing what to stage."

"I strongly suspect that when our host gets round to outlining the favor he's about to beg, it will be to act with the *Nympha* troupe."

"I'm sure you're right."

"You sound resigned to the idea."

He was amused, she saw then. She bridled and said tartly, "Well, it's happened before. There was a British man-of-war at the cape, and my father and my brother and I were invited on board, just like this, and we all took parts in the shipboard production. I," she added, "was the shrew."

"And very well cast, I'm certain."

"Well, I did better than the resident player who would have made the gruffest shrew I ever heard."

He laughed. "And the play was a great success?"

"Not really," she admitted. His eyes took on an inquiring glint, and she said, "The ship, you see, was on the way back to England after a tour of duty in the Indian Ocean, and various sultans and nabobs had sent presents by her for the queen— presents for the zoological garden in Regent's Park. The production was going very well," she said reflectively, "until the lions escaped. Royal showed more agility than I'd ever seen him display; he was the first in the rigging, but the whole of our audience was hot on his heels."

Jake said, "What?" and then shouted with laughter, the most surprised laughter she'd heard from him yet, and she was all at once aware that the newcomers were all looking curiously in her direction while Captain Mara boomed pleasantries.

She looked at Jake again and said, "And were you amazed, Jahaziel?"

"What? to find you were an actress? No, indeed, for it explained much . . . such as why you expected me to know your name. I presume you're famous?"

"Not really," she admitted.

"Ah," said he and grinned. The newcomers were moving, herded in her direction by their affable host. Then Dexter said idly, "It also explained something else."

"Yes?"

"The melodramatic tantrums." Before she had time to cast him a simmering look, the guests had all arrived.

The midshipman poured champagne while the second lieu- tenant recited the names of all present, names which Harriet forgot the instant she heard them. One of the ladies was a large toothy Frenchwoman who shrieked, "An actress? You—you a woman of the stage?"

That, thought Harriet, was phrased rather unfortunately. Jake, however, merely smiled and said, "The Gray family is famous."

"Aha," said the Frenchwoman, and, "Indeed!" boomed Captain Mara. "I hope," he went on roguishly, "to prevail on Miss Gray to take a part in the interlude from Shakespeare that our troupe is staging for our entertainment tonight. Do you think she'll do it, Captain Dexter?"

"Of course she will," said Jake, smiling wickedly at Harriet.

" 'Tis the part of the lovely faerie queen . . . Titania."

"Excellent!" Jake said.

"Do you think," he asked anxiously, lowering his voice a little, "that she knows the lines?"

"But of course she does," said Jake heartily, which earned himself another acid glance. Captain Dexter, Harriet mused heatedly, was having himself a first-rate time at her expense and no doubt thought he was having a little revenge for the bad times she'd given him on the brig. When the door opened again and dinner was announced, she, for one, was heartily pleased.

The dinner was set at a long table in the wardroom, in a sparkling display of white linen and silver and crystal. There was more luxury than Harriet had seen in almost two years. There were three different wine glasses to each setting. Harriet sat between Captain Mara and Captain Mervine of the *Savannah*; Jake Dexter and the toothy French lady sat right opposite. Then, no sooner had everyone found his or her seat, than the eating and drinking got started.

The courses of fancy food seemed endless, but not as endless as the toasting. Then men bobbed up and down with the regularity of corks in a rugged sea. They toasted Queen Victoria, President Polk, and Shakespeare. Then, by process of logic, they all toasted Miss Gray. Harriet nodded regally as the glasses were quaffed. They toasted Captain Dexter then for possessing the charm and perspicience to bring Miss Gray to the bark, and then with further logic toasted the American flag. After the men all sat down, the Frenchwoman cried out, "Tell me, Captain Mervine, tell me, what do these tales of the gold?"

Gold? Harriet blinked; she saw Jake Dexter lift his crooked eyebrows and then lower them in an attentive frown. What gold?

"The gold in California!" Captain Mara bellowed in her ear. "There be fanciful tales a-runnin' about this coast, right disbelievable stories of gold up the Sacramento River!"

California? Her eyes flew to Jake's. He said quickly, "Who says there is gold there?"

"Forget it; 'tis naught but a hoax." The answer was flat, spoken in a nasal Yankee accent. It was Captain Mervine, silent as an obelisk till then. "There was a fuss about in Monterey, in March. A feller rode into the barracks, shouting about some gold, gold he reckoned he'd seen, collected up a fork of the river, called 'American.' There be another feller up the Sacramento, a Mormon called Brannan, he hollers the same hoax. 'Tis but to hustle up business, that's all, so he can sell the goods he's got in his store at Sutter's Fort, a store full of picks and pans and shovels. He's a rogue; sane men don't heed him. California has a future, glowing, California has riches, true, but they ain't in the form of nuggets or gold dust. They can only be found in the sweat of honest men."

Mervine nodded at Dexter then and said, "Have you made port at California, ever? Have you been to San Francisco?" Harriet watched Jake Dexter shake his head. "Oho, Captain Dexter," Mervine said with no joking in his voice, "I prophesy it right now, and I mean it, for it'll come true, jes' you watch, but San Francisco is destined to be the premier port of the Pacific. The poor little town of two hundred souls that I laid eyes on first in 1846 has grown by ten times, and the most of the growth is American. Aye, I can testify it; California is now afflicted with American drive and enterprise, and its future now be inevitable."

Harriet shook her head, bewildered, and said, "But I thought California was Mexican?"

"No longer!" Captain Mervine hollered, and Harriet flinched. He was perfect puce; she felt serious alarm for his health. Then he thundered, "The Mexican War is over, ma'am, and American force and diplomacy prevailed!"

"Oh, dear," she said, "I am so very sorry," and then winced again, for the words did not come out the way she had meant them. Captain Mervine gave her a very brooding look, and she could hear his heavy breathing. She said rather lamely, "I've been traveling, Captain, and—and subsisting in the colonies. The war must have ended while I was not paying attention, Captain Mervine."

"H'm!" said he and sniffed suspiciously. "The territory will flourish now," he grumbled. "And California, well managed, will prove rich indeed."

"I'm sure you're right, Captain."

"But, Miss Gray, it will not grow rich on this problematical gold!"

"I believe you."

"And even if there were gold, the garrison will claim it, in the name of the United States government; Colonel Mason will send out a force to take possession of the mines."

"But there is no gold," she said cooperatively. "There can't be."

"You seem certain of your words, ma'am?"

"Yes, I am, for I have but thought of it, the logical proof that there can't be any gold."

"And that, Miss Gray?"

"Why, if there had been gold in California, the Mexicans would have known it, and if they knew they possessed a mine, they would have fought much harder and never, ever, let the Americans win, Captain Mervine!"

She looked about the table, smiling radiantly, and met Jahaziel's eyes. They were dancing, most definitely. She heard Captain Mara clear his throat all of a sudden, and she realized what she had said.

"A toast," said Captain Mara gruffly. "A toast . . . ah, to the Chilean flag." Harriet subsided, profoundly grateful to have the subject changed. She listened absently as everyone talked about the desperate villain, the Chilean forces that were out in town a-hunting for the rogue, and the Peruvian brig-of-war that was sailing for this port in criminal pursuit.

She paid little attention; she was mentally rehearsing Queen Titania's lines. If she missed one cue, she was certain, Jake Dexter's teasing would never give her any rest.

The stage was the afterdeck of the *Nympha*, and Titania's grassy mound was a chaise longue with a green felt billiard table blanket draped over. Harriet reclined gracefully, listening to the commotion. Captain Mara's party was going full fizz, a tremendous success.

When the dinner had finally finished the party came up to deck to drink and dance. The music was produced by a music box with drum and bell accompaniment, and Harriet had been swept off her feet. Then the drinks and box had been set to one side, and the men who had been enjoying their own fete forward had come and disposed themselves up in the rigging and about the decks. The cabin guests, of course, had chairs.

Harriet lay with her eyes shut, carefully draped. She heard a little bell and then Captain Mara's gruff loud voice. The audience hushed and she was able to hear the words. A recital was about to commence, the Irishman announced, a recital from the immortal bard's *A Midsummer Night's Dream*, a recital that would be enlivened and flattered by the most unexpected presence of a Star of the Stage, none other than

Miss Harriet Gray of the Royal Opera House, London, the
Theatre Royal, Bristol, and the Theatre Fitzroy, New Zealand!

The ensuing silence was stunned, most of the astonishment,
she was certain, emanating from the *Hakluyt* men. She heard
the actors as they made their entrance and gathered about. And
then:

"If I were only thine!" the actor playing Bottom brayed. His
tone was muffled, and when Harriet peeped he was wearing a
magnificent mask indeed, a very hairy donkey face, made of
pig bristles glued onto wire and canvas.

"Help, we are haunted!" cried the other actor-yokels, and
Harriet listened to the retreating thunder of their boots,
followed by the lighter steps which she deduced must belong to
the actor-Puck.

"I see their knavery," the actor-Bottom mumbled.

"They hope to make an ass of me."

Harriet sighed and stretched, and said, "What angel wakes
me from my flowery bed?" She opened her eyes and the first
face she saw was Jahaziel's.

Jahaziel had apparently declined to sit on a chair, for he was
leaning against the corner of a deckhouse, most disconcertingly
near. If she was about to fumble her lines he was not going to
miss it, she deduced; never had she seen his eloquent face so
amused. She scowled at him and tore away her eyes. She
smiled ravishingly at the actor-Bottom, saying, "On the first
view, I say, I swear I love thee."

"Methinks, mistress, you should have little reason for that,"
Bottom objected, and all the *Hakluyt* men came out of their
daze and hooted and agreed and cheered. "And yet, to say the
truth," the actor philosophized, "reason and love keep little
company together nowadays."

"And that, boys, is the truth," said Valentine in a loud
voice.

Harriet waited with all the patience she could muster. Then:
". . . and I do love thee," she breathed. Her fingers
brushed the air, hovered over the donkey mask, dared then to
caress the hairy hide, while the *Hakluyt* men all whistled.
". . . I'll give thee fairies to tend thee," she promised, and
right on cue four fairies arrived, clumping out of the darkness
with a dutiful clicking of bootheels. She cried out their names:
"Peasblossom, Cobweb, Moth, and Mustardseed!"

"Ready!" "And I!" "And I!" "And I!" four heavily bearded
and tattoo-ed fairies chorussed. The audience stamped with

hearty approval; never had Harriet taken part in such a runaway farce. The applause when it ended lasted quite five minutes, and it took some shouting by the mates to bring the foremast men back forwards.

Then the music box was brought out and wound again, but the male cabin company paid little attention to that. They gathered about the drinks table as it was also brought out, and Harriet retreated into the shadows by the rail, out of sympathy for her battered spirits and her overworked feet.

She leaned on the bulwarks, contemplating star reflections in black satin water, and was just beginning to relax when Jake Dexter materialized beside her. She turned her head and scowled at him, and he said in matter-of-fact tones, "My dance, I think."

Then, with no premonition at all, she found herself in his arms. He held her loosely. The music box was playing a waltz at the rate of a feverish gallop, but he made no move to dance.

She said heatedly, "Jahaziel Dexter, you are a most irritating person."

"The feeling, Harriet," he replied, "is mutual," but he grinned. She saw his white teeth gleam in the dim light.

"And I suppose you're about to taunt me with all the blunders I've made."

He laughed at that. "I doubt that Mervine will ever forgive you, but I will. And I'm certain you acted for much less rowdy audiences in Cape Colony . . . and New Zealand."

"I wouldn't be so certain of that," she said moodily.

"And your fellow actors knew their lines! I must admit it, I didn't believe you when you said that soldiers practice Shakespeare."

"Oh, but they do, and for all I know American troops share the habit. Why, even in New Zealand the soldiers staged Shakespeare!"

"Even . . . in New Zealand?"

"The men in the Albert barracks outside Auckland have a small theater, with a stage and a drop curtain; they produce their shows to entertain fellow soldiers and Auckland citizens alike, even though the people of Auckland don't seem much aware of the privilege."

She was tired; her voice was betraying her deep bitterness. She became aware of Jake's narrow frown.

He paused, and then said, "Do the people of New Zealand not approve of the stage?"

"They don't approve of anything! The colonists of New Zealand all act as if they suffer from one like delusion, that delusion being that they don't live on the wild frontier at all, but in some London district instead. Actors—and actresses—do little more in their opinion than annoy the neighbors or even worse. Mind you," she said acidly, "they do come to regular theaters, even if they do have to arrive drunk."

"Drunk?"

"Yes! We staged a week of interludes from Sheridan in that theater named Fitzroy, a pretentious tap on the corner of Shortland and High streets, in Auckland, and when the show was done we came out to find half our erstwhile audience swimming about in the canal."

"The . . . what!"

"Oh, it's more like a gutter, really." She was close to weary tears. "Perhaps they were not drunk, or perhaps only half of them, and perhaps they stumbled in, for the night was very dark. And those were the people who'd applauded us! Oh, why are you listening to me? Actors and actresses are not very respectable people, you know."

Respectable. In her mind she could hear again the clatter of the wooden soled shoes that the New Zealand colonists wore, the clatter, rattle, rattle, as they scuttled along the wooden sidewalks; she could hear the sudden silences when she entered a room, and the hushed whispers as people hurried past.

"And your brother, Royal?" said Jake Dexter's voice. She blinked, brought out of bitter memories, and he said casually, "Is he respectable?"

"Why, what do you mean?" She stared at his shadowed face, frowning. "Royal is an actor, I told you that; he's not very good, but lives a passable Falstaff."

"Lives?"

The echo was startled. She smiled a little, wryly, and said, "You will see what I mean, when you meet him."

"We'll have to find him first."

The words were flat. She shifted uneasily, trying to pin down the anger she sensed inside him. She said slowly, "I received a letter from him, in Auckland, New Zealand . . . but I told you that too. He bid me have the vessel hired, and to be in Valparaíso at the end of June—"

He said angrily, "Hired?"

"I'm sorry, Jake, But I—I was desperate."

"As desperate as your brother?"

"*What*?"

Jake Dexter said nothing for a moment but began to dance, in slow out of rhythm circles. She went with him unwillingly, very conscious of his scent, of brandy and shaving lather, and the curry powder kept in his chest to keep the moths from his shore-going clothes. Then he said abruptly, "My pack of rogues will find your brother, never fret about that; they know the places to leave a quiet word to the wise, but you had better tell me what he looks like."

She stopped start-still, and he stopped too. "Oh, my God," she said, "you think he's that desperado that the Peruvian brig is coming to arrest; oh, dear God, that's why you're so angry. You think I've involved you in a bungled criminal mess."

"You've certainly complicated my life," he agreed dryly.

She snapped, "You were already accustomed to such complications, I know it, so please don't pretend otherwise."

"*I beg your pardon*?"

She could have bitten her tongue out the instant the words had left her mouth. She said, "It was . . . nothing. And Royal, yes, is easily recognized, for if there ever was a person who looked the very strolling player, it would certainly be Royal. He's tall and thin, and walks long strides, like this, see . . ." She broke away from him and took long steps, looking at him over her shoulder. "He leans forward as he walks, like this, and he walks with his toes pointed out to the sides. His hair is like straw, in color and texture, and he has a long nose and pointed beard . . ."

Jake said flatly, "You've been gossiping with my men."

"I have not!" She shut tired eyes then, struggling for composure. Then she opened them and said more softly, "Please, Jake, my tongue blunders so tonight, it was just another clumsy phrase. I spoke the truth that night when I said I find the way you run your brig so admirable. I took advantage of your methods, yes, but I was truly desperate; you have no idea how I felt then, and whatever may lie in your past means . . . nothing to me, and I do promise that's true."

"You mean you haven't been informed yet, how I came to own the brig?"

The words were harsh. She shook her head silently, gazing up at him.

"Then it's obvious, Harriet, that you need a little schooling. Three years ago, I was given command of a fine small bark, to trade in hides and tallow on the California coast. I was but twenty-three and it was my very first ship . . . and I'd bought a little house, Harriet, and I married my sweetheart and sailed away, and the bark had an owner who fancied that sweetheart, and fancied my cottage as well."

She gasped and said, "Please, Jake, I don't want to hear this."

"You do. Four months later I made the port of Talcahuano, and I began to hear a little gossip. Oh, I didn't believe it at first, but then I made port in Valparaíso, and Callao and Tombez, Harriet, and in each port I heard the same story . . . and then I heard that the owner owned not only my wife and house but also an infant, a fine small son, so—"

He broke off. Then he said tonelessly, "So I sold the bark and used the money to buy the brig—and that brig is mine, Harriet, by every moral right, if not legally."

And he'd never returned to New England. She remembered the first night when she'd read the logbook; she remembered the sense of domestic comfort when she'd first arrived on the brig. It had puzzled her then, but now she understood. She said very softly, "I am so sorry," and reached up to kiss him gently on the lips.

Perhaps she stumbled, perhaps the ship pitched, perhaps . . . All she knew was that somehow, somehow she was tight against him. The world and the man-of-war and voices and laughter all faded, as her world diminished to the perfect fit of their bodies, his warmth and taste and her hand in the curve at the back of his head, tilted, the feel of his skin and her hair loosening so it fell into his hand and over his shoulder, his intensity and her trembling . . . and then the ship trembled too, as the air thudded and the very night exploded.

Harriet gasped. His mouth left hers. Jahaziel said something but she could not hear the words, for the night was thundering again. "My God," she cried. "Is it the end of the world?" But then she knew the answer.

The firing was a salute of guns that went on and on . . . and on. The men on *Nympha* were cheering as they ran about, and the Peruvian brig-of-war had come.

7 ❧ Early next morning Jake Dexter leaned on the larboard rail and watched all the fuss on the water. The Peruvian brig-of-war was anchored to the north of the steambark *Nympha*, and all three men-of-war in port were flying flags and bunting. It was as if, he thought ironically, the hunting down of one solitary desperado was an occasion for holiday. Soldiers lined up on all three vessels in smart and businesslike rows; those on the Peruvian brig wore white and red regimentals which looked almost spick-and-span from this distance. Loud shouting drifted over the water, and the Peruvian soldiers all stamped in unison and fired their muskets in the air. Then the steambark *Nympha* hooted a whistle in a screech of steam and weighed anchor.

The bark puffed out to the perimeter of the bay, fired at a target, missed, puffed back and forth and fired again, steamed this way and that and then at last dropped anchor again, in the very same spot that she'd left. The Peruvians fired six cannon

in reply, and the *Hakluyt* men all tossed their hats in the air and
delivered three tongue-in-cheek cheers.

The cheerleader—of course, thought Jake—was Valentine
Fish. The second mate was dressed most highly in honor of the
occasion, in buckskin pants with a mountainman fringe down
each seam and a bright red drilling shirt. Crotchet was with
him, and Tib Greene and Dan Kemp despite Tib's broken arm,
and Pablo the Chilean of course. Jake nodded to them to lower
the boat, and then, just as he braced his arm to swing over the
side, Harriet joined him in a rustle of skirts.

Jake stopped and turned and frowned at her. She was
wearing a skirt and a waist with her blue shawl on top, and the
blue ribbons he'd bought her now adorned a bonnet. He studied
her carefully, and then said, "And where, madam, do you
think you're going?"

"On shore, of course! How else will I find my brother? I
have to go to—to the Customs House and—and report my
presence, or how else will Royal know that I've arrived and
that I'm on this brig?"

Jake paused. Behind Harriet the harbor was busy again: the
soldiers on the Peruvian brig-of-war had moved in their lines.
As he watched they stamped in unison and began to file into
their boats. Then the boats began to pull in military file for
shore, the toy soldiers in them sitting bolt upright, their braid
all a-glitter in the sun, their cockaded hats set square. The
American soldiers lined up in like fashion in the boats of the
frigate *Savannah* were not nearly as beautifully decked out, but
they looked even more businesslike.

Jehovah, he thought; the steambark *Nympha* was lowering
boat-loads of military too. He returned his thoughtful gaze to
Harriet's flushed and uptilted face. She looked as stubborn as
a bumblebee and every bit as beautiful. The slim form under
the blue shawl was taut with tension, and he wondered if he
would have enjoyed watching her so much if he had not
thought her so ungainly when she'd first invaded his brig.

He braced his feet and looked past her again, at the beach.
The boatloads of soldiers were beginning to disembark on the
strand, much to the amusement of the Valparaíso populace, and
he could hear distant shouts and orders. What a mess, what a
caper, he brooded; he had every excuse and reason now to back
out of this alpaca business, but he wouldn't—because of that
kiss. He wondered if Harriet guessed how disarming that kiss
had been, so soft and girlish and then abruptly so more than

that. He wondered if she had done it deliberately, for after all, she was an actress, expert at judging an audience, but of course she had not. That kiss had been too innocent.

He grinned dangerously and said, "Miss Gray, you stop right here on my brig."

"What right do you have to order me like that?" she demanded. "He's my brother, Captain!"

"So he is," he agreed. "But if you're still determined on smuggling alpaca, you'd be extreme unwise to bandy the name of Gray about."

"I don't see your logic, sir!"

"Don't you? I think you do, for that is what you plan, is it not? You think to step into the customs house and charm them all, and pay up any trifling fine that the magistrates might charge, and then sail away scot-free."

"But how the devil will you know him if I'm not there?"

"Harriet, you underestimate yourself," said he sardonically, as he pulled down his hat brim and stared intimidatingly from its shadow. "Your description," he elaborated, "was vivid indeed, perfect sufficient." Then, while she was still staring mutinously up at him, patently marshalling argument, he turned away, said idly to Charlie, "Mr. Martin, oblige me by keeping a close eye on Miss Gray," and with that vaulted over the side and into the stern of the boat.

His last glimpse was of Harriet's red and furious face and Mr. Martin's grim nod: he would certainly make sure that Miss Gray stopped on board. Mr. Martin hadn't forgiven her yet, Jake mused, for that night she'd been tricked onto the brig. Then he forgot it, turning his attention to the confoundedly delicate task that awaited on shore.

Jake had plenty of legitimate business, enough to keep him on shore all day despite the twenty-four-hour embargo on trade that the port officials had declared in response to the Peruvian request. The inside pocket of his peajacket was stiff with ship's papers, bills of lading, bills of sale, accounts for his agent and accounts for the customs house, bills of credit signed by the traders and merchants with whom he'd done business the past four months. He had not touched port since Honolulu in January, except for Judas Island, and that of course did not count.

And, while he was about all this innocent business, Jake bent a thoughtful stare on the men in his boat. Valentine, Crotchet, Dan, and Pablo pulled at the oars, along with Joseph

the handsome black man from the Azores whom they all called
Joseph Fayal. Tib Greene, because of his broken arm, lounged
at his ease in the sheets. They all, Jake mused, looked
somewhat raffish and less than reliable in the bargain. The
forces of four nations searched Valparaíso for one lone
fugitive, and somehow he expected this unhandsome group to
succeed where all those soldiers and officers would fail.

He wondered if he was overoptimistic and feared that he
was. The most he could hope for, perhaps, was that these men
would manage to evade incarceration in the fort. They should
accomplish that, at least, for they certainly knew their Valparaíso. Jake made port here often, so that these six men knew
all the terraced streets and the sleazy dockyard area; they knew
the cock-fighting pits, the billiard rooms, the taps, and the
various alleys. They knew, too, the two brothels which the
sailors nicknamed Maintop and Foretop because of the two
hills they stood on, and they knew the crimps and the port
police.

The trouble was that they knew all the whores as well—by
name—and the proprietors of the roughest pulperías. The boat
grated on black gritty sand and then scratched loudly as the
boys hopped out and hauled the boat high and dry.

"Sunset," said Jake sternly. "Be here. I'll wait one hour, no
more." Then he threw some coins to some urchins, bidding
them to watch over the boat, and then he turned without
another word, and strode off about his various errands, which
included some personal business.

His six men stood in a straggling group watching him go,
and then they held a council of war. They did not share his
doubts about their mission in the slightest and would have been
most highly insulted if they had guessed his thoughts. They
were perfectly confident of finding this rogue Royal Gray, for,
by thunder, they surely did know their Valparaíso! No doubt
the man was not using his given name, but they knew how to
ask about, how to spread tempting hints of bribes and which
people to approach, and they had an excellent description.

"Tall," said Valentine. "Straw-colored hair," and the others
nodded like wooden mandarins. "Walks with the wind blowing
rugged behind him, with his toes stuck out to the side."
Hunting such a distinctive playactor seemed child's play: all
they needed was a rendezvous. "Maria's fandango," said
Valentine. "At sunset." That gave them an hour to get the
fugitive to the *Hakluyt* boat; that, they thought, was plenty.

They all nodded again and shook each others' hands with great ceremony, and then they all dispersed.

And such a time they had! Valentine and Crotchet took the upper reaches first. They strolled arm in arm along the steep alleys and doe-eyed señoritas leaned over fanciful balconies and called out their names. Men massaging roosters in crumbling doorways called out times and bids for fights and nodded, grinning, when words were muttered in their ears. It was just that easy: everyone in Valparaíso had heard all about the desperado, and knew exactly whom they meant. His whereabouts . . . *perdone,* that was not so easy, but the hours of asking stretched ahead, and everyone promised, *spit on my palm,* that if found, the fugitive would be directed to Maria's fandango.

And so the pleasant hours wandered by. Late afternoon found Tib and Dan visiting the tenth pulpería of their progression, staggering more than a little, their hints and queries sadly slurred, massaging maidens and teasing the wenches into dim back rooms. Pablo and Joseph were searching for the fugitive in the cafés of the opposite end of the waterfront town, Joseph sober but Pablo nine-tenths inebriated, and loud and quarrelsome with it. He was playing monté, recklessly, for money that he did not have. Crotchet and Valentine were gambling too, in taps on the higher terraces.

The game they were playing was nine-pin billiards, a game that it seemed the Valparaíso sharks had just invented, and that most diverting too. Nine pins were set up at one end of a billiard table, and the boys competed to knock them down, having but three balls to do it: the white, the spot, and the red. Crotchet played with flair, greeting each toss with a loud and urbane, "See that, suh!"

"I'm from Massachusetts," quoth Valentine to his third wench of the day, "and Crotchet hails from ole Virginny . . . and have you ever danced in Maria's fandango?" The harlot did not answer: that was the moment that Crotchet lost and found that he had none of the ready to cover his bet. He was embarrassed, as he told them all, and the proprietor of the establishment gave vent to loud and furious screeches of pain. Valentine had no money neither, so he dropped his wench and a boisterous battle commenced, as the proprietor's large family all rushed in to his aid.

This was at about the exact same moment that Tib and Dan made a precipitate escape from the murderously jealous lovers of the women they had been teasing. Pablo, at the other end of the waterfront, was battling a huge Peruvian who had cast aspersions on his honor and his honesty. The Peruvian was one of the soldiers from the Peruvian brig-of-war, but he was not fighting Pablo in pursuit of his duty: like the most of his comrades, he had succumbed long since to the blandishments of sophisticated Valparaíso, and he was drunken and as penniless as Pablo. The port police and the mates of the Peruvian brig pounded onto the scene with much Spanish hollering and blasting of whistles. They arrested the Peruvian on the spot, and Pablo escaped, followed closely by Joseph Fayal.

Valentine and Crotchet enjoyed an even more fortuitous escape from their predicament. Just when it seemed most bruisingly plain that the nine-pin billiards man and his burly built brothers and cousins would pound them into the dirt, a man driving cattle on the next-highest street lost control of his herd. Cows plunged about in every direction, harried by yapping dogs and half the town urchins. Women shrieked, and marching soldiers shinnied up creepers and drainpipes onto balconies. Valentine and Crotchet kept down low and darted between flying horns and hooves, scuttling away down the nearest handy little alley.

By devious ways and means, then, they found their way to Maria's fandango house. It was a reticent-seeming affair, in a long adobe hall, whitewashed inside. Dancers and harlots strolled back and forth with little cigars betwixt their red and shining lips, and pimps and gentlemen hung about the doors, dressed in spurs and showy brocades. The men were obviously Spanish, the lot of them, with not a straw-colored hair in sight. The sun was nudging the western horizon in a blaze of low red, and Valentine and Crotchet looked at each other rather uneasily.

Out in the narrow street the air was growing cooler, and a smoky quiet was settling over Valparaíso as the populace thought about supper. Echoes of marching boots and barked-out orders resounded among the terraces: many of the Peruvian soldiers were drunk, lost, and perhaps deserted, but it was painfully evident that evening replacement troops were coming in off the ships. First Pablo and Joseph and then Tib and Dan slid in the doors furtively and looked all about. A squad of American marines marched deafeningly by, right outside in their alley, and when they had gone in a rhythmic clatter Dan looked about and said in a piercing whisper, "Why ain't yer found the fugitive?"

Crotchet shrugged. They all paused while a gaggle of sailors from the various merchant ships came in and looked about and stayed in the hope of entertainment. "Plenty of time yet, suh," he said then sunnily. Maria the proprietress of this establishment came in from the back smiling widely at this influx of paying customers, and then she sighted Valentine and let out a shriek.

"Aha!" she cried. "The boy, yes, who plays, who sings!" and the man who strummed the doleful guitar was unceremoniously dismissed. His vacated chair was shoved up to a dilapidated pianoforte, and Valentine was urged into it by imperious Spanish hands.

> *"Yankee doodle went to town"*—the boys sang rowdily, and the sailors on liberty perked up and took notice—*"Yankee doodle dandy . . .*
> *"And there he met a winsome lass, and sweeten'd her wiv . . . candy*
> *He put his finger on her breast, a'cause he felt so . . . handy*
> *And put his finger sommat else, a'cause he felt so . . . randy!"*

Crotchet produced a mouth organ, while Tib and Dan and two dozen delighted mariners began to stamp and prance.

> *"Yankee doodle went to town . . . yankee doodle dandy.*
> *And there he met a pretty lass, and sweeten'd her wiv . . . brandy*
> *He lifted her shift and kissed her quick, a'cause she were so . . . bandy*
> *He did her quick and rubbed his knees, a'cause they were so . . . sandy!"*

"Hooray, fine fellow!" rang out a right jovial voice, and sailor boys were dancing so hard that whitewash fell off the walls and ceiling in flakes, like a storm of dandruff. Valentine strummed another cord, glanced over his shoulder, and stopped dead, astounded, for there stood a tall, thin fellow who leaned as if in a gust of wind, a man with a pointed straw beard and a long pointed nose with a drop on its reddened end. This customer was dressed in a shabby collection of South American clothes, and what's more, he stank most high. He said in a diffident English accent, "Would your name be *Valentine*, sir?"

"Tarnation," said Valentine, astonished, "you must be Royal Gray."

"I received a message in the first tap where I took refuge, and then another message in the next, message upon message, an abundance of these messages, that if I came to Maria's fandango at sunset, *and* asked for one fellow named Valentine, then that Valentine would see me right. Is that so, sir?"

"Tarnation," said Valentine again. His wits were utterly fuddled by this unexpected success of his scheme, and this at the very last moment, for sunset was gone at least one hour.

Tib Greene swaggered up in a gust of alcoholic fumes and said, "Wa-al, good Lord, this must be the young bastard hissself." Tib stopped, as Royal Gray's smell got through to him. He wrinkled his nose. "Good lord," he said again rather faintly, and the doors crashed open as a squad of Chilean soldiers charged in. The women all screamed and the sailors all fought to get out the back. The smelly fugitive and the *Hakluyt* men shoved as hard as the rest. The mass of men all struggled and strained and then the lot popped through, out of the back of the fandango house and into a cobbled back street.

The alley was as black as a witch's cat, and men scrabbled to disperse in all different directions. Soldiers charged out after them and then stopped short and ran into each other, unsighted after the bright lamps inside the hall. Shots were fired blindly into the air; more women screeched; shutters above crashed wide; orders were bawled in hysterical Spanish; and men all about, sailors, citizens and military alike, cursed and scuffled at random. Then, from the bottom of the cobbled steep alley echoed an approaching thunder of iron wheels and hooves. Everyone stopped short and fell all over each other again, the *Hakluyt* boys included, and all the time the wheels were rumbling nearer and nearer. The mass of struggling men heaved and scattered to get out of the way. Then the huge old carriage jolted into sight.

It was one of the battered equipages that the Valparaíso citizens used as omnibuses and that drunken sailors commandeered and raced about at suicidal speed for sport. This latter circumstance seemed to be the state of matters here, or so the Chilean soldiers evidently thought, for they stepped aside and laughed as they playfully fired their guns in the air. The man who handled the reins so recklessly, however, was not inebriated in the slightest. Jake Dexter was simply furious.

For God's sake, he fumed, did he always have to do a job himself if he wanted it done well? He'd relied on his rascals to ask about with devious stealth, not to inform the whole of Valparaíso that they wanted to meet the desperado, and that at Maria's fandango house at sunset! By the start of siesta the whole port had laughed about it, and captains in the saloons and offices had speculated aloud on the identity of the numbskulls. Jake had been forced to listen and hide grim consternation, and the fruitless hour of waiting by the *Hakluyt* boat had not helped his mood. Then to his dismay he'd found that the gossip had reached the Peruvian brig-of-war, for boats from the brig arrived on the beach and disgorged more troops. The soldiers had lined up and marched off, in this direction, and this—this *requisitioning* of a public coach, had been the desperate inspiration of the moment.

Goddammit, he seethed as he cracked the whip, urging the horses up the alley. The narrow street seemed full of men, and the walls were closing in rapidly. The coach's legitimate driver was crouched by Jake on the driving bench. He screeched with fear and clapped his hands over his eyes as varnished wood scraped with a scream along old stonework. Jake ignored him but sharply hauled back on the reins.

He'd just sighted Valentine, cowering in a doorway. "You damn fool, why didn't you paint your message on the custom house walls and be done with it?" Jake roared. Then he shouted, "For God's sake, tumble!"

Then he slapped the reins and stamped on the footboard. God alone knew how many Peruvians were marching this way at this very moment. Jake took an infuriated breath, as dozens of bewildered faces gauped up at him and roared again, "Tumble!" He was perfectly prepared to abandon the rescue at an instant's notice, for he had no intention of landing himself into prison. If that happened, old Scratch alone knew who would bail out these bunglers he had the misfortune to number in his crew!

Then to his impatient relief the tall fellow with them hollered, "The cavalry, by God!" and made a headlong dive for the nearest coach door. The latch gave, the door crashed open, slamming against stone. The horses snorted and tried to plunge, and Dexter fought with the ribbons. He heard six thuds as the six *Hakluyt* boys recovered their wits and tumbled in after. An indeterminate number of drunken sailors crashed in too, one of them landing on the bench by Jake, but he merely cracked the whip, and with an English holler of "God for Harry, England, and Saint George!" from inside the carriage, they were off! Chilean soldiers came to their senses then and fired madly down the street. Shots whined and clunked from wall to wall. Jake hauled the coach with a shuddering crash about a corner and the shooting stopped and off into the darkness they thundered.

The shouting was lost too, in the rumble of iron wheels on cobbles. Jake slapped the reins and stamped on the footboard, and the coach veered around another bend, for—by Jehovah!— he surely knew his Valparaíso! Lamps flickered into light in houses all about them as wooden shutters crashed open. Never, Jake deduced, had the citizens of Valparaíso seen one of their omnibuses driven at quite this breakneck pace. The anonymous sailor on the bench beside him was cheering, and Crotchet in the coach was leaning precipitously out of the window and hollering, "Alors, alors, suh!" like a very French imp possessed. Down the hill they thundered, on and on into the darkness, heading for the water's edge, leaving pursuit further and further behind in the night.

Then, with a lurch, they were there, poised on the edge of the embarcadero. The beach was near-deserted, for the Peruvians had asked for a curfew. The boat lay where Jake had left it. Jake hauled on the reins, thrust them at the sailor beside him, thrust the agreed sum of money in the coachman's outstretched palm, and vaulted onto the sand.

He nearly fell over with his momentum, skidding through black grit. Then he recovered, whirled, yanked open the coach door, and shouted, "Tumble!" The *Hakluyt* men and the desperado tumbled. The drunken sailors still inside grinned and gaped. "Drive on!" Jake roared then, and heard the sailor on the driving bench cheer and whirl the whip. The coach was taking on pace even as Valentine Fish hit the sand. Then it thundered on into the night. The door, still open, crashed back and forth, adding to the commotion.

The echoes of pursuit were still high on the terraces. Yellow lights were popping on all over town, but the bay was black and serene. The limpid satin water lapped at Jack's knees as they hauled the boat. The craft seemed impossibly heavy and reluctant, grating rebelliously, but then it was light and alive, floating in the ripples, and Jake and the others piled in.

The men at the oars seemed to take forever to get their rhythm. Jake could hear them grunt and pant. The oars squeaked, deafeningly, it seemed. Tib Greene in the middle thwart shoveled himself into some kind of sitting position, pushed his good hand over his dissolute whiskery countenance, and said with an air of vast satisfaction, "Wa-al, good Lord, sir, we found 'im."

"Good Lord," Jake agreed tersely, "so you did."

"Sir?" echoed the stranger. He scrambled to a sitting position with every lively appearance of curiosity and said, "Does that mean, sir, that I speak to the master of the rescuing brig himself?"

Brig . . . so the gossip around town was that the desperado's message came from the crewmen of a brig. It would be only time, Jake thought furiously, before the port authorities narrowed down their guesses to the name of brig *Hakluyt*. The tide was on the turn, and he'd damn well have to take it. Then the consternated faces of the oarsmen distracted his mood for the moment. When he looked around, the steambark *Nympha* was lowering a boat—a boat with officers in it. He could see the reflections of the light from the bark's cressets on their braid. He swore under his breath and then muttered, "Stern two . . . gently, gently." Two of the men trailed their oars; he leaned on the big steering sweep and the boat slid quietly into the shadow of some anonymous ship's stern.

They would approach the brig from the starboard side, the side away from the *Nympha*. The oarsmen were pulling faster, with no need for Jake to speak. The boat lurched a bit, and water splashed over the gunwales as they took on quicker pace. The English stranger flinched as spray hit him, Jake saw; however Tib Greene, lost in alcoholic dreamy reverie, did not even seem to notice. "And, what's more, sir," he mused aloud, "he do but sure talk strange."

"Like the veriest Falstaff," agreed Jake. There was a snap in his voice; he saw the actor stare and frown.

"And, what's more, sir, why good Lord but he sure do stink."

"Like a skunk," quoth Valentine Fish.

" 'Tis not my fault," said the actor. Jake could see him bridling and pulling his rags about him with an air of wounded dignity. "The odor is not mine, sirs. 'Tis llama spit."

The silence was stunned. They had arrived at the brig, but at that instant all Jake could do was stare. Then he said very cautiously, "You did say *spit*?"

"I did," said the actor angrily. Jake put out a hand to touch the brig's straking but stared at Gray all the time. Beneath his palm he could feel the liveliness of his vessel; the *Hakluyt*, like her owner, was eager to be free and away from this mess. The tide was on the full, and Jake was abruptly filled with urgency.

"Llamas, like all camels," said Royal Gray angrily, "spit when harrassed, and llamas feel harrassed very easy."

Jake watched Joseph Fayal hook the boat onto the falls, ready for heaving into the davits. Then he snapped, "Llamas, Mr. Gray? Your sister gammoned us all that you were collecting alpacas."

"My . . . *what*?"

Royal Gray's voice was entirely thunderstruck, and his patent shock hit Jake like a blow in the chest. Then, while he was still absorbing the instant savage anger, with another lurch he heard loud polite English voices hailing the brig.

The sounds came from the other side, the larboard side. Jake froze, and so did his men; he could see the whites of Joseph Fayal's upturned eyes. He recognized the voice at once; it was that of the stiff second lieutenant. The officer called again, "Brig *Hakluyt*, ahoy!"

A long pause. Where the hell, thought Jake, frozen, was Charlie Martin? Then he heard the clear reply: "Who goes there?"

It was Harriet. Royal Gray moved abruptly and the boat wobbled. Someone hushed him. Jake, gripping the straking plank he held, waited.

"Miss Gray," said the midshipman's young voice. "And how d'you do, ma'am?"

"Very well, thank you." For God's sake, Jake thought incredulously, in another moment she would be inviting them to take tea. Instead, however, she merely said, "Did you wish to speak with Captain Dexter?"

"There's a commotion about, ma'am, the—h'm!—desperado is about and on the loose, Miss Gray, a most enlivening situation! They do say that he's keeping the company of a band of loose and rebellious sailors, that he's leading them on a looting of the town; the port authorities, they say, have dire prognostications of wholesale arson!"

" 'Tis the story of the Fishmarket gang all over again, Miss

Gray!" chimed in the second lieutenant. "The like of the gang
that ravaged the country about Callao and Rio de Janiero
naught but a dozen years ago!"

"Merciful heavens, is that so? said Harriet, sounding perfectly calm. For God's sake, Jake thought; his arm was
growing numb as he held the boat steady with his hand on the
brig. He could see Joseph Fayal's hand clenched on the falls.
"Well," said Harriet then with decision in her voice, "there has
been no commotion here."

"But a word of warning, ma'am—"

"And I thank you very kindly for that warning. If any
desperado so much as scull by the brig, be sure we will fire
cannon instantum!"

"But ma'am, our instructions—"

"Instructions? But you've delivered me your warning, sir."

And the two officers said nothing: there was utter silence as
if this last had defeated them entirely. Jake waited, every nerve
taut, waiting for their departure. He could hear shouting on the
foreshore, and once a volley of shooting. The Peruvians, he
thought uneasily, had caught up with the runaway carriage and
found that their quarry had fled into the bay. The tide rippled
under the boat, and despite his tense grip on the planking the
side of the boat kept on clicking against the hull of the brig.

Each click echoed: surely if the officers were still on the
other side they would hear the sounds? He almost spoke then;
he almost thought that the *Nympha* boat had gone. Then he
heard a hiss and realized that the two officers were conferring
in whispers. One raised his voice and said, "If we came on
board to ascertain—?"

"Ascertain what?" inquired Harriet. There was a mocking
note in her voice, a note that Jake knew all too well. "But why?
It seems such a waste of time. That villain and his sailor
cohorts could be devastating the town!"

"But to set your sensibilities at rest, ma'am—"

"Sensibilities, fiddlesticks," said she, sounding the very
dowager. "Thank Captain Mara most kindly for his concern,
sirs, but I do assure you that all on board is perfect quiet;
indeed it's perfect tedious!"

Lights were glowing on the foreshore, and Jake could hear
shouting as boatloads of troops were launched into the bay. He
was holding onto the brig so tensely that he wondered he'd ever
let go; he was full of tension, that and seething rage at the
Grays, who had risked his neck and his brig and his reputation

so, and at his involvement in this antic furor. He damned the day that Harriet had boarded his brig, he—

The officers had gone; he heard them go. He'd missed the last exchange of stiff courtesies. All at once worried faces peered over the starboard rail above, and he could see the pale blob of Harriet's head. "Shouldn't you come up quickly?" she said, and Royal at the same instant said in a high incredulous voice, "'Tis Hat. It really is Hat."

Jake said nothing. Urgency hammered in his throat. He shoved Royal upward and scrambled onto deck himself. The others joined them and Jake snapped at Charlie Martin, "Prepare to heave short and make sail."

Men began to hurry on the decks, infected by his tone of crisis. Jake hauled himself onto the planks and immediately began to run, hassling men to windlass and sheets, head tipped back to watch as men obediently tumbled up the shrouds and along yards.

Every now and then he glanced about at the night. Boats were swarming even thicker on the water, heading out at random to the ships and boarding them one by one. Harriet might have prevented inspection of the *Hakluyt* in the meantime, but another time was looming fast. He tipped his head again to stare at the canvas as it billowed out loosely against the stars, and tugged his arm impatiently as someone touched it.

When he looked it was Royal Gray. He saw the actor open his mouth but interrupted tersely, "Lay aloft."

"I beg your—"

"You heard me. Get up that mast, and keep on going till you pass the topgallant crosstrees."

Then he saw the actor tip his head too and the pallor of the thin bearded face, and he saw the Adam's apple in the long craw bob as Royal Gray swallowed with obvious fright.

"But—"

"Do it," Jake snapped. Behind him he could hear men chanting softly at windlass as the anchor came up. The brig was bobbing eagerly, agog to take the tide and the damp warm wind.

"If you want to save your skin, sir, lay aloft," he grimly said and almost enjoyed the man's fear. "We'll be boarded soon, and don't doubt that for an instant. They won't hold us back, not with the tide on the full, not unless they find the man they've been hunting. So if you want to be taken for a sailor, sir, you scramble those shrouds and you do it fast. Just pretend," he said, grinning humorlessly. "Just pretend that there's a passel of lions hot on your heels."

Then, without waiting to see Royal Gray ascend the mast, he whirled and strode swiftly on about the decks. He had questions to put to Royal Gray—questions in abundance!—but in the meantime all he wanted was to quit the bay while he still had his brig and some shreds of reputation, and then to find his offing.

8 ❧ Harriet scarcely slept a wink all night. The cabin was empty when she stole through it at dawn. Jake Dexter, she knew, had been on deck the whole of the night, while the brig cleared the bay and the Chilean coast. Nevertheless it was a shock to find when she arrived on deck that land was entirely lost to view. The sea was rugged, and the wind tossed the crests of the waves, but even when the gallant brig lifted to top each billow, there was no sign of the hills of Chile.

The wind was cold and sharp with wet salt; the men on watch about decks huddled in corners, looking chilled. There was no sign of Royal. Harriet went to the amidships rail and waited, trying to look matter-of-fact, nibbling the tip of one finger and avoiding the inquisitive stares of the crew. She felt miserable and utterly apprehensive; she had lived so long with the certainty that all would come right as soon as she found Royal, but now she had no feeling that things were going to come right at all.

Then, when she was on the verge of losing all hope and
trudging down to breakfast, Royal stumbled onto deck. Most
of his rags had gone and he had a gray blanket clutched about
him; he peered about blearily, standing unsteadily, stumbling a
step each time the brig lurched. Then he saw her and wavered
toward her. The brig rolled, waggling her stern, and he arrived
in a little clumsy rush, faster than he'd evidently intended.

During the past year she had pictured over and over again
what she would say when she finally found him, but all she
could say now was, "Oh Royal." He had seemed shabby
enough in the dark, rushed encounter the night before, but the
daylight, gray as it was, proved even more cruel. His skin
seemed patched and scabbed, nut-brown in parts, pink in
others, as if the sun had burned him and then burned him again
as the injured skin peeled. By contrast his hair looked almost
white, stiff and sticking out all over his head like a very
scarecrow's. He was dirty and terribly thin, his eyes haggard
and his cheeks pouched.

Royal was twenty-two years old, but he looked the very Old
Father Time. She said again in distress, "Oh, Royal." Then,
illogically, she continued, "Where are your clothes?"

Instead of answering he gulped and then leaned over the rail.
She watched his misery as he heaved, feeling helpless, unable
to do anything but pat his back now and then. She could feel
the vertebrae under her palm, as knobbled as knucklebones.
Then when at last he had ended retching she went to the galley
to fetch him a mug of fresh water. Cookie said nothing but
rolled his eyes sideways. Harriet smiled distractedly and went
back to her brother.

Royal was sitting in a hunched miserable heap by the rail,
one long arm hooked over the lash rail to keep himself still. He
wiped at the mucus smeared on his beard with the back of one
hand and then took the mug. Harriet listened to the thirsty
gulping, and then he said, "Hat, what the hell are you doing
here . . . and where the hell is Sefton?"

She paused. Then she said evenly, "I was the one who
received your message, and I was the one who followed your
instructions. I bought passage on a whaleship to meet you at
Valparaíso, and I . . . negotiated with Captain Dexter and
his crew, and prevailed on them to find you and then to fetch
the alpaca."

He gaped at her. Then he shut his mouth and said tersely, "I don't believe you. You're a married woman; you couldn't do any of that."

She said bitterly, "Am I? Then where, pray, is my husband?" She scarcely remembered the man she had married; her courtship and marriage seemed like some ancient meaningless history. Colonel Frank Sefton, urbane, rich, gallant, American, had begun to pay court to her the day after the Gray family had arrived in Auckland; he had flattered her quite out of her senses. He had been the most eligible bachelor in the whole of the colony; she had been the envy of every woman in the town; and now she could scarcely remember what he looked like. Colonel Francis Sefton had been a man of the world, almost as old as her father, and she —she had been a silly goose-brained girl of sixteen.

She said evenly, "Sefton left me. He left me the week after you sailed from New Zealand; we had been married just ten days, and yet he left me. I've been alone for more than a year."

"But that—that ain't possible, Hat. Swamp it, Hat, the man signed a marriage contract, he signed the day a-fore you married, he gave you all his worldly goods on your marriage eve!"

"Nevertheless, despite that contract and the scheme you three men had hatched, he contrived to leave me." Harriet's voice was wooden in her ears, and she realized, furiously, that she was on the verge of desperate tears. Instead of crying she turned and stared unblinkingly at the sea, not even seeing the waves.

"But, you were his wife, stump it. You meant he up and went, without a word of warning?"

Royal's tone was frankly incredulous. Harriet paused. "Perhaps, in a way, I should have suspected it. Frank talked all the time of trying ventures in other lands. He talked much of New South Wales, and planned at one time to go there and set up a station ready for the alpaca . . . and Father seemed to think that logical."

"Well, 'tis logical. Father is right."

"Then Frank changed his mind about that. He talked instead of California, or the northwest coast of America. He told Father he was reluctant to invest in British lands again. He had been stung too badly by the New Zealand authorities, he said; he said that when he'd arrived in the colony the British administrators had been glad enough to see his money, but then when he wanted to take a profit they changed their minds and wouldn't allow him to sell at the proper price. Only those of English nationality were allowed to make money out of New Zealand."

"Well, we all knew that," Royal's voice objected. "That's why the man gave you all his property before you were married, to put his goods in English hands."

Harriet said, "Yes." Then she silenced, remembering Frank Sefton's raging. The affable urbane man who had courted her had been unrecognizable after the ceremony of marriage was done. When Sefton was angry his blue eyes flushed red, with little nasty blood-vessels standing out on the whites. He had paced the bedroom floor, shouting for hours on end.

He had scared her with his rages, even though she had hidden it. She said somberly, "He hated me because of my English blood. He had taken advantage of my English nationality to avoid the taxes, but I think he hated me always."

"Nonsense! What moonshine, Hat; I was there myself, I saw it." Royal had raised his voice, and she looked nervously about and shushed him. His expression became impatient, and she thought he would insist on shouting, but instead he lurched to his feet and vomited again over the rail.

She listened to the awful sounds, feeling sick herself. Then at last he slumped back into a heap and muttered, "Oh, God, and such moonshine you speak. 'Tis true that Sefton signed over all his property to you for a devious reason, but it was a good reason, a practical reason. It made perfect sense to avoid the taxes if he could. He discussed it fully and honestly with Father and myself; for God's sake, Hat, I helped draw up the document, and Father and I were two of the witnesses when you signed it, and that lawyer fellow was there to make sure it was legal; you must remember that. And even if it were some devious, to give you his lands like that, it still was right trusting of Sefton. The three of us could have sold it all and gone off the morning you were meant to wed, and left the fellow penniless."

"Then how come I was the one who found myself deserted?" she cried. The low shaking words burst out of her. "You've no idea what it was like, Royal, to be left alone and deserted in a place like New Zealand. They gossip, Royal, and whisper, and you know that actresses are despised in any case. You keep on talking about Sefton's generosity, but have you ever thought that the one and only reason he ever courted me was because it offered him a means of getting clear of paying the taxes?"

"Nonsense. Sefton adored you; he doted, Hat, he doted. Father would never have allowed it otherwise; you know how he feels about Americans."

Her father . . . she still had to tell him about their father. When Royal had sailed to South America the plan had been that their father would return, alone, to England . . . but Charles Gray had never sailed.

Their father. Charles Gray had certainly prated on about Americans, especially when at his most brandy-scented and philosophical. Shrewd fellows, he called 'em, amazing preoccupied with profit and money, and yet so oddly naïve withal, not quite socially right. She almost laughed with bitter humor. Colonel Francis Sefton was a scion of one of the first families of Philadelphia, and he—he had spoken scornfully of strolling players, every touch as snobbish as the most prim New Zealand colonist.

She took a long shaking breath and said, "Royal, I—I have to tell you about Father. He—he . . ."

She had to stop and try again. "Frank was talking of going, and I . . . became worried. I walked out to Father's hotel to speak with him, alone, to talk about it, before Father had sailed off to England and I'd left it too late. He wasn't there. Then, on the way back, in the street, I heard a . . . commotion. Father . . ."

She stopped. She stared blindly at the sea and said, "I found him, in the street. He'd been run over by a carriage. There were . . . people. They said . . . they said a horseman had struck him and galloped away, that Father had fallen under the wheels of the passing carriage, that he . . . that he—"

She stopped, utterly unable to go on. The silence drummed in her head. She turned slowly, blinking, looking down at Royal, and her brother stared up at her, his face so pale it was green. When he shut his eyes she could see scabs on his eyelids, and the hollows in his cheeks were intolerably gaunt. Then he said, "Oh dear, dear God, is Father dead?"

"Yes."

"Killed?"

"Yes . . . and robbed. Everything he carried was gone. People . . . helped, there were formalities, but people were kind . . . then. It took hours, and all the time I waited for Frank, I knew he'd come the instant he heard of the tragedy, but he didn't, and at last I was able to leave, to go . . . home, to Frank's house. And he wasn't there. He'd gone. He'd sailed."

"What! But where?"

"I had to ask at the customs house." That had been the first humiliation. She remembered the pitying looks, and the embarrassment. "He'd gone to Canton."

"To . . . *where*?"

"Frank had sailed to China, on God alone knows what business. And then the day of—of Father's funeral I returned to the house, to Frank's house. You spoke of that lawyer, Royal, the third man who signed as witness the day before my marriage, when Sefton gave me all he owned; you seem to remember that lawyer well, and so do I! That lawyer was waiting at the house when I got back from the burial, and he had more documents, signed by Frank Sefton, documents of ownership. Sefton—somehow—had sold him the lands, the house, even the horses that Father had given me for dowry; he owned it all, Royal, and he showed me the door, and I've lived like a pauper ever since, waiting, waiting for your letter."

"You're destitute?" She nodded mutely, listening to the desperation in her brother's voice. "But that ain't—ain't possible, Hat! Sefton was rich; dear God, Hat, but it were he who devised the alpaca scheme!"

"I know. And the alpaca are our only hope, for without those alpaca we have nothing—*nothing*!"

Then she waited. Royal said nothing for a long, long moment, and then he said numbly, "Oh, dear God, that can't be right."

She turned then, to stare at the sick bewilderment in his face. "But it don't make sense—" Royal began, and she shushed him. There was movement on the afterdeck as the companion-way door opened. Then Valentine and Crotchet came toward them whistling "Yankee Doodle."

The whistle was cheerful, determinedly so, but the boys had a chastened look about them; their cheeks were still flushed, and they were carrying their sea chests on their shoulders. "Heigh-ho," said Valentine, coming abreast with them. "Adios cabin—not that I slept there much ever—and hail fo'c'sle."

Harriet said incredulously, "You've been demoted?"

"Indeed, Miss Gray. The events of yesterday proved rather

too much for our skipper to stomach, rather too much to swallow indeed!"

Harriet shook her head, bemused and beginning to feel angry. "Captain Dexter is punishing you . . . because you rescued my brother from the Peruvian forces?"

"Well, ma'am," said Crotchet, and both boys coughed and looked at each other. "The rescue, as it happened, Miss Gray, was carried out by the captain himself."

"What?" said Harriet, wrinkling her brow, and then she listened in growing disbelief as the boys told her the story. She could picture the coach ride easily enough, for the citizens of Auckland had just the same conveyances, which the seamen when tipsy commandeered in just the same fashion. But to try and imagine Jahaziel Dexter driving a requisitioned coach in such flamboyant style really was too much. Then, just as Crotchet was launching himself into the most colorful parts of the story, the protagonist himself arrived on deck.

Valentine and Crotchet instantly silenced; they heaved up their chests and disappeared rapidly for the fo'c'sle hatch, leaving Harriet to confront Captain Dexter uneasily. Jake looked as vital as if he'd slept a full night instead of scarcely one hour. His mood, however, looked black.

He snapped at Royal, "Where are the alpaca . . . if they exist?"

Royal flinched. Then he somehow got himself to his feet, while all the time Harriet stared at Jake resentfully. There was no need to talk to Royal in such harsh terms, she thought, even if he did not know that Royal was still absorbing the news of their father's demise.

Royal snapped, "The alpaca exist, I assure you of that, sir, and I thank you for yesterday's rescue. I'm sorry if that will make affairs difficult for you the next time you make port at Valparaíso—"

"You're sorry, I'm sorry," Jake barked. "Where are the alpaca?"

Royal paused, and Harriet tensely wondered why. She watched his eyes move, hunting the seascape, and then he reluctantly muttered, "They're up the river Tombez, on the Ecuador border. A Frenchman has a plantation there, and he offered—"

"They're *where*?"

The word was a roar. Royal said angrily, "They're safe . . . on a plantation up the Tombez River!"

"But that's goddamned thirty days' sailing away!"

"I know, and I'm sorry!" Royal sounded tormented, and Harriet instinctively shifted closer to him in support. "I've had the very devil of it all, Captain; the agents I hired have not been reliable. They supplied me with beasts, and then reported them stolen to save their own skins; I've been cheated and harried, by troops as well as marauding Indians; I've been on the run for months, Captain, harried northwards and all the time knowing I had to get to Valparaíso by the end of June. I did what I could, sir!"

Jake's face was grim and growing grimmer with each word. Royal, thought Harriet, sounded like a guilty schoolboy, full of rapid excuses, and at that moment she hated Jake for doing this to her brother. She stared at him defiantly, but he did not even seem to notice. Instead he said coldly to Royal, "So I sail thirty days' worth, and then I take men up the Tombez River, thirty days before I see the sight of even one alpaca. And last night you said the word *llama*, Mr. Gray: how do I know that these so-called alpaca, sir, won't turn into common llamas when I finally get to clap eyes on them?"

"There are three hundred alpacas, I swear it! I had to have a half dozen or so llamas in with the herd, for alpacas are too disdainful to carry burdens, they're wretched beasts, I hate 'em! My God, you've no idea of the fidget and fuss that they cause, and they're shocking poor dams in the bargain."

Jake, for once, looked taken aback. He said in stunned tones, "*Dams*?"

"Damn-shocking mothers, are alpaca," Royal said with passion. "The pangs of birth are enough to make 'em flee for the most distant horizon, and if the foal drops halfway through the dash the alpaca don't even notice. It's up to the poor fool of a herdsman to make up for the beast's insensitivity, and more often than not that running alpaca was snatched up by some passing Indian who would have the face to try to sell the beast back to me!"

"You mean," said Jake with angry sarcasm, "that you did not steal the alpaca?"

"Of course I did not! I bought them, as I said, from damn dishonest unreliable agents; what else could I do? The Indians revere the beasts, and only the backsliders in the tribes will sell 'em, men as crafty and underhand as the agents who talked 'em into the sale. I've had the luck of the very devil, sir, the time of old Scratch!"

Harriet could hear Royal's heavy breathing; he was vibrating with righteous anger, and his greenish cheeks had taken on a flush of rage. Then, with an obvious effort to contain his temper, he said more quietly, "I regret the fact that I had to take the alpaca so far before I dared leave them, and I am grateful, sir, that you've consented to carry the beasts to Australia."

"Consented?" said Jake. He shifted his stance, and Harriet found the narrow green eyes on her face. Then he said deliberately, "Has your sister not told you just how she persuaded me to do it?"

Royal's expression was perfectly blank. Harriet winced, and seethed uncomfortably as she listened to Jake informing Royal how she'd joined the company and tempted the men with the alpaca idea.

The silence when he finished was awful. Royal kept darting little glances at her, and Harriet's fists were clenched. She couldn't think of a word to say in her own defense, and all the time she waited for Royal to tell Captain Dexter just exactly why she had been forced to take such desperate measures. Her nails dug into her palms with anticipated shame, but all Royal muttered was, "Devious, damn devious, I must admit it."

"At least," Jake said tersely, "your presence on the brig will lend some decorum to the situation . . . which brings us to you, Mr. Gray. You, I presume, also wish to join our company?"

"What?" Royal's mouth sagged open as he absorbed the import of this. Then he shifted, the picture of uneasiness, his eyes evading Harriet's again. He muttered, "If joining your company means fifty dollars, then it ain't possible."

"What?"

"I . . . don't have the ready. Collecting the alpaca took every sou I had."

This time it was Harriet who cried, "*What*?" She couldn't believe it, for surely Sefton had put up money for the alpaca venture, surely! Then she whispered, "Oh, dear God," for it was all in tune with what Sefton had done already. She saw Jake frowning then, the narrow eyes studying her face. He said slowly, "Perhaps your sister has the money," but all she could do was silently shake her head. Buying her own share had been a desperate gamble; it had taken about the last of her cash.

She thought Jake's expression became troubled, and she looked away to avoid the intent eyes, staring blindly again at the sea, wondering what awful shocks life still had in store for her. Jake's voice, when he spoke, seemed to come from a distance. The tone was matter-of-fact. "There's no help for it then," he said to Royal. "You'll have to work off your share."

"Work?" There was silence. Then Royal muttered, "Oh, God," and Harriet remembered his patent fear as he'd sidled up the mast the previous night. Thirty days and nights of ship work, going aloft in storm and calm, mending rigging, reaving blocks, washing decks whatever the weather: would Royal survive it?

"Thirty days will work out one share exactly," Jake's heartless voice said. "You'll find it a sure cure for seasickness too," and then, before she could turn to confront him, he'd gone.

Royal muttered, "Oh, God," and she listened to him stumble to the rail again and hang there, heaving. It was as if the word *seasickness* had started his stomach to rolling on the instant. Finally she heard him spit and curse and straighten. "What a martinet," he said with passion. "What a bastard."

Quite involuntarily she said, "No, no, he isn't—" but Royal was not even listening.

"So I'm doomed to sleep in the fo'c'sle," he muttered instead. "They swear I stink, d'you know that? They stole the half of my clothes and threw them overboard. Oh, God, I feel awful. D'you think I'd feel better if I ate some breakfast? It used to settle my intestines first rate if I managed to keep down a meal, on my other voyages . . . or do you think" he continued ghoulishly— "that Dexter will keep me starved until I've worked off my share?"

Harriet moved away from him. "You will find," she said stiffly, "that the grub here is excellent, and furthermore that Captain Dexter admires a hearty appetite."

9 ❧ Royal Gray was seasick for a full two weeks, and how the men teased the poor sad scarecrow! It did not amaze Jake that the boy should be so thin and forlorn: from all accounts Royal had run afoul of every sharp trickster in the Andes, and Jake had never yet seen a plump and smug adventurer, adventures being arduous by nature. However, the seasickness did surprise him.

"He," he pointed out to Harriet, "has a-plenty of fresh air."

It was part of their running argument over whether she should spend her days above decks or below. The sun shone hot and bright as the brig forged north, and the ribbons Jake had given her were becoming as faded as the straw hat she wore. The expression on the face in that hat's speckled shade was mutinous in the extreme. "My brother," said she primly, "has ever been a martyr to seasickness."

"What—even on the voyages to Cape Colony and New Zealand?"

"Even then."

"And what did he do when he did not have his head over the rail, take part in little plays and recite poetry?"

The glare he received, Jake mused, was simmering enough to bubble the tar in the deck seams. He could see men smothering grins about decks. Harriet snapped, "He does his share of work."

"He does," Jake admitted. After a fashion, he thought. The day after the brig had left the Chilean shores so abruptly, the men had asked for a company meeting. It hadn't surprised Jake at all: the men, he knew, wanted to register their disapproval. They wished to protest the lack of alpaca; why, they'd fully expected to see those valuable beasts in Valparaíso! And where were they? Full up the Pacific coast of South America, that's what; it was a scandal, they all averred. Royal Gray had listened to it all with an air of the most profound disbelief, but from then on, true, he surely had worked. The men counted him lucky that he was not holystoning the decks for a week, like those miscreants who had bungled their mission so in Valparaíso, but Royal made up for that in the amusement he gave them. The actor looked such a strange awkward mario-nette as he sidled about the rigging that Jake sometimes wondered if he exaggerated his movements on purpose, but he certainly provided the crew with entertainment. And that was a blessing on a passage that was so hot and dry and monoto-nous as this.

"And I, too," said Harriet virtuously, "am prepared to work."

Jake did not bother to answer that one. Harriet had offered to help old Bodfish, which had scandalized the steward yet again; she had offered to help Jake with his account books, which offer had been promptly rejected. For all he knew, she'd tried the same with the logbook and Charlie, with similar results. However then came the day that he arrived on deck to find her sitting on a tarpaulin in hat, apron, and washdress, helping the watch overhaul potatoes.

"But I told you," she said. "I want to help . . . I really do."

Jake surveyed the flushed face with no patience at all inside him. Fresh food on the brig was growing short as the days and then weeks went by and potatoes were precious. Taking off the sprouts would soon be a daily affair, but . . .

"There is no need for you to do anything," he snapped. "You own a share; you're the supercargo."

"But the men who have shares work on the brig. Anyway," she said, "I need the money."

"The . . . *what*?"

"The money. For Royal. The men," she said in the most aggrieved manner possible, "throw away his clothes."

"Oh, for God's sake," he said, and had to quench a laugh. He sent her below and sent up clothes from the slop chest, but within hours there she was on deck again.

Why did that annoy him so? It was the heat, perhaps, he thought, and the lack of fresh water; everyone on board was becoming cross. She said, "Anyway, I don't believe we're steering for.Tombez. How can we be? I haven't seen the coast at all, not even a little glimpse."

She was back at her trick of distracting him with conversation. Jake sighed and leaned with his back against the taffrail, and said, "We're well offshore, that's why. We sail well out, to take the trades, or else the winds will be against us."

"But how do you know that?"

"Every seaman knows that; ever since Juan Fernández steered such a course mariners have known that that is the way to sail north on these longitudes."

"Juan Fernández?"

And she was back at her trick of listening so enticingly. Was there ever an audience as flattering as Harriet? "Juan Fernández was a navigator," he said. "He found the course to take the offshore winds, and he made the voyage from Chile to Callao in thirty days, and because it was considered impossible they rewarded him by trying him for sorcery."

"What! I don't believe you," she said, and laughed.

"Well, believe it, for 'tis true," he said, and sent her below.

It was turning into a game; perhaps he needed the entertainment as much as the men. "Jahaziel," said she thoughtfully next time, "what do you think of those stories of gold?"

"Gold?"

"The gold in California."

"I saw no gold rush," said he tartly. He had most of his attention on the sky. Gray pillows of clouds were piling up in the air, great clouds of promise of reviving cool rain. The men were watching them as hopefully as he was.

"Gold rush?"

Gold rush: man's eternal greed for gold, and the race to get the yellow stuff first. Jake thought of the conquistadors, and old Rochester's journal, which Harriet had still neglected to return, and he said curtly, "If those gold yarns were true, do you really think all those soldiers would be content to march about in Valparaíso, even with the excitement of a desperado to hunt?" He saw her wince at that, but then she nodded, for what he had said was so very true.

"What soldier," he repeated, "would stay satisfied with twenty cents and his rations every day if that gold really existed?" He repeated it again at noontime dinner for Charlie Martin's benefit.

"Aye," Charlie concurred, and nodded with weighty emphasis. "Every man, whatever his nation, would desert first chance—if the stories were real."

"Perhaps they haven't heard the stories yet," Harriet objected.

"Ah, beg pardon, Miss Gray, but to contradict, they most surely have, gold tales bein' so uncommonly encitin'; gold is excitin', ma'am, even when unreal, and they talk about it, certain. The men need excitement, and there's not been excitement since old Uncle Moses cracked open the cider barrel, since the fair came to town and men heard of folks who had seen the elephant."

Jake blinked himself at such unexpected outflowing of poetic rumination, and it completely silenced Miss Gray, he saw. Then, like Charlie, he glanced up again at the skylight, at the thickening sky. There was hope of rain yet, and that was more interesting than the dinner, which had fallen off sadly in variety, on account of the lack of fresh provisions.

The heavens opened while the watch was shortening sail. The clouds were thick white at the edges of their dark gray masses, and the rain hissed down and bounced merrily on the decks. The air was abruptly cooler and smelled most wonderfully clean and new. The men in the rigging cheered and held out their hats and then tipped over their heads as they filled, and the watch below came yodeling up on deck, turning cartwheels and capering in the rain. Even Royal Gray was with them, his thatch of stiff beard pointing exultantly up to the sky . . . and there was Harriet too, laughing on the quarter deck.

Jake turned and stared in disbelief, as she held up her arms to the sky and laughed. He hadn't realized that she, too, had wished for rain, not until he saw her now, with the rain tumbling through her hair, streaking it down over her shoulders, darkening the gold, running down her upheld arms and soaking into her dress. He stood staring with the rain drum-

ming on his hat, soaking his shirt and pants, sticking them to
his skin; he almost laughed, infected with her joyful ebulli-
ance. For God's sake, she looked but twelve years old!

No, she didn't. Her dress was as sodden as his, skirt clinging
to long elegant lines, waist stuck tight to pert breasts, the thrust
of nipples, the round curve of buttocks. He moved abruptly and
whirled her round, thrusting her in the direction of the
companion. "Silly wench," he grunted, "get below."

Behind him Cookie was waiting by the galley door, laughing
widely, holding bars of good yellow soap at the ready. The
men, the whole crew, had arrived on deck and were dancing
about, shouting wildly, as ebulliant as she was. Jake could feel
the weight of their laughing attention, their eyes all fixed on
Harriet. "Get below!"

"But I'm wet already, Jake!"

She most certainly was. The voyage and the good *Hakluyt*
food had done her much good, a detached part of his mind
decided: her skin was radiant, she throbbed with life, her
breasts had enlarged. He said nothing. He reached out an arm
and opened the companionway door, and then he bared his
teeth in a narrow dangerous smile. She took the hint and
went . . . and only just in time.

Cookie had tossed the bars of soap, and men caught them
with hollering delight. The men in the rigging had finished
their job and were skidding down onto the planks. Rain
splashed down and they wielded the soap, rubbing down
clothes, rubbing down each other, raising a sea of bubbling
foam that ran into puddles on the decks. Then they stopped up
the scuppers so that the rain could not run away, and the
puddles rose and rose, foaming ankle deep, and the men all
vied to toss each other into the huge shallow bath that this
made. Involuntarily or on purpose they all rolled over and over
in the wet, rinsing the clothes they all still wore. Then, that
done, they stripped.

The sodden balls of cloth were tossed aside, and the bars of
soap were wielded again, this time on naked skin. The boys all
pranced and yelled as they attacked each other with massaged
lather; they washed each others' hair unmercifully, and men
swore cheerfully as soap ran into eyes and stung. They picked
up the balls of clothing again and hurled them at each other,
and then, all at once, they ganged up on Royal Gray.

He did his best to run: they chased his frantic lean buttocks
round and round the masts, and then they felled him and they

scrubbed him and he cursed most wonderfully all of the time.
"Crack your bottom cheeks!" he hollered, and, "Drench your
balls and drown your cocks!" They all cheered and jeered most
merrily, for Royal's affronted cod was as long and thin as he
was. They rinsed him then and scrubbed him again, until at last
they had rid him of his stink, they declared, and Jake Dexter,
as naked and clean as the day he'd been born, pronounced this
a moment fit to split the main brace. The boys unstoppered the
scuppers and let the soapy water out, and then they sat around
blissfully and savored the good dark rum.

Harriet was extremely sniffish at supper, Jake noticed. He
wondered if she had been scandalized or embarrassed; perhaps,
he thought, she was miffed that the men had treated her brother
so. Royal would do a deal better on the brig now, Jake knew;
the scrubbing was a kind of ipso facto initiation rite, like a
seaman's first crossing of the equator. The life on the brig had
done Royal much good altogether, he mused then; the man
might still be cadaverous-thin, but the sores and scabs of the
hard, past year had all healed. Then Charlie Martin came into
the cabin with an announcement which distracted Jake entirely
from that: the men, it seemed, had asked for a meeting of the
company.

The opening of the meeting and the reading of the minutes
seemed as endless as always. Then at last they came to the
problem on the collective minds. The problem, it turned out,
was Miss Gray.

"She spends too much time, sir, about decks," said Abijah,
and then he sniffed at the drop on the end of his nose, as
mincing as if he had never stripped and pranced about that
afternoon.

"Well?" said Jake. He turned and gazed inquiringly at
Harriet, and everyone else stared at her too. If she was
embarrassed, she certainly didn't show it: she was perfect
scarlet with temper. She glared at Abijah and snapped, "And
your reasons, Mr. Roe?"

"It don't allow the crew any privacy; it ain't decent."

"*Decent*?" Her voice rose with outrage; she was acting the
haughty dowager again, Jake decided. He shifted his stance,
leaning one shoulder in negligent style against the deckhouse,
enjoying this moment to the full, with most leisurely relish.

"No, ma'am," said Abijah, and sniffed at them all, staring
righteously about the men. "We can't even wash in peace and
quiet."

"Peace and quiet—?" The echo was indescribably affronted, and Jake frowned a little, remembering the exuberant commotion as everyone washed. Somehow, inexplicably, his sense of enjoyment was dissolving.

Then Harriet said coldly, "I apologize," in a tone that was not apologetic at all. "No doubt, Mr. Roe, you are thinking of the mass bathing I heard this afternoon, and no doubt you feel embarrassed that a *lady* was witness to such sport. I appreciate your sentiments, sir, and think them most appropriate, but please do not feel ashamed on my account, because now I know about the custom I will cope much better in the future. It only happened that I was on deck—for a very brief time—because I am not yet used to the ways of this brig, and I apologize most fervently for that. However, in future, as long as I am warned"—and Jake found himself the subject of a very darkling look—"I will take great care to keep well out of the way . . . though I do wish someone would think to fill a big tub for me, so that at some time I can take a bath of my own."

And this, Jake thought incredulously, was the source of Harriet's miffed mood: she was envious of the fun the men had enjoyed, and she wanted a bath of her own! Jehovah, he thought, and had to admire her, for Abijah was gaping most inelegant as he slowly absorbed the fact that somehow her apology had blamed him. He heard Royal Gray let out a muffled snort and was curiously certain that Harriet's brother was biting back laughter.

Then Abijah gobbled, as game as the girl he was condemning. "It ain't just the bathing, sir," said he in querulous appeal to Jake. " 'Tis the functions of nature. When Miss Gray is about the decks she can't help but see what men be about, which men go over the bows to perform functions of nature in the nets, and which men go to the urine barrel to perform other functions there."

Jake shifted uneasily. He felt angry on Harriet's behalf. However, she merely tilted her chin and said in distant accents, "If that is your problem, Mr. Roe, then I must admit that I have never noticed. I may have the sensibilities of a lady, sir, but I also have the sense to turn my back! If you are embarrassed, then there is no need, and if you feel concern that I am embarrassed, then please rest at peace, Mr. Roe, for embarrassed I am not."

And that was that, Jake saw; Harriet had won the battle, lock, stock and barrel, and the meeting broke up in disarray.

However, "See?" he muttered triumphantly as she passed him in the doorway. She merely cast him a disdainful look, and next day there she was on deck again, with her back resolutely turned to all the men.

He came up alongside her and said, "What the devil are you doing?"

"Fishing," said she brightly, and fishing she was indeed. It was no use for him to point out that it was worse then useless to expect to catch fish over the stern of a vessel that was under full sail. She merely chose to disbelieve him. "I haven't eaten fresh fish in such a long time," she murmured plaintively, and it was no use, either, to inform her that fish could be caught, yes, if they took out a boat and fished around a floating log or piece of wreckage; that fish could even be taken when sailing slowly across another ship's stern. It was no good, for the brig was doing neither of those things. The men, like Harriet, would certainly relish a mess of fresh fish, but the brig was on passage. At night flocks of flying fish skimmed twenty feet above the waves, pursued by huge, leaping predatory albacore, and Harriet watched them with the same wistful look.

It might have been a ploy to distract the men from muttering about her presence above decks, Jake noticed, but Harriet's preoccupation with fishing became a joke. One night a flying fish missed its mark and landed on the planks, and next morning Harriet was presented with the fish for breakfast, fried and tastily decorated with paper frills and a few leaves from the steward's pot plant. Harriet ate it nevertheless with excellent relish and declared it delicious. "Oh, for God's sake," said Jake, who had to laugh. "I'll show you how to really catch fish."

The fishing demonstration was timed for that night. The brig was hauled aback so she barely moved through the starlit waves, and Harriet, looking extreme suspicious, was ushered into the boat that hung from the davits. She sat down cautiously, and Jake stepped in with her and worked the falls as the boat was lowered. He was barefooted and wore duck pants and a loose French shirt. When the boat finally touched the water everything was very quiet, except for lapping against the planks and the click as the boat touched the hull of the brig and the muttering of the men lined up at the rail to watch the fun.

Jake left the boat hooked to the falls. Then he padded surely about the boat, setting it rocking as Harriet sat and watched him. He hoisted the four-cornered sail, and adjusted it so it did not take the wind. Then he lighted a lantern, turned, grinned down at Harriet's puzzled look, and bid her hold it on the other side of the canvas.

"And keep down low," he said.

"But why?"

"You'll see." The light made the sail luminescent, and he watched her silhouette. It was a ghostly shape against the lamp and the night.

Moments plodded by. "But this is ridiculous." More moments. "Are you playing a joke on me? Merciful heavens, Jake Dexter, we don't even have a line!"

He grinned; still he said nothing. Then all at once a silver-fletched arrow sped through the air. He ducked, and it crashed into the sail with a drumming plop and dropped like a felled bird into the bottom of the boat.

"My God, Jake, what was that?"

It was a flying fish, and it was rapidly followed by another, and another, and two dozen more. Jake shoveled them into bags as they dropped, too busy to talk. He heard Harriet's incredulous mirth, and still the fish kept flying into the sail. Within ten minutes he had enough bagged for the whole of the crew, and that for two meals at the least.

Then there was a pause. "Well, madam," said he to the laughing silhouette, "are you impressed?" and a two-hundred-pound albacore came hurtling through the night.

Jake's only warning was the swish as it left the water. He threw himself forward to knock down the sail, but the huge fish hit it like a cannonball first, and Jake plunged right through, grabbing Harriet as he went. His body thumped against hers, and he felt the whoosh as the breath was knocked out of her chest. He held her tight. Then his scrabbling toes felt the boat tip and capsize, water touched his feet. Somehow he reached up one of his arms, still holding her, his arms still wrapped about Harriet, and somehow his fingers snagged the boat falls.

He gripped and hung on grimly, and felt the jerk as the boat became unhooked, as it turned relentlessly upside down. Harriet's body was tight with shock. He had one knee thrust between hers to stop her from slipping, and his arm socket grated with the strain of the double weight. His pulse was thumping deafeningly in his ears, and he could feel the flutter of her breath. She moved against him, wriggling wildly, scrabbling for a hold on the rope, and they began to spin slowly, held only by his single-handed grip on the hemp.

He could feel her straining upward. Then she set a foot on his knee, and braced herself with that. For an awful instant he thought he was going to lose his grip, but then with a lunge she had a hand on the rope as well. She wriggled upward, farther, moving against him, and suddenly his mouth was in the curve of her throat, open, gasping for breath. Shocking excitement surged inside him; he was gripped with heat; all he wanted to do was close his teeth, gently, close his jaws softly on the smooth taut skin and hold her still while . . . while . . .

She lunged again and held the rope more tightly. The strain was easing on his arm; he could feel the men on deck begin to haul. They spun; she was leaning outward, her body tight against his chest; surely she must be aware . . .

She leaned back farther, even more precipitously, turning her head to look down at the sea. "Goddammit," she said. "We've lost our fish!"

She sounded furious, her mind entirely on the lost catch, and Jake began, helplessly, to laugh. In the beginning her robust language had shocked him, for a New England woman would never speak thus, but now he found it irresistibly funny. Within the space of a moment he had desired her most ardently—swinging one-handed on a rope, for God's sake!—and now as the men hauled them on deck he was shaking with wonderful mirth.

Harriet sniffed and informed him there was naught to laugh about. That most surely was true, as old Chips promptly pointed out. "You oughter watch out for them albacore, sir," he said with deep disapproval.

"Yes," said Jake.

"You could've most easily been killed, sir, and worse'n that, you mighter killed Miss Harriet."

"Yes," said Jake. Finally he calmed down, and the men turned their attention to the capsized boat. They righted it and trapped flying fish by Jake's good method but with due caution in the matter of albacore. The men then debated the notion of dropping overboard to enjoy a nice swim while the brig still lay aback. However, the sharks were coming sniffing about, so they made sail again instead.

Two days after that the coast of Peru was raised. Then, the next late afternoon, they made the Tombez River.

10 ～～～   Five men went in the whale-
                        boat with Jake Dexter: Royal,
of course, to lead them to the Frenchman's plantation, and
Pablo for interpreter. Joseph Fayal, the black Portuguese, went
too; and scarfaced Abner, who was fit and better than new; and
Crotchet for his French.

It was just dawn, but the whole ship's company gathered at
the rail to see them go. Men moved quietly and kept on looking
over the sandbar and its breakers to the still green jungle. There
was no wind at all; the only sound was the crash of the muddy
yellow surf and the whisper of myriad leaves and insects. The
brig was the only vessel in port, and the silence was uncanny.

The last time Jake had recruited here for wood, water, and
fruit seven vessels had been at anchor outside the sandbar. He
stared around carefully, his hat tipped down over his eyes, and
then he looked back up at the rail. Harriet was there, leaning
over, and their eyes met. She was frowning; she seemed very
anxious. It seemed strange to have an anxious girl say

119

good-bye; the last time that had happened . . . He pushed the thought out of his mind, and reached up to take the rifle that Charlie handed down to him.

The rifle was a pretty piece, French in manufacture. It had mother-of-pearl ornamentation set into the stock and a brass plate on the butt; the brass was engraved with a scene of ships at battle. Jake hefted the familiar weight and then set it down by his knee, bracing the steering oar in his armpit. With a series of thumps the others joined him and took their places at the oars.

The combers breasting the sandbar were foaming and angry, snapping up mud and spray. The oarsmen waited, poised, looking over their shoulders, and then with a thud as Jake said, "Heave!" they all set their sweeps. Royal was the man nearest to Jake, and Jake set his fist on the end of that oar to give Royal the timing of the stroke. The boat jumped and jinked and took in water, and then with a lurch they were over, into the mirror-calm river mouth right on the other side.

The river was narrow, so narrow that Jake could have touched either bank with his twenty-foot oar. Within yards they were surrounded by trees. It was like sculling through a green tunnel, and the tide was so low that the roots of the riverbank trees were exposed. Clumps of dead and floating vegetation bobbed along and caught in those roots, and coconut fronds and spikes of banana-palm flowers leaned far over, threatening to snag in Jake's hat. The water was the color of well-stewed tea, dusty with pollen all over the surface, so that the reflections of flowers and foliage were in shiny pools, like oil. Sugarcane grew like grass gone mad, and the smell of mud and decay and rampant vegetation was thick, almost palpable. Insects whined and alligators floated like fallen trees, watching the boat with cold bubble eyes.

The men rowed slowly; the wet heat was oppressive. Then at last, on a muddy bend, the spiles of the first houses came into sight. More spiles were set in the middle of the river, slimy and green with thick algae. These were for securing the boats that came to this place for fresh water. The boats towed empty water casks all in a line, and these were tied to the stumps and then tipped so that only the bungholes protruded, and the water flowed into the open tops. Last time Jake had recruited here the boats had had to wait in line to get to the spiles, but now the place was deserted and still.

He looked about slowly, carefully, trailing the blade of his oar, the hackles rising in a chill on the back of his neck. The miserable thatch houses were set high on stilts to keep out of the reach of seasonal floods, but naught but thin dogs and skinny roosters . . . and alligators . . . scavenged among the piles. The last time he'd been here the soggy landing pier had been wild with urchins and touts, but now . . . nothing. The men were looking about, apprehensive looks on their waiting faces, and when a bird called shrilly right above, they all flinched with fright.

Carefully, very quietly, the five oars touched the water. The boat drifted on, against the slow current, and then Jake said softly, "Wa-ay enough," as the boat touched the stage. He was the first to clamber out when the boat had been secured, and he stood with his hat tipped back, looking around, listening.

The town of Tombez was three miles from the landing stage. Usually there were horses for hire. Now the men trudged uneasily up the sodden slime of the bank. The miserable huts were all empty. Jake led the way along the track, out of the trees and through tall, rustling fields of sugarcane. The stiff drab-green leaves were shoulder-high, and when two women came out of the cane ahead, the men jumped with fright again.

The women seemed equally frightened. They wore loose clothing in the South American style and had the familiar hungry South American look. They were dirty and soil-smeared, and one carried a mattock over her shoulder. They relaxed and even giggled when Pablo teased them in their native language, and the younger one seemed willing to go back into the cane field with Abner, but they were reluctant all the same to tell where all the people who lived in the huts by the landing place had gone.

All Pablo could elicit from them was that the men had gone away. The men had simply disappeared, it seemed, and apparently the horses too, and then the women and children had gone off inland, to the town of Tombez or back to family farms. But why had the men disappeared, and to where?

They would not say. Jake tipped his hat back, staring down at the bland faces in puzzled frustration, and then, slowly, his nape crept with an indefinable sense of someone watching. He turned his head quickly and saw Joseph Fayal turn his head too. The Portuguese had sensed the intruder even before he had; Jake could see the whites of his wary eyes. Then he saw the man who watched from farther up the track.

An Indian. The man was an Indian, unmistakably, but he

was like no Indian Jake had ever seen up the Tombez River before. The man was short, and nut-brown, red-cheeked, almond-eyed, and squat. Despite the damp heat he wore many square-shaped colorful garments and a braided cap on his bullet-shaped head. He was standing very still, so that Jake wondered how long he had been there.

The Indian was a good fifty paces away but made no movement to come closer. Jake said quickly to Royal, "Who is he?"

Royal shrugged. The movement was nonchalant, but Jake could see the gooseflesh rising on Royal's bare forearms.

"Where does he come from?"

"How would I know?" Royal's expression was uneasy in the extreme, Jake thought. Then he muttered, "He comes from high altitudes, probably from the altiplano."

The Indian certainly had the bright red cheeks and barrel chest of those who breathe thin mountain air. Jake said nothing but slowly led his party forward. The Indian stood to one side as they passed, politely, and watched unblinkingly without a sound. No one said a word. The women seemed to pay no attention; they were too busy giggling and eyeing the men to be afraid, it seemed. Then, at last, they emerged from the sugarcane.

The rutted track led on through parched fields toward the town of Tombez. The reds and yellows hurt the eyes after the abundance of green. Away from the river the air was dusty, and dust clung to the leaves of coconut palms. A mile way up in the glaring pallor of the blazing sky an eagle clung to an invisible current of air, its wings widespread. Jake looked about, grimaced, and said to Royal, "Where is the Frenchman's plantation?"

Royal's expression was uneasier than ever. He said, "Four miles."

"Past Tombez?"

"No. Four miles—that way."

That way was a trail that shimmered with heat and rising dust. Jake groaned and said, "Oh, Jehovah," and then became aware of one of the women pulling at his arm. Evidently she understood some English, for she led the way up a side path that led along a high thorn hedge. The path was the way to a kind of farm, for at the end was a large shed, sheltered by mango and tamarind trees.

The shed was dim and had a cart and other equipment

stowed inside it. Harness dangled from dusty rafters, and two
oxen grazed under the trees. The two women rummaged out a
heavy wooden yoke and intimated that cart and oxen were
available for hire, an excellent bargain, scandalously cheap.
Their smiles and persuasions had a nostalgic air about them, as
if they had almost forgotten the pleasures of striking bargains
with visiting seamen.

Jake surveyed the equipment wryly: the oxen no doubt could
be easily caught, but hitching the cart would be a different
matter entirely. The wheels had been made from rounds sawn
out of some huge log. He shook his head and they all trudged
back up the path by the hedge . . . and the Indian was
waiting for them.

Once again he merely stepped aside and watched them as
they passed. Jake could hear the uneasy muttering of his men.
The women had stayed behind in the shade of the shed, but
when Jake and his party were five hundred yards along the trail
he looked back, and the Indian was following. It was peculiarly
chilling to be dogged thus by one silent man who kept an even
twenty yards to the rear. Jake had to control the urge to keep
glancing over his shoulder, and the back of his neck felt stiff.

The sun beat down from the pale sky and the air was thick
with dust. Moments trudged by, and then full hours, a hot
monotony of dust and heat and putting one boot in front of the
other. Then, all at once, Royal stopped. Jake almost bumped
into him. Then he looked up and around. The landscape
seemed the same as it had been seemingly forever, and then he
saw the path that straggled off to the left.

The path had an adobe gate, in the Spanish style, crumbling
and whitewashed and with a few terra-cotta tiles on top, but
despite this embellishment the path was merely made of
cracked clay and small stones. It led past a cockabill weather-
silvered fence to a clump of huge dusty trees and a glimpse of
a low whitewashed structure. Jake could see cattle grazing in
the distance, and the wavering heat-muddled shapes of hog
houses, but the field between the trail and the rancho house was
empty, a sere, brown empty pasture.

Jake shifted his stance and said sharply, "Is this the
Frenchman's place?"

"That is his house, yes." Royal spoke confidently enough,
but his expression was apprehensive. He squinted, and his eyes
were as reddened by dust and glare as the way Jake's felt.

"Then where are the bloody alpaca?"

"How would I know? They must be in another field." Then he set off, through the archway and along the path, and first Jake and then the others trudged after him. When they arrived in the shade of the trees it was like a blessing. Jake stopped and looked around as the men milled in an uncertain group. The house stood on one side, half-shaded by the trees. It was an ancient structure, the worse off for time and wear, the adobe crumbling and many of the roof tiles gone. Nothing moved; the house seemed as deserted as the landscape and the small village at the landing place. Royal, however, walked right up to the door and rapped loudly on the wood. The door creaked slowly open, hinges grinding, and all the men startled.

There was no one behind the door; it had opened of itself, with Royal's knocking. When a loud grunt whistled right behind Jake Dexter, he jumped with fright, and so did everyone else.

Jake was the first to recover. He turned and peered narrowly into the shade of the tamarinds and palms, and as his eyes adjusted he saw an animal . . . five animals, who all peered haughtily back.

He had never seen anything like them, not in the flesh. They had fine dark eyes with miraculously long lashes, long elegant necks, and imperious expressions on their faces: they reminded him somewhat of Harriet. He quenched his grin and said to Royal, "Well, well, so this is what alpaca look like."

Royal said flatly, "No." He was staring at the animals with an expression that was every bit as disdainful as theirs. He said, "These are llamas."

"Llamas? Then where the hell—?" Jake stopped short as his belly muscles clenched. He has just glimpsed movement: it was the Indian, the same Indian who had shadowed them so doggedly all the way from the river. The Indian was walking across the empty field, his squat shape dignified, and he was walking to join a group of Indians like him. Where the devil, thought Jake, had they come from? The Indians had materialized by a kind of magic, or perhaps they had been there all the time, blended into the landscape like the llamas.

He said tensely to Royal, "Do you know those men?"

"*I don't know.*" Royal sounded like a caged lion. "My agents . . . bought alpaca from Indians who looked like these, yes. But they all look the same!"

Jake said softly, "Oh, Jehovah." An urgent sense of danger drummed inside him. If these men were from the tribe that had sold the alpaca, they they were men who had been informed that those alpaca had been stolen—by Royal. His hand clenched on the familiar weight of his rifle stock. He snapped, "Where is the Frenchman?"

"I don't know!" Royal shouted in a harassed voice.

A man came round the corner and said, "Be you after M'sieu La Plante, sirs? For if you are, then he's gone."

There was dead silence. Jake turned and so did his men, and the newcomer grinned obsequiously back. By the smell of him, he had just arrived from a hog house, and he looked somewhat hoglike too. He was as short and broad as any of the Indians but had bristly red hair that stuck out all over his face and head, and one tooth was missing in the front of that ingratiating smile. His clothes were made up of rags and scraps of regimentals, the regimentals of an American regular.

If he had noted the Indians, they did not seem to worry him. Royal's blank voice said, "Who the hell are you?" and then in the same breath, "No, never mind that; where the hell are my alpaca?"

"You mean those woolly beasts, sir? Ah, they went."

"They . . . *what*?"

"They were a-pastured in that there field when M'sieu La Plante went off and left me in charge, sir, and then a lot of Indians came, and they put 'em in a flock, and off they went."

"You allowed them to steal my alpaca?" bellowed Royal. He was scarlet with consternation. "You watched them take my alpaca away, and made no effort to stop them?"

"Well, no, I confess not, I didn't."

"But I paid La Plante a fee to look after them!"

"You did? Well, would you ever now, eh? But you must admit it, sir, that you did not pay me."

"And how the hell could I? I've never seen you before in my life!" Royal was shaking with rage; Jake could see the veins bulging out on his neck. "Those alpaca were my rightful property!" he shouted. "I paid good coin for them, and I paid La Plante about the last that I had to take good care of them!" Royal had his hands out before him with a stranglehold on air, and as he stepped forward with each shouted phrase, the newcomer backed an apprehensive pace. The snoutish grin had entirely disappeared, and Jake was just preparing himself to prevent imminent murder, when Royal, utterly unexpectedly, whirled about and vaulted the fence.

The llamas snorted and scattered. Royal set off in a headlong sprint for the Indians. Jake said, "Oh, Jehovah," and vaulted the fence after him.

Royal hollered as he ran, jerking furious words out. "Those alpaca were my legal holdings!" he cried. "Those alpaca belonged to me, by damn!" His thunder was enough to shake the very heavens, Jake thought, panting as he ran in hot pursuit, but the Indians merely stood and waited. Jake expected massacre at the very least, but Royal, when he arrived at the forefront of the impassive group, merely halted and carried on with his bellowed tirade. "I paid good Chilean dollars, by prearranged agreement!" he shouted. "I paid all the monies I owned, gave a twelve-month of my life; my God, when I think what I suffered, endured! Am I to profit nothing, naught for all my investment?"

It was marvelous thunder, Jake decided, fully worthy of a Gray. He folded his arms, listening with interest, but Royal abruptly changed to another language, one that Jake had never heard before in his life. He supposed that it was the Indians' dialect, but it inspired as little reaction as the English. The Indians merely listened, their brown unblinking eyes set in wrinkled nests.

Then all at once Royal ran out of steam; the flow of invective faltered and stopped. There was a long polite pause. Then one of the Indians began a lengthy speech that sounded solemn and formal and elaborately courteous. Royal said nothing but was so puce in the face that Jake wondered at that moment if he might take a fit. Then the Indian finished. He bowed and nodded regally to Jake, and then he and his fellows set off back across the field to the trail, loping in a silent group.

It was startling to see how quickly they disappeared. Jake returned his grim gaze to Royal. He said, "And what was that all about?"

Royal shifted from one boot to the other. Jake could see the veins standing out on his clenched fists. Then the Englishman muttered furiously, "The bastard had the face to sympathize; he made me feel the perfect sheepish guilty schoolboy; he gave me a present."

"What!"

"Yes. He gave me the goddamned llamas, five useless bloody-minded pack beasts! I'm ruined, Jake. I don't have a sou in the whole wide world, and my God, when I think—"

Jake stopped listening. He turned on his heel and set off toward the clump of trees and the waiting faces of his men. The stranger was still with them. The ingratiating smile was back on the red-bristled face. The man lifted a hand as Jake walked right up to him, but Jake ignored that too. He snapped, "Where has the Frenchman gone?"

"Why, sir, he's gone with all the other men from these parts. He gave me this farm for a song, such was his hurry. Why, they all bought berths and sailed on the ships, all them what could raise the ready. Why, sir, they've all lit up and gone to California!"

"*Where*?"

"California, sir, after the shining gold."

Gold. The word dropped into the stunned silence as heavy and rich as the metal itself. Jake listened to the men whispering. "Gold . . . gold . . ." and then he said slowly, "Who are you?"

"Why, you can call me Honest Mill Mason, sir, late of the American forces for the Mexican War, stationed on the flagship *Ohio*, sir, only what I somehow missed the ship in Callao." A deserter, Jake thought, staring at him, a man on the run. He watched the obsequious grin widen, and then Mason said, "D'you think these tales of gold be true? I'm beginning to think so myself, sir. I'm beginning to think I made the wrong choice and should've gone with them myself, and why, sir, you may well ask, sir, but none of them have come back."

Jake paused. Then he said shortly, "What tales?"

"Ah . . ." said Honest Mill Mason, and took a long breath.

For a long time Jake did not want to believe the tales either; he didn't want to believe that Captain Mervine of the frigate *Savannah* had been so wrong; he didn't want to believe that while he'd been setting a course for Honolulu in January a man called Marshall had found gold in a millrace on the American River . . . that while the *Hakluyt* Company had been digging so arduously on Judas Island, other men had been digging wildly profitable up the Sacramento. That shrewd trader Brannan might, after all, have been telling naught but the truth when he'd run about with his hollers of, gold, gold, gold on the Sacramento River . . . but Jake did not want to think so.

But—as this Honest Mill Mason argued— the Tombez River men had gone and none of them had come back. "One ship called, sir, to take on provisions to sell at 'Frisco, and with such tales of the finds in the hills! The sailors all sweared that the gold in California be all layin' about, so thick that men

scoop it up with spoons! They had big gold nuggets to show
me, sir, but me, I thought 'twas naught but watches stolen and
then all melted down. But the others, yes, they believed the
stories, sir, for they all fought for berths to get to that place.
There were ten ships layin' anchored off the mouth of the
Tombez when that news came in, and all ten loaded up, full to
the gun'ls, and they sailed for California and they ain't come
back."

Jake stood silent, lost in thought in the dark shadow of his
hat. It made no difference if he believed the yarns or not, he
knew: he could hear the excited whispering of the men behind
him. "Gold, gold . . ." and it would go to the company vote,
this stimulating notion of digging gold in California, and Jake
thought he knew exactly what the run of that vote would be.
Gold, gold . . . It was the greatest adventure, and Jake
Dexter's seamen were all adventurers of the most optimistic
kind. Poor sailors, they all went to sea for excitement and
adventure—and what did most of them get? Exactly what Jake
had got on his first voyage: drenchings and cold, midnight
watches, and the kind attentions of a half-mad skipper and a
sadistic mate, that's what . . . unless they had the good
fortune and percipience to ship on the good brig *Hakluyt*.

Gold, gold . . . The gold would save Royal Gray's skin,
Jake mused grimly. The talk and the excitement and the voting
would distract the men from the most righteous anger they
would otherwise have felt. Five useless llamas where the
company had expected a half million dollars' worth of alpaca,
worthless pack beasts. . . . He said sharply to Mason,
"Where are all the horses? Where have they gone?"

"To 'Frisco, like the men! Would you believe it, sir, but they
say in California there be a grave shortage of pack beasts on
account of a-carrying all that gold, and anything what carries a
load be in demand. Why one cap'n who took horses to 'Frisco
asked for two hundred each and got more!"

Jake stared, thunderstruck. In some contrary way, strangely,
this convinced him more than anything he'd yet heard that the
gold yarns might be true. Two hundred dollars? "Jehovah," he
said softly, and turned and stared at the llamas.

It was late afternoon when they made the brig *Hakluyt* again,
and the tide was on the turn. The swell over the sandbar lifted
them clear with scarcely a lurch, but Jake did not notice: his
entire attention was fixed warily on the dramatic change of
scene that had happened since his dawn departure.

The brig was surrounded with ramshackle coastal craft as a hen is with chickens. The *Hakluyt* crew including Harriet lined the larboard rail, and Jake's men rowed slowly to the boat falls, underneath the aimed barrels of the muskets that the shipboard company kept leveled. When Jake vaulted up to deck he made straight for Charlie and said tersely, "What happened?"

"They came about noon, sir." Charlie was hauling at his beard and looked extremely hot and sweaty. "Bill was up the forepeak and he begun a-yelling, 'The bloody pirates a-coming, the bloody pirates a-coming!' and afore we knew it there they all were. They seem peaceable enough, sir, only extreme excited, and all they seem to want is parley, but the Lord alone knows what about, for all they screech is *California, California.*"

"California?" Jake turned and gave the assembled water craft a narrow scrutiny. It was a shabby fleet indeed, the most of the boats filled to the gunwales with hopeful-eyed men and threatening to capsize with the slightest stray gust.

"And," said Charlie with a virtuous air, "I was not prepared to take any risks."

"Well done," said Jake, but the praise was absentminded. He deliberated and then sent for Pablo. "Tell them," he said, "they can send over spokesmen, but not more than two from each craft."

Predictably, it was a noisy and argumentative process and took an unnecessarily long time. Jake waited as patiently as he could; despite the ache in his back and feet and the dust and sweat that seemed to coat every inch of clothing and skin, he stood still and watched as the message was delivered and the men on the boats squabbled about which should be allowed to the brig. There was babble all around him too of "Gold, gold . . ." The air of excitement was palpable, that and the realization of what that magic name *California* stood for. He saw Abner hold old Abijah in confidence, Crotchet waving his arms at Valentine, Joseph Fayal in deep confidence with Tib Greene and Dan Kemp. Royal . . . Royal was talking to Harriet. Jake saw her eyes widen, and her expression become red with utter consternation. Then she whitened and ran below. He thought she might be crying, with anger and shame and frustration, for she certainly had cause. Then he merely thought it was fortunate she had gone below, for the South American delegates were clambering on board.

He watched them as they came. They all looked the same in

the first cursory look: they were all black-haired and swaggering, and they all wore some form of local costume. Then, with
the years behind him of summing up mariners and adventurers
as they arrived on his decks, Jake saw the differences. Some
were callow as well as strutting, while others had a weary
seasoned air. Some were obviously used to spending, for they
had the sleek but furtive air of those who owe much to the
merchants, while others had the hollows of habitual hunger and
peonage in their cheeks. They all milled about in the amidships
deck and watched him eagerly. Then at last the final delegation
arrived and numbered six, instead of the stipulated two.

"You," he said sharply, and pointed, "step forward."

For a long moment no one moved. Then the crush of men
shifted, like an eddy in a sand dune, leaving the latest six
arrivals isolated on the after deck. They smiled insolently at
Jake, and Jake stared grimly back.

So, he thought, here were the roosters of the fowlyard, the
bosses of the perch. These six men had the arrogant look of
bullies and politicians. They had a leader, who stood a little
forward, standing brace-legged in tight black pants with gilt
buttons down the seams.

All six wore these *calcineros*, and the bottoms of the pants
were left unbuttoned so that bright silk linings and chipped and
scarred riding boots could be seen. They each wore a striped
serape too, pinned at the shoulder, and they had knives and
pistols thrust into the stained silk sashes they had about their
hips. They all smirked sneers in Jake's direction, never quite
meeting his stare.

Jake said tersely, "Your names?"

The leader spoke for all of them; they were brothers, or
brothers and cousins. They were all called Murieta, and the
leader's name began with *Don Joaquin*. Jake believed the re-
lationship, for their stubbled faces were alike in villainy, but
he disregarded the *Don*. They, like all the other men in the
hastily gathered craft, came from the Gulf of Guayaquil. So
the news of California had passed from Peru to Ecuador, Jake
mused; that was not surprising, for it must have perplexed
the neighboring state to guess where the men of Tombez had
gone; what did amaze him was that the arrival of the brig had
been reported so quickly.

It was all part of this new sickness, gold fever. "Our
business, Captain," said Joaquin Murieta in passable English,
"is of the most profitable. For you." He had a way of splitting

his sentences into sibilant fragments, a curiously threatening manner of speech. "All we demand is passage. To . . . 'Frisco. At good price, very good price. For you."

Jake paused. The South Americans on the deck stood still, gape-mouthed, waiting, and he felt the heaviness of the concerted stares. "Well . . . sir?" said the Murieta, and Jake calmly and deliberately looked away from the mob, at the jungle and the coastal craft and the sea.

The punctual late afternoon wind had arrived. The first wave lifted and broke on the bar, and then began the rush and thud of the surf. The sounds seemed deafening because of the intent, waiting silence. Finally he glanced at the Murietas again and said briefly, "I will tell you tomorrow."

"What?" The man's thin moustache writhed in a sneer. "You need . . . time? To make up your mind?"

"Tomorrow I said, and tomorrow I meant," Jake snapped. "In the meantime you will oblige me by getting the hell off my brig."

11 〰️ The meeting of the *Hakluyt* Company was scheduled for the hour after supper. Harriet went quietly up to deck ten minutes before the bell was struck, and stood at the rail with her back to the decks, staring out to sea.

Somewhere over the smeared glint of the far horizon New Zealand lurked, New Zealand where she had scrimped and saved pennies, and had planned for this day. The alpaca . . . She didn't even know precisely what these alpaca looked like, but for more than a year the alpaca had represented her only hope. She had endured . . . endured privation and humiliation while she waited and planned for Royal's letter and the instructions it held, and while she had waited she had dreamed.

Now she wondered what exactly her dreams had been, for they resembled the reality so little. The pictures in her mind had changed all the time, as scintillating as a kaleidoscope: going back to Europe with Royal, rich, settling in the Cape Colony with that one hundred thousand pounds behind them,

132

buying their own theater . . . somewhere . . . settling in the pastures of New South Wales, raising alpaca and becoming very wealthy.

It didn't matter what form her dreams had taken, she thought drearily. The alpaca had gone, perhaps had never existed, not really; perhaps they had been dreams too. She had involved Jake Dexter and the *Hakluyt* men in a mere figment of her imagination. The alpaca scheme had given her respite from the constant nightmare of Sefton's cheating betrayal, and that had been all the good it had been, for she still did not know, not really, what alpaca looked like. The bell rang. She braced herself and turned, ready for the company's pain and censure.

Instead, amazed, she saw broad grins. Even Royal wore an air of animation.

> . . . *Oh-h-h, I'm off to California, with a heart both stout*
> *and bold* [sang Valentine]
> *I'm goin' to the diggin's there, to get my lumps of gold* . . .

Incredibly, there was an atmosphere of approval. Then slowly and hazily as the meeting jogged along, Harriet understood that the men were delighted—delighted!—that Royal's alpaca business had brought them so far and placed them right convenient for an assault on the diggings of California. Jahaziel's expression, she thought, was sardonic, but even that did not dim the startled relief that filled her, relief that blurred and gilded all the motions and voting that led to the company decision to sail to 'Frisco.

Then Jake said, "There is also the matter of those assorted gentlemen in the craft out there."

The silhouette of his hat nodded at all the assorted craft, and the company looked that way too. Harriet frowned and said, "What do you mean?"

"They all want to buy passage to California."

"But of course you won't take them?"

"That," said Jake deliberately, "is up to the company."

Harriet was silent, feeling stunned; she couldn't understand why she felt so shocked. She'd gazed long enough at the little craft and the men crowded on their decks, over the barrel of a gun. The men had stared back and some had called out, some enticingly, others insolently. That had been easily ignored, for they had been out on the water and she had been safe on board

of the brig. But if the company concluded to carry them
passenger . . .

The thought was appalling. The voyage to 'Frisco took two
weeks, someone had informed her. Two weeks of an invasion
on the decks of the brig; she would have to stop below, and no
argument, but it wasn't that which seemed so horrifying. She
had enjoyed her constant game with Jake Dexter, she had
enjoyed defying and teasing him, but it wasn't that, either.
She had been so happy the last few weeks. Oh, dear God, the
voyage had done her so much good. She had eaten well and
slept well, and for quite three weeks had been touched with no
nightmare; she didn't want this gaggle of strangers on her brig,
for the brig *Hakluyt* was her meantime . . .

. . . home. The realization was like a physical jolt. Quite
involuntarily she cried out, "No, we mustn't take them!"

All the men stared at her, most openmouthed. Abijah Roe,
predictably, gobbled. "You ain't got no vote, remember," he
warned.

"But I do have a voice, Mr. Roe," she snapped. "And I do
have a mind, to think."

That mind was running desperately, hunting out logic to
forestall this terrible proposition. Then she had it. She said
clearly, with false calm, "Why carry passengers . . . when
there can be no profit in the deal?"

"No profit?" Charlie Martin echoed. The echo was stunned,
and his expression was duplicated on the faces of all the men
about him.

Harriet was terribly conscious of Jake Dexter's frown. She
said with all the calm reason she could muster, "Those men out
there, yes, will pay large sums of money to go to California,
more money than the most of them could possibly afford. You
could charge them as much as sixty dollars per head, if you
wished, and get all the customers you need to fill the brig. But
don't expect to do much with the money when you get to
California. In a place where the gold lies about in lumps, no
one is going to be very impressed with a sackful of Chilean
coinage!"

A babble began—and just as abruptly silenced. Harriet
gazed around at the blankly consternated faces and dared,
secretly, to breathe a sigh of relief. She saw the men all look
at Jake Dexter to see his opinion. She looked at him, too, and
their eyes met. In the light from the ship's lanterns his face was

all planes and shadows, his eyebrows a-kilter. "My God," he said, and grunted with wry amusement. "She's right."

Harriet savored internal victory but kept her tone matter-of-fact. "Furthermore," she pointed out, "those captains who carried the men from about here certainly charged for the passage. If they had found profit in the business, don't you think they would have come back for more?"

"P'raps the cap'ns be all a-diggin' on their own account," said Dan Kemp, and some of the men laughed.

"You could well be right," said Harriet. "Which proves that there is more profit in that than there is in the passenger trade. Unless, of course," she added with a chuckle, "the trade was carrying passengers out of California, for then they would pay in lumps of gold."

Men chuckled along with her; the atmosphere was relaxed and easy, and Harriet at that moment was jubilantly conscious of having won just one small victory, a tremendous improvement on her state of mind when the meeting had begun. It was certain which way the men would vote on the passenger-carrying notion, she thought. Jake Dexter said sharply, "We've forgotten one ship."

Silence. Harriet stared at his face, as puzzled as the rest. "We've forgotten the ship that came with the news of the gold," Jake said. "The ship that called here for provisions to take back to California."

Silence, still that blank silence. Harriet saw Jake look at her, and when their eyes met he smiled. "Miss Gray had the right notion," he said. "Paying in kind is an excellent idea! We won't charge our passengers in money, we'll charge 'em in goods—in fruit, vegetables, rice, flour, salt pork and salt beef, all the recruits I normally buy in this place. And when we get to 'Frisco, why, we'll sell 'em . . . and that is when our profit will be made!"

He didn't even seem to notice that Harriet, aghast, did not return his smile. Instead he grinned about at all his men, his manner relaxed and complacent. Harriet said nothing; she could think of no argument. She looked down at her folded hands, listening to the enthusiastic babble, and felt tired, hopelessly tired, awash with a sapping sense of defeat.

It didn't matter that she had no vote: it would have been just one vote against many.

At midmorning next day Jake Dexter bid Pablo send the message to the craft all about that he was ready to see their

representatives. Two from each craft, he added in an incisive
voice, and that ruling applied to the Murietas as well as the
others. Harriet, listening quietly, drifted up onto the afterdeck
ahead of time and stood in a half-hidden corner by the taffrail,
in a shadow cast by the deckhouse. She had slept very badly,
haunted again by worry and a sense of oppression, but she
found it impossible to keep away from the coming confrontation.

Over the night the boats had bobbed away from the brig with
the changing tides. Now, as the word passed along, men
scurried about the rickety hulls, struggling to get them closer.
Then they vied to be the first to send delegates onto the brig,
stamping and pushing at each other. The air of hopeful
suspense was palpable. As before, the Murietas arrived last.
Jake Dexter's instruction had registered, it seemed, for there
were but two of them, the leader Joaquin and one other. Their
sneers were just as insolent as the day before, however. When
Joaquin looked about, swaggering, Harriet inadvertently
caught his stare. He preened, tucking in his buttocks so his hips
jerked in her direction, lifting his upper lip in a leer. She very
quickly looked away; when she looked back Jake Dexter had
arrived on deck.

He stood facing the crowd in a stance she knew so well by
now: hat tipped back, legs braced apart, his thumbs hooked in
the loops of his belt. He was taller than any of the other men
there, rangy in buckskin pants and his thin leather weskit. The
sleeves of his loose shirt were pushed up to the elbow, and dark
hairs gleamed on the brown skin of his forearms. He looked
experienced, very competent and businesslike, she thought,
and she listened to his brusque voice explain the system of
payment for passage to San Francisco. The cost of passage had
been fixed at sixty dollars, he said—sixty dollars' worth of
recruits.

The silence was blank, utterly uncomprehending. Insects
buzzed in the hot quiet air, and men absentmindedly waved
them away while all the time they gaped at Captain Dexter.
Harriet, in her corner by the deckhouse, had her arms folded
very tightly, holding her elbows tightly in her hands. Then she
listened to Jake explaining how, as the recruits came in, Mr.
Bodfish—as ship's purser—would inspect and put a value on
them and give the owner a promissory note in exchange. All
kinds of goods would be acceptable, he told them: potatoes
both Irish and sweet, rice, flour, beef and pork, vegetables and

fruit, oranges particularly, and bananas if they were green. Live animals might be accepted as well, depending on space; the brig would be carrying five llamas as pack beasts to California, so good fodder would be acceptable too. Wine, molasses, the local brandy and sugar would all fetch good prices, but all payment would be made in the form of those promissory notes.

Those men who collected sixty dollars' worth of notes could have a berth in the hold. Salt tack and hard bread and a ration of fresh water would be provided, and time at the galley stove to cook their own meals; any other food would have to be provided by the passengers themselves. Ninety dollars would buy passage in the steerage, and proper meals at the cabin table. Once the brig was full, the brig would sail, but those men who had not collected enough of the notes would not be cheated, for they could exchange the notes for money at the brig's agent in the port of Paita.

Then he stopped. The South Americans all waited, as if there was more to come, but Jake had put it all clearly, Harriet thought, more than clearly enough. Then the Ecuadoreans began to look at each other, and shift and mutter. There was an air of bewilderment that was tinged with anger, swiftly turning into an atmosphere of menace. The hairs on the arms Harriet had folded so tightly across her breasts shivered with half-felt danger.

Then Joaquin's sneering voice said, "Salt beefs, you want? Salt porks?"

"Yes."

"And potatoes?"

Jake nodded. Harriet saw the hands he had propped on his belt curl slowly into fists.

"Beans? Fruits? Flour?" He nodded curtly at each word. "*Caray*, sir. We do not deal in such things."

Caray. Harriet had never heard the word before, but it was not a nice word, she knew. The Ecuadoreans all shifted forward, almost imperceptibly, and Joaquin's sneering upper lip was lifted. Harriet saw the *Hakluyt* men all glance at each other, and then they shifted too, closer to each other and their captain. She began to wish very much that she had not come up on deck.

Joaquin Murieta smirked, his hips thrust forward again. She saw his eyes slide in her direction, and shrank back quickly, deeper into the corner. She thought Jake's eyes would follow the Ecuadorean's, but his shoulders did not move. His right fist, however, had dropped from his belt and touched the deckhouse wall. The broad back was alert; she could see the kite-shaped muscles over the shoulder blades ridged with tension.

He said nothing. Joaquin Murieta swaggered, his eyes sliding about again. "*Caray*, I do not. I not deal in beefs, porks. I am not peasant. Take," he said, and thrust his hand inside his shirt.

Everyone hissed, a swift intake of breath. However, instead of a weapon the Murieta brought out money. He pushed the fist toward Dexter, smirking. Harriet could see the glint of coins sticking out between the shut fingers. "Take," he said. "Money. Enough. Me, my brothers, all six. In the steerage, eat at the cabin table, all nice, very polite."

Jake said curtly. "I see you did not understand what I said. I will take no money; I will only accept notes."

"Notes?" Joaquin's tongue clicked in the Spanish gesture of contempt. Then with slow insult he opened his fingers little by little, so that coins began to trickle out and drop one by one to the deck. Some fell with a single rattle, while others rolled round and round to a wobbling stop. One ran all the way to the scuppers, but no one bent to touch it. Most of the Ecuadoreans were grinning, their expressions stupidly sly.

Then, at last, the sounds stopped. Jake had not moved, not an inch. When he spoke, he spoke softly, so Harriet had to strain to hear. He said: "And still you don't understand. I do not accept money; I accept only notes. Take that money away. If you don't comply with that arrangement, then the answer is simple: you do not sail passenger on this brig."

"*Comply*? What is this *comply*, Capitán. I do not, yes, I do not understand it." Then with a jerk of his chin Joaquin Murieta moved. He and his brother strutted to the rail, and Joaquin said contemptuously over his shoulder, "Pick it up, Capitán. Pick it all up. We will be here, yes, when you sail."

Jake's hand moved so swiftly Harriet almost missed it. He gripped the rifle leaning on the wall, swung it up, around, and said very crisply, "Hold it."

The Murietas kept on going. Breaths hissed all about the deck—and Jake pulled back the hammer.

The metallic click seemed very small to Harriet, but the Murietas instantly halted. Jake was standing very still, poised.

The Murietas turned; their eyes wavered; they looked at each other. Jake's voice was soft. "Pick up the coins."

"Señor . . ."

"You heard me. Pick up the money and get off my brig."

Silence. Every man on board was rigid, suspended in a silent pause. Then, slowly, Joaquin Murieta and his brother knelt. They picked up the coins; they even found the coin in the scuppers.

Then they went. It was as if some spell were broken. Harriet heard breaths let out, and then the Ecuadoreans all shifted and began to babble. Somehow, she thought, they all looked smaller, as if the defeat of the Murietas had somehow diminished them all. "Pablo and Mr. Bodfish will explain it all again, if necessary," Jake said; he sounded brisk, incredibly matter-of-fact.

Then, without any more ado, he disappeared below.

Bodfish certainly had to explain it all again, for the remaining Ecuadoreans seemed to find the plan perfectly incomprehensible. The poor old steward became extremely harassed: if he'd had any hair to pull he certainly would have pulled it out, and Pablo, likewise, was reduced to hauling at his own black glossy locks. In the end Harriet forgot propriety and attempted to help them, but she fared just as badly. She tried to explain the scheme in her most ringing clear tones, but all she achieved was the exasperating sight of stupidly admiring mass grinning and Jake Dexter's abrupt arrival on the deck.

He had, it seemed, heard the echoes of her explanation through the skylight. "If you want to help," he informed her sharply, "you can help below . . . in the pantry."

"What?" She stared, shook her head, and stared at him again. "But what would I do there?"

"What Bodfish is normally doing there at this time of day."

"Cooking?" She stared, appalled and angrily aware, too, of the *Hakluyt* men and Ecuadoreans alike all grinning at her discomfiture.

"Exactly. I'm certain Bodfish will find that this job will go a great deal more smoothly and that he will get more attention paid to what he says, if your pretty and distracting presence, my dear, were removed from the deck."

To her fury, Harriet felt her cheeks flush scarlet, and the widening of Jake's grin told her that he saw it. "You've told me more times than I can count that you want to work," said he, and he even had the sauce to heave a sigh. "Or have you forgotten?"

"Of course I haven't forgotten," she snapped. "And I hope you don't regret it!" Then she flounced down the companion. Once in the pantry, however, her problem became paramount, for the steward was in charge of cooking the fancy food for the cabin table as well as bread and cake for all hands, and Harriet knew with sinking heart that she was no kind of fancy cook.

She could buy a pie and a mug of milk or ale, and rig a curtain in a dank and dirty backstage corner so she could improvise privacy while robing or disrobing for a part; she could learn that part in less than three hours and go straight on the stage and play it; she could, indeed, play four different parts in the space of one week and groom a horse and act from the back of that horse if need be. But persuading dough to rise and then baking it into a fancy, soft loaf was beyond her. Nevertheless, she put her attention to a bowl, a spoon, and some flour.

The result was not encouraging. The bread did not rise and was sour in the bargain, and her subsequent efforts fared no better. Predictably, the company held a meeting to register their general dissatisfaction.

"A man cannot work with such ballast in his belly," declared Jonathan, and the men all nodded in severe unison.

"A man cannot do 'is best on such provender, and in particular such work as what we now do," pronounced old Chips. The crew of the brig was all spoiled rotten, Harriet decided, fuming, but there was nothing she could say in defense. The men were certainly working very hard. The coastal craft had sailed away as the Ecuadoreans at last understood the system, all gone off to procure the stuff that would magically buy them the coveted passage, but the brig still rang like a barrel of nails, with unstowing and readying for the stuff to arrive. As Harriet struggled in the pantry she could hear the commotion of the half cargo of lumber all heaved on deck, and the sawing as planks were made ready for the manufacture of berths.

Over the next two days fussy Bodfish took back the most of his job, and she did her best to learn from him, but no sooner had she begun to pick up the niceties of proving a loaf than the Ecuadoreans began to come back. The craft arrived in gaggles, loaded to the gunwales with stuff the men exchanged for notes before sailing off to fetch more. Sacks arrived with corn, both grain and ground, and little barrels that oozed molasses and brandy. Sacks of coconuts came too, and sugarcane, gourds, squashes, and bananas, along with boxes of oranges, and Bodfish became as busy and important as a colony of beavers, inspecting each lot as it came and allotting a value to each load.

The South Americans hovered in loud and eloquent suspense as they waited for his judgment. Harriet loved to watch them covertly if she could. They watched every mincing motion of the long lanky steward, and unconsciously imitated every expression that crossed his long magisterial face; they smiled eagerly when he smiled, and frowned most piteously when he frowned. Then, when he pronounced his judgment, the heavens above were informed of the unfairness, every saint being called upon to witness their wretched lot.

Then as the week went by the salted-down meat came too, arriving from the hinterlands of the Tombez. Bodfish went on shore and lived there in the hayshed near the sugarcane fields, and Harriet was deprived of even his advice. "I would have thought," said Jake, "that with practice even you would have improved."

Harriet did not deign to favor this jibe with an answer. Instead she concentrated on Bodfish's precisely scripted recipe: surely, she thought despairingly, she could make passable biscuit. The loaves she'd produced that morning had been about inedible, raw dough inside and hard scorch on the crust. It was hot below and noisy too with all the clatter on deck. Her hair straggled down and stuck to her cheeks, and the waist strings of her apron had come untied.

"Did you never learn to cook?" asked Jake.

She said briefly, "No," and wished he would go away; surely, she thought, there was more than enough to occupy him elsewhere.

"But your mother . . . ?"

"Never learned to cook either; she never had the need. You forget that I am an actress, Jake; you forget I come from an acting family. Why, for that matter, we never had a home."

"What? Then where is your mother now?"

Harriet paused. Then she said steadily, "My mother died when I was ten. I'm an orphan, even more of a waif than you thought."

"I'm sorry."

Jake was behind her, so Harriet could not see his face, but his tone seemed more than merely polite. Then she felt his fingers: he was gathering up the waist string, tying her apron.

It felt strange, matter-of-fact and yet so intimate. Harriet stood very still, her head bent over the recipe, and then Jake said, "And she was an actress?"

"Of course. She was very talented, but not in the way of cooking. My mother could not cook any more than I can; acting families have no need of culinary expertise, Captain; they spend the most of their lives in boardinghouses." Harriet could feel the bow being tugged into shape, patted neatly in the back curve of her waist. She kept still and said conversationally, "We had our favorite boardinghouses, of course, or my father did; we returned every year to the good ones. There was a Mrs. Grubbins in Bristol, who was famous for her pies and ale, and my father was particularly fond of a Mr. Kelly. He was such a funny little Irishman who smelled of horses; all the boardinghouses had to have stables of course, that was part of the agreement with the theater managers who hired us, but Mr. Kelly had a particularly deft hand with the gees. He had an even defter hand with a bottle of port," she confessed and turned her head.

She couldn't see Jake's expression, for he was hunkered down gathering up the lower ties of her apron, the ones that tied about her skirt and which she very seldom troubled to fix. His head was bent, as if the fiddly little task took all his concentration. Harriet turned her head again and studied her floury hands in the bowl; the confines of the little pantry seemed very small.

"And then, in the London season," she said, "we stopped, of course, with my Great-Aunt Diana, in her house in Redcliffe Square. We would not have dared to try and cook there! She had a housekeeper, a most severe woman called Mrs. Pink, who ruled my aunt with an iron hand and had a weakness, too, for a bottle of port. There were servants, too, whom she treated very strictly; she was only lenient with my father."

"Because of that fondness for port?"

"No doubt," she said, and heard him chuckle.

"And in New Zealand?"

Harriet froze; the spoon she was holding hurt as it bit into her fingers. She thought in that awful moment that Royal had told Jake about Sefton. She remembered the pity and the salacious speculation in other male faces, and thought she couldn't bear it if she glimpsed that in Jahaziel Dexter's expression. She heard him stand up and quickly looked away.

She said very carefully, "When we arrived in New Zealand we lived in a hotel."

"No servants?

She wondered why he had asked that, and said, "Servants are very scarce in New Zealand, there being so many men and so few women, but there were maids and cooks at the hotel, of course."

"I was thinking about the time after your father died. I was wondering how you coped."

His voice was neutral, but nevertheless her eyes stung. Even Royal had never asked her this, how she had managed in New Zealand alone. She said as lightly as she could, "I acted. After all, that is all I can do. Manager Buckingham was pleased enough to employ me."

"At the Fitzroy, the one with the canal?"

"The very one. Green room it did not have, nor any kind of apartment for robing. It was a dirty, flea-abounding, ill-lighted stink-hole, but yes, indeed, it had Ligar Canal."

"And how much money did you get for such a life, pray?"

"Oh." She shrugged and laughed a little. "Money," she said. "You don't really think of it in terms of *money*. Lodging at a boardinghouse is included, as I told you, that and meals—of a kind—and stabling, if you have a horse."

"But you did not have a horse?"

"No."

Despite herself she looked him fully in the face. Jake's face was wry, his brows tilted, and his head a little on one side too. Again she was very conscious of the closer quarters of the pantry. He said again, abruptly, "How much?"

"Ten shillings a night." Two dollars fifty.

He said, "Not much."

"I could only afford one share in your company," she pointed out, and he was silent. The silence seemed eloquent, more speaking than the questions and answers they had exchanged. Harriet felt inexplicably near to tears: if he questioned her further, she thought distractedly, if he expressed any kind of sympathy, she would embarrass herself and him by dissolving into sobs. She thought of the gossip that had run about Auckland, of the preachers and editors who had prated about the theater: they had called it, "The greatest threat to public morality in the whole of the colony." She thought of the men who had sent her flowers and poems and invitations, how they had slyly approached her in the street, and she braced herself for Jahaziel Dexter's own prating or pity.

Instead he said, musingly, "And throughout that time you had no time, no doubt, to practice cooking biscuit."

"I beg your pardon?"

"Biscuit," he said, "is a weakness of mine. I must confess I have a great fancy for well-cooked biscuit."

"And you don't trust me to cook it the way you like it?" she said incredulously.

"That," said he, "I do not. I've never tried my hand at biscuit either," he confessed. "But I see that Bodfish has writ the recipe in a most legible hand, so if you'd excuse me . . ."

"With pleasure," she said tartly, and left without wasting another word. To her chagrin the biscuit proved excellent, and Jake Dexter as smug with his success as a cream-fed cat. The men pronounced it first-rate, exclaiming loudly about it, and so did Charlie Martin at the supper table. Captain Dexter's expression became more and more complacent.

Then: "I saw such a sight this day," Charlie added with sublime disregard for spoiling the appetites of his companions. "Such a gruesome sight I never did see, and that in a cask of salt pork."

Harriet gaped at him and heard Jake say, "What?" At least the smugness had left his tone. "Where?"

"On shore, in Bodfish's shed, what he calls his store. The carts come in from the various farms, all laden with barrels of salt pork and salt beef. 'Tis impractical for Bodfish to ask for all the casks to be opened to judge the quality and price, so he chooses one at random, as a sample, you understand, and he orders that open and judges the whole by that."

"I see," said Jake. Harriet nodded; it seemed to her to be practical, as commonsense as most of what Bodfish did.

"Wa-al, today, when I were witness, that was what happened, only the sample tub turned out to be full of naught but heads and trotters. There were even rings, still, in the snouts, all gone greenish! The owners roared their astonishment and innocence, but old Bodfish held firm. He sniffed and ordered them all away."

"As severe as Mrs. Pink," murmured Jake as he raised a crooked, humorous brow at Harriet, which she ignored with hauteur. The fuss about her terrible cooking still rankled; as far as she was concerned, Captain Dexter the consummate biscuit baker could do all the cooking, and welcome.

However, he was far too busily occupied to do such a thing, supervising the stowing of the provisions as they came. The bags and sacks and boxes and barrels were all packed tight in the empty hold, two layers high. Then carpentering gangs laid boards on top to make a kind of floor and built the berths about the bulkheads with a long rough table along the middle. These would provide the common accommodations for the passengers who had been able to accumulate sixty dollars' worth of notes. It was all very noisy and involved a great deal of shouting and hammering, and it meant that Harriet was left alone to cope with the cooking as best she might.

The days went by but the job became no easier, simply because the *Hakluyt* crew demanded fresh provisions. They had become heartily tired of soft potatoes and salt meat on the thirty days' passage to this place, and now they wanted grub that was fresh and varied and tasty. Accordingly, Harriet found all kinds of fruit and vegetable matter dumped by the galley door each morn, and somehow or other she had to devise some means of serving it up in acceptable state.

Bananas were easy; she knew of bananas, even when the fruit was a strange orange-red. Some were tiny, furthermore, the size of baby fingers, while others were enormous, and huge woolly spiders lurked in the bunches. When they sprang out she leapt back and screamed and made the men laugh. Mummy apples arrived too, looking reassuringly like pumpkins which could be made into pies, but proving deceptive, and other strange fruits called *apple*: sweetsop, soursop, cherimoya, and pappaw, which proved just as difficult to cook. Alfalfa came as a fodder for the llamas, and she mistakenly tried to cook it as a vegetable. The fruit from prickly pears bewildered her entirely. She made stews, which came out as strangely colored soups, and soups, which thickened most mysteriously into stews. Once she cooked some sweet-looking berries, and when Charlie Martin tasted the concoction he emerged with blistered lips. He forgot his company: his language was definitely unhandsome, and Harriet rushed into the pantry and slammed the door. Beyond the wood she heard Jake Dexter laughing, and she put her apron over her head and did dissolve into tears.

Perhaps the men heard her weeping; perhaps they did not. Charlie Martin, however, was most contrite and begged her pardon often, and Jake Dexter suggested that she might like a jaunt on shore, for she'd not been up the river yet.

Harriet went willingly enough, though she mused as the boat

set off that it was odd, strange that this was indeed her first trip ashore in more than four months, and yet she'd never felt restricted on the brig. She held onto the side of the boat and looked about with interest. Valentine at the steering oar broke into jovial song.

> . . . *My creditors gave me a week, to pay 'em what I ought*
> *So I thanked 'em very kindly, and sailed to Tombez port*
> *Now I sail to Sacramento, where once the river rolled*
> *To fill my trouser pockets, with the bright and shining gold!*

Sacramento, she thought uneasily; the valley, surely was some distance from San Francisco . . . and what would Jake Dexter conclude to do with the brig if the company voted to go up the river to the mines? It was inconceivable that he should abandon the vessel, an even more appalling notion than agreeing to take the Ecuadoreans passenger to 'Frisco. Surely he wouldn't do that, for the brig was his home, too. She turned her head and watched her home while the boat lifted and then dropped over the sandbar, and then the men pulled about a narrow curve, and the brig was out of sight.

Cool green enfolded them; it was like rowing through a sea bottom. Insects as large as reef fish buzzed and hovered, and long fronds leaned down and touched the river surface and waved with the river current. The men pulled strongly, and she could hear them grunting with each heave. Alligators floated balefully, their cold egg-eyes all fixed on her, and:

> *Beneath a hot and burning sun I'll work for many a day*
> [sang Valentine] *Certain sure I'll strike it rich and soon be*
> *sailing away*
> *I'll find a monstrous heap of gold and dig it with my hands*
> *And get some boards and box it up and sail for Yankee lands!*

Harriet stepped carefully when the boat nudged the pier, and walked with her skirts held fastidiously high. The smells of warm dirt and slime and pigs and rotting leaves and squashed bananas enfolded her. Then when she arrived at the end of the track through the sugarcane field she was instantly aware of thick, enervating heat. She stopped, looking about, and then saw Royal. He was sitting in an untidy huddle in the shade of a thorn hedge, and five strange beasts were nervously grazing not far away.

She found a gate and climbed it, and then she said, "What are those?"

"Llamas."

"What?" She walked up to one, and the beast skittered a bit, but then was still. Llamas, she thought, the sheep of the Andes; old Captain Rochester had drawn enough of them, some in amongst the bears and dragons and such in his deceptive map of Judas Island. She walked about the beast, her head on one side, and the llama stood still, turning its head on its long flexible neck to meet her eye to eye throughout the inspection. Captain Rochester, she remembered, had wondered in script if the llama fleece had been used by the conquistadors to sieve the fabled gold.

She sighed, then turned and went to sit on the grass beside Royal. "You know," she said, "those llamas remind me of someone—Great-Aunt Diana. Do you see the resemblance? She had just such a neck, I'd swear, and the same sloping shoulders and haughty expression."

Royal favored this attempt at humor with a grunt, no more. Harriet said wistfully, "Do alpaca look like llamas, I wonder?"

He frowned and said in terse tones, "'Twould make no difference, even if the alpaca had been here. The company is full set on chasing to California."

California, she thought and sighed. She looked about and saw Bodfish standing in the front of a big ramshackle shed. That, she deduced, was his store, but the area about him was empty. She wondered if enough provisions had been taken on already, if Captain Dexter and the company had concluded already to sail. Three South American women had arrived at the gate and were standing still, staring at her as inquisitively as she had gazed at the llamas. Harriet gave them an uncertain smile and looked back at her brother and said, "The men seem utterly sure, yes, that they will dig a fortune in that place."

"But of course they will! My God, Hat, you haven't heard the half of the wonderful yarns. Why, I heard just yesterday of a Mormon settler in the Sacramento valley whose wife was so lazy she failed to sweep away the dust of the cabin floor each morning: instead she shoveled it into a cask that was set by the door. When her husband heard of the gold he took that barrel of dust-sweepings and panned it out and made himself two hundred dollars."

Two hundred dollars; it sounded pretty paltry, she thought

cynically, when compared to half a million for a breeding flock of alpaca. "And did that Mormon keep that gain, pray?"

"What d'you mean?"

"An American officer, Captain Mervine of the frigate *Savannah*, a man who knows his California, and that right well, why, he informed me that if the tales were true the gold would profit the American government solely, for Colonel Mason of the garrison at Monterey would move in forces to claim it all."

"And that," said Royal with passion, "would be typical American high-handedness. However, Hat, it will not happen."

"And why so sure, pray?"

"I'll tell you another gold tale, Hat, and that will give you the reason. Why, the day before yesterday they told me of two men embroiled in a duel. A wild shot scraped on rock in ricochet and revealed such a vein of gold that the quarrel was forgotten in an instant. And the day before that I heard of a man who threw a rock at his mule, and that rock was a two-pound nugget, perfect-pure. Tales like this spawn in litters, Sis, and once those tales race about the world another race will begin—to get to the yellow stuff first. Colonel Mason and his force would have to wage war to confiscate that gold; within weeks they'll be outnumbered."

Would that really happen? She thought about it, nervously pulling up sticks of grass with her fingers as she did it. She wondered what old Captain Rochester would have thought of California. Would he, like the conquistadors of whom he wrote, believe these gold tales without a qualm?

She said angrily, "Who spread those yarns around?"

"They began with a man by the name of Honest Mill Mason, if you credit the title."

"Then where is he now?"

"Back at the Frenchman's plantation, selling pork and beef to the Ecuadoreans who vie to buy."

"And you, Royal? Do you believe these yarns; do you plan, too, to dig the gold for yourself?"

"Not for myself, but for the *Hakluyt* Company," said he tersely. "And 'tis no use repining, Hat, for it was your devious device that landed us both in this fix; not," he added in hasty tones, evidently noting her outrage, "that it were not damned convenient, the way things were at the time."

She said furiously, "And what happens to me while you go off to the diggings, Royal?"

"I'm sure Jake Dexter will devise occupation for you," he said. Harriet guessed with fury that he was referring to her cooking. She opened her mouth to snap, but he forestalled her, adding in casual tones, "Is Jake Dexter your lover, Harriet?"

For a moment she could not believe that he'd said it. Then she flushed hotly and quickly looked away. "Of course he is not! And I think poorly of you for saying that, Brother!"

"Why so? 'Tis on the cards," he drawled.

She was shaking—with rage, she thought, and consternation, and yet he was right; it was on the cards. Their own parents had neglected for years to get married, and there had been whispers of affairs that even she had heard. And Great-Aunt Diana . . . when the old lady had passed away, only slightly faded in her elegance, they had found out at last just which prince of the realm had paid for the household in Redcliffe Square. The royal descendants had politely and firmly stated the facts of the case and taken the mansion away. It had been the major reason for the venture to the Cape Colony and then to New Zealand.

" 'Tis a concommitant of a life on the stage, dear Hat," said Royal with a patronizing air. "You know the reputation of actresses even more than I do. Why, I'd wager all the gold I'm going to find in California that you had more than twenty pressing invitations to grace some colonial manor or other, once Sefton was obviously offstage."

She could have wept, and bit her lip furiously to stop the outburst. Royal was horribly, mortifyingly right. She remembered the invitations to dine, the men who had passed her unheeded in the daytime streets but who had thronged adoringly at the backstage door. Bouquets had been tossed over the whale-oil footlights, with enticing notes inserted in the stems. For the first time she realized why Royal tactfully—had not asked her how she'd coped in New Zealand after their father had been killed and Sefton had sailed. Then all at once she remembered how Jake Dexter had asked, with such seeming kindness, how she had coped. She remembered how he had tied her apron while he had asked. She had been on the verge of tears then, grateful for his kind concern, but now, horridly, she wondered if he had been merely curious, if Jahaziel, too, had pictured her as some man's mistress.

It would be logical if he thought her a sporting woman, for

so many women of the stage were just that, but nevertheless she felt hot with shame: it was even worse than the abrupt fear that he had found out that Sefton had married her, disdained her and deserted her, all in the space of two weeks. Then she was saved by another memory. Jake Dexter had been motivated solely by the prospect of well-cooked biscuit.

She snapped, "Captain Dexter has never entertained the notion."

"You think not?" Infuriatingly, Royal's tone was scathing in the extreme. "Prove it."

"He's . . . a veritable puritan; he said to you himself that a recompense for your inconvenient arrival on the brig was that it would make my position on board more respectable! You've heard him go on about me showing my face about decks. He . . . he treats me like a child!"

"And so you are." And Royal had the sauce to laugh in the most derisive tones possible. " 'Tis a part of your dewy attraction, my dear, that and your spirit. And don't believe for an instant that he does not admire that. He finds you extreme diverting, Hat. He enjoys the game of teasing and pestering just as much as the men enjoy to watch. How old did you say you were, when he asked, pray?"

Harriet wavered; to her fury she wasn't able to hold his taunting look with her own angry stare. She looked away and muttered, "Almost nineteen."

"What! If my memory serves me correctly, dear Hat, you're older than eighteen by no more than two months."

"I'm nearer nineteen than I am to twenty, Brother!"

"Such sophistry," he derided, and laughed again. Then she heard him clamber to his feet. "And here he is," he said.

She saw Jake herself then, arriving with a group of *Hakluyt* men at the end of the sugarcane track. She scrambled to her own feet hastily, hot-faced and flustered, unwilling in the extreme to face Jake at that moment. Instead she looked at Royal and said quickly, "What's happening?"

"We're collecting the llamas, Sister, collating the bunch to get 'em out to the brig."

"Already?" Her tone held dismay; she hadn't realized that the day when her brig would be invaded by unwelcome Ecuadoreans had come so soon.

Royal, however, looked animated. His pointed straw beard jutted at the sky as he seemed to scent battle. The llamas seemed to scent it too, Harriet observed, for they skittered and pranced more warily than ever. "We must introduce 'em to their transport, Sister," he declared. "They must become submissive to their lodgings. Like women, dear Hat, they must learn duty and patience; their digestive systems must become resigned to the peculiar motion of a ship! Tell me, Captain," said he to Jake as their skipper arrived in the field, "have you ever viewed a seasick llama?"

"No," Jake admitted. He shot a glance at Harriet, and his expression was eloquent: this, he seemed to say, was extreme diverting talk from a man with a system as delicate as Royal Gray's.

"Neither have I, sir, neither have I, and I must admit further that I have no ambition for the experience. So, with thought and wisdom I hope to avoid it, by starving the beasts for four and twenty hours afore we sail, to render their systems barren, in a word."

"An excellent plan," Harried said tartly, "a plan that certain men would be wise to emulate." However, Royal ignored her. He set off at a lope to encircle his flock, and the llamas trotted about even more nervously, their long necks swiveling to keep everyone in view. Then Bodfish arrived to increase the number, and said, "Can I help?"

"With pleasure!" Royal declaimed. He began to sweep a bow, but a llama chose that moment to make a bid for freedom, galloping along the hedge and then suddenly clearing it in one agile and utterly unexpected bound, proving to them all, Harriet thought with growing amusement, that the llamas had remained in the field up to now purely in a mood of cooperation. The other llamas bolted after their leader, followed on the instant by a hollering mob of most animated men. Chaos reigned for a few muddled moments, and then the dust settled, and the llamas were more or less together, trotting nervously in a mutinous muddle down the canefield track.

Everyone walked slowly forward, down the track in line, keeping the llamas ahead. The woolly beasts skittered on fat trotters, their lashes fluttering as they looked this way and that. Their long necks bobbed as imperiously as those of swans. One made a break for freedom just as the river came into sight, but Davy Jones Locker neatly foiled the attempt by thrusting out a long arm. The llama turned a complete circle in midair and dashed to the river instead, heading for the landing stage, followed by its fellows.

And they were there! "Yo ho!" cried Royal, whirling his

hat. "Got 'em, by thunder, and never more easier! 'Tis the least trouble the beasts have delivered yet!"—and a large alligator swirled in the water, and all the llamas bolted in various ways.

Two shot back up the trail, neatly leaping Davy's hastily leveled arm, two dashed away upstream, and the fifth lay down with its neck stretched out. It emitted heartrending groans, apparently on the point of expiring, and with a terrible curse Royal flung down his hat.

Then he shook both fists at the sky. "Oh, mighty Gray!" he roared. "How has the mighty name of Gray thus fallen; have we sunk so low, are all our plans and schemings, our glories, triumphs, dreams, all shrunk to this little measure, that we should be humbled so by a pack of bloody llama? Unfair!" he hollered, shaking those fists at the indifferent heavens. "Unfair!" Alligators sloshed away in fright, and the prostrate llama surged to all four feet and took off, apparently straight up in the air but finishing down an alley and disappearing fast.

"Such eloquence," sighed Bodfish. His bony palms were clasped. Jake Dexter, predictably, was laughing helplessly, and all the others hallooed at once, and set off in exuberant pursuit. It was a romp, a marvelous caper for high-spirited men, and the llamas gave them a fine chase indeed. It was a lengthy business, too. In the end Harriet clambered into the boat that was tied to the pier, and sat and observed the sport. Every now and then a llama galloped into view, closely followed by a *Hakluyt* man. Then, with roars of triumph, the llamas were clinched and shoved back onto the landing stage.

Even when caught, they did not make the job easy. They had to be felled and thrown, trussed and tied, and the men had to evade flying green spit all the while. The first one was lifted, Harriet hurriedly quit the boat, and the tied-up llama arrived in her place. The other llamas were no easier. Any opportunity for liberty was seized on the instant. One broke loose from the hold of three ropes, and Abijah Roe was kicked hell west and crooked right into the river. Then at last the two boats were laden, bobbing frantically with llama struggles. There was scarcely room for the oarsmen. When Captain Dexter invited Harriet to take her seat with a low-swept bow she hastily declined. She, she declared, would wait on shore until a boat returned, so he, he declared, would wait with her. Bodfish and Davy Jones Locker stopped on shore too, and Harriet silently watched the boats' erratic progress until they finally breasted a curve and pulled slowly out of sight.

Then it was very quiet. It was late afternoon and very humid in the shade of the riverside jungle. Insects hovered heavily, and even the birds were silent. When Jake turned and strode up the bank toward the trail to Bodfish's store, Harriet was glad to follow him. The sugarcane stalks leaned back and forth in the small dusty wind and made a rustle that clattered secretly in their massed ranks of leaves.

Bodfish was beside her. "So we sail tomorrow," said the steward ruminatively. "Or the day after that at the latest. I anticipate trouble with the Ecuadoreans, Miss Gray, and I don't mind admitting that I do. Such men can be quarrelsome and vengeful. The females on the other hand, are generally lively, beautiful, and interesting."

"Yes," said Harriet, not really listening. She held her skirts with both hands and watched Jake Dexter's back as he strode ahead of them, and the black shadow of his pulled-down hat. She thought that the women who had stopped by the gate and inspected her so inquisitively earlier had been rather too weathered to be beautiful; but it was rather too hot to think.

"The premonition of trouble is a-constant on my mind, Miss Gray!"

"Yes," she said. She could hear the quiet plod of Davy's feet as he brought up the rear. The ex-slave was as silent as their captain.

"The evenings will prove the worst," Bodfish's doleful tones promised. "They will gamble and fight and be altogether restless. The Spanish," said he with heavy disapproval, "are allus thus inclined. They wake up with the dark when more practical men have done their day's work, and instead of resting they sing, Miss Gray, and fight and generally make an unholy ruckus."

"But what can we do?"

"Why, we entertain 'em, Miss Gray!"

"*What*?" She gaped at him and saw Jake turn his head and stare, but Bodfish beamed on regardless.

"We preoccupy those dangerous evenings! I've thought long and hard on it, Miss Gray, throughout my sojourn on shore; the problem has been with me a-constant! We have a piano and the bestest chantey-man I ever did hear, and we could read poetry, do interludes from Shakespeare, sir!"

"Jehovah," said Jake. His dancing eyes searched out Harriet's, and he said with false solemnity, "But they don't understand English, Bodfish!"

"I'm certain that don't signify, Cap'n, for even those of Spanish blood should be conscious of the grateful favor of being privileged enough to view true art."

"Tarnation," said Jake. Harriet, doing her best to avoid his eyes, thought that Jake would explode with his mirth. They soon emerged from the canefield and onto the trail that led inland, and she saw the laden ox-drawn cart that was lumbering toward them.

Away from the cane and the trees the air was so hot to be scarcely breathable. The progress of the cart threw up pale dust, which hung in slow clouds which were constantly augmented with each plod of hooves and rumble of solid wood wheels. The cart was still two hundred yards off; Jake, without a word, led the way along the thorn hedge to the shed where Bodfish kept his store. The cart moved more quickly than Harriet would have thought possible; when she arrived at the shed and stepped into the straw-scented hot shadow, the ox and cart seemed right on her heels.

The ponderous wheels rumbled and squeaked, and when the oxen stopped outside the open front of the shed, silence seemed to take over the world. Harriet could hear the grunt of the draft-animals' breathing and Davy Jones Locker's softer breathing in the shadows behind her. She was only just inside the shed, with Jake Dexter nearby. Bodfish was in the forefront as proprietor of this temporary place: she could see the hot sun reflecting on his shiny bald head. Far above in the sky an eagle hung, unmoving as it wheeled in slow circles, the outspread feathers of its wings quite still.

There were three men on the cart, all Spanish in appearance. It was hard to see their faces. Their sombreros were pulled low, and the shadow cast by the glazed leaf of each was quite black. They all stared, and Harriet could feel the weight of their curiosity as they searched out the interior of the shed. They were Murietas, three of the Murietas. Harriet unconsciously moved and found she had nervously shifted nearer to Jake. He was standing brace-legged, silent, his hat tipped back, staring at the cart and the men. The Murietas' tight *calcineros* were dirty and dusty, with spatters of what looked like grease or blood all down them. They had got down from the cart and were standing close together, facing the steward. They said nothing, not a word, and Harriet's nape was prickling.

Then: a scurry of wind, the way the late wind came up in this place. Palm leaves rattled, and dust spun in spouts. Joaquin

Murieta stuck his thumb back over his shoulder and said, "Salt porks. From the Frenchman's plantation."

They all looked at the cart. It was loaded entirely with barrels, the fat short barrels that Harriet knew were used for pickled meat. Then she heard Jake say crisply, "Where is Honest Mill Mason?"

All three faces jerked toward the sound of his voice. Harriet saw mostachos lift as the Murietas all sighted her. Joaquin's teeth gleamed and he said, "Cap'n?" but he was looking at her, instead. Harriet's arms were folded tightly; despite Jake's closeness, she felt vulnerable, almost scared. Captain Dexter did not have his rifle or any kind of weapon, and the Murietas had knives and pistols thrust into the sashes that were tied round their waists.

Jake said, "I asked about the man who looks after the Frenchman's plantation, the American soldier." Harriet could feel his tension.

"Ah . . ." However, Joaquin merely smirked and thrust his thumb over his shoulder again, in the direction of the plantation, she guessed. It was the same gesture that had indicated the barrels of pork. Then Bodfish cleared his throat with an important noise, and everyone looked at him.

He said, "You know how I choose one cask for inspection?"

The Murietas nodded. They were back to sly smirking. Harriet looked at the cart to avoid their stares. The barrels looked identical. Their staves were delineated by marks where the brine still darkened the cracks. The wood of the round tops was dried to a gray shade by the dust and hot sun. The palms and trees around the shed rattled again with a gust of wind, and Harriet heard thumps as mangoes fell off onto the roof.

Joaquin said to Bodfish, "Which one we open? You choose quick, quick." The tone was bullying; Harriet heard Jake shift restlessly. However, he said nothing.

Joaquin said as he stared at the steward, "That one?" His hand moved. A flash of hard light left his hand and one of the barrels *thumped*. Harriet's mouth went dry.

The flash was a knife. It stuck, vibrating, in the side of one of the casks. It caught the red light of the setting sun. Joaquin grinned, his eyes sliding to Harriet, and he said to Bodfish, "We open . . . that one?"

"No," said Bodfish. His voice cracked, and he cleared his throat and said again, "No." Then he pointed, seemingly at random, well away from the singing knife.

"Ah . . ." Joaquin did not seem disappointed. He and his two silent brothers teetered the chosen cask off the cart and onto the ground, making a noisy process of it. Neither Jake nor Davy moved to help them. Then the Murietas opened the top and stood back, and one of them reached up and plucked the knife out of the barrel. It left an arrow-shaped mark where it had been.

The opened cask held good pink pork, the best Harriet had seen in a very long time. She watched Bodfish nod importantly and would have believed him quite at ease except for the visible tremble of his fingers as he wrote out the notes of exchange. Then the Murietas heaved the rest of the load off the cart, and still Jake and Davy did not move. The process seemed to take forever, and all the time that Harriet watched she counted in her mind. Twenty casks, twenty . . . How many berths on the *Hakluyt* would these twenty casks buy? *I anticipate trouble with the Ecuadoreans . . . I don't mind admitting that I do . . .*

Yes, she thought, yes. When the cart turned and ground away back along the trail to the plantation, it was growing dark and rapidly cooler. Birds began to call, eerily, crying, *Whip, whip, whip poor Willy, weep, weep, weep, poor Willy . . .*and the hairs on her nape and forearms all rose with a weird chill.

"Oh, my God," she whispered. "What is that? What kind of bird is that?"

Davy moved, in the dark behind her. "Why, they be goatsucker birds, Miss Gray," he said in his soft hesitant voice. "In Guiana, why, we say that they be the ghosts of poor dead slaves."

"Oh, dear Lord," said she, shivering, and despite herself moved closer to Jake.

12 ⬗ At dawn next day the South American argonauts began to come to take up their berths on the brig. The little craft came in with the tide and other groups by land. Small boys and ancient grandfathers came on the boats, to pilot them back home, and

> *Come listen to me adventurer boys and a story I'll relate*
> [sang Valentine]
> *It'll come about in the valley land of Sacramento state*
> *Down to the bottom lands brave boys will go so bold*
> *And work like hungry tigers, when we think about that gold!*

The argonauts brought promissory notes that were folded so carefully that they threatened to fall apart, most of them filthy and all of them hoarded like the yellow metal itself. Those who had not been able to accumulate nearly enough sold them to others at a premium, and those who had not quite enough brought along more provisions to make up the balance, so that Harriet was forced to cope with even more amazing things. There were sacks of strange nuts and corn in bright unfamiliar shades and smokedried strips of what she was assured was meat.

The meat was even brought all alive-still-oh, including a gross of furious chickens. To Harriet's relief old Chips took over the stowing of those. He made coops by the simple means of putting two barrel hoops crosswise and then weaving them together with rope yarn. Then the trapped, indignant hens were slung by nails from the stern. Another man brought a complete live bullock that had to be heaved up with the windlass. Within a trice he was lowing sadly in the pigpen, with two dozen small black pigs scuttling about his bewildered feet, squealing like rusty hinges.

Then it was another dawn, and the tide was on the turn. The sky was as pale as new milk, and the wind gusted fresh, fair for a swift passage to California. Thank God, thought Harriet, for the time to weigh anchor had come, and that with no sight of the Murietas.

> *A-all hands on deck, our first mate cries* [sang Crotchet]
> *His shouts like thunder's roar—suh!*
> *All hands on deck, brave boys reply—*
> *'Tis the signal for Cal-ifor-nia . . .*

And men labored at the windlass, and others in the hamper loosed the canvas. The argonauts cheered and waved their hats and fired their pistols in the air. The excitement was intoxicating, even for Harriet: she crept up the companion and stole into a corner by the taffrail.

> *Go loose your tops'ls, boys, he cries*
> *Fly-jibs and jibs let go—suh!*
> *Haul home those sheets, I say, brave boys*
> *And for 'Frisco gold we go—suh!*

Then, all at once, the chantey stopped short. Harriet frowned, wondering why, and the men in the yards were all looking sternward, shading their eyes. A whaleboat was coming down the river. It crested the bar, took on water, and jinked. The oarsmen baled and then pulled again, steering for the brig. Everyone watched, everyone was silent, and the *thump* as the boat touched the hull of the brig seemed very loud.

Harriet still could not see the oarsmen, but she felt chill with uneasiness. Then she heard Charlie Martin say, " 'Tis the Murietas, Cap'n."

Harriet's gaze moved swiftly to Jake's face. He was frowning. Then he moved a pace forward, and she heard the thump of boots and scrambling as the six Murietas arrived on deck. The six stood in a line when assembled, just like the first time, with Joaquin a little ahead of the rest.

Their expressions were furtive, secretly grinning. They looked filthier than ever in the clear dawn light. These, Harriet thought somberly, were the true descendants of the conquistadors. Their great-grandfathers had lit slow fires under half-throttled Indians thirteen at a time to commemorate Christ and his twelve disciples; they had forced Indian women to watch while their men were roasted and their babies spitted alive. . . . They had buried more than twenty nuns alive in a cave on Judas Island because the nuns had not told the secret of where the Panamanian gold had been hidden.

Joaquin said, smirking, "We come . . . with notes, enough notes. For passage to California."

He pushed a fistful of notes at Captain Dexter. The papers were filthy, stained most foully. Harriet, frozen, watched Jake count them. Then he said, "Yes. There is enough here for six berths in the hold . . . more than enough."

In the hold. Thank God, she thought; at that moment it was impossible to contemplate how awful it would be to have to share the cabin table with these men.

Then she saw that Joaquin was pouting. "How much more," he said, "for six, in the steerage?"

Jake said curtly, "Sixty."

"Ah . . ." The sound was long-drawn-out. Then Joaquin sneered and said, "The boat."

"What?"

"The whaleboat. She . . . she is yours. Good boat, worth more than sixty."

Silence. No one moved. The crowded decks were utterly still. Everyone waited. Harriet's arms were tightly folded as she stared at the back of Jake's head and willed him to turn the bargain down . . . Jake Dexter, who had the most need of any man she knew to prove himself honorable.

He turned, just as if he felt the weight of her concentration.

His eyebrows were tilted, eloquently wry. He looked away again and said crisply, "Very well. You have six berths in the steerage."

A steady sou'easterly wind and the nor'ard current carried the brig well off the land and continued fair the following days. Their passage bid to be speedy, and that, Jake mused, was no small blessing. At no time was it possible for him to forget that he was carrying passengers, and at all times he remembered, ruefully, how he'd refused to carry passengers before.

He wished most heartily that he'd adhered to that belief, for his cargo of argonauts proved arrogant, noisy, quarrelsome, and dirty. At the very first dawn they picked a fight with the *Hakluyt* watch which within instants developed into a brawl that Jake and Charlie Martin had to quell with shouts and fists. Their grievance, the Ecuadoreans declared, was on account of the washing down of the decks. The argonauts had chosen not to sleep in their berths but find soft planks in the lee scuppers instead, and the *Hakluyt* men had been more than careless with the way they used their swabs and buckets.

Their brawl set a pattern. The argonauts fought constantly, with each other as well as with the *Hakluyt* men. They spat and shot off pistols and carved in the woodwork, and they stole each others' wine and tobacco. If Harriet had not broken his pattern of never carrying passengers, his brig would not now be such a kettle of discord, Jake thought passionately. The worst of his passengers, by far, were the Murietas.

The problem was that the Murietas ate at the cabin table. They had been informed over and over again that they had no place in the mess cabin until after Captain Dexter and Mr. Martin and Miss Gray and Davy Jones Locker, the second mate, had eaten. However, every time Jake arrived in the cabin the Murietas were there. They sprawled on the benches, and dug in the tabletop with their knives, and when they ate they used those knives to spear their meat and ate off the blades. Then when they'd finished they used those same knives to dig about in their teeth and fingernails. When Jake snapped at them to move they did move, but the next time he went below they were there again.

He commented on this sharply the next time Charlie was at the table with him. "But I do my best, sir," said Charlie, injured. "I send 'em off each time I see them." His eyes, however, were evasive, almost scared. The Murietas, Jake

thought grimly, had intimidated young Charlie and old Bodfish
and several other of his men as well.

There was very little he could do about it, for the Murietas
were passengers, with passengers' rights. He looked at Harriet,
knowing it was unfair of him to blame her, but blame her he
did. She, too, avoided his eyes; she watched her plate but
ate very little. He had never known her so wan and quiet; he
thought of all the times she had teased him by declaring she
needed fresh air, and then thought that she had been right, for
she looked so very pale now. She was sitting on the bench on
his right, so close he could have touched her, but somehow,
oddly, she did not seem to be there. Somehow, illogically, he
missed her.

They exchanged so little conversation these days, he thought; at
times he wondered if she was avoiding him. The instant Charlie
or Davy left the table she would stand and leave too, with scarcely
a word, going straight into her stateroom and pulling the latch-
string through to her side of the door. He felt as if she were
punishing him for something. Most of the time he thought that she
was angry because he had adhered to his bargain and agreed to
carry the Murietas.

"They gamble," gloomed Charlie. "All of 'em, they gamble, and the Murietas, sir, be the worst."

"What kind of gambling?"

"They call it *monte*, but it ain't the three-card stuff you see
at Valparaíso. They throw down a serape and mark it into four
quarters, and they throw down four cards and bet on what the
next card will be face up."

"That's *monte*," said Jake. He sighed, his eyes still on
Harriet's bent head. "Do the *Hakluyt* men play too?"

"Crotchet does, in his watches below."

That, mused Jake, was inevitable, given Crotchet's nature.
He said, "Does he win?"

"Wa-al, the last time I seen 'im, yes, sir, he were playin' the
Murietas, and he were winning a deal, it seemed."

"Good," said Harriet. The unexpected word held passion.
For the first time in what felt like weeks her eyes met Jake's,
and she smiled, very ruefully. He smiled back, wryly, and
thought, oh, Jehovah, yes, how he'd missed her, and he sighed
again as he stood and went to the companion door. His black
mood returned as he climbed the stairs; he had to brace himself
for the now-familiar sight of dirty argonauts sprawled all over
his decks. It did not occur to him for quite some moments that

Harriet had stood too when he left the table and had gone at once into the stateroom, leaving Charlie alone.

Next noon it was Davy Jones Locker who left the table first to go on deck, and Harriet, again, immediately stood. She was in her room with the door clicked shut and the string pulled through before Jake could stop her to ask the reason. Then, while he was thinking about it, the steerage door creaked open.

Joaquin Murieta came a short way into the cabin. Jake could smell the rank stuffiness of the steerage behind the Ecuadorean, and his frown became intimidating. Joaquin, however, did not look daunted. He smirked and said, "You not finished? Not yet?"

"No," Jake said flatly, and stared.

"Ah . . ." Joaquin looked furtively about and lowered his voice to an insinuating mutter. "There is trouble, yes, with the pretty *gringa*?"

"I beg your pardon?"

"The pretty. The señorita. Such a pretty filly, yes. One woman alone, too, and so many men. She is yours?"

It took a long pause for Jake to fully take in the implication of that *yours*. Then it hit him, in a jolt of anger. He snapped, "I don't know what you mean."

"You are not . . . not protector?"

"Miss Gray is a passenger, sir, like yourself."

"But." Then Joaquin was silent, his furtive eyes running past Jake and looking about the room. "But . . . the steward, yes, the servant, he say she an actress, yes?"

"I say again, I don't know what the hell you mean. And I repeat, Miss Gray is a passenger, and like all passengers she is under my protection. Her profession has nothing whatever to do with it."

"Ah . . . Capitán . . . beg pardon, señor." However, the leer was in no wise apologetic. Jake stared at him, and the yellowed eyes as usual slid away from his. The man radiated malicious stupidity, and Jake abruptly had had enough of it. He set down his mug with a bang, stood up, and left without a word.

Similar stupid stares filled his decks, however. Oh, God, he thought, and thanked God when he took a sight and noted the figures on the slate by the wheel and saw how close they had come to California. The fair wind had served him well. He'd be grateful even for a storm, he mused, if it would get them to 'Frisco even faster.

At dinnertime next day that casual prayer was rewarded. He and Charlie had but settled down at the table with Harriet than a squall swirled upon them, a white squall out of a peaceful blue sky.

It was only Davy's vigilance and speedy reaction that saved the brig from catching aback. When the first big gust arrived and the *Hakluyt* pitched, Jake left the table in a lunge and made for the stairs with Charlie Martin close on his heels. However, even before they made the deck the courses were hauled up and the topsail reef tackles hauled out. The brig was dancing and pitching her head, but Abner and Joseph Fayal were out on the boom furling the jib. The canvas was slatting and old Sails was pulling at his whiskers, but the squall spent its strength and there was no sail damage.

The whirling gusts had gone as quickly as they'd come. The South Americans were all babbling and milling about with patent fear on their stubbled faces, but there was no need to keep the brig off and haul down the staysail. Within minutes the brig was back under all canvas . . . but the weather bid rugged, Jake decided. He looked at the horizon and the fleeting long clouds high in the sky. There was a sharp briskness to the wind; the squall was but a presage, he thought, a warning of what was a-coming. He gave orders for a sharp eye to lookout, and then went down to his transom cabin.

There he set out his charts and became so absorbed in marking a course that it took a moment for him to respond when a tap sounded on the door. He looked up and listened to the sea and the creak of the ship, expecting Davy's face at the door with news of a faster-than-expected change in the weather. However, it was Bodfish, looking more than usually awkward.

He said, "Sir, 'tis Miss Harriet."

"What?" Jake straightened quickly. She had been at the table when he and Charlie had left so abruptly; he remembered the alarm in her expression with the first sharp gust. He said alertly, "What's wrong?"

"She's—" Bodfish coughed; he shuffled and blushed. Then he said with extreme diffidence, "She's in the fo'c'sle, Cap'n."

"She's—*what*!" Jake was utterly certain he had not heard a-right; it was unthinkable for a female to visit the abode of the foremast men. He said blankly, "She can't be!"

Bodfish fidgeted and said, "But she is, sir, and . . . I think she's in a passion."

Jake said, "Oh, Jehovah." That, he knew, was perfectly possible. Then he ran up the stairs, two treads at a time, in a thunder of boots.

It was gusty still on deck. Spray spat over the weather rail and the scuppers foamed. The sky was scudding with thickening cloud. It was less than comfortable topsides, but the decks seemed more packed than Jake had seen them yet. He had to force his way through grinning gape-mouthed men. He shoved angrily, certain that they were getting in his way deliberately. They jostled him and moved with utterly infuriating sloth. Then he was at the hatch to the fo'c'sle, and the Murieta brothers were there, all six of them. They, too, were grinning. Then Jake shoved past them and he saw the leering faces falter.

Then he heard Harriet's voice, from the fo'c'sle. "For God's sake, Royal," she cried. "You're my brother! Try not to pretend to be a worm!"

Jake heard stupid sniggering all about the deck. He hesitated no longer but tumbled down the fo'c'sle ladder two rungs at a time.

Harriet was standing in the clear space at the foot of the foremast, and the little room seemed perfect-full of silent *Hakluyt* men. Were none of his crew on deck at all? It certainly seemed that none were; Jake opened his mouth to roar—and Harriet turned and he saw her face.

Her hair was down, tousled and tangled, half covering her eyes and cheeks, and for a terrible instant he thought she was weeping blood. Then she thrust the hair away with one hand and he saw the long cut high on one cheek. His belly clenched; he shouted, "What the hell has happened?" For a long moment no one answered; silence reigned, filled only with the sounds of the brig and the sea and the waiting hush from the Ecuadoreans on deck.

Then Harriet said fiercely, "No doubt you're angry, but don't be angry with your men, Captain. If you want to shout then shout at me, for this is all my fault entirely."

It was like the time she had boarded his brig and instructed him not to be cross with Charlie Martin. Jake said blankly, "Then what the devil—?"

"The Murietas were a-tormentin' her," said Chips's gruff voice. "We all know for certain, Cap'n, that it be improper for Miss Harriet to come a-callin' here, but circumstances begged it, for Miss Harriet were plumb in dire need. She tumbled down the ladder in a rush, and begged a refuge, all on account of the Murietas."

The Murietas. The rage kept down for almost two weeks rose inside him, seething. Jake snapped, "But why the fo'c'sle?"

Without realizing it he had gently gripped Harriet's arm, drawing her near to him. He could feel her trembling, but she threw out her other hand, pointing, and shouted, "I came to see that—that worm!"

She was pointing at Royal. Her brother was in his berth, all hunched up in a very strange untidy position. Royal had his head in his hands in the most eloquent attitude of despair, and his long legs were all wrapped up like the legs of a jinn, as if he wished himself out of here and in some inconspicuous bottle.

He said, "For God's sake, Hat—"

"All you needed to do was show some spirit, Brother! You know what bullies are like—all you have to do is raise your hackles and roar, and they retreat in disarray, sir! My God," she said. Jake could feel her shaking with rage; he was holding her tight, close beside him, and at that moment he thought that without that restraint she would lose all control and fly at Royal. "My God," she said. "Those goddamned Murietas, those infinitesimal bandits, why they caught me in the mess cabin alone, Captain, they insulted me most scandalously, they—they called me a gray filly, sir, they pulled my hair and tried to cut it and cut my cheek instead, sir, they called me a harlot, they had found out somehow that I am an actress, and—"

"She wanted me to fight a duel for her honor!" Royal interrupted. He was as fierce with outrage as his sister. "Swamp it, Captain, she asked the impossible!"

Jake was shaking himself with anger. A gray filly . . . *such a pretty filly, yes . . . she is yours . . . ?* Oh, Jehovah, he thought tightly, yes, damn it, yes. He had given Joaquin the fainthearted answer, and Harriet had been the one to pay for his prevarication. He said nothing, but moved, turning Harriet, guiding her up the ladder, following her closely onto the deck. The Ecuadoreans had all gathered in the foredeck, and the Murietas were there, smirking. Jake could hear sniggers, but when he stopped and stared around, all the sniggering stopped.

He was holding Harriet, close by his side. Then he shouted, "You may be passengers, passengers with rights, passengers with whom I made a decent man's bargain, but by God I tell

Joan Druett

you all that the next man who lays a finger on Miss Gray will be flogged!"

Then he set himself in motion, holding Harriet close by his side. Men fell back, their eyes gone frightened, and when Jake saw Joaquin he reached out and shoved. Joaquin Murieta stumbled and got out of the way so fast that he slipped and fell sprawling, rolling into the puddle in the scuppers. No one helped him up. Someone giggled nervously, and then Jake had arrived at the companionway door. He reached out and slammed it open, and when Harriet stumbled he held her more tightly. He felt her loose hair tumble across his cheek so vividly that he could swear he felt every soft strand, and then they were down the stairs and in his transom cabin.

He set her on the sofa, and then, still holding himself in tight control, he fetched out his medicine chest and hunkered down beside her. When he touched her face she tried to wince away, but he held her chin firm in his broad cupped palm. The cut was deeper even than he'd thought, dangerously close to one eye, and the anger twisted inside him again. There were tears of fury and pain on her lashes, and he brushed them away gently with a hunk of clean cotton before moistening the cotton from a bottle.

She said, "Not alcohol, Captain Dexter!"

"Hush." She twisted her head away, but he held her still. She yelped and flinched when the cloth touched the cut, and he said, "Don't be such a baby."

"Then don't treat me like an infant." However, she submitted. He sponged carefully, drawing out blood, thinking of the Murietas' filthy knives, how they used their knives to pick their teeth and their nails.

The filthy, filthy Murietas. He said, "I wondered why you left the table so quickly each mealtime."

"I couldn't risk being caught alone; they made their foul intentions plain from the very first day . . . They had poor Bodfish so frightened."

And yet she had been right: all bullies were cowards, underneath. All it had needed was for one man to shout in her defense. Jake said angrily, "Why didn't you tell me? Why didn't you call out? I was only in the bloody transom, right here!"

"It happened so fast; I knew if I screamed they would know I was frightened, and then it would have been even worse. They were trying to herd me into the steerage, like—like a filly

in season, Jake! So I went . . . and kept on going, up the
steerage ladder and up onto deck."

Like a filly in season. Jake trembled again with rage. He said
with soft savagery, "I'll kill them." She said nothing but
smiled faintly, then shut her eyes as he gently spread simple
ointment. He could feel her soft breath on the back of his hand,
and then he drew back and surveyed her, and the long lashes
still shadowed her cheeks. He waited, but she didn't move. Her
eyes stayed shut.

He thought she dozed, or even slept, reclined as she was on
his transom sofa. She belonged there, he thought with a
fiercely possessive corner of his mind, and then the creaking of
the brig drew his attention. There was an uneasiness in the way
the *Hakluyt* met the rising waves, and he could hear rhythmic
splashing as water got over the taffrail. It was time there was
an extra hand to the wheel; even as he thought it, he could hear
Charlie shouting out on deck. "Stay here," he whispered, and
didn't even know if Harriet heard it. Then he strode up on
deck.

By noon next day the brig was pitching and heaving as if
she'd jump the sticks right out of her. All hands were on deck
as they had been all night, taking in sail piece by piece until
they were running under double-reefed topsails and jib. Even
with reduced canvas the brig was making twelve knots an hour,
plunging toward 'Frisco with every bump and splash.

The wind was rugged but the wind was fair; but the argonauts were in no condition to appreciate that good fortune.
"They're a-travelin' by rail," said Charlie Martin with glee.
The Murietas might have scared him, but now the sea was
giving him revenge. The Murietas, like most of their Ecuadorean fellows, had their heads all bent a-heaving over the lee rail,
having learned the hard way to avoid the one on the weather
side of the ship. Like the argonauts, too, they were cursing and
praying, beseeching the unforgiving saints for mercy.

"Some of 'em are a-hidin' theirselfs in lockers and such, so
the storm won't find them," said Charlie in gloating fashion.
Even Royal Gray was not seasick, nor the haughty llamas, but
the Ecuadorean argonauts were in a most satisfactorily miserable state. The Murietas were out of sight as well, being now
forbidden the cabin. Harriet, however, was not at the table
either. Jake, as medical officer, had bid her stay in bed.

At nine that night she opened her eyes and blinked at Jake

rather blearily. He was standing in the small clear space at the head of her berth, and the lamp he'd hung on a hook swung wildly. He looked huge and reliable in his oilskins. He had his medical book in his hands and was frowning as he looked from the page to her face and back again.

She said tartly, "Oh, go on deck and nurse your brig instead." He grinned but looked weary. She listened to the creaking and the thump of waves on the starboard quarter and thought that he would spend another night on deck.

Then she said, "Where are we?"

He said nothing for the moment but hunkered down and set to dabbing at her cheek with a cool solution on a cloth. She winced, but the cut was not really sore. She smelled his scent of salt and warm leather along with the sharpness of the varnish of his coat. Then he said, "It looks good. I've done well."

He sounded as smug as he had when he'd baked his biscuit, she thought. However, when he stood she smiled at him. He grinned back and said, "We'll be in the Bay of San Francisco tomorrow, thank God. With grace and favor and our cargo of prayers the wind stayed fair for California."

California, she thought. It still seemed unreal; she could not picture what they might find there. California, next day. It wasn't credible. Instead of answering she shut her eyes, and the next time she opened them it was morning.

The brig, however, was scarcely moving. The *Hakluyt* wallowed, making little headway, and the view outside Harriet's sidelight was full of drifting gray cotton. Fog . . . and the lee shore of California was hidden in the thick damp mists. She crept out of bed, expecting Jake to come in and discover her mutiny any instant, but he did not arrive, and the cabin, when she opened her door, was empty. She softly climbed the companion stairs and eased open the door at the top. Mists clung stickily to the rigging. She could hear breakers distinctly, and everything dripped. The sail loomed unnaturally close, ghostly gray, and the oilskins that the *Hakluyt* men wore were black and shiny with wet. Harriet closed the door again and went quietly back down the stairs.

But not back to bed. Three hours later, when she was eating dinner from a tray in the transom cabin, the door opened and Jake came in. His eyebrows lifted as he saw her, but he made no comment. He had taken off his foul-weather gear, and there were droplets like cobwebs in his hair. He looked tired, she thought, and wondered if he'd had any sleep at all in the past forty-eight hours.

Still he said nothing. He sat down beside her and picked up the book she had been reading. Then he looked at her again. He said, "Well, so at last I regain my property."

It was Rochester's logbook. She awaited a scolding, but instead he gave her one of his lopsided grins and said, "So this is how you filled your time when you shut yourself in your stateroom."

She paused. Then she said, "I've been trying to puzzle out the letters at the top of the map."

"*I A S*?"

"Yes. You said once that the *I* might be the downstroke of a *D*, and I've been thinking about that, wondering if the *A* is truly an *A*. Do you think it might been an *H*?"

The book was open at the map, and she saw him frown and look down at it. Then he said slowly, "You think it's *I H S*?"

"Yes. They make up the Greek symbol for *Jesus*."

"But that makes no sense, Harriet."

"I know." She sighed, and Jake put the book down and began to help himself from her tray, reaching across her to pick up the pieces of food. Again, as in the pantry, she was beset by a sense of intimacy. She swallowed and said carefully, " 'Tis the opposite of Judas."

"It still makes no sense." The words were flat, but still he felt—so close. There was a tap on the door and he straightened, moving away from her, and Bodfish came in with hot coffee. The steward inspected them with his long benevolent face, and then picked up the tray and went out.

Jake said when the door was shut, "Perhaps all three letters are suspect. Do we trust the *S*?"

His drawl was amused. She was being teased, she knew, and she tried to feel angry, but did not succeed. "What about the *I*?" he said. "It could be all manner of letters or parts of letters. How about an *L*?"

"As in, *L A S*?"

"As in *las*, the Spanish for *the*."

"But the . . . what?"

"What indeed? Mystery upon mystery, dear Harriet." Then, while she was still trying to feel vexed at being so mocked, he moved. It happened before she knew it. Jake put his emptied coffee mug on the floor and then he stretched out, full length on the sofa. His head was in her lap.

She sat utterly still, listening to her heart thump. His long legs were crossed at the ankle. He was wearing rough woollen socks . . . how Great-aunt Diana's Mrs. Pink would have disapproved. Jake's eyes were shut, he looked so weary. He shifted, wriggling to make himself more comfortable, turning his head, burying his face in her lap. Then he was still, and where he breathed, deep inside her, was a terrifying responsive warmth.

She wanted, desperately, to pull him closer, lie down beside him, pull his face into her breast. She had never felt like this before; she had never before felt this demanding inner hollowing, this shocking heated craving to be filled. With him. With Jake Dexter's hard body. *Is Jake Dexter your lover, Harriet?*

It was indeed on the cards, oh, most surely. Oh, dear God, she thought, oh, please, and all the time she struggled with herself to keep utterly still.

She watched his chest rise and fall in long slow breaths, and then the breathing became soft, and she knew he was asleep. The thick short lashes were shut, and his face had smoothed out and become very young. She whispered, "Jahaziel," and he did not move, so she softly touched the a-kilter brows with a gentle loving fingertip.

Is Jake Dexter your lover? If she had turned around into his arms that day in the pantry, would things have turned out different? Perhaps if she'd gone to him when the Murietas had first pestered her she would be his mistress even now. His mistress . . . which was all she could offer. She hadn't told him about Sefton yet, perhaps because she had been too proud; she hadn't wanted him to despise her, to realize that she was nothing more than the discarded relict of another man's contempt. But would he accept her on those terms?

Jake Dexter was such a Puritan; his faithless wife had made him that. Harriet remembered his severity when he ordered her to keep off the decks, all his fussing about her reputation and the impropriety of being the only woman on board. He was a complex man, consciously honorable as if to make up for selling the bark that had bought this brig. But all Harriet could offer any man was her body and her promises.

She had asked about divorce in Auckland. It had been one of the humiliations. Someone had told her that the wives of American men could sue for divorce in certain circumstances, so she had saved some money and then she had consulted a lawyer.

The counsel had been curt to the point of rudeness. She could divorce Sefton only if he created a public scandal. That was somewhat more than the wives of Englishmen could do, as the lawyer sniffishly pointed out, but cruel desertion was not considered a public scandal. It happened too often. Men left their wives penniless all the time while they searched for fortunes in other lands.

Oh, dear God, she thought and touched his face caressingly, treasuring the moment, until a shout from deck roused Captain Dexter in urgent summons.

The fog had lifted like a theater curtain, and the Golden Gate to El Dorado lay ahead.

13 ◈ The entrance to the Bay of San
Francisco was framed with a
vista of hills and mountains that marched boldly down to the
sea. Waves dashed up against the black and brownness,
making rainbows, and water birds made patterns in the sky.
The brig tacked slowly up a strait where a giant rock appeared
to block the way, and the water was like a glinting jewel, set
in a coronet of peaks and valleys; it reflected stands of cypress
trees and the sere browns of rounded hills and the heavy
granite-gray of cliffs. Even Captain Mervine's enthusiasm had
not prepared Jake for such beauty, and Jake's charts were
inadequate for showing the way. When a sloop beat out and
then hailed them, he took on a pilot with some relief.

The pilot was a grizzled old customer with a seamy face and
toothless gape, but he seemed to know what he was about.
Jake's charts told him that a man named Richardson, a deserter
from some whaleship, had acted as pilot here for fifteen years,
and this man's gruff knowledge seemed to mark him as that

man. "Haul in port main braces," he said, and Jake was content enough to leave him at his job, for there was more than enough to see.

The shore of the bay curved. There was an island, he knew, a lump of dirt and rock called Yerba Buena, where whalemen often called to take on water and wood. Jake had heard that about twenty whaleships called each year on this inoffensive business; the rest of the time, he'd been told, the bay was about deserted . . . so why were more than two dozen vessels lying at anchor here? He stared, utterly puzzled: the beach in the curve of the bay was marked, as on the charts, with three rounded hills, so that the anchorage looked like an amphitheater. More than twenty ships, definitely, all rode at moorings but were huddled in an untidy cluster, as if the winds and currents had more to do with their state than the guidance of men.

The *Hakluyt* men in the hamper who had been exclaiming so loudly were eerily silent, and all had one hand raised, shading bewildered eyes as everyone stared at the abandoned ships. Abandoned they certainly were; all of Jake's mariner instincts told him that. The silent hulls were splotched with bird droppings, streaked with rust about davits, catheads and hawseholes. Their yards were struck or left hanging all cockabill, and there was no sign of movement about the decks. Jake said swiftly, turning to confront the old pilot, "What goes on with those ships?" but before the taciturn old man deigned to reply, the brig passed the inlet of a peninsula and Jake saw the frigate *Savannah*. For a horrid instant he thought the man-of-war abandoned like those enigmatic ships, but then as he stared he saw a signal raised, and a boat begin to lower.

Captain Mervine, evidently, felt as much urgency to see Jake as Jake felt to ask questions of him. Jake wondered how long the man-of-war had been here, and he turned to the pilot again. The old man was smirking, a wrinkled smile to himself. He said, before Jake could ask, "There ain't a ship in port, sir, save that man-of-war, what has hands enough to weigh the anchor—and the *Savannah* keeps sailors, sir, by the threat of floggin' and worse. Ain't nothin' else what anchors here but loses all his men; they all go off to the diggin', sir, off to the fabled mines. You'll lose your men," he said, his tone almost triumphant, and spat a gob on the deck.

Jake snapped, "I think not."

"You think not? Har-har, you'll see different, like all the rest of the skippers. A man can dig a thousand a month, up them fabled diggin's."

A thousand. There was utter silence all about decks, and then an instant babel. It was as if no one, not even the Ecuadoreans, had truly believed in the gold till this moment. A thousand a month! The old man was sniggering to himself at the effect of his words but still did his job nevertheless. Mr. Martin relayed grunted instructions, and the brig slowed, hesitated, heeled, easing to an anchorage upwind of the clustered ships. Then the anchor chain clattered as the links ran free, and everyone was abruptly silent again, because of the silence of the town.

There were small squat buildings scattered about on the brown slopes, some of them clapboard, most of them adobe, but there was no sign of life. The arms of a distant windmill swung jerkily, but that was the only movement. Even the crying of the seabirds was eerie. It was high summer, but the air was dank with the afterchill of the heavy fog, and Jake shivered despite his pea jacket.

Then all at once the Ecuadoreans seemed to come out of a spell. They all shouted at once and pushed at each other and informed the *Hakluyt* men in a demanding babble that they had paid for passage to 'Frisco, yes, and that bargain included passage in the *Hakluyt* boats onto shore. They all had their bags full and swung over their shoulders, and they were all, every man jack, ready to quit the brig.

And not before time, Jake thought tersely. Then he found the old pilot insinuatingly beside him. The old man had his palm out.

Jake said curtly, "How much?" Then he winced as he heard the price. The old man spat on the coins and then tucked them away somewhere in the depths of his garments. Jake said, "Are any American whalemen here?"

"Whalemen, sir? Ah . . . the whaleship *Flora*, yes, she be here, over there, over to Whaleman's Harbor, but it ain't no use goin' a-callin', for she be as deserted as the rest. See them davits, see how they be empty? She come in June, the *Flora* did; the cap'n saw the danger, tried to get away a-fore he lost his men, too late, crew all mutinied, all refused duty, gagged the watch, escaped off to the mines. Cap'n and mates saw naught could be done about it, off they went theirselfs to the hills."

Jake said softly, "My God." It seemed utterly impossible

that any righteous New England skipper would leave his ship like that.

"Ah, it ain't for nobbut more'n a few weeks—or so they all tell me a-fore they set up river. I'll warrant me them chains 'n cables be sufficient strong to last till they comes back."

Jake didn't believe it: these abandoned ships looked neglected for years, not weeks. The boat from the frigate *Savannah* had almost arrived. He said, "You must hear talk. Are any American merchantmen or whalemen expected?"

The old man's face worked in ponderous thought. "The *Isaac Walton* be in Monterey, or so Cap'n Mervine told me, dischargin' her oil while she still got some men. Others be plying the coast, carryin' passengers in place of oil; another one still be up to Sutter's Fort, all done up for the boardin'-house business."

"The . . . *what*?"

"At Sutter's Fort—one hundred 'n fifty miles up river." The old man cackled, seemingly first-rate amused at Jake's patent stupefaction. "No need to be astounded," he said. "The wind blows fair from February to October, fair upstream, and the river be a noble one. She's navigable all the way to the fork with the American River and all the way to the Feather. I'll pilot you meself, if you conclude to go up the Sacramento yourself! The brig will make it easy, even now, at the end of dry season. I know the way, and don't you doubt it, for I were the fust mate of that very same whaler what be up at Sutter's now."

Jake said blankly, "But I thought you were the harbor-master, Captain Richardson."

"What? Me?" This gave the old man a deal of amusement; he cackled until the tears ran down his dirty cheeks. "No, no," said he as his mirth subsided, "Paddack's the name, late fust mate of the whaleship *Humpback* . . . and I do think, yes, that I have seen this brig a-fore. Off Judas Island, was it not?"

"What?" Jake stared. Then he was distracted by the arrival of Captain Mervine. When he turned back to the pilot again Mr. Paddack the late first mate of the whaleship that had brought him Harriet was gone. Harriet herself was coming hesitantly on deck, drawn by the noise of the Ecuadoreans' departure, but Jake's full attention was instantly claimed by Captain Mervine.

The soldier looked more bustling and self-important even than remembered. "What d'you think?" he cried, when barely in earshot. "What d'you think? Ain't it a scandal? Look," he bellowed, "look at that bark." Jake turned to contemplate one ship that seemed every bit as abandoned as the rest and that eons in the past, and Captain Mervine shouted, "*Amity*, her name, came in but yesterday, this morn the master found but six men on board, he's on board the *Savannah* right now, laying a most earnest complaint. Oh, we'll punish the scoundrels, when we find 'em; confiscate their gold, make spread-eagles of 'em all! I've lost seven men myself! Seven hundred dollars lie now on each of their mutinying disloyal and dishonest heads, seven hundred! Good morning, Miss Gray!" he hollered, and then Jake found a preemptory hand gripping his elbow. "Come," Captain Mervine urged, "come ashore, tell me what you think, sir!" He went into the *Savannah* boat without a word, so compelling was Captain Mervine's manner; the last Jake saw of Harriet was her frown as she stared about at the scene from the larboard rail. The red line of the cut stood out on the pallor of her cheek.

The oarsmen in the gig pulled for a narrow gritty beach. Some of the Ecuadoreans were there already, wading through shallow water as they made their way along a bluff, but Captain Mervine urged Jake directly up the hill. The wind cut through him despite the exertion, and Jake climbed with his hands in his pea-jacket pockets, listening to Mervine's heavy panting.

At the top of the bluff it was even colder, and there seemed to be naught to view except short brown-gold grass and brown-gold dirt all exposed in the gullies. Then, all at once—signs of habitation, rows of houses, mysteriously only half-built. There seemed to be so many, and, eerily, they were all at about the same stage of construction. It was as if some strange pestilence had carried off the builders in the space of a moment. There were even ladders left propped against half-built walls, and stacks of shingles alongside the eaves of raftered gaping roofs.

Then dogs cringed around corners, as lonely as the two or three Ecuadoreans who had made it thus far and were now staring about, bewildered. It was a chilling scene, palpably weird.

"Fifty," Captain Mervine barked. "Fifty houses a-building, according to the plan they were, rising according to the plan when I left this place in May. Artisans were being paid eight dollars a day, the highest in the land, and where are they now? Up the mines, sir, up the diggin's!"

Mervine seemed to regard the exodus as a personal insult, Jake mused. He stood still, staring about, his hands curled into fists in his jacket pockets; the scene was fully as weird as the first sight of the landing place at Tombez had been. Jake said, "Did they all go at once, in a body?"

"Two thousand men, sir! And two-thirds of them American! They went in June, they tell me, and then after that, in July, another two thousand followed in their path. They all came to 'Frisco and kept on going, in a hungry horde up the Sacramento River! But is that latest number American? No, sir, that they ain't. The men who flood through here, Captain Dexter, the men all intent on filling California and robbing the territory of rightfully American gold are not our citizens! They be Peruvian, Chilean, Ecuadorean, sir, Russian, French, even— for God's sake, and pardon me, sir—the miserable Mexicans and bloody arrogant English! Our natural-born enemies, sir, come to steal our rightfully won treasure, come to rape the territory that we claimed with American blood!"

They were walking again, more slowly, and the narrow streets widened and became uphill and downhill, often with one side of the road a full few feet higher than the other. There was a deserted market, fenced with rawhides on wires, stinking most foully, and then substantial buildings, many made of stone . . . but still, still there was no sign of life.

Jake said slowly, "But in Valparaiso, Captain, you declared there was no gold."

"Well, there is." Again, Mervine made it sound like a personal insult. "Colonel Mason and Lieutenant Sherman, they went to the hills to make a survey . . . and they're just back and reported, sir, what the gold in them hills is like."

Jake waited. Then he prompted, "And?"

"You've no idea," Mervine said sourly. "Sir, you ain't got a notion. Two ounces, they reported, was a usual day's work. While Mason were on the very spot a-watchin' two men dug seventeen thousand dollars' worth, just in the space of an hour."

Jake said softly, "Oh, Jehovah." It didn't seem possible. "In an hour?"

"And that with naught but Indian baskets to pan the nuggets. Them with proper pans and simple cradles can work out even more."

"And this is what Colonel Mason reported?"

"He did indeed, sir, and he writ it down, and tomorrow we sail, sir, bound to Monterey, to escort the schooner *Lambaye-cana* out of Monterey to Paita. There will be a loyal lieutenant on board of that schooner, Captain, and he will carry that report, along with a tin tea caddy of samples of the gold, all the way to Washington."

Mervine was positively bristling with importance. Jake said slowly, "So Colonel Mason begs more troops?"

"What, Captain? What do you mean?"

"You informed me in Valparaíso that if the gold did indeed exist, then Colonel Mason would claim it all in the name of the United States government."

Captain Mervine stopped at that and cleared his throat with a loud harrumphing noise that seemed to echo among the deserted stone façades. "If we take deserters—and we will board all outgoing ships to inspect for deserters, I assure you of that!—then, most certainly, sir, we will confiscate their ill-gotten gold and make spread eagles of them all! But," he added with every evidence of most extreme distaste, "Colonel Mason has been forced to confess that he and his forces are capable of no more than that."

"What! Why, pray?"

"Because of topography, sir, and the base nature of man! The placer has proved to be fully five hundred miles in length! How can a small force of men patrol that? And desertion, Captain, desertion! What allurement is a private's pay of six dollars a month compared to the stories from the mines, eh? Colonel Mason keeps the flag flying with naught but a small force—ever-diminishing!—of loyal officers and men. 'Tis a scandal, sir, an utter disgrace, that American men should prove thus disloyal, and this at a time of great national danger!"

He himself had predicted this, Jake remembered. However, he kept his counsel and for a moment the street was silent save for the thud of their boots, echoing about the dusty corners and blank facades. "Look at it," Mervine muttered. His head turned from side to side like a bulldog's. "Ain't it the truth, Captain, that it be a confounded scandal? When I think of the bustling *American* place I left in May . . . Why, there were two newspapers, two! A sure sign of American energy and initiative, Captain, but both have died, and died from what? Starvation, that's what, for no paper can survive when the writers, editors, printers, and readers have all gone off to the mines. Gold fever," he mumbled, and made it sound like a curse. "Have you ever seen a place so emptied?"

Jake thought of the landing place at Tombez, and he wondered, uneasily, what other towns on this coast had emptied. Perhaps Paita, Callao, and Talcahuano were in the same condition, and all on account of the tales of gold. "The rain's will fetch the men all back, the rains when they come in October," said Mervine. He grumbled and said, "You should be about here in October, Captain. You'll see 'Frisco all a-bustlin' then, all the way to February when the rains stop. And then, no doubt, they'll all be up to the hills again . . . and more and more furriners with 'em! My God, sir, and beg your pardon, but it sure bites hard, that the gold in this territory should be taken away by the very men we fought to keep out. 'Tis a time of great national danger, sir!"

"So you said, Captain Mervine."

"Aye, and I was right. And that is why Colonel Mason had devised his report, so all red-blooded patriotic American boys can get to hear of the gold! You know what will happen when the report all gets about? Why, American boys will come in their hundreds and kick all the furriners out . . . and 'tis your patriotic duty, sir, to do exact the same!"

"I beg your pardon?"

"Your duty as an American, sir, is to take your brig upriver and add to the number of American citizens! Show the flag, sir, wave it high!"

"Jehovah," said Jake, astounded. For a moment he almost laughed, so incredulous was he. A shut door in the imposing facade of a store at his right bore a ragged notice. It read: Closed on Account of Going to the Mines. "Jehovah," he said softly again.

14 ⟨⟩ Jake Dexter dined on the frigate *Savannah* and did not return
to the brig until Harriet had gone to bed. She lay listening until
she heard his voice and step, but even then she did not sleep.
She felt oppressed, beset with terrible forebodings. The thumps
and metallic scrapings as the abandoned ships tangled further
with each change of tide seemed unutterably doleful. However,
none of the men seemed to share her mood, for the dawn watch
woke her with their cheerful singing. Chill San Francisco fog
drifted about her sidelight, but:

> *Oh-h-h—'Frisco be a damn fine town* [sang Royal]
> *A very famous city*
> *Where all the streets be paved with gold*
> *And all the prospects pretty!*

"I see no gold," she said tartly to him when she arrived on
deck.

"It's in the hills, Hat, in the hills!"

"So they say," she admitted with a sigh and stared out at the bay. She saw little but slowly swirling gray cotton, and the wood of the rail squeezed dampness onto her palms. She was wearing a woollen shawl hugged about her shoulders, and yet it was high August, nearly September.

"California is the modern-day Araby, Hat! Folk will talk and sing about this forever."

"No doubt you're right, but I just cannot credit that every man who has come here has made himself a fortune. 'Tis like the boasting of a man who has mortgaged himself to buy a new carriage. He dare not say he made a bad choice, for then all his sacrifice will serve for naught, so he's forced to boast, all of the time! Even the true stories must be embroidered, tales told by men who know other men who have been to the fair and seen the elephant."

"Such eloquence," he scoffed, mimicking Bodfish. "But 'tis the tales, true or not, that will bring the adventurers to California, and Colonel Mason knows that full well, shrewd fellow."

"Colonel Mason?" she echoed, startled. She had to pin down the familiarity of the name, and then the dining table on the steambark *Nympha* was vividly in her mind.

"Colonel Mason has written a report that describes the wealth and extent of the gold here, 'tis the most fanciful gold yarn yet—and all it is is bait, to tempt thousands of American boys here, to thin down the numbers of hated aliens. Colonel Mason and all his garrison are most dreadful miffed that the territory they won so hard should attract hordes of the very men they fought to keep out, scandalized utterly, Hat, and at dawn the frigate *Savannah* sails to Monterey, to escort that Mason report on the first state of its journey to Washington, and they take a tea caddy of gold as well. Marvelous bait, Hat, and that is truly all that it is. Oh, these Americans," he sighed, and laughed. "They think themselves so subtle, when they are all so very transparent."

"If they don't like foreigners digging in their mines," said she tartly, "you are not going to be greatly welcome, Royal."

"You may well be right, but nevertheless I am a true-blue member of a true-blue American company," he said, and chuckled. "Anyway, off they go in the morning to attend to that report, and, I hear, Jake Dexter goes with them."

"On the *Savannah*?" She stared dismayed, with shock. "But why?"

"Perhaps he thinks to inspect Colonel Mason and his tea caddy of gold bait and the Mason report for himself. However," he added lazily, seeming most amused, "I do hear scuttlebutt that Jake has a wife, tucked tidily away in New England. He hasn't viewed her in a number of years, so he journeys to Monterey to speak with the skipper of the whaler *Isaac Walton*. That man, it seems, was once Jake's neighbor, and would certainly know how Mrs. Dexter fares."

Harriet said nothing; she couldn't. Her fingers felt nipped with cold, and then numb with her grip on the rail. It was as if the fog had crept through her skin and entered her blood; it was impossible to feel emotion, for all she could feel was the sullen thud of her heavy heart. It was like the numbness when her father was killed, the terrible numbness that preceded grief. She didn't even notice Royal speak or move away, not until Chips loudly declared a company meeting, and she blinked and roused, painfully, and realized that she was alone.

Then Jake came on deck and looked all around, his every manner vital with energy. Harriet moved slowly, her limbs feeling like wood, and she scarcely thanked Crotchet when he brought her a seat, or remembered sitting down in it. Long strings of ducks hooted in the distant, slowly clearing sky, and she heard their crying instead of Bodfish's monotone reading the minutes.

The men evidently paid little attention too, for the voice that moved the minutes be accepted as correct was very impatient. Then there was silence, and when Harriet looked up everyone was watching Captain Dexter, and every face was expectant.

He said, "I guess you've all heard of Colonel Mason's report. It certifies that the gold yarns are based on nothing but the truth. Men in the lower mines are digging two hundred dollars a day on the average. You might have heard, too, the tales that ran about Valparaíso concerning a Mormon trader called Brannan, who started off this gold rush by running about the streets here waving a little quinine bottle of gold from the American River. I was informed in Valparaíso that Brannan only did that as a ruse to sell mining goods from his store at Sutter's Fort. It was a device that worked—he did trade that week to the tune of thirty-six thousand dollars!—but the story was never a lie. The gold in that bottle was real, and it came from the American River, one hundred and fifty miles up the Sacramento valley."

He paused then, looking around. Everyone watched him and no one said a word. He tipped back his hat, looking reflectively at Harriet, and said, "Perhaps, too, you've heard of Sutter's Fort. As I said, it is a hundred and a half-hundred up the Sacramento, but the Sacramento River is by repute a noble stream. It is perfectly possible for us to take the brig there, and that is what I propose we do."

Predictably, this bewildered some of the men. Harriet listened to Jake's patient voice go on and on, talking about current, tide, drift, and bottom. There were marshes and sandbars in places, he said, but all of them were negotiable. As always he was honest and fair, making sure that all the men understood. All they needed to understand, she thought wryly, however, was that the river passage would get them all a hundred and a half-hundred nearer the hills and the gold. But what would happen to the brig, she cried silently, and what would happen to her? No one asked, she thought desperately, no one cared about either.

Her hands were clasped tightly in her lap as she struggled with shameful self-pity. She had coped before on her own in a foreign land, she told herself fiercely; and, dear God, she could cope again. She looked up at Jake again, her shoulders consciously squared, and found his thoughtful gaze contemplating her still.

He said, "We must give thought to what we will do when we arrive at the junction of the rivers. Sutter's Fort has a substantial landing place which they call the Embarcadero, so mooring the brig will be no problem. However Sutter's Fort in this month of August 1848 must be the place with the most potential for profit in the whole of the world—so what we must do is to make up our minds how to get that profit for ourselves."

He paused again. The men all gaped at him; they had had naught in their minds, Harriet deduced, but going to the hills and digging much gold. The idea that there were alternatives befuddled them completely.

Jake said, "We're carrying a possible fortune right here," and he tapped one boot on the deck in meaning fashion. "It is fortunate indeed that we asked for foodstuffs rather than money from our passengers, for the provisions we carry will bring us much wealth. We could sell the provisions ourselves, or sell through an agent. Either way, we'll make thousands, if we do it properly."

"You mean, sir, you want us to set up as traders?" exclaimed Abner. His tone was affronted, almost insulted. "But we came to this land for gold, sir!"

"And gold we'll get," Jake promised. "Let me give you an example. The flour we reckoned on at fifteen dollars a barrel off Tombez will fetch fifty at the fort—if we're stupid enough to sell it in bulk. We can make still more if we bag it up into one- or two-pound lots. And let me give another example: the oranges that we counted at eight thousand for sixty dollars fetch fifty cents at the fort. Fifty cents. Each. Fifty cents per fruit."

The mouths of the staring men were sagging open, and Harriet found herself in the same state. This was incredible, a yarn to match the gold yarns themselves. "And," said Jake, "the payment for these high-priced provisions is not given in coin. It is given in gold."

Gold. The word dropped as warm and heavy as the metal itself into the astounded silence. "Gold, not coinage, is the currency in this place," said Jake. He nodded, looking from one to another. "A teaspoonful fetches this or that, a pinch buys a drink, a nugget a meal. A sack of gold dust is the stake in a game of monte . . . and a palmful of nuggets buys a passage up the Sacramento River."

Harriet found her voice. "Passengers, again?" she said, and her voice was high with horror in her ears.

Jake smiled, ruefully. "Mistakes have been made," he admitted, and smiled, no doubt trying to coax an answering smile, but Harriet, shocked, merely stared. "Mistakes," he added, "which I will not repeat. If we agree to take passengers on the passage upriver the fare will get nothing more than a berth in the hold or a plank on the deck. The passage takes three or four days only, and the passengers will have to fend for themselves and carry their own food."

His eyes were still on her face, trying to meet hers; it was as if he was trying to say, *you'll be under my protection this time*, but Harriet knew, desperately, that Jake would not be there. Jake, if Royal had told the truth, would be on the frigate *Savannah*. Perhaps the scuttlebutt was wrong, she thought with a snatch of hope, but that hope was destroyed on the instant. "Mr. Martin," said Jake to them all, "will take the brig upriver."

No one seemed surprised; they had all, Harriet knew, heard the rumors too. She said, trying to hide her desperation, "But how will you rejoin the brig? And what if—what if there's trouble?"

Her voice had shook only a little, but nevertheless he was frowning. He said, "There will be one passenger in the steerage."

"*What*?"

"He will be the alcalde of the Feather River settlement, a kind of sheriff or mayor. Alcaldes are men given the responsibility of keeping law and order in this land. He's an Englishman; his name is Don Roberto Ross. There will be no . . . trouble, with an alcalde on board."

Jake's voice was oddly urgent, as if he wished to reassure her, but Harriet, dumbfounded by the oddness of his information, could only gape. She was conscious of the men shifting about, looking at each other and muttering, but could not remove her stare from Captain Dexter's face. Their eyes clashed; it was oddly intimate, like the day he'd tied her apron strings, as if they were alone, lost in private conversation.

He said in that persuasive tone, "'Tis only four days' ride from Monterey to Sutter's Fort. Captain Mervine assured me most earnestly of that. I . . . have to go to Monterey, on a private matter, it is of the first importance, and when I get to Sutter's Fort—"

Abijah Roe interrupted, crying, "But what about the gold, sir, what about the diggin's?"

The Gold. For a long moment Harriet thought that Jake had not heard. Then his eyes, at last, left her face, and he looked impatiently at Abijah, saying, "You're determined to try the mines?"

"Aye!" and men all about were echoing the sentiment.

Jake paused; he was frowning, as if he was trying to choose careful words. Then he said, "You've all heard the wonderful stories, but I want to warn you that it won't be easy. The season is a-drawing on; the cold and rains begin in October. The rains, I hear, are no small matter; they come in cataracts, in floods. Once they've commenced in earnest all the trails will be impassable, and the men in the hills will all be trapped. Many will starve; some will die; and none of them will be able to dig. At most there is six or seven weeks of the digging season left."

Six weeks, six weeks! Harriet could feel the abrupt urgency inside all the men. The passage up the river would take four

days, and then they would have to wait for their captain, and
then God alone knew how long it would take them to get to the
hills and make a claim. The men all looked about and then
began to babble, and Jake raised his voice, shouting, "But
there are alternatives!"

"But if we wait till February all the good claims will be
gone, sir, we'll have got here in season, through luck and
chance, sir, and we can't sit back and lose that luck!" That was
Dan Kemp, and his crony Tib seemed every bit as anxious.
"Why, good Lord, sir," said he, "we've all of us put up with
wet and cold a-plenty; it don't make no diff'rence to us."

"Perhaps you're right," Jake said. His voice was very even.
"You all know your own strength and capacity. Form mining
parties if you wish, but remember this well: *I'm not having the
brig abandoned.*"

His voice rose with this last, with a snap, and Tib, being Tib,
caved in on the instant. "Abandon the old *Hakluyt*, sir?" said
he. "Why, good Lord, sir, that would be the lastest thing on
everyone's minds."

Jake snapped, "Good. I presume, too, no one wishes to
abandon the chance of making profit from our cargo?"

"And that's another truth, sir, and I freely admit it, that I
do," said Tib. He was scratching his head with every lively
appearance of perplexity, and the other men all watched him,
their mouths a little open as they struggled one and all with the
problem. "The fact is," he admitted with an air of candor then,
"we have a program that be too plumb full, and not enough
time to do the tenth of it all, Captain."

"But the answer is obvious," Jake said smoothly. He looked
around at all the men, and Harriet sat quietly and watched him.
He even smiled, but seemed as unaware as all the rest that she
was sitting there. "All we need is a little organization," said
he, and then he began to talk. The talk went on and on and was
all about forming into separate groups, about one part of the
company going into the hills, establishing a claim and digging
in until spring, about another group stopping on board, about
trading and setting up as a kind of boarding house, about sizing
up the possibilities of Sutter's Fort. It seemed to Harriet as if
none of it had aught to do with her. After a while she stopped
listening.

At dawn there was another fog, in the way that 'Frisco had,
but nonetheless the frigate *Savannah* prepared to make sail.

When Harriet came on deck all the *Hakluyt* men were at the rail watching, so she joined them, standing aft, a little apart.

The rail under her hands was clammy with moisture, and this air of high summer was cold on her cheeks. The shouts from the frigate echoed emptily in the soggy air. Birds cried out far above, and the sails as they dropped seemed luminous with mist. Harriet could see the rows of men in the yards, and hear the bos'un's whistle. Then, a clangor as the chain rattled up and the ship hove short. Then, slowly, slowly, the frigate began to move.

A cannon from the Presidio on shore thudded hollowly, and the frigate replied. Harriet could smell the heavy sour smoke. The big flag fluttered, dropped, and then, like the sails, took the breeze. The fog, too, lifted with the rising breeze, and low sunlight glittered on the tips of little waves, struck sparks from brass fittings, made stark the black shapes of gunports.

Then, another salute. Harriet heard the cannon and then saw the frigate lurch as she fired. Then all at once the stern of the man-of-war was presented. The sails filled with an audible pattering as the frigate hauled round.

Then the frigate was gone, and Jake Dexter with her. The mists swirled, eddied, and then were gone completely. Harriet turned and went below, to wash and brush for breakfast, and to tidy up the accommodations before the passengers for the upriver passage came on board.

15 ～   It was an amazing invasion. Four glum and querulous Yankee merchants came along, grumbling about the scandalous price of passage, and the skipper and five officers and men from the latest abandoned vessel, equally sour-faced, still all fired up with the impertinence of the rest of their crew in fleeing their bark and taking off for the hills. If those runaways were ever found, Harriet deduced, they surely would rue the day they'd succumbed to this gold fever.

Other Americans came as well, furtive men in tatters of badly disguised uniforms, surely deserters from the American forces who had come out hiding with the departure of the *Savannah*. There were kanakas too, Hawaiian men who had run away from the Sandwich Islands' traders, round-faced and musical by nature, sadly ill-equipped for the winter in the hills. Better adapted were the few South Americans, who knew the altiplano.

Other kinds of men hailed from the north: heavily garbed,

tallow-scented Russians and shifty beaver trappers who spoke
a kind of French. There were black men like Davy Jones
Locker, perhaps like him, escaped slaves. Silent pigtailed men
came from the land called *East*, and Harriet was reminded most
unpleasantly of Canton. She wondered briefly what Sefton had
found there; then she wondered if he'd heard of the gold in
California, but she quickly pushed the thought to the back of
her mind, for she remembered, too, how he'd talked of settling
in this place. Then, mercifully, she was distracted by the
arrival of the single passenger for the steerage cabin, the
mysterious English alcalde, Don Roberto Ross.

Charlie Martin brought him down the companionway. Charlie was pulling at his beard even more distractedly than usual,
looking a deal uneasy with the responsibility of getting the brig
upriver, and behind him trotted a sight from some pantomime,
an unbelievable flamboyant figure of fun.

Don Roberto Ross was a middle-aged fellow, a fat little man
with a most abundant paunch. His legs, by contrast, were as
skinny as sticks, and despite their funny shape they were
crammed into Spanish calcineros. He wore a serape draped
along one arm; it was striped in black gray and ginger, as if to
match his flowing beard. The leaf of his glazed sombrero
measured one foot from crown to rim, and when he swept it off
he revealed a yellowed pair of small blue eyes and a rather
large port-wine nose. His accent, when he spoke, was pure
Cockney.

"Why, Gawd'n bless me," said he in thunderstruck tones.
"A lady!"

"Miss Gray belongs to London too," said Charlie Martin,
beaming. "Miss Harriet Gray," he amended proudly.
"Perhaps, Don Roberto, you may've viewed her on the stage!"

"Miss Harriet Gray," the newcomer echoed. His tone was
reverent, and Harriet found her hand enfolded in a moist warm
and relentless grip. "I've been a Mexican since 1839, through
a most remarkable set of circumstances, Miss Gray! But do I
know the name, sir? Yes, I do believe I do."

Harriet said nothing, smiling politely as she tried without
success to retrieve her hand from his grasp. She declined to
believe him. What had she been doing in 1839? She had played
the circuit as a cherub in board-and-feather wings, and she had
acted the juvenile in *The Orphan of Geneva* and *The Maid of
Milan*. Her first success had been her rendition of a song called

"Home Sweet Home," but she refused to believe that this flamboyant fellow had even heard the tune.

"London, London," quoth this Don Roberto, and he even had a sentimental tear in his eye. "Such recollections as the name do bring back! I've been in this here California," he confided, "as I told you, since 1839, came 'ere looking for adventure, Miss Gray, for a fortune indeed, Mr. Martin! I arrived in that memorial year wiv a letter of introduction from the British consul at . . ."

Charlie Martin, Harriet observed, was not listening at all, for all he tried to look polite. He kept on looking up at the skylight at the busy sounds on deck and jumped visibly as the boat bringing the old pilot was hailed. Thuds on deck and metallic clanging from the anchor chain and . . .

". . . consul at Lahaina," quoth this unstoppable fellow. "Found the Mexicans exceedin' 'ospitable." Don Roberto didn't even seem to notice when Charlie found the courage to forget courtesy and mutter an excuse and escape up the companion. ". . . and I bought sixty thou' acres at a most excellent price up the North Fork of the Feather River, and I've been 'ere ever since, Miss Gray, never regretted the move . . ." Harriet, benumbed and battered with his endless talk, felt on the verge of helpless hypnosis. Surely this Cockney would run to a stop!

But he didn't.

The brig anchored at sunset, at the end of the first leg of the passage upriver, thirty-five miles from 'Frisco at a pretty place called Benicia. Benicia had a fine harbor and a fine view of grazing lands, and Harriet went up on deck, partly to look at it, but mostly to avoid Don Roberto's endless conversation. Jake Dexter wasn't there to tell her nay or to inform her of her impropriety, but he would have had no need to do so anyway, she saw after some moments: the passengers paid her almost no attention whatsoever.

They were instead engaged in gauping at the llamas. The five llamas lived on the foredeck in the pen that Chips had made them more than two weeks before, and the passengers, oddly, lined up in a neat queue to watch them. The men, she saw, studied the beasts solemnly and seemed very reluctant to move on, but move on they did, to allow the next fellows in the queue to have their turn at looking too. It was all very odd, she thought, and the llamas evidently felt the oddness too. They were becoming more and more restive, and then, inevitably, they spat. The audience scattered in cursing disarray and stared at smelly green splotches on their shirt fronts and complained at length, and noisily.

The complaints, inevitably, were passed on to Charlie Martin. Harriet, quenching inner amusement, watched poor Charlie haul at his beard as he heard out the story. The llamas, the Yankee spokesman then said, not only spat, but they stank. In fact the whole brig stank, and all the crew did too. It was no doubt on account of living with the smelly spitting beasts for so long. It was pointless for Harriet to point out that Benicia stank too, for her nose had soon told her that Benicia had slaughter yards, and those right close to the beach. Everyone ignored her, because she was merely female. The *Hakluyt* crew made things snug for the night in a wounded silence, but no sooner had full dark come down than the brig was attacked by a horde of blood-thirsty mosquitoes. Within minutes the spokesman was back with a renewed complaint. It was the stench of the brig, the crew, and the llamas that attracted the pests, he said.

Poor Charlie was too distracted and distraught to eat much in the way of supper, and then Bodfish became sniffish too and banged about in the pantry because of what he considered an insult to his provender.

He was clanging about in the pantry again at dawn when Charlie ordered weigh the anchor. Then, while Harriet and the loquacious Don Roberto were eating breakfast the brig stood up with the tide in her favor, sailing into Suisun Bay. Harriet escaped onto deck as soon as she could and stood at the rail to view the amazing scenery. Within one bend the brig was surrounded by vivid marshland, a gold-red-green sea of marsh and tall bulrushes. Bulrushes? "Toulies," said Don Roberto, arriving beside her. Harriet bit back a sigh.

Don Roberto talked on and on. Standing on the deck of the brig seemed more at times like standing on the floor of a dray. Ducks and geese rose hooting into the pale air, and then they were sailing up the Sacramento proper. It seemed impossible that they should be able to sail upriver; as a child Harriet had learned beyond doubt that the current of a river flowed always to the mouth. The Sacramento was a noble stream too, truly, a full hundred yards wide even at this dry time of the year, or so Don Roberto informed her. The waters certainly rippled strongly, and the banks were no shallow obstacle, either. They were lined with long stands of oak trees and sycamore, many with trunks with a girth of more than six feet. Their great boughs leaned over the water, but still the brig sailed upriver, against the current, the wind filling her topsails sweetly.

Beyond the trees: more trees, and rolling slopes of gold-brown grass. Then elk were glimpsed, bounding about in the shrubbery, and the passengers demanded, one and all, that the brig pause while they lowered boats and went off a-hunting. They all fired off their pistols to emphasize their point, and Charlie, tearing frantically at his beard, grudgingly gave in and let them have their way.

So the brig loitered about while the men who stopped on board made wooden pickhandles and sheet-iron washers. Then when the tide had turned against them the hunters returned with various bloodied booty. They gave out these freely, declaring they had eaten their fill on shore. The truth of this was confirmed by the sight of their campfires all gone out of control. Harriet wondered aloud with alarm what effect this would have on California, but Don Roberto informed her at length and indulgently that the toulies caught alight all the time, and no harm was wraught. Then, just as the fire went out, proving the Cockney correct, the brig grounded on a bar.

Next morning the crew was on deck at dawn and struggling to get the brig back afloat. They took kedge anchors and dropped them and returned and heaved at the windlass to haul the brig up to the kedges, but all they accomplished was the loss of the chain and the anchor with it. They came back on board downcast enough, ate supper, and went to bed with nothing more than a minor scrap with the most belligerent of the passengers. Then at three in the morning the westerly wind blew fresh and the tide was on the full. Poor harried Charlie called all hands on deck, and they managed, at last, to get the brig afloat.

And all the time Don Roberto talked; my God, thought Harriet, battered beyond belief, how the little fat Cockney talked. It was as if he'd been forced to silence since that memorial year of 1839, and now the dammed talk was all pouring out. "Sixty thousand acres," he told her, and, "Other men 'ave done it, yes, but I be the first, Miss Gray. I've been a pioneer in the breaking frontier business, I 'ave a fort myself, up to the Feather River where it be narrow enough to bridge. A fort were plumb necessary, Miss Gray, for the state of lawlessness 'ere be beyond belief, you knowing full well, I be certain"—and here he lowered his voice and looked about the empty cabin in most confiding manner—"what a rambunctious lot Americans be. The trappers and hide-and-tallow traders, why you ain't got no notion! Drunken I call 'em, but shrewd enough too, and some of the *wide* ones have been wide enough to see the opportunities, ma'am, and settle like myself in this new land. Some even become an alcalde like me, with jurisdiction over a province and a pueblo! Ain't that strange enough, a native born Londoner reaching the state of alcalde?"

At four in the afternoon the brig fetched a settlement called New York. Harriet, amazed, went on deck again to view this unlikely city of the west. New York was at the junction of two fine rivers, the Sacramento and the Joaquin. It was made up of two houses and two riverboats. The *Hakluyt* men all had a good laugh about that, and their mirth made the passengers more vexacious than ever, it seemed, for they all promptly laid another complaint. While one and all slapped energetically at bloodthirsty mosquitoes they complained about young Bill.

Bill, they all declared, had been stealing. He was naught but a nasty common little thief. They all demanded to know where he'd come from, and they all guessed, darkly, that he hailed from the penal colonies of Australia.

The basis of their complaint was that Bill had more money stowed away in his breeches than any little rascal had any right to own; he had more dollars, *fips* and *levies* than any boy could rightly stow in his pockets. Where did he get this hoard, that's what they wanted to know. Bill refused to say. Instead he defiantly informed Don Roberto, who had importantly taken up the role of judge, that there would be a lot more where this lot had come from.

His face was contorted in the most frightful scowl Harriet had seen yet. He denied all charges, and two of the Yankee merchants took over. They collared him, clinched his squirming form, and poked fingers into his breeches pockets. He squirmed and screeched until both men let go of him with a curse, and he shot like a bullet into the rigging.

Bill did not stop till he reached the foretop. Then he turned, steadied, adjusted his breeches, took aim, and pissed with startling accuracy right down on the heads of his tormentors. Both Harriet and Royal found this excruciatingly funny: Harriet laughed until the tears ran down her cheeks, and the Americans all stared, declaring her behavior scandalous. Then the *Hakluyt* men found out how Bill had made his contentious fortune: he had made it by charging the passengers money to look at the llamas! The *Hakluyt* men had their own laugh then, and the passengers all muttered most foully.

Don Roberto did not laugh: somewhere since 1839, Harriet deduced, he'd lost the robust quality of English humor, and, in any case, he had been one of those rained down upon. Even that, however, did not stop his endless flow of information. "A pueblo, now, you may not be familiar with that word, Miss Gray, for *pueblo* be Spanish for village." His pueblo, he informed her, was situated on the Feather River, a half-day's march west of his fort. It was called Pueblo San Marco. Don Roberto received a fee for his work as alcalde, it seemed, and it was easy money, too, for legal proceedings in California were a deal less complex than the workings of the law in London. "For a start," said he, confiding, "there ain't no writ-down law."

"Merciful heavens, is there not?"

"And the jurisdiction of the alcalde be about boundless. The Mexicans devised the system. They established the pueblos and then sold the land in fifty-vara lots. Then they appointed an alcalde and gave him the money to start off the town. Whenever an alcalde needs more money all 'e 'as to do is sell more land! Easy at that," he said, and nodded profoundly at her expression.

"But what about crime, Don Roberto? You told me yourself that the state of California is lawless beyond belief. What do you do with a robber . . . and what if a man commits murder?"

"That do be a problem, and I do admit it freely, Miss Gray, but still the system makes things easy! There ain't no jails, I grant you that, but who needs a jail where there is a tree, and that tree 'as a good strong branch, and you 'ave a good strong rope to hang it from?"

"But who decides if a man is guilty—and what if the man is truly innocent?"

"Ah, but that be simple too, Miss Gray! If there be any doubt at all, any suspicion that the charge be unfounded, why then, the man be given twenty-four hours to quit clear of the alcalde's territory, a full day and night. Then, if he be still about at the end of the deadline, then he be dead indeed, ma'am, for we string him up without argument. We take it, you see, as a confession of guilt. I told you, 'tis easy!"

"Good heavens," said Harriet, wondering. Don Roberto sat with his knees apart, beaming in most unaccustomed momentary silence. He opened his mouth and she mentally braced herself for yet another flood of conversation. The passage upriver seemed endless, but at supper Charlie wearily reassured her.

He was certain sure they'd make Sutter's Fort next day. The old pilot had told him that.

It rained in the night, and when Harriet arrived on deck the trees and grass were all washed and shining. Beyond the hills and clumps of trees the mountains were a distant gray and beige. The passengers were all up and staring at those distant promising hills, and the *Hakluyt* crew paused often in their jobs to gaze hitherward too. The old pilot, as always, was standing at the main shrouds with his hunched back turned toward her, and—as always—Harriet looked at him often, trying to pin down a sense of familiarity.

Each time she saw him she was struck by the sense of recognition, and yet it was impossible, she thought. This old man knew the river and knew this California; it seemed logical that he had lived here for years upon years, and she'd never met anyone from California. All seamen looked the same in their weathered old age, she told herself, even if that seafaring happened on a river instead of in the sea; they all got seamed in their water-beaten faces. She had never spoken to the old man, and he had never come into the cabin. He lived on deck, and bedded down in a locker. He did not speak to anyone save Charlie, and spoke to him solely to convey his instructions. He was a sour old man, dirty and unsociable, and when Don Roberto trotted up to her side Harriet turned her head, intending to ask him about the identity of this pilot.

However, the Cockney forestalled her. He grinned as broad as if he'd done a wide trick, threw out an arm, and said, "New Helvetia!"

"I beg your pardon?" Then Harriet heard the men in the hamper all calling out. The passengers rushed as one to the starboard rail, and the brig heeled over with the weight. Mr. Martin yelled. For a few moments there was utter commotion, and throughout it all Harriet could see nothing to warrant such excitement.

She gazed wildly all about at the same blue-brown river, the same clumps of yellow-green trees bending over their red-green reflections. Mud, gold-colored grass, crisp despite the general wetness of the landscape, a smell of mud and humid warmth, more scattered clumps of thickly foliaged trees, and then . . . in the middle distance, walls, the thick solid adobe walls of a fort. Harriet could glimpse the blunt witches'-hat shapes of corner bastions, a huge high gate that seemed designed for some ironwork portcullis, the terra-cotta tiles of a square building within those solid walls, a bright proud flag. She looked up, envying the *Hakluyt* men their vantage in the rigging, and saw Royal up the mainmast, his arm flung out like Don Roberto's, his beard jutting out against the shrouds. He looked medieval, like a herald from old Outremer, and the scene was almost Arabic too, like some ancient defensive structure in an oasis in the desert.

Then the trees thickened as the brig sailed on slowly, slowly, past the fort toward an embarcadero, and the fort was almost lost to sight. There was a path running alongside the riverbank, but it could only be glimpsed in snatches too, in gaps in the thickets. Harriet saw ox-drawn carts, horses, men hunched over with the weight of burdens on their backs, a half-beached riverboat with a notice up that said Trading Post and then the larger hull of some ship, wedged tightly into a thicket so she couldn't see the sternboard. The old pilot was talking to Mr. Martin, and Charlie hollered orders out. The brig slowed and slowed as the topsails left the wind, and then the *Hakluyt* sailed toward the bank, toward the squared timbers of the landing . . . the landing of what?

The passengers were rushing about all over the deck, fighting each other to get to the gangway first, as eager to quit the brig at this place as the Ecuadoreans had been to leave her at San Francisco. Harriet scarcely noted their departure, and the departure of the old pilot too; she was a deal too busy with studying this fabled gate to . . . what?

Surely not El Dorado! She could see the outlet of a small river that flowed toward the distant walls of the fort, and a lake, pastures, cattle grazing, wheat fields more than ready for the scythe, and gardens of South American corn all neglected and trampled. A path ran alongside the stream, crowded beyond belief with drays and horsemen who galloped back and forth, halloing, as if on errands of the most urgent importance, galloping endlessly from the Embarcadero to the fort and then back, through . . . fields. Whips cracked, but for no apparent reason, and all the shouting, or nearly all, was in Spanish. This, surely, was still the frontier, even if men called it *El Dorado*.

Then she saw the three soldiers. They were working

incomprehensibly, extremely preoccupied with strings and stakes. They had a little handcart to carry all their gear, and in contrast to the hollering throng on the path and on the Embarcadero, they made a most miserable trio. Their scruffy regimentals were muddied and ragged, and they had a most dogged look about the way they did their work.

What the devil were they doing? "Laying out the town," said Don Roberto, laughing most heartily at the expression on her face.

"What town?" said she derisively.

"Why, this town—what the sailors call Embarcadero, Miss Gray! They're a-laying it out American style, just like a grid, streets numbers one way and lettered the other, all neat and tidy-oh, United States fashion!" Then he chuckled again and waved a plump arm and cried, "But there be a future 'ere, Miss Gray! Can't you see that future, can't you see the promise?"

Harriet said nothing. If there was a future for this unlikely place, she mused, then it was merely in American male heads, for the present of this place was almost entirely all on paper. Except for the fort, she thought then, except for the fort. The massive structure had her fascinated, and when Don Roberto offered to escort her there, she accepted with enthusiasm.

They walked, joining the throng that crowded the path alongside the little river. Harriet had to hold her skirts high to avoid mud and heaps of steaming horse manure, and men on all sides pressed close to stare at her, and she heard many Spanish comments.

The way was uphill, for the fort was sited on a rise, and a little river curled about the north wall, as medieval as a moat. There was a chunky little bridge, which added to the fortress appearance, and the walls were as thick up close as they had seemed from a distance. They were more than two feet thick at the level of Harriet's waist, and three times higher than her height. They were tan colored where the whitewash had flaked, and the humped roofs of the bastions showed over the tops. The path ran on past the entrance to this imposing place, to a double-storied adobe building two hundred yards or more farther on. Don Roberto told her that the latter was the one-time barracks, and Harriet could see the fenced corral that lay before it. Then, like the men that pressed around them, Harriet and Don Roberto turned into the entrance of Sutter's Fort.

The portcullislike gate poised high overhead was made of

huge timbers studded with spikes. There was a guardhouse on either side, adorned with small barred windows. Then, directly inside, a huge compound made of bare beaten earth, sheltered by large trees in many places, dominated by the squat three-level dwelling place in the middle.

Like the path outside the compound was full of noise and color. It was like an ancient eastern market, Harriet thought with amazement. She felt buffetted by commotion, for the place was so bustling, so astoundingly complete. Every trade was carried on here, and that at the top of men's voices. Gamblers set up striped calico awnings and rang little bells and called out bets; traders with trestle tables of picks, pans, tools, and provisions, all shouted out their allurements too. Beehive ovens were set here and about, steaming red-hot with the loaves that sweating bakers constantly made to sell to the waiting lines of men. Other fires spat with spits with whole carcasses revolving over them, while other fires burned under metal grilles that held gobbets of meat buccaneer-style.

All around the inner sides of the fortress walls adobe cottages had been built, many of them seemingly manufactories, for Harriet saw blacksmiths sweating over forges and coopers shaving staves. There was a candle-making house; a room where Indian women patiently worked at blanket looms; another where Indian men made whiskey, brandy, pisco; kitchens that turned out priceless hams; and stonewalled pantries where equally valuable butter was churned.

Harriet wandered about as openmouthed as the stray Indians and gauping Yankee backwoodsmen and sailors. There was even a room where hides had been tanned, with its own distinctive stink. Most of the tanning had been done in a hut over by the American River, near where the three soldiers were laying out their mythical streets. Curing hides and the making of tallow had been the prime industry here, but the discovery of gold had put paid to all that. Now the soldiers lived in the tanning hut, and the tanning room here was hired out by the night as accommodation.

"What?" said Harriet. She shook her head and laughed. "But why don't the soldiers live in the barracks?"

"All of the buildings," said Don Roberto, "are hired out for the hotel trade." Several of the houses inside these walls had been rooms for Sutter's vaqueros, but they were rented out too. There was an old ship moored at the Embarcadero, and even that was turning huge profits as a boarding house. Sutter's house was not exempt, Captain Sutter being at the mines himself. "They pack 'em in so tight in the attic," said Don Roberto, chortling, "that when one wishes to turn in the night, why, they all 'ave to turn, so the one who wants it gives the signal by hollering 'Spoon.' "

And how much did men pay for this uncomfortable sport? One dollar at night, meals and blanket extra, Don Roberto told her and laughed most heartily at the expression on her face. It was all so amazing, this uncommon fever called *gold rush*, and no one enjoyed the amazement more than Don Roberto himself. "You just wait till Colonel Mason's report gets out! The mines will close down soon as the rainy season comes, but in February 'twill all be different. You may think things are bustling now, but you just wait, Miss Gray; you just wait for the memorial season of 1849, and then you'll truly see doings."

They walked back to the entrance then, and Harriet paused a moment to look out at the scene. The path was as crowded as before, and she could see the Embarcadero and the brig anchored. She could see men in the rigging and men on deck, but supposed a lot of them were exploring, as amazed as she was. There was a flag flying from the rooftop of the long double-storied building that she now knew was the barracks; she could see horses in the round corral, clustered about an old well, but they were travelers' horses, she supposed, and the flag was naught but a show. A barracks—a boarding house! She shook her head at such an extempore solution, but Don Roberto waved a short plump arm and said, "But things will get better!" Then he pointed at the soldiers and their charts. Harriet hesitated and then followed him as he trotted in that direction, saying, "Who bid them to survey this place?"

"Why, the son of Captain Sutter, of course! He might be Swiss or whatever, and only jus' come to California too, but he 'as the business head, and the kind of head needful in this place."

There was no *of course* about it, Harriet silently thought, and then observed the three soldiers straighten as they saw her coming. They looked no less morose at close quarters, and they stunk very highly too, no doubt, she mused, on account of their living quarters. Their horses were grazing in a rough corral nearby and looked as muddy and miserable and bitten as their owners. She marveled that they were there at all, the enticements of the mines being such a contrast to their present state.

The three soldiers, moreover, were all lieutenants, Harriet learned. "Lieutenant William H. Warner," said the first one. "William Tecumseh Sherman," said the second. The third one was named Ord. Not only did they have to do this confounded muddy surveying job, they one by one informed Harriet, but they had to fend for themselves as well. Lieutenant Warner looked after the horses as hostler, Lieutenant Sherman did the cooking, and Lieutenant Ord was *supposed* to clean the dishes. However, the first two told her, sounding as sulky as school-boys, they had just found out that Ord cleaned the plates by the simple filthy process of wiping them down with wet grass from the horse paddock.

Harriet, quenching slightly hysterical inner laughter and breathing shallowly through her mouth to avoid the common stench, shook three exceedingly muddy hands. "Lieutenant Sherman," Don Roberto informed her, "was assistant to Colonel Mason during the investigation that led to the report on the mines."

"Actual, ma'am," said Lieutenant Sherman dourly, "I were cook there as well." He sniffed as his drooping musta-chio, which matched his straggling black hair in lank abun-dance.

"But the gold was truly there in the hills?"

"Ma'am," said he heavily, "the Colonel estimated that more'n ten million dollar' wo'th be taken from them hills since May."

"Ten million? Surely not!"

"Ma'am, I assure you, I do not tell a lie."

All three officers were glowering at her, and Don Roberto was seeming all at once peevish too. Harriet said very hastily, "I do assure you, and that most sincerely, that I do not doubt your word for one moment—"

"Men in them hills, ma'am," said Ord with heavy emphasis, "be runnin' about like hogs in an acorn patch, pickin' up nuggets the way hogs pick up groun'nuts."

"Merciful heavens," said Harriet rather faintly. "Is that really so?"

"Indeed it is, ma'am," said Warner, and shook his head at her continued disbelief. "Men are pickin' up ten ounces a day; they reckon on making a dollar a minute."

"Seven men staked a claim within my jurisdiction," chimed in Don Roberto, sounding more self-important than ever, "up the Feather River mid-July. You know 'ow much they've dug from there since?"

"No, I do not," said Harriet sincerely.

"Well, Miss Gray, I know it for fact, that they've dug three hundred pounds all but twenty, and that in seven weeks!"

Harriet was silenced at that, by a strong conviction that whatever exclamation of amazement she might make would be taken again as disbelief. After a moment she turned to Lieutenant Sherman and said cautiously, "And it is facts like these that form the content of the colonel's report?"

"Indeed, ma'am, those facts or other facts like 'em. And when the facts all get about back East, why, they'll all come in their thousands, and they'll all come through here, ma'am, and render this city bustling."

This was as difficult to credit as all the rest, Harriet found. She looked about, at the trees and canvas shelters, the tanning shed and the muddy corral. The fort on its rise in the distance seemed miragelike, an illusion. She said, "And so you survey this . . . town?"

"'Tis the situation!" Lieutenant Warner trumpeted. "'Tis the confluence! American River one way, Feather River the other, and fabulous mines on each of 'em! It all stands to reason, that this place will be a second New Orleans!"

He sounded as inspired by this as he had been about the gold, and Harriet suddenly thought, of course—for these three men, morose as they were, displayed a most remarkable loyalty to their country and their flag. Their fellow officers and the soldiers they had led had deserted in their dozens, off to claim some of that gold for their own, but these three men had proved stalwart despite shocking conditions and pay, so of course they had to show good reason for their actions.

Once she had gauged the reason for their sincerity, however, she was even less inclined to believe them. She looked about at this uninviting tract of land again and heard Don Roberto say, "Look, Miss Gray, look hard but try to imagine this place at this time next year. 'Forty-nine will be memorial, I warrant it! There will be stores and other trading places where you see naught but trees and grass, and taverns and taps and groggeries too; saloons and gambling 'alls, theaters, even! This place might turn out to be low-class, even fast-paced, for men will be men, and wish to do more when they find their gold than shout EUREKA! They'll want to buy provisions when they come 'ere first, and celebration when they come 'ere next, and the Embarcadero will provide all that, and become the boomingest little town in the whole country while it does it."

Harriet said nothing. Her mind was abruptly too full for her to form any words, that one word *theater* filling the whole arena of her brain. My God, she thought in a rush of wild inspiration, the three lieutenants and Don Roberto and Colonel Mason could all well be right, and if they were right . . .

"My God," she said softly, theaters. If men came from the big cities, from New York, New Bedford, Charleston, Cincinnati . . . the numbers would have to include fanciers of the stage, managers who would be prepared to risk all on a theater here. Managers? My God, she thought, not managers, but owners. As in any enterprise it was the owners who raked in the profits, while leading actors had to be satisfied with ten shillings a night with board and lodging and stabling for horses and the occasional benefit night . . .

She said swiftly, "How does one claim land in California?"

The three men gaped at her as if she'd taken leave of her senses. Then Don Roberto said, "Why Miss Gray, have I not told you the system before?" Before she could shake her head or nod he was in full self-important flow, then: "No claim be more'n one hundred feet square, no man can own more'n one current claim, no man shall own a claim and not work it, unless 'is tools be left there, all claims soundly staked with a notice, no man can jump a well staked claim or one with men or tools upon it, all disputes taken to the local alcalde, who decides the rights on payment of a fee."

"Yes, Don Roberto," she said impatiently. "Yes, you have told me that, but how do I buy a piece of the land that these gentlemen are surveying here?"

All four men could not have looked more astounded if Lady Godiva and her horse had come strolling by, Harriet thought with exasperation. "You, Miss Gray?" hooted Don Roberto. "*You* . . . buy land?"

He looked as scandalized as any American; Harriet said with little patience, "Not me, then, if that offends you, but—but the men on the brig, the *Hakluyt* Company."

"But why would they want a plot of land 'ere?"

"You've just been extolling the future of this place," she pointed out. "Have you changed your mind?"

"No, of course not, but . . ."

"All we want to do is make our fortune, like everyone else."

The men all shuffled and looked at each other, but this, it seemed, made more sense to them than anything else she had said, for Lieutenant Warner said with an air of benevolence, "And which plot do you fancy, ma'am?"

She looked about and pointed at random. "That one."

They all looked at the lot. Then Lieutenant Sherman looked at the charts. "On Front Street," he said. "On the block between I street and J."

Giving the lot a description seemed, somehow, to make it more real, and the men, accordingly, more cooperative. Don Roberto said musingly, "You'll 'ave to buy through the alcalde of this place—Sutter's son 'imself."

"Do you know him?"

"Of course, Miss Gray, of course!"

"Can you arrange it?"

"Certainly, ma'am!"

At a fee, no doubt, she thought cynically, but was too enthused to let it spoil her inspiration. She said instead, "How much should we offer?"

"A thousand."

"What! But that's terribly expensive!"

" 'Tis a bargain," said Lieutenant Warner. " 'Tis a bargain," said Lieutenant Ord. All four men nodded.

"Then I shall speak about it the moment I'm back on the brig."

"But what, if I might ask, ma'am, would you do with such a purchase?"

"We'd build a theater on it, of course! What else?" she inquired.

The transaction took a full four days, and still Jake Dexter had not arrived. He was still not back on the fifth afternoon, when Harriet stood poised in the middle of her plot of ground. The *Hakluyt* men all watched, some indulgently, some wise-cracking to fit the occasion, lined up along the starboard rail with a good close view, for the lot was right on the waterfront. Harriet waited, hammer in hand, and Don Roberto trotted up to her and handed her the precious notice.

She nailed it to the stake with her own hands while the *Hakluyt* men all threw their hats in the air and cheered with simple and good spirits. The notice stuck to the stake, and Harriet stood back to admire it. The words were in English.

NOTICE!

THIS PIECE OF GROUND, FORMERLY PART OF
THE RANCHO OF SUTTER'S FORT AND CON-
TAINING ONE THOUSAND SQUARE FEET OF
LAND, IS HEREBY CLAIMED, FOR THE PUR-
POSES OF A THEATER!

At the bottom it was signed by Don Roberto. "Congratula-
tions," said he, and shook Harriet's hand. Harriet laughed, and
all at once the nape of her neck felt aware.

It tingled. There was someone behind her, studying her.
Then she heard a most familiar chuckle; she turned very
quickly—and there was Jake Dexter.

He was standing by a hard-ridden horse and was holding the
reins. He was sun- and wind- and mosquito-bitten, and he had
his hat pushed back. He was grinning down at her, and for the
life of her she could not hold back the welcoming radiance. She
exclaimed entirely without thinking, "Oh, Jake, oh, Jahaziel,
'tis so good to see you!" and stood poised to throw her arms
about his neck . . . and a hoarse voice from the Embarcadero
said, "Ah, there you be, Cap'n Dexter, and you still owe me
the thirty dollars' fee for piloting your brig upriver."

She saw Jake frown, and she knew the old pilot's voice. In
that dreadful instant she remembered where she'd seen the old
man before. Not in California, but in Auckland, and then on
the whaleship *Humpback*.

He had been dirty and taciturn and unsociable on the
whaleship, too, and seldom had come down to the cabin.
Harriet turned slowly, feeling like wood, and with dreadful
inevitability she heard him say, spitefully, "Afternoon, Mrs.
Sefton."

Mrs. Sefton. She had traveled on the whaleship under her
married name. Oh, God, she thought, and numbly said, "Mr.
Paddack."

"Ah," said he, and nodded sourly. "I see you know me now,
Mrs. Sefton, for Paddack be indeed the name. I've been up the
Feather River, Mrs. Sefton. I've been up to see your
husband—or p'raps you disremembered too that Colonel
Sefton be a settler up the Feather River now. I thought to
meself he might be pleased to hear of ye and be interested, too,
in the happenstance that you don't sail on the brig under your

married name, and I were right, for he paid me well for the information, Mrs. Sefton, and he's not far behind me. He's a-coming to fetch you right soon."

The he spat to one side, barely missing her skirts, and Harriet, feeling sick, was able at last to shift her eyes. The first face she saw was Don Roberto's. His expression was strange, almost aghast, but she didn't have the strength to think about it then. Instead, she looked at Jake Dexter.

She expected to see embarrassment, and contempt, the expression she had dreaded for weeks. At least, she thought drearily, she had not embroiled him in this mess by confiding her problems; she had saved both of them the embarrassment of falling in love.

Then she saw the terrible disbelief and shock in Jake Dexter's face, that and the awful cynical pain, and she knew then, desperately, that she had been wrong.

16 ⤳   When Jake returned to his brig that night, Don Roberto insisted on accompanying him. The little alcalde seemed anxious and talked far too much. Jake strode with long angry paces along the path from the fort, and Don Roberto hurried along with trotting steps to keep up, panting but chattering nevertheless.

"Colonel Sefton is a most prosperous settler," he said, and, "Like Captain Sutter's son, he came late, only arriving jus' last fall, from Canton with money and a Chinese servant, and a Chinese ward and all, bought hisself a farm across the river from Pueblo San Marco, in my area of jurisdiction, thought of very highly by the Californian folk there, a most influential family named Vidrie. 'E even 'as a bank, the Bank for Miners, in Pueblo San Marco . . ."

Jake stopped listening. He said curtly, with pain and anger, "And did you know he had a wife?" as he turned onto the gangway to the deck of the brig.

Don Roberto scurried after him. "No, that I did not know," he said in those worried tones. "Miss Gray, yes, I knew she were from New Zealand, and Colonel Sefton mentioned once—" He broke off, looked around in the darkness, looked again at Jake, and said in furtive manner, "I had not a notion that Miss Gray were married, otherwise I would never have allowed 'er."

Jake stared, bewildered. "To do what?"

"There was a small matter of business, a signature—"

Don Roberto broke off, abruptly, and then belatedly Jake became aware that Bodfish had happened on the scene. The old steward was hopping about on the afterdeck, looking more than a little embarrassed. Jake forgot the alcalde on the instant, saying, "What is it?"

"Ah . . . sir, there be company in the transom, awaiting."

"What?" Jake frowned and then sighed, wondering what more this dreadful day held in store for him. He said curtly, "Who is it?"

"When I said company, sir, I didn't exactly mean guests." The steward's eyes avoided Jake's puzzled glare, as he said unhappily, "As a matter of fact, sir, it be Miss Gray."

"Oh, God." Jake had himself arranged hotel lodgings for Harriet, in Captain Sutter's house in the fort. He had gone to a great deal of trouble and expense to arrange it. He said savagely, "What the devil does she want?" He watched the old steward's mouth open, but forestalled him, turning to Don Roberto and saying brusquely, "I'm sorry, Mr. Ross, but I must ask you to leave."

"Don Roberto," said Don Roberto.

"What?"

" 'Tis the Mexican custom, sir, and bein' by law a Mexican citizen . . ."

Jake said nothing; he merely stared. Don Roberto started as if come all at once to his wits; he looked about and then with a lot of peevish flaunting of serape he went, trotting busily down the gangplank. Jake watched him go. When he turned again Bodfish had made himself scarce. Jake sighed again, braced his shoulders, and went below.

The door at the bottom of the stairs was open. Harriet was sitting on his sofa, her head bent in the position he knew so well, the light shining from the single lamp kindly on her downcast lashes and her hair. She must have heard him, he knew, but for a long moment she did not move. He stood and watched her, and for a moment all he wanted was to sit beside her and take her into his arms and bury his head in her lap. Hot angry craving wracked him . . . and then she looked up.

The spell was broken. He folded his arms as he stood over her, and he said curtly, "You mutiny, Harriet?"

Her lips twitched, making him angrier than ever, and she said softly, "Yes."

"I expected you to remove to the fort."

"I won't go until we've talked."

"Talked." The word was bitter. "You mean you've concluded at long last to convey the truth of your situation?" Then, unable to keep back the violence, he shouted, "Did I not have the right to know you were married?"

He saw her lips press together. Then she met his eyes and said quietly, "Of course you did, and I'm sorry I didn't tell you, more sorry than you would ever believe . . . but 'tis no use telling you that, I suppose. The day after I arrived on the brig I asked you if it would make any difference to my situation on board if I were married, and you said, No . . ." She looked away then, and her hand rose in a helpless gesture. Then she said softly, "Of course I should have told you, but there was always so much else to talk about; I enjoyed teasing you so, and I was . . . so happy on this brig, for the first time in more than a year I was so content. Can't you see that I was scared to spoil the happiness with telling you my problems? The world out there seemed so far away and unimportant . . . and then . . . and then, Royal told me that you were off to Monterey, that scuttlebutt had it that you were anxious to learn about the welfare of your wife."

He shouted, "I asked about my wife in Valparaíso too, if that holds interest! And the news I heard then encouraged me to ask further!" He was shaking, almost out of control, wracked with rage and humiliation that he should have been cheated twice. "And at Monterey I heard that the rumor was right, that my wife had divorced me, that I am now an unmarried man; *she divorced me* for stealing the bark that belonged to her lover, *she divorced me* for causing a public scandal, *she divorced me* and now is remarried, to that same lover—and they live most comfortable in the house I built before I left."

Harriet said. "Oh, God." Her voice was shocked, her face so white he could see the pink line of the healed cut on her cheek. Then, incredibly, he saw her try to smile. She said softly, "It must be a wonderful house."

He nodded curtly, unable at that moment to speak. He'd built that house with his own hands, honor-built, sailor-built, paid for with his money from his last voyage as mate and the legacy left by his parents. Everything he had owned had gone into that house; he had invested in the best bricks and most lasting cedar shingles. He had run to the extravagance of sixteen-paned windows and to the devil with the resulting taxes; he had pictured it half a century hence, filled with exuberant children, with a shell-and-coral wreath fastened to the door to tell passersby that this fine house belonged to a seaman.

Then he heard Harriet whisper, "I am so sorry, Jahaziel."

Sorry? He had been delighted when he'd heard for certain that he was no longer a married man; he had thought himself free to capture and claim this enticing waif. The last time Harriet had said she was sorry she had reached up and kissed him on the lips—and it had been that kiss that had done such damage.

He shouted, "How often do I have to tell you not to call me that!"

Harriet flinched, and he saw her go white; at that awful moment he felt as if he'd struck her. She cried, "Can't you find it in your heart to forgive me? Won't you listen, and try to understand me . . . and repent your decision to send me away from the brig?"

He said curtly, "Whatever I think and believe makes no difference. When your husband comes to claim you neither you nor I will have any choice. He's your legal husband; he owns you."

She shouted, "Never!" She was up on her feet, trembling, close to him, and his world narrowed to her wide stricken eyes. She cried, "You have no right to punish me by sending me back to that man; I have done nothing to deserve being shamed so utterly. Can't you understand that I was *ashamed* to tell you I was married?"

"Ashamed?" Jake's echo was blank. Then rage seethed; he was reminded of past nightmares, the endless awful self-questioning. Had his wife been ashamed of him; was that why she'd fallen so readily into the bed of an older, richer, man?

He shouted, "No decent woman is ashamed of being married!"

"No?" she demanded. Her breasts were rising and falling, rapidly. Then she said passionately, "I did not expect to be ashamed, Jake. I too thought that marriage implied honesty, responsibility, and loyalty. I married Frank Sefton gladly, because I thought I loved him, because I was convinced that he loved me. For God's sake, Jake, I was only sixteen, and he was a man of the world, more than forty! He was wealthy, a landowner. He went to New Zealand from Philadelphia and invested heavily in New Zealand property; my father was greatly in favor of the match. I knew there was some kind of business arrangement, but I thought little about it at the time. Arranged marriages, perhaps, are more common in England than they are in your land."

This last was wistful. Jake stared at her in angry perplexity. Arranged marriages in New England were unheard of; he'd thought they only occurred in exotic eastern countries. He said tersely, "What kind of business arrangement?"

She paused, as if choosing words carefully. Then she said quietly, "I know you will find this hard to believe, but Frank Sefton married me for my English nationality. As I said, he had invested heavily in New Zealand. Then, when the British took over the colony, they imposed discriminatory taxes to force the American investors out. Most went, but some, like Frank, hung on. They were hoping for a change in policy, no doubt. Instead the British government imposed a requirement that Americans give over their property, that they should donate it or sell it to English nationals, and if they sold it, the price was to be no more than the amount they had originally paid. So," she said, and sighed, "Sefton and my father devised a tidy scheme. The day before our wedding Sefton signed over all his holdings to me, putting it in my name as a dowry. My father and Royal—and a lawyer—witnessed the transaction."

Jake frowned, trying to puzzle this out. Then he said slowly, "Sefton gave you everything?"

"Yes, to avoid the taxes. As an Englishwoman, I did not have to pay them."

"And is that why you are ashamed, because you were party to such a devious plot?"

His tone was scornful, and he saw her flush red. "No! Sefton shamed me the day he left me! The day my father died I went home to find that he'd sailed away without a word."

"To California."

"No! He—he talked at times of California, yes, but the ship that carried him away from New Zealand was bound to Canton."

Canton; that, Jake remembered, was what Don Roberto had said. He folded his arms tightly and said in a low bitter tone, "You can't pretend that you're not married after all, just because your husband sailed off to another land to make his fortune. Men all over the world do that, and their wives do not think themselves deserted."

"But do they leave their wives homeless and destitute?" she shouted. Her eyes were wide and shiny with fury; for a moment he thought she might hit him with frustration. She cried, "I don't know how he did it, but somehow Sefton sold everything that he had given me, all the lands and property that were rightfully in my name; he sold them all at a gratifying profit, and then he took all that profit with him; Frank Sefton somehow cheated me and shamed me, and left me destitute and despised in an utterly foreign and friendless land!"

Jake paused, listening to the heavy thud of the blood in his throat. It was like the day she'd run to Royal instead of to him when the Murietas had attacked her. Then he roared, "Why didn't you tell me all this before?"

"Because I didn't want you to despise me too! Because—" Then she stopped. Her eyes left his and she looked down, her demeanor almost shy. She said very softly, wistfully, "Can't you see that I wanted you to think well of me, Jahaziel?" Then, slowly, she gazed up at him.

He was silent. Her lashes were long and shadowy, her eyelids heavy, almost blue, her lips just a little parted, the lower lip gleaming just a little, enticing. The bodice of her gown was cut in the English style, so much more revealing than any dress a New England woman would have worn, and he could see the sweet full curve of her bosom and guess at the inviting thrust of nipples. For the long space of a heartbeat he moved toward her; their breaths mingled; her eyes shut even further; he almost took her in his arms.

Then sense returned in a rush. She was an actress, she was trying most deliberately to seduce him into forgiveness and protection. He jerked back a step and shouted, "I don't believe you; despite all you say I refuse to credit that Sefton cheated you! How could he—if your story is true—for all the property belonged to you! How could he sell what he no longer owned?"

She was growing whiter with each curt word, her eyes stricken. Then she cried, "I don't understand it either, Jake, and don't think for a moment that I haven't worried it over and

over in my mind! I don't know how he did it, but Frank
somehow left me penniless; I even had to scrimp to pay for
Father's burial. Please don't make me go back to a man who
treated me so foully!"

"I have no choice; he's your legal husband."

"How can you call a man like that *husband*?"

"It makes do difference what I call him," Jake said bitterly.
"The fact remains that you are married, and I do not rob other
men of their wives."

Harriet said softly, "Oh, God, you really think that I'm
lying." Her eyes closed for one long moment, while he stared
at her and grappled with his own bitter pain.

Then she opened her eyes and said tonelessly. "I'm a
member of the company; you cannot send me away without
consultation with the men."

"You want to call a meeting?" he said incredulously. "And
air your problems to the men?"

"But we have to call a meeting, to discuss the land we
bought, for the purpose of building a theater."

The theater. Fury rose inside him. At a time like this, he
thought savagely, she was intent on her career; at a time like this,
when he was wracked so cruelly with disillusionment, she could
think of a theater.

Bodfish and Charlie had told him about it, how Harriet had
called a meeting the night the brig had made this place, how
she'd told them that she'd found a chance for a fine investment.
I can put a piece of most profitable business your way.

She had charmed and persuaded them all, and Don Roberto's
reasoned recommendations had done the rest. The men had
collected one thousand dollars out of their own pockets, in the
innocent belief that when their skipper returned and they had a
proper meeting, the company would repay what they'd shelled
out. "Once it was alpaca," Jake said curtly. "Do you really
think that a theater will do any better?"

She flashed, "It was not my fault that the alpaca were not
there! And," she added, albeit reluctantly, "it was not Royal's
fault either."

"And what, pray, led you to the delusion that I would want
to build a theater?"

She snapped, "You're a shrewd businessman, Jake, and I
thought you'd see the possibilities. A theater here cannot but
do well! I've told you, I'm certain, that men in far-flung spots
always turn to theater for recreation."

That, he thought unwillingly, was true. In Monterey Colonel Mason had shown him a little playhouse the soldiers had made. It was perhaps the first theater in California—or that was what Captain Mervine had declared. It was set up in a wing of an old adobe hall, with pit, scenery, stage, a wooden drop curtain.

Harriet was watching him, her eyes intent on his expression, and as if she read his mind she said swiftly, "Now that we have the land, the rest is easy. You've concluded already to moor the brig here for the winter, and leave a gang of shipkeepers while the rest of you dig into the hills and watch over a claim until spring. The shipkeepers would have time a-plenty to build the structure. We have the timber, once the berths in the hold are dismantled, we have the material for the walls. You've seen the calico buildings here! And we'll have custom enough, once February comes. Why, the passengers on the river passage were willing even to pay Bill coins in order to view the llamas!"

"And who would play, on this stage you think to build so easily? Royal, perhaps?"

She flushed at that, rebelliously, but said only, "No."

"What? Your brother does not share your vision?"

She bridled at his sarcasm and snapped, "Royal wants to try his luck at the mines."

"What?" said he, and started elaborately. "Well then, what players will you employ? Surely not Crotchet or Valentine!"

"Crotchet and Valentine are certainly talented," she said curtly. "However, yes, they wish to try the diggings too. But there are always players to be hired."

"What? You think there will be actors begging for employment, when the mines are so uncommon beckoning?"

"There are certainly fortunes to be made in California," she said defensively, "but you told me yourself that those fortunes can be made in other ways than digging."

"And you? Would you go on the stage, for the entertainment of men?"

She went bright red at that, and with obvious fury she shouted, "Don't act the righteous prig with me now, Jake Dexter! I've been 'entertaining men,' as you put it so nicely, ever since I was born, for my mother acted Rosalind on my birthday! You forget that I come from a stage family: I learned my first words from listening to my mother, father, aunt on stage; I learned to read from the scripts of comedies and melodramas! And how can you play the prim Yankee? You're a self-admitted adventurer and resourceful too: you know full well how to make a profit by doings right flamboyant. And the men who come here will be the same sort: lawyers, medicos, shipcaptains and soldiers, farmers and writers, merchants and whalemen, and they'll pay good gold, the lot of 'em, for the privilege of theatrical entertainment!"

"Ah, yes," said Jake bitterly, "we're all adventurers, and we all need our grubstake, and no one more than you. You learned your eloquence from your family, too, no doubt, and no doubt these were the very impassioned arguments that you summoned when you duped some of my men out of a total of one thousand dollars, just to set yourself up in the theatrical trade."

She went white again, staring at him. Then she said furiously, "You bastard. I would never, ever, cheat your men, and you know it."

"Oh, yes? What I do know," he said with savage pain, "is that you stopped to talk to me for this reason and no other. You did not stay to explain your silence, or even to beg my forgiveness. What you wanted was to make sure of your theater, to get the thousand dollars' backing for your scheme."

She stared at him, her eyes wide and unseeing, her arms folded so tightly over her breasts that he could see her knuckles on her elbows turn bluish. Then she said in a shocked, toneless voice, "You don't really think that." He said nothing; he was unable to move or do anything but watch her with that awful rage and pain locked inside him. She shivered and whispered, "Oh, dear God, what will they think of me?"

And still he was silent. For a long moment the only sounds were the bumps of the brig against the wooden wharf and the low silky rush of the Sacramento River flowing along the brig's coppering. Their eyes were tangled, and again he was tempted to forgive her, to take her as his mistress, to stop here and give her a theater . . . or to sail away, forever. His hand even began to lift, but before he could touch her she turned.

She began to walk out of the transom cabin with short quick steps. Then her head turned so that she glanced at him over her shoulder. "Tell your men they will get their money back," she said crisply. "I will repay this debt too—the way I paid all the others."

Then, before he could stop her, she was gone. He heard her steps rattling on the gangplank. Then he heard Bodfish's voice, hailing her, and the steward's hurried footsteps as he pursued her. The old man was still calling out, in a voice that rapidly faded with distance.

Then nothing, nothing but silence. After a long moment Jake moved. He looked about, stiffly, not sure what he was seeking. Then he sighted the brandy bottle. Then he sat down on the sofa.

17 〰️ The room that Jake Dexter had arranged for Harriet was in the central building of the fort. Bodfish escorted her there, once he caught her up, and Harriet listened distractedly to the old steward's embarrassed mumbling, feeling the heat of her anger turn inevitably to the cold of near-panic.

She couldn't stop here, not in California where Sefton would find her and take her to his house or desert her again according to his whim. She stumbled along the path, holding up her skirts to save them from being dirtied by unmentionable things in the dark. It was night, but men and animals jostled all about, and the clouds flying across the face of the moon lit up gleaming faces and the trappings of harnesses in melodramatic spasms. The walls of the fort loomed up suddenly out of nowhere. There were Indians seated all about the entrance, some with blankets pulled over their heads. They all smelled of ardent spirits, and one reached out as she passed. She moved away nervously, frightened that he would snatch at her skirts. Then they were through, into the compound.

Smoky red fires were all about, and the mysterious dark shapes of tall trees. A sharp voice called out in Spanish, in a kind of challenge. Neither Harriet nor Bodfish answered, but Harriet quickened her steps. She could smell manure and flies and scorched meat turning bad, urine and sweat, both of horses and men. The gamblers still plied their trade in the shifting light of small cressets, but very few men responded to the ringing of their little bells; very few men seemed to be awake. Coming to El Dorado, Harriet mused, was a tiring business, and then her mind turned and nagged at her awful problem again: How in the name of dear Providence was she to get away from California?

They were at the outside flight of steps to the upper stories of Captain Sutter's house. Harriet silently followed the bobbing shapes of her baskets on the steward's shoulder, up to the second-floor entrance. When she followed Bodfish inside she was instantly aware of the presence of many men. She could see them lolling about on benches as they tried to sleep upright, or sitting crouched over small books or packs of cards. Some were writing—perhaps letters home or journals. There was a massed creaking from the ceiling where men slept crammed together in the attics, that and the pit-saw sound of concerted snoring. The air was so stuffy that it was about unbreathable. Bodfish stopped and Harriet stopped, too, to watch him as he tapped at a door.

The door, she knew, led to the room where Jake had booked her a bed. Prior to this summer it had been Sutter's dining room, where he had entertained Californian guests. As Bodfish tapped, the door creaked open, but no one came out. Instead of a questioning voice, all Harriet heard was more snoring. Then Bodfish pushed her baskets toward her and Harriet roused herself and took them.

He muttered a good-night and made to go off, but Harriet softly called him back. "Tomorrow," she said, and, "I will find the money, I promise." He merely nodded, mumbling awkwardly again, and Harriet, sighing, found herself alone.

She moved hesitantly into the dark room and shut the door. It was all at once pitch dark. She stood with her back to the door, the baskets at her feet, and waited while her sight adjusted. It was like the night of the day of her father's burial, the night she had abruptly found herself without a roof over her head. Then she had removed to the hotel where her father had lived; she had taken over his room and found in the morning that she had not only to pay a good round sum for her night's lodging but was presented with the unpaid bill for her father's past lodging as well.

But she refused, refused, *refused* to feel self-pity. She had managed then and would cope with this too. Instead of weeping she concentrated on getting her bearings, listening to the feminine snoring from the bed in the other corner, on sorting out which bed was hers. Some man in the loft above cried out hoarsely in his sleep, and other men cursed him for waking them up. It sounded then as if an awkward brawl broke out; there was some shouting and commotion, and then abruptly all was snoring quiet again. Harriet moved stiffly.

Her bed had a thin straw mattress, and there was no blanket. Harriet undressed to her shift and then took her wool shawl and lay down under it. She did not close her eyes but stared into the noisy darkness instead. California . . . she had to escape California. She thought of San Francisco then, and the abandoned ships: it seemed chillingly evident that few ships if any quit these shores. California was a golden trap, and she . . . she had very little money. Joining the *Hakluyt* Company had been a desperate gamble. Oh, dear God, she thought, but refused to cry. After an endless interval she went to sleep. When she woke up she found she had wept in her dreams, for the pillow was damp, and the sky outside was weeping too, gray and drizzling outside the single window.

The humped shape in the other bed was silent. Harriet got up and dressed stealthily, reluctant to face any kind of conversation. There was a single washstand in one corner, with one pitcher, one bowl; and looking glass, comb, and toothbrush all chained to the stand to prevent theft. The jug and bowl were empty; Harriet took up the jug and hesitantly opened the door.

Men sat hunched in chairs under blankets, while others were curled in tight spaces on the floor. Above, in the attics, there was a great commotion of rousing men. Some were even singing, apparently glad enough to be here, even if the hills were veiled in streaming rain. There were more men out in the compound, rain blackening their hats, waiting in yawning queues at the well and the steaming ovens. Before she joined the line for water Harriet walked out to the entrance. She could see the Embarcadero in the mile-long muddy distance. The brig was moored snug, and a schooner had joined her.

A schooner. Harriet turned quickly, illogically afraid that someone on board the vessel would see her. When men spoke jocularly to her at the well she scarcely heard them and did not reply. Her head bent, she carried the water to the house and upstairs.

The other occupant of the room, she immediately saw, was awake. This female was sitting on the edge of the other bed, contemplating a tumbler of clear liquid that she held raised in one hand. She wore only shift and petticoats, which did little to disguise an exuberant figure; she was middle-aged, or at an age that she no doubt considered *interesting,* and her abundant coarse hair was dyed black.

Harriet said rather cautiously, "Good morning," and the woman turned to look at her. Then she applied her attention to the tumbler again. As well as liquid it held teeth, and as Harriet watched, unwillingly fascinated, the teeth were extracted, popped into the waiting mouth as if by magic, and then the liquid was drained at one gulp.

Then the lady smiled, radiantly. "Good morning!" she cried. "Though that statement be not true, I see, I do verity an injustice. 'Tis not good at all, for I hear and see rain, and—*hist!*—we miserable folks be all drenched again."

Harriet gaped; she couldn't help it. Not even on the provincial circuits had she met a woman so eccentric. Her silence did not seem to faze her companion in the slightest; instead she looked about, grabbed up a gown, and commenced to haul it over her head. "Does my manner of speech intrigue you?" Her demand came muffled from within the folds. "I have a gift for rhyme and cannot leash the facility; it demands to be ever unleashed!" Then she wriggled, came out red-faced and panting, and said, "Mrs. Abiah Marchant!"

"Miss Harriet Gray," said Harriet. They shook hands, American style, and Harriet became all at once aware that the liquid in the glass had been gin.

She didn't mind that; throughout her childhood she had been used to sporting men and drinking women. Instead her mind was abruptly touched with hope, for here was not only a fellow female in this place that was so greatly dominated by men, but a female, moreover, who spoke English, albeit with a broad Yankee accent.

Here, perhaps, was the key to her escape from California. She said carefully, "Have you been in Sutter's long?"

"Naught but one week, Miss Gray!"

"But how did you get here?"

"By ship," Mrs. Marchant said airily, and waved a hand. Then she allowed Harriet to read the journal she had kept on passage. To Harriet's further bemusement the diary proved to be a tiny handmade book, stitched together and measuring no more than two inches either way. Its contents—of course, thought Harriet, marveling—were in verse.

> *"May the eight, eighteen-forty-eight*
> *On the good ship* Magnolia *I my berth did take*
> *To calafornia for to go*
> *To seek my fortune, weal or no . . ."*

"Merciful heavens," said Harriet, and turned another minute page.

"Ain't it, Miss Gray, ain't it a wonder?" quoth the complacent diaress. Harriet nodded, beyond words, and continued reading.

The diary ended in 'Frisco.

> *". . . The hills of calafornia are very high and green*
> *But the adobe dwellings are thought to be mean*
> *The journey is over, this journal is done*
> *The captain's wife yesterday bore him a son."*

"I am in the throes of composing another versifying journey," quoth Mrs. Marchant then. "Based on my own travels, but nonetheless most fanciful. 'Twill be the story, Miss Gray, of a young miner misguided enough to bring his wife to this extempore place. On their very wedding day he catched the gold fever and couldn't make up his mind 'twixt love and lust for the yellow dust, and carried her along, the dithering fool. How romantic the tale will be! Like the captain's wife, this young miner's lady will bear him a son, and expire soon thereafter."

"But what happened to the real captain's wife?" asked Harriet.

"Who knows, Miss Gray, who knows?"

"But I can't imagine why she consented to come along, or what you are doing in California either."

"But the poem tells you!" hooted Mrs. Marchant. "I came to make my fortune, of course!" Then she produced a visiting card, which Harried took rather warily.

It announced that Mrs. Marchant taught the gentle art of painting on velvet. "*Here*?" said Harriet, unstoppably amazed.

"But the gentle pursuits are of the most essential in this rough and extempore land, Miss Gray! Without the presence of the gentle arts the men of California will be lost beyond cure in pursuit of unlawful pleasures and indulgence in enervating vice."

"But . . . here, in Sutter's Fort, *velvet painting*?"

"Nope, not here," said Mrs. Marchant, for the first time sounding impatient. "The rains will come, they come today, for just look out to see rain hold sway . . . and, for certain, I'll do better business in 'Frisco, as the inhabitants return, to await the drought of spring. And then . . . and then, aha, we'll see!"

Harriet ignored this last, however, seizing on the possibility of return to San Francisco. The port might be only the first part of a journey away from this land, but it was certainly a step in the right direction. She said swiftly, "How will you get to 'Frisco?" but the lady ignored her.

"Breakfast," she said compelling. "I hear the merry bell, that tells us preparations all go well." Harriet heard no bell but went with her.

The dining room turned out to be a large long house tucked against the northern wall of the fort, hard up against the kitchens. It was deafeningly noisy, crowded with men. A greasy pine table took up the length of it, and the benches on either side were full of hollering customers who voiced their impatience by hammering with their jackknives on the tabletop. Other men lay on the floor all rolled up in blankets, while others sat and scratched their heads, evidently in the places where they had slept all night. More men walked about, kicking bottles and bags. Harriet stood in the doorway, blinking and feeling dazed, and a fat man came out of the doorway that led to the kitchens, looked about, and then hailed Mrs. Marchant.

This gentleman, Harriet found, was mine host, the man in charge of this restaurant and all the lodging places; he was the agent appointed by Captain Sutter's son. She sat in the chair that was miraculously produced by this man, and Mrs. Marchant, not looking diffident in the slightest, sat beside her with Mr. King on her other side. Then, in procession, the food arrived, all borne on huge tin platters by sweating pigtailed Chinese cooks.

Meats: stewed meats, roast meats, fried meat, and huge elk steaks, chops all sliding about in quivering gravies, sliced meats and hashes. The smells of grease and sweat were overpowering, and a greasy steam rose into the rough-hewn rafters. Hard bread and biscuits and frijoles were served up, too, and molasses in little dishes, but there was not a fruit nor a vegetable to be seen. All the time that Harriet watched the dishes go by, Mr. King and Mrs. Marchant held vivacious conversation. Harriet did not have a single chance to insert a question about getting to San Francisco.

The air was redolent with flirtatiousness as well as steaming meat, and as the talk went on Harriet deduced that Mr. King and the versifying female were somewhat more than acquaintances. Perhaps Mrs. Marchant, she thought, saw the fortune she desired in the person of this fat man, and Mr. King seemed certain sure of making his own fortune too.

He would do it with the accommodation trade, he told her. He was highly delighted with his venture thus far and told Harriet all about it. He quoted prices, profits, numbers of guests, and his voice rang out with more than sincerity, for the rest of the room was most unnervingly silent. All of the men at the table were eating like wolves, and none of them spared time for talk. As Harriet watched in disbelief men poured molasses onto platters of meat and then demolished the mixture with their knives, with no resort to spoons or forks. The only sounds were the rattle of tin dishes and knives, the champing of jaws, and Mr. King's talk.

Mr. King planned to build a hotel of his own, somewhere on the Embarcadero, at the place where the soldiers were surveying the streets. Harriet said swiftly, seizing her chance, "Have you made that purchase yet?"

"In the spring," he boomed, "in the spring!"

"But why not before that?" Harriet countered. If she sold him the ground she had bought for the theater, some of her problems would be solved, she thought. She had the deed to the land, and the ground was properly staked and claimed. She could ask a little more than one thousand dollars and get funding for her escape as well as the repayment for the *Hakluyt* men.

"Spring, Miss Gray, will be time enough!"

"But won't you build your hotel this winter?"

"No, no," he chuckled, and seemed highly mirthful. "It rains here, in cataracts, ain't you seen the rain out there yet?

No, no, off to 'Frisco I do go, and with me my dear Mrs. Marchant." He reached across and jocularly slapped a large thigh, receiving a playful push in return. "And I'll make my plans!" he cried. "It'll be a true Yankee hotel in true American style. Carpets!" he cried. "Chandeliers!" Then, while Harriet stared at him in suspense, waiting her chance to insert another question, a bell rang.

The men at the table all stopped eating, all at once and together. It was only fifteen minutes since the bell to start had rung, but the men all stood and walked out of the room with many regretful over-the-shoulder glances. Some picked their teeth as they went, and others hauled tobacco cuds out of the places where they had stowed them and set them back betwixt their jaws. "Fifteen minutes be time enough," said Mr. King severely. This, it seemed, was one if the secrets of making a tremendous profit. The Chinese cooks came in and hastily wiped down the table and then went back for more huge platters of meat and little dishes of molasses; there was, it seemed, a second setting, and a queue of eager men awaiting the bell to take their places.

The bell rang. Even Mr. King had to stop his talking as men shoved and fought to get onto the benches, for the noise was so tremendous. Harriet, however, had a voice that was trained to overcome the ruckus of the noisiest of pit audiences.

She shouted, "If you are going to San Francisco, how do you get there?"

"By ship, of course!" he bellowed.

"But what ship, pray?"

"The old ship, the boardinghouse ship, the one set up at the Embarcadero," he said. His voice rang out all at once as the men set to their chewing, and his laughter was even louder as he surveyed Harriet's expression. "Didn't you see her?" he demanded. "They've been setting up her rigging; the folks what run her have made their fortune, yes, and now they sail for 'Frisco and the seas beyond."

They were? Oh, dear Providence, Harriet thought, here was her chance at escape indeed. She opened her mouth to ask price, time, date, to offer her piece of land . . . for what? one thousand dollars plus one hundred and fifty? But Mr. King was distracted by the arrival of a bowl of steaming stew, which was placed on the table in front of him.

This was evidently a treat, judging by Mrs. Marchant's exclamations, and Harriet nodded when Mr. King made to fill her plate˙too. She said rather breathlessly, "Mr. King—"

He said loudly, laughing, "They might've made their fortunes, yes, but they be going one year too soon, they are, for this time next year even greater fortunes will be made in the lodging trade. Bathtubs!" he cried.

"I beg your pardon?"

"In my new hotel. It'll have bathrooms."

"With bathtubs?"

"That's it! Long tubs, tubs what a man can stretch his bones in."

Harriet paused. Both Mr. King and Mrs. Marchant were beaming at her expectantly, and her mind was so full she didn't know what to say first. Then Mr. King forestalled her by saying, "Like the stew?"

"It's delicious."

"'Tis coon," said he, beaming . . . and Frank Sefton walked into the room.

18 ❧   Her husband. For a terrible moment her mind went blank and she did not recognize this man. Then Frank Sefton took off his hat and his fine hair gleamed in the light from the doorway. She thought, that's Frank Sefton. Men all about were obliviously bolting food in California style, and Mr. King had risen to his feet, exclaiming happily; Mrs. Marchant had her hands clasped together, but nevertheless New Zealand was all around Harriet. She remembered the day her father and Royal had brought this admirer to her attention, and Colonel Francis Sefton looked just as he had on that day

He was urbanely handsome. Weirdly, she felt relief, for she'd lain awake so many nights wondering why she had been such a fool as to marry such a man. His suit was more than damp but of excellent quality, and his face was as sleek as on the day he'd first declared himself enchanted. His manner, too, was as courteous: he went over Mrs. Marchant's tremulously extended hand as gallantly as he did over Harriet's.

He said: "I came the very moment I heard of your presence in this land, dear Harriet; I crossed the river and boarded my schooner and ordered sail set that very next day."

She stared at him. His words seemed meaningless; she was aware only of the smooth hand holding hers. She pulled away her fingers and wanted to wipe her palm on her skirt, but instead she said, "Schooner?"

"My schooner, Harriet, moored at this moment at the Embarcadero. You will soon see what a beautiful vessel she is! She is but newly made, my lovely schooner, made for the river trade, and is nameless yet, but now that you have come at last to join me, dear Harriet, the name for my beautiful schooner is obvious. 'Tis a crowning jewel to my success in this land! Harriet, my dear, you have not a notion, you will not believe that a man could do so well in such a brief time. I have a bank, a rancho, all kinds of profitable speculations in Pueblo San Marco up the Feather River; what I have accomplished is the embodiment of what ingenuity can accomplish in this golden land!"

Mrs. Marchant, beside Harriet, was palpitating at the presence of so elegant a man; she was like the women of the colony of Auckland, when Colonel Sefton had been the most eligible bachelor in the whole of New Zealand. "My dear Harriet's arrival could not have been better timed," he exclaimed to her. "I have such invitations, extended by the first families of the upper Feather, the Californian dons named Vidrie. We will have fandangoes, bear-baiting, bull-fighting, and all the variations of the California sport, and we will extend many invitations of our own. Do say, my dear Mrs. Marchant, and you, Mr. King, sir, that you will be able to accept one or two of these?"

Mrs. Marchant fluttered. Obviously she would have adored to sigh an affirmative. However, Mr. King cleared his throat and gruffly said that, no, it wasn't possible, for they were leaving Sutter's bound for 'Frisco, the very next day. He didn't sound too regretful, Harriet thought. Mrs. Marchant's so obvious admiration of another man had made him a trifle jealous, no doubt, but Harriet's mind was too preoccupied to think much of that. "Perhaps next spring," Mr. King said gruffly, but Harriet was thinking, the ship to San Francisco sailed the next day . . . next day!

All she needed was the money for her fare and the chance to get away. She said desperately, "Do you sail upriver soon?

Surely not, when I have made such friends. Delay a day, please do," she said to Sefton.

If he noticed that these were the first words she had spoken to him, he did not allow it to affect his complacent attitude. He smiled, in the pouting rosebud smile she had almost forgotten she hated so much, and said, "Harriet, Harriet, after all this time, surely you will consent to come quickly to the home I've prepared for you in this land?"

"But I must see Royal—"

"Ah yes, Royal," he said. His face was the smooth face of a cardplayer, she thought. "What wonders we have to show your brother, truly! But he has signed up, it seems, for a mining company, or so I learned from an . . . informant. Such dreams of gold as he harbors! He will come to stop a while, my dear, once he has made the strike he no doubt expects most confidently to make in the hills. But my fortune, dear Harriet, is even more golden, golden with promise! Cattle, horses, grazing lands, I can't even begin to enumerate them all."

Nonetheless, he enumerated them. So he had not even seen Royal yet, Harriet thought drearily; both men, no doubt, would be glad to see no sign of each other, there being the prickly topic of alpaca to be discussed between them. "How the Californian women will envy my wife's blond beauty!" he rhapsodized to Mr. King. "But I shall not allow the men to look, for I am wild with jealously already, dear Harriet, as wild as I was when no letters came in reply to mine."

"*Letters*?" she cried. "*What* letters?"

"Letters go a-missing, you know that," he said reprovingly. His mouth was pursed again. "I assure you I speak no less than truth, when I say that I made every effort to get word of your welfare. How could you believe any less of me, when I am your loving and lawful wedded swain?"

Harriet kept her mouth shut; she was shaking too much to speak. She felt sick, and her skin felt clammy. "Come, my dear, you must pack your belongings," Sefton said, and she found her elbow gripped in an implacable hand, turning her toward the door. Still she said nothing; the bell rang at that moment, and with a clattering and commotion the second setting was forced to quit the room.

Harriet went alone up the stairs to the second-floor entrance of Sutter's house. Her last glimpse of the compound was the sight of Sefton standing in the rain, impassively watching her.

Surely he wouldn't stop there, with the weather so inclement? She shut the door and collapsed onto the edge of her bed, her arms tightly folded, hugging her breasts as she tried to stop the shuddering, tried to make plans.

The door clicked open. Harriet's heart tried to lurch into her throat. Then she saw it was Mrs. Marchant. The woman shut the door again and whispered piercingly, "You could've knocked me down with the veritable feather, most truly! Everyone knows of Colonel Sefton, he is second only to Captain Sutter in prominence! But no one knew, and I must confess it, that Colonel Sefton owns a wife. Tell me," said she most confiding, "do you have a reason, perhaps, for calling yourself *Miss Gray*?"

Reasons? Harriet could think of more than one hundred if she felt like trusting this inquisitive and garrulous woman. Instead she said carefully, "Miss Harriet Gray is my stage name; I'm an actress."

"An actress?" It was a shriek, and Harriet flinched. "Oh!" cried Mrs. Marchant; she had her hands clasped before her bosom again. "Such poesy sublime, Miss Gray! And, ah yes, I must confide my little secret, that I myself—yes, me!—I have ofttimes longed to tread the Thespian planks. I've faltered often on the threshold of drama's shadowy land, drama's hands have beckoned me, thrilling from the strand."

"They have?" said Harriet blankly; she felt enmeshed in an illogical nightmare, but the strained quality of her silence did not seem to affect Mrs. Marchant, if indeed she noticed Harriet's tension, for she dropped her voice to a whisper.

"And furthermore, Miss Gray, I must confess it, that at times I too have played a role, with grass as stage and moon and stars as illumination. It was in the very best of causes, in the case of the salvation of others. Certain camp preachers vied to procure my services as an actress, in their mission to find sinners and make them repent. You've not a notion how often I have stood and listened to the sermon, and when the preacher cried out, Repent! I were the first to cry, I do repent, I do! Oh, the times I've been reformed, Miss Gray, the times I have fallen to my knees and cried, Amen! and, Glory, glory! and the preacher has cried out to others to follow my example, Miss Gray, and I can tell you with all modesty that my example was never known not to bear fruit."

"My God," said Harriet, staring at her. For not the first time it occurred to her that Mrs. Marchant was no better than she ought to be and was probably an adventuress and perhaps a sporting woman. With that thought she made up her mind and said in a swift low voice, "I'd be in your debt forever, Mrs. Marchant, if you would lend me money."

"Money?" Mrs. Marchant's eyes bulged. "What for?"

"To get away."

"From Colonel Sefton?"

"Yes."

"But don't you have money of your own?"

"No," said Harriet wryly, "I do not."

"But how much do you need?"

"Enough to buy my fare to wherever that ship that leaves in the morn might be going." She paused, her eyes intent on Mrs. Marchant's speculative expression, and then added, "I can give you security, in the form of a deed to some land, land which I think Mr. King might be willing to buy."

Silence. Then as Harriet watched, the woman's expression became illuminated, salacious. Mrs. Marchant said in a piercing whisper, "You have an . . . arrangement, perhaps, with another man; your heart lies with another?"

Oh, Jake, Harriet internally mourned; an "arrangement" was just now the most unobtainable of her dreams. Nevertheless she lowered her lashes and said demurely. "Yes."

"Ah . . ." Mrs. Marchant drew back and her manner became conspiratorial.

The arrangements did not take long. Harriet left her packed baskets for Mrs. Marchant to bring along when she boarded the ship herself that night, and then, money in hand, she stole to the door. The room beyond was empty, and there was no sign of Sefton at the bottom of the outside stairs. The whole compound, indeed, was about empty; the rain, she assumed, had driven all the men indoors in other places.

Within a hundred yards she was drenched and cold and shivering despite her rapid pace. It was not yet October, but winter had come. The path was mired with mud and slimed manure; she remembered how Don Roberto had described to her how the trails into the diggings became impassable by the end of the month. Down by the waterfront the scene was even more miserable. Even the three lieutenants had gone, perhaps packed up until spring. Harriet slipped and stumbled in places, and then all at once she was at the gangplank that led to the boardinghouse ship.

She hesitated, looking up at it. After the brig the hull seemed huge. There was mud dripping from the planking, no doubt the results of being moored here for months. She had scarcely noted the ship before, because it was hidden so in the riverside thicket, but now, unpleasantly, she was assailed by a sense of familiarity. She paused, looking around, trying to pinpoint the horrid sensation. A hundred yards up the path the brig *Hakluyt* was moored, and, beyond the brig, the schooner. Sefton's schooner. Harriet moved quickly, darting up the gangplank to the ship.

She arrived on deck and was immediately beset with still more insistent misgivings. The deck planking was in two layers, the upper being chipped and stained; there was a brick furnace built in the waist deck; the whole deck stank, of . . .

Of oil. She was on a whaleship. She was instantly transported to the miserable passage across the southern Pacific, to . . . to Judas Island. Oh God she thought; she felt sick; she saw the short, bow-legged figure of Captain Smith heading her way. She was on the *Humpback,* and all her plans for escape were tumbled about her. There was Mrs. Smith heaving into view, her huge breasts swinging the way they always had; Harriet swallowed on a dry clenched throat, remembering how Mrs. Smith's chin had always stuck out thus, like a knobbled boot.

Both captain and wife stopped short in front of her. Mrs. Smith nodded curtly and said, "I cannot say I'm glad to see you, Mrs. Sefton, for we're a deal busy for callers; it ain't convenient."

"It was never convenient!" Harriet cried. It was like a nightmare; she wanted to pinch herself, for then she might wake. Oh, dear God, how these people had tricked and cheated her, and now, incomprehensibly, they were here to frustrate her again. "Why did it have to be you?" she shouted, shaking. "Why did my luck have to be so foul? Your reason for foisting me onto Captain Dexter was that you were bound home about Cape Horn and did not wish to stop, so why, why, *why,* are you here?"

"Ain't your business," said Mrs. Smith. "We spoke a-ship and a-heared about the gold here, steered this-a-way, profited by that, but it ain't your business whatsoever."

"Isn't it?" said Harriet drearily. "Isn't it?" Then, without waiting for an answer, she turned and walked away. It was not until she stumbled that she realized she was weeping with anger and frustration. She was still holding the money that

Mrs. Marchant had given her. She turned when she arrived on the path and walked blindly toward the *Hakluyt*.

There was a man on the path coming toward her. She stopped short. It was Jake. He stopped; they faced each other in silence. He looked haggard, dreadful, unshaven, wonderful. She could sense the bitter anger inside him, and she said very tentatively, "Jake?"

He said nothing. Instead his eyes moved to look at something behind her. She heard the steps, then, and knew who it was before Sefton's hand gripped her arm. When she turned her head Sefton's expression was bland, but the grip of his fingers was vicious.

He said in his smooth voice, "Captain Dexter, I owe you a debt of gratitude. You could not have done me a greater favor than to bring my dear wife to my side. Name your price, sir, name your price! All you need to do is send an accounting to my bank in Pueblo San Marco, and that price will be paid, and that right prompt."

Harriet said nothing; she couldn't. Her mouth was parched with the desperate words that she could not voice; her mind was leaden with utter despair. Jake looked so . . . unforgiving. He stood quite still, warily, in the pose she knew so well. The rain dropped off the brim of his hat, but he did not seem to be aware of it.

"And," said Sefton, smiling, "I have this for you, as well."

Harriet felt him move, then, and watched him reach with his free hand into an inside pocket. Sefton brought out a folded paper and reached out to give it to Jake.

Jake was slow to take it. "What is it?" he said curtly.

"A note for one thousand dollars, sir, money that I owe you."

"For . . . your wife's passage?" Still Jake did not look into her eyes; he said stiffly, "It is far too much. I don't want any payment."

"But 'tis recompense, Captain! My wife's theatrical notion must not leave you and your men in unnecessary debt."

It took a long incredulous moment for Sefton's bland words to sink into Harriet's mind. Then her stomach lurched, and she cried, "My . . . *what*?"

"You heard me, my dear." Chillingly, Sefton seemed disdainfully amused. "My wife, Harriet, was such a bewitching little girl when I first met her," he said patronizingly to Jake. "Such a pretty young charmer, and I see that charming naïveté yet. She thinks to build a theater in this place, surely against your better judgment! Look at the rain, silly goose," he said to Harriet while she stared at him in fast-growing consternation. "Picture the way this place will be in one-month's time, naught but a tract of swamp, just the way it was last winter, just as it will be next year. Build a theater in this place? Nonsense."

Harriet was shivering. She said in a hiss, "How did you find out the idea was mine, Frank? Who told you?"

Sefton stared at her, his mouth pouting, but Jake moved abruptly before the words came out. Jake snapped, "Was this your wife's idea, to give the money back?"

"But of course, Captain! Who else?"

Harriet flinched; Jake was staring at her with bitter hurt, as if he hated her, and she couldn't bear it. She shouted, "Frank, answer me! How did you know that I paid one thousand; how do you know that I borrowed it from Captain Dexter's men, and how in God's name do you know that it was I who signed the bill of sale?"

Sefton's eyes blazed; they went red the way she so horridly remembered. At that moment she truly thought that if Jake had not been there she would have been throttled. However, his voice was as bland as ever when he said, "Take it, Captain Dexter, take it; as Harriet's husband I hold myself responsible for all her debts and obligations."

His hand moved then to propel Harriet along the path on the way to the schooner. Her sight was blurred again, but she saw Jake take one step to block their path.

His tight voice said to Sefton, "Keep your bill; I don't want it."

Sefton stopped. Harriet tried to tug her arm away but failed; she would have bruises in the morning, she knew. She blinked wildly at tears of pain and frustration but learned nothing from Jake's face.

Sefton said curtly, "You're a fool if you don't accept the sum, for the land is mine by right, because my wife signed the bill of sale. The decision of what to do with the land is entirely mine. According to law I don't have to pay you at all."

Harriet said bitterly, remembering other documents she'd signed as blithely, "Is my signature worth so very much?"

"Harriet, my dear," said Sefton, who gave her another little shake, "your signature is worth precisely nothing; that is what I am trying to explain."

Nothing. Was that true? Harriet's mind seemed trapped in a circle, endlessly seeking some kind of sense. "But how did you learn that it was my signature?" she said, but was too weary with despair to wait for the reply. She looked at Jake, yearningly, desperately, and she said, "Take it."

Jake shifted. He looked the way she felt: caged, frustrated, wracked with fruitless longing; he looked a full ten years older than the man she had known on the brig. He said, "But—"

She said, "Please." Then she allowed Sefton to lead her away to the schooner.

The schooner certainly was beautiful, varnished and shiny above decks and below. Harriet thought bitterly that it was little wonder she was expected to be so impressed, for the vessel certainly boasted that her owner was a rich and successful man. The schooner was large for these waters, only a little smaller than the brig *Hakluyt*, but the crew was a small one, of but four men and one sailing master. All five men looked furtive and were wearing scraps of regimentals; they were deserters, she wearily assumed, driven out of the mines by the rain but too frightened to retreat to 'Frisco where the officers of the garrison and the men-of-war were hunting down runaways like these.

The holds of the schooner were spacious, furnished with long low benches; the vessel, Harriet deduced, had been designed for the passenger trade. There were only two private cabins: one between decks for the sailing master, and one on deck for the owner. Harriet disdained both. Despite the rain she much preferred to stop on deck, where at least the air was fresher and she had a chance to avoid her husband.

The scene did little to distract her from misery, however, for the Embarcadero was so overwhelmingly miserable itself. It was almost impossible to believe that a place could become a mire of ankle-deep mud so quickly. As Harriet watched, canvas tents were hastily struck by mud- and water-drenched occupants, and the area that the three lieutenants had surveyed was naught but a swimming tract of mud. Harriet could no longer see the stakes, and one stake in particular.

It was quite impossible to guess just what bit of ground was the ground she'd bought . . . so unwisely. Sefton, contemptuously, had taken Mrs. Marchant's money away from her. He had gone to the fort and returned it himself, no doubt spinning benign explanations every instant of the time. Then he had brought back Harriet's baskets, and the deed that Harriet had given Mrs. Marchant as security. He showed her the document

before he stowed it into his inside pocket again, his cold
chuckle like a sneer.

He said, "So you have come to the land of gold for a
theatrical notion."

"It would be profitable," she snapped.

"The very idea is nonsensical."

"I don't agree. Any kind of theatrical entertainment would
be successful here, even if the performers lacked any kind of
talent." Her voice was tired in her own ears; it was like a chill
echo of that terrible quarrel with Jake. "Men will pay—and
have paid—to see common soldiers perform on a stage. In this
very year of 1848 the garrison in Monterey have staged *The
Golden Farmer* and the *Omnibus*, and a Russian comedy called
Feodora, and each and every effort was enthusiastically
received."

"By common soldiers."

"By common whatever. The men who come to this place are
forced to take their entertainment at the fort, but if a decent
theater were established here the gamblers would lose half their
custom." Then she had lifted her chin and said very deliberately, "I am not coming to live on your rancho, Frank, I no
longer consider myself married."

"You don't?" He stared at her, and she gazed levelly back, but
for a long time the silence went on, endlessly. Then he smiled.

It was a small, cold, cruel smile, chilly with contempt. He
said, "You think of divorce? And on what grounds, pray? Is
Captain Dexter your lover?"

She snapped, "How dare you say that. He is an honorable
man."

"Then why, I wonder, did his manner convey the most lively
look of a man of great jealous passion?" He laughed at the
expression she could not hold back and said tauntingly. "Then
on what grounds will you sue for divorce, my dear? You have
just informed me that adultery is out of the question, and yet
my behavior, too, is beyond reproach! Have I been unwise,
have I created a public scandal to cast blemish on our name?
No, no, your case is well and truly lost, dear Harriet, for my
intentions have all along been of the most benevolent, and you
can never prove them otherwise."

Harriet said nothing: it was just another humiliation, and she
knew, drearily, that there were many more such moments to
come.

Then, as Harriet stared at the blurred landscape, the schooner got underway. The vessel reached the middle of the flowing
river and heeled. She closed her eyes to force back tears, and

when she opened them again the schooner had rounded a bend, and Sutter's Fort was out of sight.

The wind was with them, if not the current, and the rain tautened the sails so that the schooner scudded swiftly. It was a streaming landscape, of brown-green water with a ripple on its surface, clumps of trees in thickets along the banks, rolling golden hills of grass that were rapidly mildewing with wet, and then, beyond, in the distant fastnesses, the blue and purple-gray foothills of the sierras.

In the middle of the afternoon they passed an Indian encampment, a miserable place in the rushes by the river. Women and children lifted their heads to stare remotely as the schooner slid by. They were so close Harriet could see their expressions of bleak dumb endurance. The children seemed bluish with cold, and their coverings were scarce and pitiful. Harriet stared, horrified, and didn't hear Sefton's arrival until he spoke in her ear.

He said, "Waste not your sympathy on these people."

Harriet said nothing; she scarcely glanced at him. She clutched her shawl more tightly about her and returned her gaze to the sodden encampment. The houses were pits in the ground, covered with plaited willow thatch and piled up mud. She wondered where all the men of the tribe had gone. Were they, like the other gold seekers, dug in at the mines? Perhaps, she thought uneasily, some of them were at the fort, and she remembered the drunken Indians of the night before.

"They have benefitted greatly from the arrival of Americans," Sefton said.

Harriet said curtly, "They don't look rich to me."

"But they are, my dear, if a comparison is made to the way they lived before. Many of the rancheros employ them to work in their claims; 'tis a great improvement to the way the Mexicans treated them. Under Mexican rule the Indians here learned theft and treachery, they stole valuable horses . . . for food, Harriet, imagine that, food!" His tone was scandalized in the extreme. "They learned too fast about guns and grog; they fell into bad habits from rogues and scoundrels. The administrators of Sonora and Chihuahua were forced to put a bounty on their heads, such was the state of affairs!"

"They . . . *what*?"

Sefton smiled, his plump lower lip round. "Two hundred dollars for the scalp of a warrior, one hundred for that of a woman or child."

Harriet said, "Oh, dear God in heaven," feeling physically sick. She said with bitter disgust, "And how, pray, do the authorities distinguish between the scalp of a man and that of a woman? Surely the system begs deception?"

"That's so," Sefton admitted. He seemed most thoughtful. "Whatever," he said then, shrugging, "the system brings trade, a trade in scalps that offers reward to the chiefs of rival tribes as well as to bounty hunters."

Then, to Harriet's unbounded relief, he moved away, still looking pensive. Harriet concentrated on the scenery. Bounty hunters, scalps. Dear God, she thought, what kind of country is this? But then the schooner tacked about yet another bend, and the miserable encampment was lost to sight. The country-side was quiet and tranquil, a most deceptive land. It was a landscape of high banks and russet-colored riverside thickets, of great evergreen oak and sycamore trees, all with branches spreading to touch the face of the water. Dark purple pine groves marched down the flanks of the hills beyond, and beyond the hills . . . great rock faces, gray and black in the lowering light, and a hint of lofty mountains. Here it was easy to believe, yes, that fortunes in gold lay in those hills.

They arrived at Pueblo San Marco at sunset. The little town was a mere scatter of streets and terraces, built on the side of a hill as pretty as Don Roberto had promised. Then, while they were still securing the vessel to the wooden embarcadero, night fell, with more rain. The gangplank dropped, and Harriet felt Frank take her arm in an implacable grip. He led her down the plank and along a cobbled strand and then down some steps to where a boat was waiting.

It was a ferryboat. A small man was waiting beside it, a lamp in his hand. When she got closer Harriet saw he was Chinese. His name, Frank said, was Ah Wong. Ah Wong said nothing but bowed a lot, and smiled all the time, seeming most intensely nervous. Then Harriet was in the boat, sitting straight with her heavy wet shawl clasped tightly about her, and she watched Ah Wong as he propelled the boat to the other side of the river.

He stood in the middle of the boat to do it, grunting as he hauled at a rope. It was a double rope that apparently stretched all the way across the river, and it appeared to work with a number of pulleys. Despite the pulleys it looked very hard work, and the Chinese man was very small and thin. However, Frank made no attempt to help but sat in the bow looking

forward. Ah Wong had to reach up for the rope, and the wide
sleeves of his loose blouse fell back past his elbows. Those
elbows were thin and sharp, but the arms were corded with
knotty muscle.

Then, with a bump, they arrived. There were horses waiting,
one with a side-saddle. They mounted them, and then set off
into the darkness. The wet night was very black.

Harriet knew when they were near the house because the
hooves of her horse suddenly rattled on gravel. She could smell
wet dirt, a garden, and then the stone smell of wet adobe. The
house loomed up, massive in the darkness. There was a lamp
set on either side of the entrance, and that door was huge. Her
horse stopped and Harriet slid down slowly, feeling stiff and
very wary.

Sefton arrived at the door before her. He watched her over
his shoulder as he pushed it slowly open. His expression was
odd, gloating, enigmatically sly. The door swung open. There
was no one behind it. Harriet stepped inside reluctantly and
found herself in a huge feudal-looking hall.

This cavernous room took up the whole front of the house so
that three of the walls were adobe, whitewashed. The single
inside wall was strange, like nothing Harriet had ever seen. It
was oriental in appearance, a huge wooden screen which rose
fully up to the high raftered roof, so intricately carved that
Harriet could glimpse fragments of light from the room beyond
in the chinks where the carver's chisel had gone all the way
through to the other side. The writhing carvings were mesmeric, shaped into serpents, dragons, twisting waves. The hall
smelled . . . strange, of some heavy perfume, like burning
sandalwood, and when Frank Sefton moved Harriet found it
difficult to tear her eyes away from that screen.

When she looked he had gone. She was alone, in the huge
strange hall, with only chinks of light and darting shadows for
company. Harriet looked about apprehensively, holding her
wet shawl tight about her . . . and she heard the ghost of a
taunting giggle.

It sounded like a child, and it came from the other side of the
great screen. It was high-pitched and feminine, and something
rustled as the unseen female giggled . . . and Harriet heard
Frank's soft, gloating voice but could not tell the words.

The sounds were feverish, perfectly uncanny, and Harriet
whirled, facing the partition, moving her head back and forth
to catch the source of the phantom laughter. Her skin crawled

with a sense of being watched; she could feel a derisive inspection from the other side, as people, a person, peered at her through the chinks cut into the screen. Sefton called out in a louder voice and she whirled at that with fright . . . and the giggling sounded again, from that end, from this, while the rustling ran back and forth like autumn leaves, and Harriet's hairs all tried to stand on end.

The door opened; she bit back a scream. Ah Wong stood there, his manner apologetic. He had her baskets. He said, "M-m-miss?"

Did he have a stutter? She said, short of breath, "You gave me a fright."

". . . a fright." It was so unexpected, this echo, that she flinched with fright again; she wondered if she had imagined it, or if it came from behind the screen. However, the room behind the screen was silent. Ah Wong said more clearly, "So sorry, miss." Then he ducked his head and said, "Follow, follow."

He went through a door at the end of the screen. Harriet followed him apprehensively and found herself in a long, wide passageway. It was lit only faintly. Her heels rattled quietly on a wooden floor. Then Ah Wong opened a door and stood to one side. The doorway led to an enormous bedroom.

It was cold inside. One lamp was lit, but there was no fire in the drafty grate. The floor was made of short pieces of wood set in a parquet pattern and was waxed. The furniture was huge, black and ornately carved, somehow Chinese in fashion, and the bed was huge, too, a gigantic bed with tapestried curtains. Ah Wong said, "M-m-miss?" and Harriet jerked her eyes round to look at him.

He had put down her two baskets. "Excuse please," he said, and smiled very humbly, showing big teeth. "Colonel come soon, please, soon," he said, and backed out of the room. The lamp flame flared up as the door shut and almost went out, but then burned more or less evenly again. Harriet listened to the soft footsteps shuffle away, and then turned her gaze, shivering, to the contents of the bedroom.

The huge bed was heaped with quilts, and she could see the sag of its canvas bottom; it was, she thought, very old. Was the wood it was made of ebony? There was a table too, with spread-out legs carved like dragon's feet, twirled carving on the supports of a washstand, a commode with a velvet seat . . . all ebony? Great-aunt Diana had had furniture like this, made of black wood called *ebony*, made in some oriental place. But this—this was old California. Then Harriet realized why this room reminded her so of her childhood: it was because she felt so vulnerable, so intimidated and dwarfed by the size of the room and the fittings.

She felt the child that she had been on her wedding night. It was terribly cold; Harriet was shivering in long shudders that were almost convulsive. The quilts on the bed looked inviting . . . deceptive, she thought. Frank would come soon, her lawful wedded husband, he would come as he had that night in New Zealand, smelling of tobacco and brandy, gloating over her body with merciless self-indulgence, destroying her innocence in a multitude of ways.

She undressed slowly, her fingers numb and clumsy, remembering what he had done to her, the long contorted hours before Frank Sefton was sated. Then she crept under the quilts and waited, cold and tense inside, watching the door. She heard his step . . . and then she heard a giggle.

The half-hysterical little sound came from the passageway on the other side of her door, coming closer, closer, and she heard light steps, oddly uneven . . . stumbling footsteps, off this way, off that, off along the passage, back and forth, punctuated by the crazy soft laughter. Then the sounds faded, smaller, shriller . . . and Frank Sefton chuckled, right outside Harriet's door.

The door opened. She thought she would scream and bit her lower lip to stop it. She sat bolt upright, the covers clutched about her, and met Frank Sefton's stare.

He had taken off his jacket, and his stock was all awry. In the flickering light she saw the unblinking shine of his eyes and the flush of excitement in his cheeks. He was smiling, and the tip of his tongue poked out and circled his lips. Harriet's heart thumped with panic against her ribs, and a door along the passage slammed, and Harriet's lamp flickered high and went out.

She nearly screamed again. Her fists were clenched convulsively, and her heart jerked wildly in her breast. She could see the gray of the doorway and Sefton's black silhouette, but that was all she could see . . . and she heard nothing. Then slowly, her door shut, and she could see nothing. The dark was still. The sounds had stopped . . . or gone away. She was alone. After a long, long time she went to sleep.

19 ⮜⮞   When Harriet woke the creeping sense of being watched was with her again. She didn't dare move or even open her eyes. Instead she lay utterly still, every nerve taut as she listened. She heard the soft sound of someone breathing and held her own breath as she waited.

She was lying on her right side, facing the window. Bright light shone on the other side of her eyelids. Then, fractionally, she drew her lashes apart. A dusty yellow quadrant of light sprung from the window, ruled off with the shadows of iron bars.

She turned her head; someone was there; she gasped. Then she recognized Ah Wong. He was standing by the bed, watching her, his expression closed and sad. She said, "I didn't hear you come in," and sat up in a quick defensive motion, gripping the covers about her. Then, just as uncannily as on the evening before, she heard his faint echo, ". . . come in, come in."

She said, "What do you want?"

He flinched visibly at the snap in her voice, and she immediately felt sorry. He looked so small, so easily hurt, and he said, "I . . . sorry. I bring . . ."

He seemed to have lost the word and looked around wildly for it. Harriet looked too and saw the tray that had been placed on the table. "Breakfast?" she said.

". . . breakfast, breakfast." Ah Wong seemed to be tasting the word: why did he do this? Then he said hesitantly, "Colonel, sir, he told me . . . when eaten, you, yes, I take on inspection, of the house, rancho."

Harriet said nothing. It amused her, dourly, that Frank was not showing his possessions in person. She nodded and the Chinese man went. She watched the door swing shut, and then she dressed and ate. She kept on stopping to listen as she nibbled, listening to the house. Outside her barred window trees rustled and unseen cattle lowed, but the house was perfectly silent. The sun shone as quiet as dust in the window. At length, hesitating, Harriet opened her door. The passageway was empty. She walked slowly to the entrance hall. It seemed even more cavernous in the daylight, and was empty. The big door was open, and two horses waited outside on the road. One of them had a sidesaddle, so Harriet walked out into the open. Ah Wong, she saw then, was waiting too, his expression still most anxious.

Once mounted, Harriet set a fast pace; the jolt and thump of the trotting progress was soothing, and the fresh cool air felt almost like normality. Ah Wong followed her, and Harriet tried to ignore him. She made for the path alongside the river, toward the place where the ferryboat had landed; she wanted to see in daylight what she'd passed in the dark the night before.

The river was the broad powerful serpent that she remembered, rushing green with brown in the curl of the current. The land to her left was certainly lush; Sefton, she thought, had invested well. Grass grew lavishly, still not halted by the chill of autumn, and groves of thick oak gave substance to the landscape. The edges of their leaves were claret-colored in the low autumn light. Then Harriet reined in; they had arrived at the beached boat, and the town of Pueblo San Marco was on the other side, a hundred yards away from her, across the tumbling river. The double rope of the ferry was like two strands of a spider's web, and Harriet could see the moored schooner.

Beyond the town the hills marched on, climbing up to the distant crests, clumps of red oak ubiquitous on the distant dun slopes. That, she thought, was the way to the mines, and wondered if Jake and his men would tramp that way.

They were no doubt busy on the brig right now, mooring her up tight at Sutter's for the winter. There would be precious little trade to be done there in the rainy months . . . if the mud was as deep as promised. She pushed the thought out of her mind and turned her horse into a wild gallop. Hooves pounded up grassy slopes, over pastures, cleared thorn hedges in wild leaps; Harriet ducked low to avoid overhanging branches but did not care—not really—if she was knocked from her steed or not. Sefton's place was certainly prosperous, she saw in a blur. She galloped past stables, haybarns, grazing cattle, and gauping vaqueros pausing in their work, and she slowed only when Ah Wong's entreating voice reached her.

She hauled in her horse outside the entrance of the house and slid down without his help. She was hot and sweating but felt a fraction better. The hall was as empty as when she'd left, and the rest of the house, when Ah Wong anxiously guided her through it, was equally deserted.

There was a kitchen and stone scullery, but no maid or cook. Ah Wong sometimes answered her and sometimes did not, but she gathered from his fragmentary sentences that the wives of some of the vaqueros came in to cook and clean up. The house was built in the old Mexican style with an inner courtyard. There were mosaic tiles about the small fountain, and Harriet wondered if it became so cold in winter that the fountain froze up.

That, however, was one of the questions that Ah Wong did not answer; he merely whispered, as if to himself, ". . . fountain, fountain." Then they were back in the hall, and Harriet said, "What room is that on the other side of the screen?" and the echo came again, ". . . other side, other side."

Oh God, she thought; she was at the end of her tether, harried and perfect desperate, and this taunting echo seemed to epitomize her loneliness and fear. She shouted, "Why do you imitate me, Ah Wong? Why do you repeat everything I say?"

The little man looked utterly aghast, and she was immediately conscience-stricken, feeling even worse. He clasped his hands so they disappeared in the folds of his blouse and blurted, "Oh, sorry, please sorry."

He seemed terrified and darted glances everywhere, staring

fearfully at the screen as if he expected, too, that someone might be spying on them through the crannies. Then his eyes jerked back to her face, and he whispered, "I came to this land intent on self-improvement, Mrs. Sefton, please forgive that I try so hard." He was shivering with anxiety, she saw with wondering pity; drops of sweat stood out on his face. "I seek the true euphonious English speaking," he hissed then. "For how may I learn the good English from—from an American?"

She said blankly, "Well, for God's sake," and gaped; she couldn't help it. The notion that Ah Wong found Sefton's cultivated Philadelphia accent not worthy of imitation was most remarkably diverting; she trembled, incredibly, on the verge of laughter, and there was a rustle from behind the screen, and a footstep. Harriet whirled, and Ah Wong scurried out of the room.

A woman came out from behind the screen, a tiny woman, Chinese. She had bright, narrow eyes, and her hands fluttered up to cover her mouth as she giggled. She looked past Harriet, giggling, and Harriet turned to see Sefton come in. He was as dapper as always, though he smelled of horses. "Mei-mei, my Mei-mei," said he, and held out his hands to the Chinese girl. Mei-mei obediently scuttled forward. "Harriet," he said indulgently, "meet my ward . . . and, Mei-mei, meet my wife. Mrs. Sefton."

Harriet said nothing. The Chinese girl ducked her head but not before Harriet saw the hatred. It was a grimace of scornful loathing . . . for her or for Frank? It was impossible to tell, and horridly chilling. As Harriet watched, the woman bent, sliding her palms down her silken thighs; when she straightened, the porcelain face was unreadable again.

Sefton said, "I bought Mei-mei in Canton. In her homeland girls are sold or put to death: can you imagine the waste? There Mei-mei's people despise such pretty blossoms, but here her beauty is paid due homage. And see, she wears naught but the finest silks."

Mei-mei's silks were in pastel shades, in several layers. Then, as Harriet stared in perfect disbelief, Sefton began to turn the girl around and around like a doll.

As he turned Mei-mei he removed the silks, one by one, layer by layer, until the floor at her feet was swathed in rustling fine fabric. Then, at last, Mei-mei wearing naught but loose trousers.

The trousers were made of silk too, in a pale yellow. Her

breasts were like pigeons, polished pale gold in color, with
dark-brown pouting nipples. Sefton's palms moved slowly,
hypnotically. Mei-mei stood still and did not seem to mind.
Harriet felt sick but could not look away. Then Frank said
abruptly, "Perhaps you wonder about Mei-mei's feet."

There was a feverish note of excitement in his tone. Harriet
had heard of the custom of foot-binding, but nevertheless her
skin crawled. Sefton stooped to pick up Mei-mei, set her on a
chair. The Chinese girl was so small her feet did not touch the
floor. Then still more incredulously Harriet watched as her
pompous, urbane husband kneeled on the floor in the humblest
of postures, and with his own hands removed one of the little
black slippers.

Underneath, the foot was tightly wrapped in bandages, but
its shape spoke clearly of past ill-usage. The toes had been
broken and bent up underneath to set into the curve of the
instep. Mei-mei's face was perfectly serene. " 'Tis a most
strange custom," Sefton said pensively. He even shuffled on
his knees to one side, so that Harriet could have an unimpeded
view. "When Mei-mei was the perfect age, when she could
walk but her little bones were still very soft, her feet were
broken and fastened like this. The pain must have
been . . . unendurable. Even now, if the bandages are removed, she suffers the most excruciating agony . . ."

His tone was reminiscent. Harriet's skin crawled. His fingers
hovered over the tiny travesty of a foot, tugging at the bandage
as if he made up his mind, rubbing and cupping the blunt
implement-like shape of it . . . and Harriet abruptly could
stand no more. Before she even knew what she was about, she
had run out the door and leapt up into the saddle of a horse.

It was Ah Wong's horse, the one with an ordinary saddle.
She yanked up her skirts and threw one leg over to sit astride,
galloping every instant. The gravel spurted away from under
her horse's hooves, and then she was pounding along the path
to the ferry. She heard Ah Wong's distant wail and Frank
Sefton shouting, and ignored both. The wind of her progress
yanked her hair out of the pins, so that it flew about her face
and shoulders, blinding her at moments, but she did not slow
her pace.

Then she was at the ferryboat, and hauled her steed to a
wheezing stop. The horse was shuddering, foam spotting
sweat-soaked flanks. Harriet slid down and looked about
wildly: the boat was there, hauled up on the strand, still

connected to the double rope. Ah Wong had done it, had
hauled the boat unaided across with two passengers; she could
do it, if she worked out how. She looked across the river to
gauge the distance and the size of the task—and stood still,
frozen in disbelief.

The brig—the brig *Hakluyt*!—was sailing into view, the
brig! She saw the vessel with preternatural clarity, while her
panting breath rushed in her ears. Jake Dexter had altered his
decision; he had concluded to leave the muddy wastes of
Sutter's Fort and come instead to this place . . . to Pueblo
San Marco. It was all a guess but seemed miraculously right,
for Harriet, scared to blink, saw the brig slow and edge to the
wooden embarcadero, downriver of Sefton's schooner.

Sefton. Belatedly she heard the pounding hooves of his
horse; she heard it thump to a stop and Sefton vault down, and
then his hard fingers gripped her arm. "Come, my dear," he
said. "We expect callers—the Vidries." He sounded calm; he
was scarcely panting at all.

20 ❧   Jake Dexter stopped at the top
        of the first climb and looked
down, down to the town of Pueblo San Marco. The air was
crystalline, like wine, and the leaves of the trees were turning
to wine colors too, dark red and yellow gold. The slope they
had climbed was ornamented with stands of fine oak trees, with
a thick carpeting of acorns under their widespread branches.
The weather was brilliant but unseasonably cold, as if the spell
of heavy rain had brought winter early. The Feather River
wound silver as ice, and the up-and-down streets of the village
looked braced for snow. Jake could see the arms of the
windmill turn briskly where he'd left grain for grinding; he
could see, too, the stump shapes of the masts of the brig, short
now that the topgallant masts and the yards had been struck.

 Across from the brig was a distant riverside path that led to
the barely glimpsed shape of a rancho and its buildings. Jake
turned abruptly and set himself to walking again. Ahead his
men straggled, the younger, hardier ones, who had opted to dig

instead of looking after the brig. That job had been left for the older fellows who would run the brig as a trading- and lodging-post until spring; the younger ones were looking forward to their ordeal with most lively anticipation; they yarned and some whistled or sang as they breasted the chilly slopes.

Jake was silent. The llamas trotted serenely ahead of him, making soft plodding sounds with their fat-insulated hooves, as graceful as woolly swans with their long necks bobbing. Their packsaddles were thick, soft cloths with leather bags called *parfleches* slung over them. Royal had showed them all how to pack a llama; the parfleches prevented the contents of the packs from splitting with branches or rocks.

The packs held provisions for a winter, even a stove, and saws and hammers to make a good shelter. They carried three gold-washing cradles too: in Pueblo San Marco, Chips had made three of them for less than twenty dollars, and a well-used common cradle cost three ounces, or forty-eight dollars, to buy in the stores. Such were the fortunes, Jake mused dourly, that could be made from this California.

The citizens of the pueblo, however, had been helpful enough. They'd shown the *Hakluyt* men the gold-panning tricks right willingly. The men who had come down from the hills for the winter had told them, too, how to dig a ditch about a tent to take off the rain, and how to throw the mud up against tent walls to make them more windproof. There had been a note of pity about it all; those men reckoned they knew enough to come out of the hills even though they lost their claims by doing so—claims that the *Hakluyt* men planned to take over and hold until the spring allowed them to mine them.

Four months—they would be dug in out of contact with the outside world for four cold, wet months, while Harriet . . . Harriet . . . Jake doggedly tramped, bringing up the rear, biting down his hurt and angry jealousy, listening to the cheerful sounds of his men. As the party tramped down the slippery shingle of the hill the wind was freezing, but the men, like the llamas, did not seem to mind. The llamas had their lashes lowered to keep the cold from their eyeballs, and their wool was fluffed up. Davy Jones Locker was at the head of the procession, stalking up the farther slope with the leading llama, a long-limbed mythological figure with striped serape billowing about his triangular back.

Then another crest was reached, and the party scrambled

down the shingle slope on the other side. Loose stones rattled
down to the stream at the bottom, a stream that had to be
forded. The water was even icier than the wind. Tib Greene
slipped and stubbed his boot, and with a fizzing curse he fell,
wetting himself near all over. Dan Kemp hooked him out with
a well-placed grip on his collar, and Tib shook himself like a
dog, then kept trudging on. At the top of that hill the wind
gusted nastily about a corner, turning Jake's bones to ice, but
Tib, like the llamas, did not complain.

"'Tis like Peru," said Royal's meditative voice, and Jake
glanced around to see Harriet's brother beside him. "Once one
of my vaqueros was kept out all night, an Indian in the Andes,
and when he arrived back he was frozen solid in his saddle. We
carried him, horse and all, in to warm by the fire. 'Twas a
strange and wonderful sight," quoth he, "to see that horse thaw
out. It dripped, it steamed, it moved, and the Indian fell to the
ground, restored to life."

Those in hearing laughed, but not Jake. He contemplated
Harriet's brother with little liking: Royal, too, had deceived
him about Harriet's married state. If he had but told that
well-kept secret, Jake would not be hurting so with jealous
rage.

Royal was also a deal too cheerful; he was as merry as
everyone except Jake, obviously relieved that the problem of
his sister was out of the way. Royal had gone to Sefton's
rancho, albeit reluctantly and only at Jake's insistence, but had
made little comment about it. Jake said curtly, "Sefton does
well?"

"You know he does well," Royal said shortly. His expression when he looked at Jake was resentful. "You saw his bank
and his business interests; I saw his rancho, his house, and his
cattle. My brother-in-law is rich and no doubt getting richer
with the passing of each day."

"But you did not see your sister."

"How could I? She wasn't there, I told you. An old
Californian family had heard of her arrival, had come to call,
had invited her most insistently to stop with them on their
rancho; they were the first family of the area, a family called
Vidrie. Sefton had much to say about them, all of it praiseful.
He will join my sister the moment his business allows it. I tell
you, Jake, he's the devoted husband."

Then he moved away, no doubt to avoid any more unpleasant interrogation, before Jake could ask the question: But why

would a devoted husband allow his wife to move away, when they had been reunited only a matter of days? Perhaps Royal had that question in mind too, Jake thought grimly, but Royal did not want to spoil the way affairs had turned out; if Harriet were still living on the brig, Royal would not have been so complacent about trying the mines. Jake himself would not be here . . . but Harriet, Harriet had made stopping on the brig impossible for many reasons, not the least of them being her hairpins.

Jake had found those straying pins everywhere, in deck planks and sofa cushions. Now his hand wanted to slide into his pea-jacket pocket and touch his little hoard of pins again, but instead he set his boots deliberately to the trail. The jar in his muscles felt good.

Davy's serape was a guiding banner in the fading light. All the men moved with confidence, despite the rough terraine; they all knew the way to the mines, had pored together over charts enough and consulted the returned miners of the pueblo. This narrow, treacherous trail led to Don Roberto's fort at the headwaters of this fork of the river, and from the fort another trail pointed the way to the various diggings.

They had even chosen which arroyo they would try first: it had the nursery-rhyme name of *Bedstead Gully*, a nonsensical title but not as nonsensical as most. More than seventeen thousand dollars' worth had come out of there last month. It was a hard half-day's trudge from the fort: they would have to stay the night with Don Roberto. Darkness was nearly upon them. The men and the llamas moved fast. The path was no more than eighteen inches wide, and the rock face to which it clung was streaming with moisture, wet that threatened to turn to ice in the night. The men sidled cautiously, strung out over the cliff, and then, to Jake's relief, the vista opened out. He could see the narrow rushing river far below and a bridge that spanned it and the squat fortified shape of Don Roberto's home.

The path straggled downward. Some of the men skidded on the loose stones, and had to windmill their arms to stop from pitching headlong. Then they were at the bottom, on the path to the little bridge. The cold waters of the river were very high, lapping at the planks; soon that bridge would be impassable, Jake thought, and he wounded what Don Roberto did when this access to the trail back to Pueblo San Marco was closed.

The fort was a square massive adobe shape, not near so large as Sutter's. The huge wooden door was firmly shut, but the men hammered and shouted, and at length a shuffle of steps sounded on the other side. The gate creaked open then, to reveal an ancient vaquero with a lamp in his hand. They all pushed past him into the cobbled courtyard.

Don Roberto was not at home. The old man informed them of this in a high-pitched whine. Don Roberto was off, it seemed, on alcalade business. Jake informed him curtly that that made no difference, and then he paid the twelve dollars that the old retainer demanded next. Then, having stowed the coins away, the old man shuffled off into the darkness, leaving the lamp with them, headed, it seemed, for a fireplace in some hovel.

Don Roberto's house was square and ugly in shape. There were no lights in the narrow glassless windows. Jake bid Dan Kemp take Tib inside and light a fire before Tib expired of consumption. Then he turned his attention to the llamas. Stables were built on the inside of one of the walls, just as in Sutter's Fort, and Jake, with Royal and Davy, drove the llamas in there. The air reeked of mildewed hay, and the stables were as empty as the house and yard. The llamas milled about unhappily, and Jake did not blame them.

He wondered if the inside of the house would prove as dank as the stables, and his first expedition inside with a load proved him right. The house had two levels but only three rooms, two below and one up above. The smallest room measured not less than forty feet one way and twelve the other. The next smallest room held a battered billiard table and naught else. The upper bedroom held a lot of heavy old furniture, all of it in damaged condition. Each room had its own enormous fireplace. When Jake went back down to the smallest room he found Tib and Dan heaving logs about, rummaging purposefully in the pile of wood that was stacked beside the grate. Jake stopped short and pushed back his hat, but then it became evident that the two hardy salts were looking for snakes, for they found one. The machete that Tib wielded cut off its writhing head at the very same instant that Dan fired a pistol at it. Miraculously, neither of the friends was hurt.

When Jake left they were back to hurling wood at the grate. When he went back in with the next load they looked a deal more comfortable. They had a fire roaring and were cooking bacon that foamed like suds in its own liquor. Tib and Dan had liquor too, some kind of pisco or rye whiskey, judging by the

pale color. There was plenty of it; by the time the llamas were
unloaded and the rations were cooked the atmosphere was
more than merry, and by the time the grub was eaten most of
the men were snoring asleep, all spread out like the spokes of
a wheel, their feet to the flames, their heads on their bags.

Not Royal, however; he took a bottle into the next smallest
room and sat crosslegged like a djinn on the billiard table.
There was a fire in that grate too, and he held up the bottle to
the light. It was a fine brew, whatever it was, perfectly
palatable and with a good knock, pale gold in hue. Wind
whistled in the chimneys, setting the flames to leaping and
twisting, but Royal was determinedly cheerful.

Jake, lounging by the fire, studied him broodingly. "Come,
thou monarch of the corn," declaimed Royal to the upheld
bottle. "Agile Bacchus in Kentucky born! Cup on!" he cried.
"Cup on!"

Then he tossed it. Jake caught it and drank, and Royal
looked pleased. "An odd old customer, Don Roberto, don't
you think, Captain?" quoth he. "One of London's odder
gentlemen." Jake kept his silence, and Royal stood up, looking
restless. "Shiver my timbers, sir," he said. "Do you think this
house on her beam-ends?"

Then he posed on the billiard table, wavering visibly; Royal,
Jake observed, was more than a little drunk. "What a house!"
he cried.

'Tis mostly a muddle of tumbledown walls
And the carpetings flap in the stormy squalls
The tiles on the roof all knock like hell
And you pay good coin when you ring that bell
The dogs all yap and the llamas make a din
But 'tis a damn fine house, for the shape it's in!

Then he spied someone behind Jake, someone coming into
the room, and he cried, "Sing, sir, sing . . . join me in a
song!"

When Jake looked around he expected to see Valentine or
Crotchet, but instead to his surprise it was Davy. The silent
black man was grinning, the happiest Jake had ever seen him;
it was as if gold fever had made him as cheerful as the rest.
"Sing?" said he. "I tell you sing, I show you sing the way we
do it."

Then, to Jake's amazement, the tall black man began to

dance. It was like nothing Jake had ever seen, an agile jangle
of long arms and legs, accompanied by an almost meaningless
scrapbook of phrases: ". . . slap, clap, slap, clap, wind do
this, rain do that . . ." It was intoxicating, as infectious as the
gold fever itself, a wild collation of jumps and bounces. Davy
danced, bent over almost double, forward and then backward,
arms weaving out, long feet kicking, hands clapping, beating
a strange broken rhythm on his thighs.

Then, all at once, it was finished, and Davy stood still,
laughing. Jake was laughing too, surprised into good humor.
Royal said innocently, "My God, Jake, but we might've
judged right-wrong, for if we built our theater, this man be just
right for the stage."

Good humor vanished in a flash. Then Jake saw that Davy,
too, was sobered. "The stage, sir Royal, you think the stage,
you really figger white folks would pay to see a black man?
Why, even black folks would not do that!"

Then, shaking his head, he went out of the room. When Jake
looked back at Royal, Harriet's brother seemed stunned,
scandalized, and angry with it. He said sharply, "Is that so,
Jake? Would a black man really not be allowed to perform on
a stage?"

Jake shrugged; he didn't know. He felt angry himself, for
Royal's incautious remark about Harriet's theater had made
him wonder if, after all, he had been too severe in his
condemnation of the idea.

She had been so scornful; he remembered her furious voice:
*You're a shrewd businessman, Jake . . . I thought you'd see
the possibilities.* A theater—in that mud? Ridiculous, he
thought, ridiculous, but he still felt uneasy and angered. Did
Harriet still brood about it now?

"Swamp it," Royal muttered. "You Americans make me
feel foreign, strap me if you don't. My father met an American
once, a fine jolly fellow called Irving, name Washington, a
humorous dramatist indeed. He had to write his plays twice
though; once bawdy enough to divert English audiences, the
second all sobered out to suit his home-country folk. Can you
credit that?" he demanded, just as if Jake were not American
but a foreigner too. "And yet I heard that in Cincinnati women
and men do not picnic together, for they'd commit the
indecency of sitting on the same grass, and I heard too, that
women in Boston pin little skirts about their piano legs, to
make their instruments modest. So perhaps, yes, I have to

credit that Americans are capable of all that's amazing. How could they have developed so different, when their country ain't even a century old yet?"

Jake snapped, "You had few scruples about marrying your sister to an American."

"What?" Then Royal's eyes became evasive; he looked at the door as if he wished that they were not alone, as if he wished someone would wake and come in. He lifted the bottle and took a swig and then muttered, "I don't know what you mean."

"Harriet informed me that her marriage was arranged; that it was a piece of business between your father, yourself, and Sefton."

"But Sefton was a fine match; a most astute businessman. I told you, he's rich, his rancho and cattle are the finest I've seen."

Jake paused. Then he snapped, "And the alpaca?"

"I do admit that the alpaca, yes, were his idea, but it was not his fault that the Indians stole 'em back."

"But did he fund you? or your father?"

He stared challengingly, and Royal's eyes were more evasive than ever. He muttered, "That has naught to do with Hat's marriage."

"No? I thought money had everything to do with it. She told me," Jake said deliberately, "that Sefton married her to avoid paying the discriminatory taxes."

"She did? My sister did not marry against her will, I assure you of that! Sefton was besotted with her, or my father would not have allowed it."

"She said that Sefton devised an arrangement, which you and your father witnessed. It was an agreement which allowed Sefton to get away without paying taxes on his dealings."

"She told you that, did she?" Royal demanded derisively. "Did she not tell you, then, that all this business happened before her marriage and not after? For God's sake, Dexter, the truth remains: no doubt you think it a devious scheme, but the fact must be faced that Sefton signed over all his worldly goods before they were married! If she'd altered her mind and decided not to wed she would have left him a pauper. Tell me, does that sound like the action of an untrustworthy man?"

"And yet, somehow, despite his gift, Sefton was able to sell it all and leave her destitute," Jake snapped.

"I don't believe that!" Royal was shouting, his manner like

a caged lion. Sounds of men shifting about in disturbed slumber came through the doorway. Royal looked about and lowered his voice.

He said, "Look, I don't know what happened after I left New Zealand. All I know is that they seemed perfectly content: swamp it, Jake, they'd only been married a day. There were lands, a great house, the horses that my father had given Sefton for a dowry. Why, Sefton looked as prosperous then as he does in California now. It just ain't possible that he could have sold everything without her signature, for all his property was in her name. For God's sake, you know yourself the man is honest!"

Jake said blankly, "What?" but was scarcely aware that he had said it. His mind was full of the word *signature*; the scene on the Embarcadero was abruptly all about him. He could even feel the rain, smell the mud, hear Harriet's voice as she cried out to her husband, *Is my signature worth so very much*?

And Sefton had said, *nothing*; her signature was worth precisely *nothing*. At the time Jake had scarcely registered the contempt in Sefton's voice, but he heard it very clearly now.

He said very slowly, "I don't think Sefton is honest at all."

"But he must be—and you must admit it. Didn't he pay you back for the money she spent on that worthless bit of swamp at Sutter's Fort?"

Jake was silent, thinking, remembering. He had the note for one thousand dollars still in his pocket; he had gone past Sefton's Bank for Miners often, had even stepped inside it once or twice, but somehow he had not been able to bring himself to exchange it for the money. He had paid back the men who loaned it to Harriet out of his own pocket. Why? Because, he realized grimly now, he had recognized that note for what it was—a boastful taunt, a gesture of contempt.

He said curtly, "If you hadn't told him about the sale of the land and my reaction, he would never have produced the note."

"What?" Royal's expression was startled, then blank, staring at Jake in the flickering firelight. He said, "I didn't tell him Hat had bought that land. I assumed that you did."

Jake bit out, "I did not." When Sefton had called on the brig that foul morn at Sutter's, he had merely advised him of the whereabouts of his wife. Then, when Sefton had seemed disposed to stop and sneer, Jake had instructed him to get the hell off the brig.

Jake had been drunk but remembered the episode as clear as

glass nevertheless. Now he frowned and said in puzzlement, "Then how the devil did Sefton find out about it? When he gave the note to me he knew it all, that Harriet had signed for it, that she'd paid one thousand dollars, that some of my men had advanced her the money. He even knew that she bought it for the purposes of a theater."

But Sefton could have learned that last from the notice on the stake that claimed that piece of ground, he remembered. Nonetheless he demanded, "How did Sefton learn all that?"

"God knows," said Royal frankly. "For I don't."

"Who else knew of the sale, then?"

Royal was quiet a long moment, staring into the fire. He was back in his sagelike attitude, cross-legged on the tabletop. Then he said, "The men knew, of course, and the three surveyor-generals knew too. And Don Roberto, of course."

"Don Roberto?"

"Yes. He was the one who organized the sale."

And the one who had presented all the recommendations to the *Hakluyt* men. *Don Roberto*, thought Jake. "Of course," he said grimly.

21 ◈ The day dawned pink and murky, and by the time the llamas were loaded cold rain had set in, a gusty drenching rain that made every surface unpleasant to touch. When they arrived on the bridge the llamas jumped about, looking restive, and the men had to drag them across. The river had risen a foot in the night, and the foaming current that covered the planks was ankle deep. Another day, Jake mused, and the bridge would be impassable. Then they arrived at the fork in the path where they'd left the track the day before, and turned east, trudging immediately uphill.

The going was worse than it had been previously, slippery and treacherous in the extreme. Abner slipped once and cried out with fear, and Tib Greene grabbed him just in time. There was a strange sense of ambush . . . why? Because the land was so empty, because the weather was so grim? All the men were tense, Jake saw; he himself kept on involuntarily breaking his step to look about. The rocks dripped incessantly, and soaked foliage hung low. Every precipice was half-hidden in cloud. Once the clouds drew apart with a stray gust of breeze, revealing the full extent of the cliff face they were traversing, and Dan Kemp swore in a yell of fright. Stones rattled ahead, and the roar of a hungry hunting bear rumbled about the cliffs. Jake was on the verge of shouting out himself. Everyone froze, and then the bear roared again, farther away.

They moved on into the mountains. At times the path was so narrow that the men were forced to sidle with their backs to the rock face. The llamas despite their burdens were the surest-footed of them all. The cliff face was pocketed with the nesting burrows of a multitude of swallows; in summer, Jake thought, the going would be more treacherous than ever. Perhaps even the llamas would take fright at the diving and swooping of the birds. Pebbles rolled treacherously away from their feet, and then, at last, they were in the valley at the bottom of the cliff.

The valley was thick with bracken and ferns and foliage. It was possible to see where the mule trains had made a path, because of the torn branches where the animals had foraged. A creek ran in the bottom, as water did in all the arroyos, and then the valley opened out into a choice of paths. There were signs of men a-plenty here; they had left notices pointing down the tracks, many of the notices frivolous. One board pointed the way to Olé Olé Hole, another to Pancho's Fortune; there were Old Dead Bar and Black Man's Luck, and Dry Bones Gulch, and Bedstead Gully. Davy led the way, onto the last; the others followed. Boughs flicked heavy moisture at their faces and fern soaked their feet and legs. Then, from the gully ahead, Jake heard an unearthly Indian wailing.

He stopped short. He could see Joseph Fayal show the whites of his eyes in fright, and Dan swore again, more softly. Royal whispered, "Oh, my God, what is it?"

It was a weird concert that shrieked with pain and rage and loss. Then the wind gusted . . . and brought with it an appalling charnel scent, of burning flesh and hair. The terrible screaming rose in volume, and Jake began to run.

He ran up the gully, toward the terrible sounds. He heard some of the men call out hoarsely for him to come back, and then Davy and Tib were running beside him. A thicket rose about them, and then Jake shoved his way about a bend in the track; he shoved through the thicket and . . .

Stopped short. There was a wide open space, and an Indian camp. The Indians were dancing, dancing about a fire, dancing in the rain. They threw their torsos back and forth while they shouted out their terrible screams. Bedraggled black hair streamed about their contorted faces as they danced in wide circles about a fire. The thing that was burning on that fire was a human body.

It was a funeral pyre, Jake understood then; he stood numbly. A gust of rain fell, and the flames drew back with a hiss, revealing what lay on the sticks. The body was dressed in a blanket. Grease spat and black smoke billowed and huge smuts whirled with the gust. The dancing Indians threw more fuel in to the flames as they circled: bowls, baskets, food. Then Davy moved and ran into the encampment before Jake could stop him. He jerked into movement himself to follow Davy and fetch him back, but Tib's hand gripped him. "No, Cap'n," the seaman hissed; Jake could feel Tib's bitten-down terror.

He watched Davy walk up to a woman; the female was crouched by the head of the pyre. Davy crouched down, too, and talked. The woman had something on her back, like a hump. Then Jake realized it was a cradleboard, with a baby in it. As Jake watched, the ex-slave took his bag and opened it and gave the woman some food. Jake thought—hoped—she would eat it or give it to her infant, but instead she threw it into the fire.

It was like a signal. The whole heap of burning branches collapsed, and the corpse shriveled and collapsed too. Everything disappeared entirely, like some ghastly illusion. Then Jake realized that the fire had been built over a pit dug in the ground, and the ashes and embers had all fallen into that hole. When he looked at Davy again, the tall black man was coming back.

Tib said angrily, "Why did she burn that grub? And them blankets? There's a hard winter a-comin'; how could she put them things to waste?"

Davy shrugged. He did not answer. The bag was back in its place on his shoulders, and he set off again along the track. The valley narrowed ahead, plunging into a claustrophobic defile. Jake followed him; he could hear the rest of the men hauling the terrified llamas along behind. Then the Indians were out of sight but not the smoke, not the smell, and not the loud mourning. Tib demanded, "Who was he, that man what they were burning?"

Davy said, "He was the chief, the woman's husband."

"But why burn 'im? Did he die of some pestilence?"

Davy paused, and all the men watched him. The defile had become no more than a thin corridor between two cliff faces. Slow echoes drummed back from the tramping of their boots. Davy said somberly, "He did not die a natural death."

Tib said angrily, "That's what I asked you."

"I saw his . . . head; I saw his skull bones."

A flicker of movement caught Jake's eye, and he tipped back his hat to stare ahead. There were mules, horses, men, at the end of the defile, coming toward them in single file. Above the heads of the cavalcade a huge boulder lay suspended in the rock, wedged insecurely between the two cliffs. One day it would come down and block the path, Jake thought distractedly; his eyes were taken up with the men ahead, and his ears with what Davy was saying.

"What d'you mean, his skull?" Tib said; his tone was aggressive with the aftermath of primitive fear.

"The—the men who killed the chief, they took away his hair." Davy's tone held bewilderment.

"Oh, God," said Royal. Scalped, Jake thought with revulsion. Then he was distracted by utter incredulity. The men coming along the defile toward them were close enough to recognize. The first was Don Roberto. The fat Englishman sat astride a fat mule, riding in inelegant fashion. The six other men in the party rode horses and led more mules. The pack beasts were heavily laden with soft parfleches that looked most suspiciously as if they held gold-dust, and the horsemen were, unmistakably, Joaquin Murieta and his five brothers and cousins.

The Murietas—*here*, with Don Roberto? For a wild moment Jake wondered if the fat little alcalde had them all under arrest, but he quickly saw the impossibility of that. Joaquin said, "Capitán," and smirked. Jake ignored him. The sneer was no more threatening then remembered, and Jake was more interested in the fat little alcalde.

"Don Roberto," he said grimly. The space in the defile was a little broader here, and men and beasts milled restively. Don Roberto's mule tried to edge away, so Jake held her still with a hand on the cheek strap. There was sweat in with the rain on the alcalde's face, and his hands fiddled nervously with the reins. His eyes hunted the landscape, rather than meet Jake's stare.

Jake said deliberately, "You've been about on alcalde business?"

Don Roberto's mouth opened. His tongue touched his lips, and then he said snappishly, "I am."

"Then I wonder what the business might be, when you travel with such men." Jake nodded at the laden mules and their fat, heavy burdens and said, "That looks more like the result of digging business than alcalde business to me."

"Whatever it be, it ain't your business whatsoever!" Don Roberto yelped. "And whatever you say, whatever you think, Cap'n Dexter, the business—and these men—be all legal. These men are my lawful, legal sworn-in deputies, and you just take notice of that!"

"My God." That was Royal's voice, awed. "Which fool would give such authority to such blatant rogues?" he said, and Jake could hear the mutters and exclamations from the rest of the men.

However, he didn't look around but kept his stare on Don Roberto's sweating face.

"I need deputies!" the alcalde shouted. Spittle flew out of his mouth to join the rain. "I 'ave to 'ave deputies, and these be fit men! I need deputies that can dig, and deputies what can guard my mule trains ag'in robbers, and I need 'em regular, claim-jumpin' bein' such popular sport!"

Jake paused. Then he said, "What claim jumping?"

"Which one, he asks," said Don Roberto sourly, and laughed without mirth. "There ain't a week what goes by without someone or other sendin' for me to complain that his mine 'as been jumped. And this be my jurisdiction, so what am I forced to do? To drop all activities, that's what, and travel to the disputed claim, that's what, and listen to all the clamor and shoutin' and then decide the rights of the matter. And 'ow am I supposed to make up my mind, eh? I need time, that's what I need, but time ain't what I got, so I make that time instead."

Then he sniffed, peevishly, at the sweat and rain on the end of his nose. Jake scowled, grasping for sense. Then he said slowly, "Is that why these mules are a-carrying gold?"

"Gold?" said Don Roberto, and sniffed again. "Well, I do admit, yes, that you be right, for 'tis indeed gold what them mules be totin'. But I'm just carryin' it off for safekeeping, to stow in the vaults of the bank while I ponder the merits and demerits of the case; when I decide who rightfully owns that gold, then that person will get it all entire! With the exception of my fee, of course," he added as an afterthought. "And my deputies' fees too, for I have to 'ave them deputies! I need deputies to dig all the gold out of that disputed claim, to pan it and bag it, and then load the mules all up. Then I need 'em to guard the gold while we're takin' it into the pueblo, and no sooner that all be over and the gold all safe in the vaults of the bank, then another claim gets itself jumped, and the business starts over again!"

Bank? Which bank? Jake snapped, "And the bank—does it get a fee as well, in the form of a percentage, perhaps?"

"But of course!" Don Roberto hollered. "You can't expect Colonel Sefton to look after all that disputed gold for nothing."

So the unasked question was answered: It was Sefton's bank. Jake pictured all the gold piled up, waiting in Sefton's vaults while Don Robeto made up his mind. So much could happen while Don Roberto paused and thought and prevaricated: the contestants could die or move on to other places or make a pile somewhere else and forget about that gold in Sefton's bank vaults.

He said grimly, "I have a note myself, writ on Sefton's Bank for Miners."

If Don Roberto was surprised or intrigued by this, he certainly did not show it. When Jake produced the folded note the alcalde merely shook it open and glanced at it. Then he said indifferently, "It'll be good," and handed it back.

"Good?"

"Colonel Sefton be a substantial man, the way I told you. Any of his notes are worth their face value."

Jake said quietly, "I am more interested in the reason Sefton gave it to me. He said it was repayment for the money Mrs. Sefton borrowed from my men to buy that piece of ground at Sutter's."

Don Roberto shuffled in his saddle. Everyone, Jake observed, was staring at the alcalde, waiting, as he was, for an answer. The silence dragged on, heavily, and Don Roberto looked everywhere except at Jake, his demeanor most oddly embarrassed.

Then he muttered, "I do admit, Captain, yes, indeed, when I realized the true state of affairs I wished myself most heartily in another place. But it was not my fault! It was Mrs. Sefton's deception. 'Ow was I to know she was married, 'ow was I to know that that *Miss Gray* was naught but a stage name, 'ow was I to know what a blunder I'd made, when I sold that lady her own husband's land!"

"What!"

"Yes. Colonel Sefton owned that very piece of ground at Sutter's. He got it as collateral on a failed loan. He owned that bit of land that Mrs. Sefton chose. How's that for an awkward coincidence, Captain, eh?"

Jake said softly, "Oh, Jehovah." So that, he thought, was how Sefton had known that Harriet had signed the bill of sale, and that was how her husband had known the exact circumstances of the affair. It made the return of the money more of a taunt than ever, a contemptuous gift of a rich man to a poor one.

Don Roberto said pettishly, "So 'tis uncommon generous of the colonel to think to repay the money, for by law he don't 'ave to: the money and the land are legally his."

Jake snapped, "I don't believe that. If I conclude to keep the land, then it is mine, for the *Hakluyt* Company bought it and paid for it, so by right and law 'tis ours."

Don Roberto hooted, "But you can't!"

"And why not? Didn't you recommend the purchase yourself? or did you lie about the good prospects of that ground at Sutter's?"

"I did not lie!" the alcalde shouted. The mule whickered at the sound, and the horses moved restively, their ears flicking at the llamas, who snorted and puckered thick threatening lips. Don Roberto stared on nevertheless at Jake, shouting, "That land will do well, I warrant it! It may be swamp now, but within a year—perhaps sooner!—a city will rise up in that spot to rival New Orleans, for all it needs is levees to hold the river waters back!"

"Then," Jake said evenly, "there seems to be no reason why I should not hold onto that land and return Sefton's note."

"But you can't!"

Don Roberto's voice was a wail, and the llamas and mules and horses all whickered in echoing complaint. The animals seemed very nervous, and Jake thought he heard thunder in the air. The rain fell even faster, but he kept his stare on the alcalde's face.

Then Don Roberto said angrily, "Can't you see it, no matter how I explain it? Mrs. Sefton 'ad no right to sign that bill, she 'ad no right to sign anything legal, for a wedded woman's signature ain't lawful. It ain't valid, for all she owns belongs by law to 'er husband, and that includes her signature! Sefton still owns that land, for his own wife signed for it; he does not even 'ave to return the money, for once she signed for it that land became his, land that 'e owned already!"

Jake stood still, abrupt understanding rushing inside him in a wave of misgiving. Don Roberto nodded curtly and tugged the mule out of Jake's grip; Jake scarcely noticed him trotting off. The Murietas went too, and Jake stood still in the shadow of the suspended boulder, lost in horrid speculation. Then he roused and looked around. When he saw Royal he launched after him and stopped him short with a grip on his arm.

The other *Hakluyt* men were moving up the defile; Valentine and Crotchet were behind Jake, in the rear. Jake said tensely, "That's how Sefton managed to sell all his properties in New Zealand, even though they were in Harriet's name, that's how he did it! She spoke nothing but the truth when she said he married her for her English nationality. He took a gamble when he gave her everything to avoid the taxes, but not much of a gamble, for when he married her he got it all back! My God, once she married him she was doomed." Urgency filled him. He looked around wildly and said, "I must go back."

"But you can't; what would you do?"

"I'll find her, I must. She could be in danger. That's why Sefton sent you off to South America, to have no witnesses. It was right lucky for him that your father—" He stopped short again, and said, "How did your father die?"

He saw Royal grow white; he was still gripping Royal's arm and felt him flinch with terrible realization . . . and from directly above the hunting bear roared.

Men shouted form both ends of the defile; the Murietas had turned their horses and were shouting and pointing. Pablo looked up and screamed. Jake looked up too; he was directly under the poised boulder, Royal's arm still in his grip. A rattle of loose stones, high above . . . and the bear roared again. Hugely. Right above. It was on top of the stone. Then it plunged. Down the cliff face, setting stones and mud rolling, falling with the falling mud. Jake yelled out and shoved, pushing Royal ahead of him, rolling frantically forward, and the bear plummeted onto the back of the rearmost llama.

The llama shrieked, like a human, terribly. It collapsed under the horrid weight, broken-backed, screaming. The bear snorted, its muzzle full of blood, and all the men fired guns at once. Jake threw himself flat, forward, hauling Royal with him, and glimpsed Valentine and Crotchet in the rear, rolling, too, in the mud and gravel. The bear roared and shook its great head while the llama still screamed and its fellows bolted . . . and the rock above thundered like the bear.

The rock moved. The whole world shuddered as the great boulder shifted and shrugged in the niche where it had been set for so long, and then like a steamer it *fell* and took half the precipice with it. With a mighty crashing that went on and on the rock and mud and stones all fell . . . and then at last the commotion was over, with only an echoing memory of the horrid double scream that had shrieked out as the rock fell onto the llama and the bear.

Valentine and Crotchet and Don Roberto and the Murietas were on the downriver side of the defile, and Jake and Royal, the four surviving llamas, and the *Hakluyt* men were firmly trapped on the Bedstead Gully side of the ravine. There was no way out until the rainy season that had just begun was finished. Like the other gold hunters who had elected to wait out the winter, the *Hakluyt* gang was forced to dig in.

22 ❧ That night it poured with rain; rain poured the whole next month, and digging in was an urgent business. Mining was perfectly impossible, for as fast as holes were dug those holes filled up with icy mud. In Bedstead Gully men made rude wooden huts and lived cooped up inside, arguing with each other, thinking, thinking, brooding over maps. Some talked of going a-prospecting, in the higher hilly fastnesses where the place of mud was taken by snow. They talked of the Towallomie, the Macalamo, the Merced, Fremont's, and the Juba, the upper Feather and the Bear, *and* all their goddamned forks, but few of them packed up and went. It was very boring, dug in at the placer, waiting out the rain for spring.

It was every bit as tedious, waiting out the winter in Pueblo San Marco. The trail to Don Roberto's fort was impassable, the river was running too high to be crossed, and Sutter's downriver was naught but swamp: there was nowhere to go and little to do. The streets were all filled up with men who'd come

upriver or downriver to wait until spring; many of them lived
as boarders in the hold of the brig *Hakluyt*, and during the long
day and longer night they lounged about the streets, fighting,
drinking, gossiping and yarning, and most of them gambled, a
lot.

Nine-pin billiards was very popular, no doubt because so
many of the waiting miners were South American in origin.
However, the biggest game in town was monte, monte in the
Peruvian style, and the biggest place to play the game was
Abrigo's café-restaurant.

Abrigo was a native of this place, a hugely fat man who had
been running this establishment for God alone knew how long.
He owned the place and worked for himself with his wife a
croupier, and must have been reaping an incredible fortune, but
nonetheless looked poor. Abrigo looked poor and dressed poor
too. He wore duck pants instead of calcineros, perhaps because
he couldn't cram his bum into his national dress. His shirt was
thin and wet with sweat even in the coldest weather, and was
invariably so lacking in buttons that it revealed a large brown
hairy paunch that had more expression than Abrigo's face.
Abrigo's appearance fascinated Valentine and Crotchet, but not
as much as the game.

Monte was a simple game, relying entirely on guesswork
and good luck. The tabletop was marked into four rectangles,
and a card was thrown into each rectangle, faceup. The players
then bet on the suit and color of the next card to be faced,
laying down their bets beside the card with the suit or color of
their choice. Then, the betting done, the card was faced. Those
who had won got back their bet plus an equal sum; those who
lost had the pleasure of seeing their hardwon gold join the little
mountain of similar lost dust in the center of the table.

Because there were so few of them, the *Hakluyt* men ate
their supper together on the brig. "Five hundred dollars," said
Valentine yearningly.

"You want company funds . . . for gambling?" Abijah's
voice, inevitably, was scandalized to a string.

"But we'll win; our luck is famous."

"Luck," quoth Bodfish wisely, "is not altogether reliable."

"Why don't you come and watch?"

"The devil's drawing room and the devil's tickets are not my
idea of entertainment," sniffed Abijah Roe, and Valentine and
Crotchet rolled their eyes at each other.

Crotchet said nothing. Instead, like some courtly diffident

magician, he began to play a kind of knucklebones, tossing heavy gold bones up in the air, catching them on the back of his hand, tossing them again. The rattle was loud in the sudden silence; every man seated about that table had his eyes fixed on those up-and-down shapes. Then, inevitably, one missed its mark. It fell onto the tabletop with a loud little thump, and then rattled to a stop. Bodfish picked it up and held it up to his nose as if to sniff it.

"What is this?" said he suspiciously.

"Gold, of course," Crotchet said easily.

"And where did you find such a nugget as this?"

"Won it at Abrigo's, suh," said Crotchet casually . . . and smiled. The boys got their stake of five hundred dollars.

They ambled into Abrigo's at a little after ten that same evening. They were wet with rain, but Crotchet seemed in no hurry to commence his assault on the tables. Instead he gambled with a little of his own gold, and watched others as they gambled more. As Valentine watched, a greasy French beaver trapper laid down half a hat of gold dust and took that fur hat full of dust away. A Californian lost his dust, then the silver spurs from his feet, the gold buttons from his calcineros seams, the serape from his shoulder, and finally the horse at the hitching post outside. The caballero went off then, as dignified as ever, and Crotchet quietly took the vacated place at the table.

He played cautiously and won a little and then lost a little more than that. Valentine, at his shoulder, watched anxiously every second of the time. Then Crotchet, without even waiting for his luck to change, began to play with *Hakluyt* money. Valentine had his heart in his mouth.

Crotchet won a little, lost a little—and then abruptly won a lot. The five hundred was all at once one thousand. A buzz of comment began to rustle all about the room, and men left other tables, coming to crane and watch. The thousand quadrupled; Crotchet could do nothing that was wrong. All the other tables were suddenly empty; men were coming in from the street. The only men who seemed unmoved were Crotchet—and Abrigo. The fat man made no comment, and no expression crossed his face.

His fingers moved like fat caterpillars, flipping cards, gathering them up, shuffling them so that they blurred. Then all at once Valentine heard Crotchet say, "Suh, I challenge for the tap."

Tap? For a wild instant Valentine could not even remember what the little word meant. He heard Abrigo cough and clear his throat and then say, "Pardon?"

"Suh, I wish to tap for the bank."

Then Valentine remembered what that word *tap* meant, and he couldn't help it: he let out a grunt of pure horror. Crotchet was betting all that he had on the throw of one card, in the hopes of taking the whole of that yellow shivering mountain of dust on the table. He looked about wildly and became aware then of the perfect hush in the room. Men craned to see, from chairs, from the tops of the other tables, and no one breathed a word.

Valentine returned his apprehensive stare to Abrigo's face. Abrigo looked unusually thoughtful. He had his head a little to one side, so that his neck on that side was fatly creased. He nodded. Then he shrugged and moved his hands a little. Four cards floated out from the pack by pure prestidigitation, one landing in each rectangle, tidily face up: the four of hearts, the two of clubs, the ace of diamonds, and the king of hearts. Three red cards, one black.

Valentine held his breath, waiting for Crotchet's bet. His friend had his head to one side too and seemed as pensive as Abrigo. Then, with a casual motion, he set their stake, the whole of their gold, the *Hakluyt* gold too, all in the square where the two of clubs lay. Abrigo's face showed no reaction. He gave the stake an indifferent look, began to move—and Crotchet said, "Stop."

Abrigo stopped. "Señor?"

"I choose to deal the gate."

It was Crotchet's right to challenge if he wanted, but nevertheless it challenged Abrigo's honesty. Valentine heard a hiss of comment start up in the room, and then silence again as men strained to hear. Still the fat man showed no trace of expression: Abrigo, with no comment, handed over the pack.

The cards were greasy and well worn about their black edges, but Crotchet handled them with reverence, his flat gambler's palm smooth. Then he shuffled while everyone strained not to blink, and then—flick! A card flew up, floated, arrived faceup on the table. Everyone craned to see. The silence was taut.

The card was a court card, a woman on a horse. It was the queen of clubs. The whole room erupted in a burst of laughter, while men shook their heads disbelievingly: Crotchet had won!

Crotchet said bashfully, "And now, suh, I wish to tap again."

"But the bank, señor, is bursted."

"I'll bet everything—everything on the table, against the stake of this fine establishment."

"*What!*"

The cry burst out, not from Abrigo's mouth, but from Valentine himself; in that shocked horrified moment he was not aware that he'd shouted. Other men cried out their astonishment; for a moment no one could make himself heard, but then Abrigo said pensively, "You ask me to wager my business?"

"Yes," said Crotchet seraphically. His smile was bashful and beautiful.

Then: silence. Everyone waited. Abrigo was staring at the table; perhaps, Valentine thought, the years of running this establishment were parading through his mind. Then, with a shrug, Abrigo nodded.

He took the pack, dealt three cards out. They arrived faceup on the table: the three of diamonds, the six of clubs, the jack of hearts. The fourth one seemed to stick. Abrigo's tongue touched his lips as he freed it, and then it floated onto the table. It was that lady equestrienne again; she lay there and seemed to smile primly at them all, that queen of clubs, but most especially up at Crotchet.

Crotchet blinked, his head to one side again. Valentine wanted him most desperately to bet on the lady of clubs again. Then, smiling faintly, Crotchet shifted all their winnings and put them by the jack of hearts.

The knave, whose smile was insolent. Abrigo murmured, "The heart, señor, you bet it all on a heart?"

"Yes, suh . . . and I deal."

Abrigo again handed over the deck. Crotchet held it, looking not at the pack but at the table. Then, with a swift decisive movement, he faced the top card without bothering to reshuffle.

It was the six of hearts.

"And now," said Valentine with great satisfaction to the *Hakluyt* men on the brig, "we can drop this poor-profit boardinghouse business, and put all our effort into running the café-restaurant instead." That, he mused, would be a deal less tedious. Ah, that gamble, the gamble that Abrigo had fixed the deck had been a marvelous caper. For the first time Valentine was grateful to the bear that had left them both a-stranded in Pueblo San Marco.

23 ❧ "Bear-baiting," said Don Manuel Vidrie. He offered his arm to Harriet. "You celebrate Christmas in London with spectacle, perhaps?"

"No," said Harriet. "I have never seen bear-baiting." And London, she thought; Christmas in London had never been like this.

It was cold, but the weather was fine, the sun shining briskly on the little Californian town that the Vidrie family owned. It was set in the foothills of the sierras, and vineyards extended up the slopes behind the little adobe houses, just as perhaps they did in the Vidries' native Spain. The small cottages were built about a little plaza; there were cracked flagstones, a chapel, a turretted well. It all reminded Harriet, every day, somberly, of the village on Judas Island. The big stone house that the Vidrie family inhabited was set a half mile away from this place, built over the cellars where the wine casks lay in fat series, alongside the press house, with its cool stone and adzed timber interiors, and the constant stinging smell of grape skins.

London had never been like this, nor Christmas. Such a commotion as the festival had brought! The dressing up had begun at dawn, with all the Vidrie women vying for places at the looking glasses, competing to see who could wind her raven hair the highest. Harriet, as usual, had felt shabby as she quietly joined the procession to church. The women and their guests were adorned as if for sale, in flowers, silk mantillas, dresses even less modest than the English styles that Harriet wore. Their bare arms were heavily adorned with bracelets, ungloved fingers equally weighted with rings; parasols, lace handkerchiefs all adorned their vivacious persons, and they had long trains to their skirts that were allowed to trail in the dust and the cobbles.

Then, another bustling changing of apparel, for breakfast, served at twelve noon: stews, soups, rice done all different ways, eggs fried in garlic, chocolate cups about too sweet to drink. Ah Wong was one of the servants who waited on the table; he watched Harriet constantly, but she paid little attention to that, for Ah Wong eyed her anxiously all of the time. She often felt, uncannily, as if she had disappointed Ah Wong in some way but didn't know why. She listened absently to the Spanish clamor, understanding all of it but saying very little. The Vidrie women found her amusing, she thought. In the beginning they had paid her vast amounts of attention, had vied for her company, had exclaimed about her hair, her form, her clothes, her manners, but now they were often less than polite. Harriet knew that they gossiped about her and her marriage, but she did her best to ignore them as they giggled behind their fans.

Then, siesta. The Vidrie women, the most of them, treated the rest hours as another social occasion. They gathered several to a bedroom, and the echoes of their laughter filled the stone walls of the old house. Harriet sat alone in her bedroom, as usual, looking out the window at the scenery she knew by heart, with old Rochester's journal on her knee but seldom read, thinking, thinking instead. She thought about many things, including Judas Island. She had too much time to think, she thought.

Now, the bear-baiting, whatever that was. Harriet allowed Don Manuel to guide her along. His talk was courteous, but Harriet sensed the same covert disdain that she heard in the feminine laughter. She thought she knew the reason for the

underlying contempt and thought it understandable; she tried to
ignore her sense of shame, looking about her instead.

There was plenty to see; the Vidrie estate was wild and
beautiful. The house was built of quarried stone, slate-roofed
with ornamental iron grilles over all the windows. On the tilled
slopes behind it the lines of grapevines marched, brown at this
time of the year, the vines twisting shapes on the wires.
Beyond the vineyard the grassy slopes rolled into the distance,
dun-colored, with cattle grazing, and then, farther . . . the
lofty fastnesses of California, the mountains that had mothered
the golden lode. Pine forests, gray granite cliffs, snow-topped
peaks, birds cawing, calling, rising in flocks from the distant
silver thread that was one of the farthest forks of the Feather
River. Nearer: more trees, the solid shapes of live oak, and a
trail among those oaks that led over the foothills to Don
Roberto's fort, fourteen miles to the west, and to Sefton's
rancho, many farther miles yet.

Sefton. Harriet pushed the thought of him out of her mind
with distaste, and looked at the pit where they were arriving
instead. She and Don Manuel were about the last to arrive, she
saw, for a chattering horde of Vidries and guests were all
clustered about the round fence. The Vidrie women had
dressed yet again, in shorter gowns and shorter shawls, all in
rainbow colors. The men were dressed to suit, in gold and
braid and velveteen, like peacocks.

The air of the festival was palpable, full of excited talk. The
pit which had drawn them all was a kind of sand arena,
surrounded by a stout high fence. The posts on the inside of the
fence were clawed and gnawed about, evidently by some large
angry animal, but for quite some moments Harriet did not
recognize the bear for what it was; except for the body of a
dead dog, the arena looked empty.

Then the bear moved, and she saw it. It had dug itself a
shallow hole in the sand and lay inside it like a shaggy rug.
Harriet saw it move, and gripped the fence in front of her,
horrified. The bear was huge and lunged to his hind legs; a rank
smell rose with him, a charnel smell of rotting meat, and when
its huge mouth gaped wide she saw the yellow snaggled teeth
and the bloody gums. Ropes of saliva dangled. Then the bear
lumbered over to the body of the dog. To Harriet's horror the
dog came alive and attempted to move its broken body away.
The bear swiped, the dog flopped back and screamed like a

woman; the bear swatted again, and the body flew over the fence, into the crowd.

Women scattered and screamed, and men jerked back and laughed. Then, with a horrid lurch, Harriet saw Sefton. He was there, in the crowd, men and women all clustered about him, laughing, chattering. Harriet had not a notion how long he had been there; he had made no effort to make his presence known to her, his wife. She jerked her eyes away but saw him look in her direction nevertheless. Every fiber of her body tensed; she thought he was moving over toward her, but then she saw him stop, distracted like them all as some large animal bellowed.

It was not the bear; the bear was back in its hollow, as if lying in ambush. Men on the far side of the arena were harrying some animal forward, and it was this beast that bellowed. It was a bull, black, its powerful body shiny. The rancho hands that harried it along were all shouting and waving their hats, laughing and cracking their whips. The bull charged, they eluded him, and then the bull charged again, right at the fence.

A gate was hastily opened, and the bull charged right through. The gate was shut, the bull stopped short and scraped the ground and bellowed again. Its viciously horned head was low, swinging from side to side. Its red eyes turned about in the sockets, and women screamed in delicious fear. It was a bull in its powerful prime, huge genitals dangling, horns lowered, perfectly wild. Then it sighted the bear.

It charged. There was no hesitation. Harriet gripped the rail convulsively, her fingers hurting on the wood. Some of the men laughed with excitement; Harriet recognized Sefton's voice. The bear rose like doom, huge, upright, utterly fearsome, and the bull rammed its head straight into the shaggy chest.

The sound was loud and sodden, like a breaking nut. One horn was buried deep. The bull's head twisted, but the horn was stuck. It twisted again, setting its hooves, shaking its head powerfully. The bear grunted, no more than that. It bent over, slowly, over the bull's head, and gripped the massive shoulders in two powerful forelegs, the huge claws set deep in the sweating black hide. Then slowly, inch by inch, the bear began to scrabble backward, sinking slowly back into the hollow, taking the bull with it. The bull's sharp hooves cut grooves in the sand as it resisted, but the bear's great weight prevailed.

Men in the crowd were shouting, some shouting encouragement to the bear, others urging the bull to do his utmost. For the first time Harriet realized that bets had been placed on the outcome. She heard Frank Sefton's voice shout loud, "Toss him, brave bull, press on!"

The bull's neck muscles bulged and ran with sweat. Hooves scrabbled frantically, and clots of sand flew, but the bull was still held fast by the horn it had buried in the bear's side. Then with a sick snap the horn broke at the root. Both animals howled as they drew apart. The bear slumped, and the bull lurched back, spraying blood from its nose as it snorted. One eye hung by a string, and Frank Sefton's voice cried out jovially, "Brave bull, brave bull, the brave bull has won!" Harriet looked down at her clenched hands, fighting nausea. The Vidries and their guests milled about, hailing each other, lost in festivity, shouting, *Merry Christmas!* and Harriet seized her chance and moved away, to the blessed solitude of the vines.

She knew all the walks about the groves and the vineyards; she had had time enough, she thought wryly, to find them all out. She had her head down as she returned to the house and walked quickly along the corridors to her room. She could hear the Vidrie women at it again, dressing up and giggling as they prepared for the evening dinner. Then when she opened her door her heart jumped in her breast: Frank Sefton was on her bed, lounging, smiling coldly and smelling of wine. She stopped short, her back against the shut door, and he smiled and inquired, "Avoiding me, my dear?"

She paused, and then miraculously her voice was steady. She said curtly, "Most would think the reverse."

"What? You have missed me? What devotion, Harriet!"

"Devotion has naught to do with it. I'm tired of living with these people, and they are tired of me."

"I trust you have done nothing to shame me?"

"I have done nothing at all save play the grateful guest. I've played it for three months," she added deliberately, "which is a season that is ten weeks too long."

Three months, she thought, three months of listening to polite Spanish conversation, a full autumn and early winter of watching the Vidrie women flirt and dress. She snapped, "I've outworn my welcome, Frank; I wonder now if I'm deserted again, and I'm sure the Vidries wonder that too."

"Desert you?" he echoed, and sat up against her pillows, watching her sideways, laughing secretly. "I know the Vidries do not think that; how could they? I've told them often enough that you are my bright star, the adornment of my life; I only permitted them to take you away because of their most pressing requests. The Vidries were all insistent that you stop here. They declared themselves fascinated, truly. How could they possibly believe that I have shifted my husbandly responsibilities onto their shoulders? For have I not come to wish my wife a merry Christmas, and have I not come bearing gifts?"

"Whatever the gifts might be, I do not want them."

"But you must accept them all, for they are beautiful gowns, made of Chinese silk, lovely shawls, created in the East, and I insist that you wear them. As the devoted husband that I am, I must pay due homage to your beauty, and you, as a dutiful wife, must be an adornment to my reputation too. The business acumen of a man is never more shrewdly displayed than in the person of his wife."

He swung his feet down as he spoke, so that he sat on the edge of her bed. His manner was expansive; his smooth palms waved in time to his words. Harriet looked at the round unblinking blue eyes with hatred and snapped, "I'm sure the Vidries are sufficient impressed already."

"Ah . . . ," he said. His smile pouted at the corners of his lips. He stood and came toward her, and Harriet stood utterly still, her back against the cool wood of the door. His hand came out, touched her face, pinched her cheek, and he whispered, "Do I take it, my dear, that you are desperate to come back to my rancho? Such a testimony to your devotion is most flattering, my dear." He paused, staring down at her, and then his fingers nipped hard and he hissed, "Or perhaps you plan to cross the river, to get to the brig. Perhaps you think, yes . . . to run to Captain Dexter's protection."

"How dare you insinuate that! Captain Dexter is an honorable man."

"Then why, I wonder, did his manner convey every lively look of jealous passion, h'm?"

She couldn't help the gasp in her throat, and the speed of her question: "Have you seen him?"

"Not since Sutter's, my dear," Sefton purred. His voice was soft, but his fingers moved, harder, more cruelly. "But 'tis useless to dream . . . and I'm sure you dream . . . for your brother paid a call and told me much, and much of what he said concerned plans to go to the hills for gold, and those plans, yes, definitely, included Captain Dexter."

So Jake was in the hills, and Royal with him. Harriet stood

very still, controlling the flutter in her throat, concentrating on breathing slowly. Then she said steadily, "The brig and Captain Dexter and my brother have naught to do with my need to leave this place. I'm tired of living off the hospitality of this family, Frank; I find it shaming, for I know they are tired of me."

"But you have your own room, feminine company, your own servant—"

"Ah Wong is as unhappy here as I am. He is treated as a curiosity by the rancho hands and the other servants. They have never seen a Chinese before, and I think they are sometimes cruel to him."

"Poor Ah Wong," he murmured. "And my poor, poor wife." There was mocking laughter in his voice. "Perhaps I'll think about it . . . later. I have much business; I have concluded to turn my bank into a public company, I've decided to sell it off in shares . . ."

She said nothing, trying to work out what he meant; his eyes had gone glassy with thought. His fingers moved over her face, pinching, probing, but the movements seemed oddly automatic, as if his mind was busy, sorting out faraway schemes.

Then, all at once, his hand fell away. "Later," he said decisively. "I'll let you know my decision later, and until then . . . au revoir, my dear."

Then he went; Harriet watched the door shut and listened to his busy footsteps retreat along the passage. Later: what did he mean?

Later was a long time coming. It was February before she saw him again.

It was February and Royal was exhausted to a string. The trail to Don Roberto's fort and Pueblo San Marco was still impassable, the defile blocked still by the fallen boulder and the shingle that had fallen with it, but as winter turned grudgingly to spring the upper ravines had become accessible. The *Hakluyt* men had thought about it, had pored over mildewed maps, and consulted at length, and they had concluded to send out parties a-prospecting. Three or four men took a tent and pans and a dirt-rocking cradle, and then they tramped off until they found a likely spot, and then they settled in that place for upwards of a week, digging exploratory pockets. The trouble, as Royal complained, was that all the places looked promising, and none lived up to their looks.

They were all the same, these lofty fastnesses of California, all the same in their rough beauty. Royal's party, which included Pablo and Joseph Fayal as well as himself, had chosen this particular ravine simply because they had stumbled onto it at the time of day when men began to think about the coming night and where to pitch a tent. This ravine was the usual long arroyo with a stream bubbling through rocks and sand at the bottom, with red clay, bluish in places. There were the usual thick pines and gray rocks and the sounds of bears and Californian dogs about at night. It was rockier than most, so that it was all Royal could do to find a flat place to put his bones at sleep time, but they'd stopped there, digging their exploratory holes, simply because this arroyo that had no name was so near to the far-famed Dry Bones Gulch.

So much gold had been found at that gulch that a town had sprung up in that valley. It was a wild enough town too, by all accounts, but this ravine could have been twenty miles from it instead of two, for all the noise the *Hakluyt* men heard. Pine trees and oak trees and various other shrubbery blocked any sound in the air, and the ravine was full, all the time, of the cheerful babbling brook. And Royal's less-than-cheerful grumbling.

This place was as empty of gold as it was of other men, he said and added, strenuously, "C'mon, *vaya*, let's go." Pablo and Joseph did not bother to answer, which was no more than Royal expected. Pablo was digging while Joseph rocked the dirt-washing cradle, and Royal's job was to bring up water from the stream. Instead he said, "Let's go."

"One more bucket," said Joseph Fayal.

"No," said Royal. "I mutiny." His pants were wet to the middle of each thigh, and his boots sloshed with icy water. Those thighs ached sorely from constantly bending down to the water, scooping, and lifting the icy weight, straightening, and trudging out and uphill, pouring the bucket into the cradle, then trudging off to do it again. He wanted the scanty comfort of the hut back at Bedstead Gully. The sun was still high and the air was growing warm, and there were dark gray clouds a-gathering with a hint of springtime showers. Bedstead Gully was twenty hours away, and Royal wanted to pack up and get going along that tedious track.

"One last pail," said Joseph patiently. "For this last pan."

Royal looked at it. The dirt that had been rocked through the sieve in the top of the cradle had been scooped out into the gold-washing pan, to be swished by hand to reveal any traces of yellow metal. He said with perfect confidence, with weary experience, "There ain't no gold in that there pan, sir."

"But why not try? We've dug it, rocked it, sieved it, and now have panned it, so why not make sure?"

"No—" said Royal stubbornly but setting off with his bucket nonetheless, for this was such a well-born routine . . . and the heavens opened in a deluge. All three men sprinted for the tent and vied to dive in first.

It was a tight fit, but they were used to that. "When the rain is ended . . ." said Joseph.

"Yes," said Royal, and sighed. They all stared at each other as they waited, all three desperately bearded. Pablo's long black hair reached to his shoulders, and Joseph's glossy curls and Royal's strawlike locks were in no better condition. "And so we are reduced," said Royal, and paused. The rain had stopped with the abruptness of a tap turned off, a rainbow had spun into the sky, and his two fellows had left him.

Royal felt a deal more reluctant to quit the scanty shelter. "One more bucket," he muttered like a curse, "and another and another—" and then he heard a wild shriek, a holler of *EUREKA-A-A!* that made the very mountains ring.

The bucket of water was no longer necessary: the rain had done the washing for them. The pan of dirt lay where Joseph had dropped it, and the rain had exposed the clump of pea-sized nuggets in the bottom.

24 ～～ It was February in Bedstead Gully and Jake Dexter was boiling up medicine for his patients. Abner and Jonathan were lying stretched on two of the wooden berths built along the sides of the hut. Jonathan was quiet, but Abner muttered and tossed. His lips were blistered and his legs were dark and swollen; his bitten tongue stuck out between his bleeding gums and teeth. He had scurvy, and so did Jonathan, as did Davy, who had brought them in. The three men had been too conscientious, Jake brooded; they had lived entirely on salt provisions and hard bread rather than spare the time from prospecting to hunt for fresh food. However, he didn't scold them, for they also had all the symptoms of the dreaded Californian ague.

Some of the men called it *mountain fever*, while others argued that it was an intermittent fever brought by men from the Isthmus of Panama. Whatever it was called, it had laid many of the miners low, perhaps because the conditions in

which they lived, dug in over the winter, had reduced their
natural resistance. The best Jake's book could advise him to do
was to administer doses of number 41: the Peruvian bark called
quinine. The medicine he was boiling was a sprucc-tips tea and
was his own, home, remedy. Now he stared down at Abner's
contorted face and looked at the scar and remembered how
Harriet had assisted at that operation. It was a fine scar, a scar
to be proud of, for Abner to show off to grandchildren . . .
and then Jake heard Royal calling.

Royal came down into Bedstead Gully from the lofty
fastnesses like a herald from old Outremer. He was grimy and
bearded and tattered withal, and he'd evidently slept by the
track in the night, but he cried out wonderfully, "Ho!"

Jake went to the door. Then he waited. Royal stalked right
up to him and said, "Swamp it, Jake, we've done it! We made
our find, and by God, you spell that *find* with a capital F, the
biggest F in the book."

"Find?"

"In a word," said Royal seraphically, "eureka."

Eureka. That word proved better medicine than any quinine,
any amount of spruce-tips tea; the only problem was believing
it. "We dug all about," said Royal intoxicatingly. "We dug east
and west of it, and verily north and south, and running west we
found this vein. 'Tis four feet down, two feet wide, and a full
fifty feet is accessible."

"And no one else knows of it?" demanded Tib.

Dan said, "Are you certain?"

"We *Hakluyt* men were the only men there. Dry Bones
Gulch is but two miles away but could be further than the
moon, for no one has stumbled on our valley yet. It didn't even
have a name, so we gave it one. We named it, we did, and we
named it *Hakluyt Gully.*"

Dan sighed and smiled at Tib, and Tib grinned and nodded
at Dan. Somehow that naming made the find more credible;
even the patients all nodded and sighed with exultant relief.
Davy was up and about and seemed almost better, and Abner
and Jonathan were taking nourishment. Jake watched them
narrowly, for he had only Charlie, Royal, Tib, and Dan, and
though he didn't say it, the sound of the proximity of Dry
Bones Gulch worried him. He knew how fast the gold yarns
ran, and how often claims got jumped. The stronger his party,
the better.

In the morning Abner and Jonathan were awake and blinking, and Davy was as good as new; the decision was easy. Within an hour Davy was left with the medical chest and the recipe for spruce tea, and Jake strode off with the men. They took the llamas with them and left a map. Soon . . . soon, perhaps, the trail to Don Roberto's fort would be open again, and miners would come back to the gully. All at once, Jake mused, every prospect looked more cheerful, and all because of the find.

The clouds closed in and it began to rain and they were forced to camp by the wayside. They did not catch much sleep, however, and were up before dawn next day. The skies were gray but the mists soon rose, and the footing became less treacherous. The bells that the llamas wore rattled gently with their trotting. Then, near noon, they arrived at Dry Bones Gulch. As Royal had said, it was a sizeable town, with several buildings and a beginning to wooden sidewalks. At least three-quarters of those buildings were taps. Jake stared about, frowning, uneasiness shifting in his mind again. The town was quiet . . . way too quiet.

He said sharply to Royal, "Our gully is only two miles away?"

"That's what I said."

"And you didn't stop here on your way to Bedstead Gully . . . not for a celebratory drink?"

"Of course not!" Royal's tone was wounded, but Jake did not feel any easier. Joseph Fayal was shy and reliable, but Pablo was a braggart. Royal muttered, "We did everything *pro forma*, Jake; we marked our claim with a stake, a notice, our men, and our tools. What more could we do than that?"

Nothing, Jake thought, but his muscles felt tense, as if he was braced for something dreadful. He resumed his silence and followed Royal as the Englishman left the town and breasted the further slope. They walked single file along a ridge, zigzagged, and then arrived at the top of a hill. There were spruce trees growing along that hill and pine trees on the other side, descending majestically down to the stream—and the mining camp.

There were more than two dozen tents set up along the creek, and more than fifty miners hacked away at the clay. Jake's chest felt tight. The fact that he had dreaded this, had half expected this, made it worse, not better. He snapped at Royal, "This is the right valley?"

"Of course it damn-well is!" Royal's voice was shaking; it

was like the day they had found that Royal had lost his alpacas. As in Tombez, Royal's face was red with consternation, and he shouted, "I tell you, we had this whole goddamned valley to ourselves!"

"Then where is our claim?"

"There is our tent—over there."

His long finger shook as he thrust out his arm. Jake recognized the tent then, the canvas gray rather than the more common calico-blue. The tent looked mildewed; it sagged on its posts, pegged close to the ground, tied shut. Jake shouted, almost out of control, *"Where is our claim?"*

Royal said wildly, "That one!" He pointed surely, but the direction did not make sense. There were men digging there, but not Pablo, not Joseph. The men had long black Spanish hair, but they were not Jake's men. Jake said, "Oh, God," and began to run, sliding and slipping as he half fell down the slope. He heard Tib and Dan and Charlie shout and run after him, but he kept on going. Then he slid to a shaking halt by the digging, and the three men who were working there straightened slowly and stared at him.

Three men. One was Joaquin Murieta, the others were two of his brothers. They smirked, stupidly. Jake shouted, "Where are my men?" There was icy foreboding inside him; Pablo might be unreliable, but Joseph Fayal would guard this claim with his life. Jake could hear mutterings and rattlings behind him, as miners set down tools and came over to view the confrontation, and he slowly, warily, turned his head.

The crowd all gauped at him. The men looked much the same as any other gathering of miners, all attired much alike in torn pants and stained shirts, their feet in double-cleated boots. They were all heavily armed, but that was not unusual, either. What was strange was the feverish air of excitement; the all-pervading scent of bloodshed and fear. The faces of the young ones were shiny and scared, and the eyes of the oldsters flickered warily everywhere.

Something had happened. Then Jake heard Royal's voice snap, "You've jumped our goddamned claim!"

"We . . . have?" Joaquin sneered. "There was no . . . stakes. No notice, nothing."

"By God, there were, for I staked it myself . . . liar, *ahijuna*!"

All three Murietas stiffened. Jake's hackles rose; every man had his hand on a gun. Then an oldster spat to one side and said, "The scoundrel tells the truth, for all he is a scoundrel. There weren't no marked claim here, not when we arrived."

"Then where the devil are Pablo and Joseph Fayal?" Royal shouted. His voice was shaking; he seemed on the verge of running out of control. Jake gripped his arm and Royal shouted, "I left Pablo and Joseph here, right here, digging this very claim, not three days ago!"

"Ah . . ." The old man meditated. "Would one be a kind of black Spaniard, and the other a regular one?"

Jake swallowed tensely, every nerve and fiber taut. Then he said quietly, "That certainly sounds like my men."

"Ah . . ." Then the crowd shifted, as men shuffled and stared with open ghoulish excitement. The old man jerked his chin, and said briefly, "This way."

Jake, ice inside him, followed the old man to the *Hakluyt* tent. The front was tightly tied shut. The oldster said nothing but bent and gripped the canvas and jerked.

Jake said, "Oh, Christ." The smell hit him. It was too early for flies, but flies buzzed, heavily. The two pairs of feet stretched toward him were stiff, and in the shadows two pairs of glazed eyes stared, still open. He lurched with the sickness that rose in his throat, and then said huskily, "Who murdered my men; who killed them?"

"That be for the alcalde to decide, not that it'll be a hard matter." The old man's tone was matter-of-fact. "If you jest look at this, you'll see what I mean," he said. "He bent and gripped a pair of feet and hauled with a grunt at one body. "Injuns," he grunted.

The corpse was Joseph Fayal's. Jake heard Dan Kemp swear and spit nausea. Royal made a noise, like pain. Joseph's face was openmouthed, frozen forever in ghastly terror. His skull where his hair had been was a clotted mass of blood. Jake heard Charlie curse thickly, stumble off to one side, and vomit. Then the old man bent again and hauled Pablo's body out.

"Injuns," the old man said, and spat. Pablo had been scalped too. Jake swallowed on a clenched sick throat as the old man said thoughtfully, "Them Injuns must've throwed away your stakes and tools, for there weren't nothing to show that claim were taken, not when I got here. There ain't nothin' to show that claim be yours'n. We found these poor boys, God rest their souls, off over there, in them trees. They'd been struck down, no doubt, in the act of running . . . and who c'n blame 'em, huh?"

Jake said nothing; he couldn't. Instead, in a kind of hopeless prayer, he looked at the sky . . . and four men were watching them, from the top of the slope.

One was the alcalde Don Roberto. He was seated on his mule. The other three rode horses, and they were the other Murietas.

It was February still in Bedstead Gully, and Davy Jones Locker was sick. Abner and Jonathan kept on whining for water, and Davy did his very best to oblige them, but he was very thirsty too. In the end he gave up the ship and rolled up in his blanket. When he woke up the fire had gone out and he was shuddering with cold.

He stumbled to his feet, dazedly, not knowing where he was or what had happened. Abner was crying out . . . Abner was fiery hot, Abner's blanket was soaking wet. Davy didn't know what to do; he called out for Captain Dexter, and then remembered that the captain was not there. He didn't know what to do so he built up the fire until the whole hut sweated. Jonathan was quiet, thank all holy; it wasn't until dawn that Davy found that Jonathan was dead.

Davy went out and dug a grave, confusedly. He talked to himself a lot, and crooned little songs. He hacked at the clay as he sang, and sweat ran down his naked torso. Jonathan's body seemed impossibly heavy, but somehow Davy wedged it into the hole. Then he covered it up. He found a board too, to put at the head of the grave, but didn't know how to write, so called out for Captain Dexter. Still the captain did not come, so Davy stumbled off down the track in search of him.

There was an obstacle in the track, a great shifting pile of dirt and gravel. It took Davy a long time to realize that it was the boulder that had fallen down and trapped them so long ago. It was raining; the cool rain fell down and soothed his hot dry skin. It ran over the dirt and shingle too, making slippery mud of it. More dirt and shingle fell down all the time, from the top of the cliff . . . the cliff was collapsing over the rock, turning it into a rounded slope.

It was a high slope, but it could be climbed, so Davy climbed it. Twice he slipped, but it was easy to start again, for the soft rain and shifting gravel helped him. Then he was at the top, then he was sliding down the other side. The trail to Don Roberto's fort was open again; he, he, Davy, had opened it!

Davy called out to Captain Dexter to come and see what he had done, but still Captain Dexter did not answer.

But Davy did hear a voice; he blinked dazedly, astonished. It was a woman, an Indian, her small rough hands were pulling at him. It was the woman whose husband . . . had been . . . scalped. Davy remembered her and told her so, amazed.

She seemed pleased. When she urged him up the track and along the defile he obeyed her.

25 ❧ It was February on the Vidrie rancho, and Don Manuel announced a fiesta to celebrate the improving weather. Soon, he said, the river would fall sufficient so that the bridge by Don Roberto's fort could be crossed; traffic would move freely between the towns and the farms and the hills, and then . . . then such a prosperous season would dawn, the memorial season of 1849. This year such wealth would be reaped in this land—and a bear-baiting spectacle was truly fitting for the occasion, and to mark the last day before Lent.

Harriet made no comment. Instead, on the day, she made her excuses: she had the sick headache, she said. She stopped in her room while the family went to greet guests by the arena and sat in her usual chair, gazing out the window at the same old scene, wondering if ever she would be freed from this shameful situation. Old Rochester's book was on her knee, but as usual she scarcely read it; she gazed at the view and tried to ignore the distant shouts from around the pit. Then, at last, the roaring

faded, and steps and voices rattled along the stone corridors of
the big house. The Vidrie family and their guests were coming
to change and primp for dinner. Harriet sighed, putting her
mind to what she would wear, and the door jerked open.

She flinched with fright, and the book fell from her lap to the
floor. Sefton came in, bent, and picked it up, then said blandly,
"Did I frighten you, my dear?"

She had her eyes on the book in his hand and not on his face,
and she had to school herself not to grab when he handed it to
her. She said shortly, "I had no word that you were coming
Frank. I thought perhaps I'd seen the last of you."

"But I have come back, my dear, I have . . . and I've
brought three guests with me, American speculators just
arrived, and you must take pains to enchant them. I have also
brought gifts," he added, but his voice had become vague. He,
Harriet observed uncomfortably, was staring at the book in her
hand.

He said, "What is that?"

She said curtly, " 'Tis mine."

"Your book, my dear? An old journal, kept by yourself,
perhaps?"

She said again, " 'Tis mine," and then swiftly added, "What
gifts do you bring this time, Frank? more clothes?"

"Clothes?" Still he seemed preoccupied; then he stared at
her and his eyes cleared and he smiled and said, "You
remember, my love, that I considered the notion of turning my
bank into a public company? Well, I have done it, and 'tis so
successful . . . so successful that I wish to celebrate by
making you one of the principal shareholders."

"Me?" She stared. "But why?"

"Why, do you ask? But I've just told you! 'Tis an affirma-
tion of my affection, a memorialization of doing so uncommon
well."

She paused, studying him warily, every suspicious sense
alert. Then she said slowly, "I'm certain that you do nothing
that is not to your advantage, Frank."

"That could be said about every shrewd speculator, Harriet." He smiled and sat on the edge of her bed, facing her, his
expression indulgent. "All I want is to benefit you, my dear, all
I want is to make you a gift of twenty thousand shares in my
bank; it will make you wealthy, in the end; even if I died a
pauper, you would never have to exist on the charity of
others."

"No?" she flashed. "I don't see why not—when I live on the charity of others right now. Do you ever plan to take me away from these people and their hospitality, or do you intend to leave me here until the day I die?"

"Such melodrama," he chided. "The Vidries speak most admiring of you; they enjoy your company, my dear; such charm and beauty never palls! Come, be tranquil, accept my gift in the spirit in which it is offered, take the shares. See, they're in your name already!"

He had the documents in an inside pocket, thick folded parchment. Harriet watched him guardedly, while the bed bounced in time to his movements. Then, when he produced them, she put Rochester's journal on the floor to the side of her chair and took the papers reluctantly.

They were certainly impressive and looked businesslike enough. As he said, her name was inscribed in flowing copperplate on each of them. She counted them: they numbered four, each certificate being the worth of five thousand shares in Sefton's Bank for Miners. In the distance she heard the bell that was the first summons for dinner; it chimed no more insistently than the alarm bells in her mind.

She said, "What am I supposed to do with these?"

"Why, keep them, just keep them! In a safe place, of course," he added. He smiled; even his eyes warmed, he was the very picture of innocent benevolence. Then he added, "To make it all lawful I need but your signature . . . on this paper, here . . . and then you can sleep easy, knowing that you will always have wealth, even if I die penniless."

The bell rang again, but she scarcely heard it. She said slowly, "Why do you need my signature for that?"

"Only to make it lawful, my dear, so charlatans can never rob you. 'Tis but a precaution, in your own interests."

"But . . . at Sutter's Fort you made it plain, Frank, that my signature is worth nothing. You said a married woman's signature has no standing in law. So why is this different?"

" 'Tis different because I will countersign the document, Harriet; I'll make it legal with my signature. That is why you made such a blunder when you bought that piece of land, my dear. You did not consult me first."

His every tone was reasonable and kind, but the hairs on the back of her neck were rising with foreboding. She said curtly, "If there is a difference, I do not understand it . . . and I still don't understand, Frank, how you found out not only the precise amount I paid for that land, but also the fact that I'd borrowed it from some of the *Hakluyt* men."

"Ah," he said. His smile pouted the corners of his cheeks. "You'll have to ask Don Roberto that."

"What?" she cried. Then she thought, *of course*, and could have wept at her own stupidity, for the source of the betrayal was now so obvious. She stared blindly out the window for a moment, uncomfortably conscious of the weight of Sefton's stare on her averted cheek, and then when she could control her voice she turned again and said, "I still don't understand why my signature should be valuable here but worthless at Sutter's. I don't want to sign your document, Frank; you can keep the shares, for I do not want them."

"But whyever not? You don't make any kind of business blunder here, for you have the shrewd advice of a husband to guide you."

"I remember the last shrewd advice you gave me," she said bitterly. "And I remember the last time you asked for my signature . . . and I remember, too, how I lived to regret it."

The bell rang, more insistently. Frank Sefton was silent; his eyes had gone opaque, and for an instant she was eerily aware of his intense anger—eerie because his smooth expression was unaltered. His voice, when he spoke, was equally mild. "But 'tis no crime to avoid taxes, if one can do that legally. Your father and brother approved of my device. They were realistic enough to know that the more wealth I managed to keep safe from the taxgatherer's hands, the more prosperous my wife would be."

"Prosperous?" She almost laughed, wildly.

"Yes," he said, and stood up. The bland mask was firmly in place. "Think about it," he urged. "And keep those certificates in a safe place. Soon, I know it, you will think better of your decision, but forget about it now, my dear, and set your mind to being both beautiful and charming . . . for I have three guests whom you must impress . . . you must, for I insist!"

Then he went. Harriet watched the door shut. It was a long moment before she stood and put her mind to dressing. Sign his document? Never, she thought, never: every nerve and sense in her body warned her that something was wrong.

She was the last to make her appearance for dinner, and the last to meet Sefton's three friends. As he had promised, they were Americans, true-blue Yankees who had come by sea, from around the Horn. They had landed at Sausalito, and then had hired horses in Sonoma and had ridden by stages to Sefton's rancho. One was middle-aged, the other two much younger. The oldest one was named Giles, and he had more than three times the experience in his face than both of the others put together. The younger two were traders, and for quite some time Harriet found it difficult to tell them apart, even though they were not related. One was called Prender-white, and the other man was Chaffey.

"But we have not come to California to dig the shining gold, no, Mrs. Sefton," said Mr. Chaffey effusively. "We have other schemes to improve our fortunes."

"And you will!" declared Sefton. "Some men will make vast fortunes at the diggings, but others will make surer fortunes by shrewd investment and trading."

"And others by gambling," said Prenderwhite. His expression was wry. "I brought two dozen roulette wheels with me and sold them within moments of landing . . . for one hundred dollars apiece. Now I wish I'd had the foresight to bring twenty dozen more."

"Or waited to charge five hundred apiece," said Sefton. Harriet watched Prenderwhite's expression turn to one of chagrin, and Sefton declared, "That was your first mistake, sir! 'Tis a mistake that men will make over and over again, if they don't have the wisdom to ask the advice of the old settlers. If you'd asked Don Manuel here, or his brothers or his cousins, or even asked for my thoughts, you would have waited until the first lucky diggers come down from the hills, when your single roulette wheel could be worth one thousand!"

Don Manuel nodded and sipped wine, and said, "It's true," and some of his brothers and cousins said it again, in Spanish. Mr. Prenderwhite's expression, Harriet thought then, was quite a study. However, the rueful reaction did not silence his questions or those of his friend Chaffey either, and did not stop Sefton and the male Vidries from offering much pompous suggestion. Food arrived in the usual procession of soups and meats and rice all garlic flavored, and the room was full of American blatter as well as vivacious Spanish. Harriet was by far the most silent person at the table . . . except, she noted then, for Mr. Giles.

Mr. Giles was the oldest one, the one most wearily experienced. His mostachos were long and drooping and stained with tobacco juice; his eyes were equally yellowed, their expression definitely jaded. He drank rather a lot, Harriet thought, and he watched Sefton all the time, even when her husband was not speaking.

Then Frank's complacent voice said, "That is the best advice a Californian settler can give: to ask the advice of others like himself. Only the men who live here are full-aware of the possibilities. It is better to go into partnerships or buy shares in businesses already established that are the substance in the rich brew that is California now, and not just merely the froth on top! You enjoyed the spectacle of the bear-baiting today, and don't deny it, for I saw you; and California, if you allow me another similarity, sirs, is like that very sport. Like the bull that strives to toss the bear high, the California market is rising. But next year, or the year after that? California may well be the bear, that endures to drag the bull down."

"Bravo!" said Chaffey; he seemed enchanted with this trick of simile. Don Manuel sipped wine and smiled importantly, and the women all looked uncomprehending. Mr. Giles, Harriet observed, merely buried his nose in his glasses. He had a most sardonic look to his brow, she thought.

Then he lifted his face, brushed limply at his damp mostachos, and said, "But how, Colonel Sefton, sir, do we brash Yankees persuade the settlers who are riding this here bull to shift over and make room?"

"But I tell you, the settlers will do that right willing, Mr. Giles; for 'tis in our benefit, too, to spread the risks and welcome investment. Why, I myself owned a fine flour mill in Pueblo San Marco till six months ago. A Yankee miller worked the stones for me for a percentage, and did so well that I gave him the chance of an eighty percent share, and my bank even loaned him the mortgage to buy it!"

Everyone looked impressed, save the questioner. Mr. Giles said wearily, "It amazes me that you should be so generous, if the profit was really there."

"You malign me, sir!" Sefton, Harriet thought, was growing angry. He said sharply, "Provisioning the miners is about the most profitable business around."

"If you don't count gambling."

"That is true, yes, but the greatest profit of all is in buying up shares in the gold business itself, and by that I mean in buying up shares in the bank."

"Bank?" Mr. Chaffey stared. "I didn't know there was one."

"Indeed there is, I own it myself. Sefton's Bank for Miners, it's called, and as soon as the river is passable I shall be over in Pueblo San Marco, checking the accounts, setting things to rights, for I've turned that bank into a public company, sirs, and am offering the once-in-a-lifetime chance to men with the will to sign up for shares."

Mr. Giles said in tones of patent disbelief, "You have a bank, Colonel, that you can't even visit? because it's on the wrong side of the river?"

"That is immaterial! The bank was established in Pueblo San Marco because I saw the possibilities; the town is at the gateway to the hills. I live across the river because my rancho happens to be there, and for the most of the year that is no disadvantage at all. The river will be down within days, sir, it may be passable at Don Roberto's fort even now, but I feel no concern whatsoever that when I get to the bank I'll find anything amiss, for 'tis supervised by Don Roberto himself, the alcalde of the parish. The bank, whatever its position, is an investment of the most prime kind . . . simply, Mr. Giles, Mr. Prenderwhite, Mr. Chaffey . . . because within months there will be a grave overabundance of gold."

The silence was everything, Harriet mused, that Sefton could have wished: the three Yankees looked thunderstruck. Chaffey said in a scandalized whisper, "Too much *gold*?"

"Yes." Frank paused then; he was back in stride now, Harriet thought, for he'd removed attention from the gadfly Mr. Giles and firmly onto himself. Then she saw what his hands were doing. He'd spread a little piece of white paper on the table, and his fingers, with fussy movements, were shaving flakes of tobacco from a plug of the stuff onto the paper with a knife.

Don Manuel and the other Vidrie men were smoking cigars, and their women were smoking miniature paper-wrapped versions of these. It was their custom; Harriet disliked the smell but had become used to the habit. Like the Vidrie women, Sefton neatly rolled the paper, trapping the flakes inside; he gave it a little twist and set it between his lips, and one of the women, flirtatiously, held a lighted taper to it. Sefton thanked her with a charming smile and then leaned back in his chair.

"They tell me," said he conversationally, "that the use of tobacco is popular with travelers, for cannibals dislike the taste of humans who have indulged in the habit."

Then he chuckled, while Mr. Chaffey and Mr. Prenderwhite

grimaced. Mr. Giles murmured, as if to himself, "Is that so, huh?" Then he said in a louder voice, "You were telling us, sir, about the danger of digging too much gold."

"It is not that the gold is too much, sir. It is that there is too little coin! Gold is the currency here, as you've all observed, and that gold is becoming debased. The first bank to establish a mint will fill a need and make a fortune, and I intend that bank to be mine, sir. Can you see how I need outside investment?"

"But," Mr. Giles murmured, "I was under the impression that you were anxious to lend us the wherewithal to do it."

"That is so, indeed; you are not mistaken, sir. I will lend the money . . . and take the shares in the bank as collateral. That is how much faith I have in my plans."

"A persuasive argument, Colonel."

"Then you will buy some shares, Mr. Giles?"

"No, sir, I will not. I have other plans, but I thank you."

"Plans?" Sefton echoed. He was staring at the other, unblinking, and Harriet uneasily saw that the whites of his protuberant eyes were turning red, a sure sign of fury. He spluttered, "But what plans could be better?"

"I plan to start a paper, sir, and have the doings with me; I plan to set it up, sir, in the place that they call Sutter's."

Sutter's, thought Harriet, and quenched a grimace; she remembered Don Roberto's prognostications for the place, and his unluckily persuasive arguments. If he had been lying, then he'd cheated her and the *Hakluyt* men with her; if he truly believed in his arguments, then that was no reason, either, for betraying her business to her husband. The women were rising from the table, but she scarcely heard them, for Sefton snapped, "You think to set up in Sutter's? Then you're mad, Mr. Giles, for the town of Sutter's don't exist."

"I was under the impression," Mr. Giles drawled, "that there was a fort there of some substance."

"There is a fort there, certainly, but my wife, Harriet, can tell you that the land about Sutter's is worthless, for 'tis naught but swamp and overflowing river." Harriet was standing, leaving her seat in belated recognition that the Vidrie men had all risen courteously to bid good night to the ladies. She froze when Sefton said sharply, "Harriet, my dear, tell him that . . . tell him that investment in Sutter's is money lost, for any project there is doomed to failure."

Harriet was silent: she was so accustomed to being ignored

at this table that she had forgotten what it was like to speak. Everyone was staring at her. She lifted her chin and looked steadily at her husband and said very clearly, "All I can say is that I have heard arguments for both sides. The place when I last saw it was muddy most certainly, but others who should know this California spoke to me most persuasive concerning the future of the place. Don Roberto, the alcalde, a man who has been in California for a decade exactly, assured me fervently that within a few years a city will rise there that will rival New Orleans."

Then she moved. She nodded regally at all the men, and left the room in the company of the other women. Her last sight of her husband was the grim set of his face, and the reddened color of his eyes.

26 ❧ When Harriet woke in the
morning she woke with a lurch,
her skin cold with a sense of danger. The house was as silent
as the grave, but the light in her window told her that the sun
was well up. She sat up in bed. She was alone; she had been
alone all night . . . or had she?

The feeling was indefinable; she wondered if she had
dreamed it. She had taken so long to fall asleep, listening,
creeping with the knowledge that she had made her husband
furiously angry. Doors had slammed, there had been sharp
footsteps in the passage outside . . . and then, and
then . . . she had fallen asleep and had dreamed that someone had come in and had moved with stealth in the dark of her
room.

She'd dreamed it, of course she had, and yet she got up with
a sense of urgency. Things were not as she'd left them when
she'd gone to bed: gowns had been shuffled on their hooks, and
drawers were partly open. Her baskets had been moved.

Apprehension gripped her; she looked about wildly in all the customary places. Then she remembered that she'd put the journal down by her chair to take the documents from Frank; she remembered the expression in his eyes. She fell to her knees, hunting on all fours beside the chair, under the chair, and then, in desperation, behind the chair, hauling it out . . . and she had not been dreaming at all, for old Rochester's journal was gone.

The book was gone. She dressed quickly, washed and brushed with furious haste, and then ran out of the room. The passageway was empty. There was still no sound in the house, not even of servants. The polished floor stretched before her as silent as a looking glass. The quick rustle of her skirts seemed deafening. She stopped, looking about, apprehension touching her, a voice behind her drawled, "Good morning to you, Mrs. Sefton."

She whirled. It was Mr. Giles. He looked even more played out than he had at the dinner table. The pouches beneath his yellowed eyes sagged almost to his stained mostachos, emphasizing his world-weary look. Mr. Giles had a cold chop in one hand, half-gnawed, and he nibbled at it while he watched her face.

She said angrily, "You gave me a fright."

"So I observed, ma'am."

But neglected to apologize, she thought tartly. Then she put her mind to her immediate problem and said swiftly, "Have you seen my husband?"

"That I have indeed, yes, this very morning."

"Then where is he?"

"That's a little difficult to answer, ma'am, being as I don't know how far it be to Don Roberto's fort. The men could be there, or not quite there yet."

"*What*?" She gasped, incredulous that Sefton should have gone and left her yet again, and abruptly furious, for he'd not only gone and demonstrated again how he disdained her, but he'd also stolen her book and taken it with him. Then her heart jerked and she cried, "What men?"

"Why, all of 'em, ma'am. Don Manuel and his showy male relatives, Chaffey and Prenderwhite and all, quite a little gathering for a solitary alcalde to entertain." Mr. Giles paused then, his attitude thoughtful, and while she watched him with implications rushing through her mind he finished the chop and threw the bone out the nearest window. Then he lounged off toward the dining room, and Harriet was forced to follow.

There were bowls of fruit as well as platters of bread and congealed meat on the table. Harriet sat down uncertainly in the chair she'd occupied at dinner, and Mr. Giles sat down opposite. He reached out and plucked another chop from its quivering gravy, and then said casually, "Who is this alcalde Don Roberto?"

"He's a Londoner; his real name is Robert Ross. He has been in this land for a long time."

"Ah," said Mr. Giles, and nodded. "The fellow with such grand prognostications for Sutter's Fort. Did you say London, Mrs. Sefton?"

"I did," she said impatiently. "He's a Cockney."

"And you, by your accent, belong to that city too."

His tone was insinuating. Harriet stared at him with dislike and then took a plate of bread and preserve. She spread with emphasis and said, "There is no connection, I assure you of that. I met him here in California."

"But 'tis an odd kind of coincidence, I think."

"Think what you like," she snapped. "Don Roberto is certainly an oddity."

"So I guessed," said Mr. Giles, and nodded knowingly. "I reckon California will soon get acquainted with the odd kind of thing, if it ain't already." Then, with such an abrupt change of topic that she blinked, he said, "And you met the colonel, your husband, in London?"

"I did not."

"Surely not in Canton?"

"I met him in New Zealand . . . if that holds interest."

"Oh, it does, it does. I wonder often about your husband the colonel, Mrs. Sefton."

So did Harriet; she said nothing.

"I wonder about the circumstance that he be so anxious to sell off shares in his bank, ma'am."

"You were not tempted to buy any?"

"Ma'am, I'm naught but a poor roving printer."

"Then we have much in common," she said broodingly, "for I am—was—naught but a poor roving player," and she saw his jaws stop short as his eyes opened wide.

"An *actress*?"

"Yes!" Her retort was sharp, but he did not seem to notice her anger, for he appeared so much astounded, lost in meditations and chewing at one drooping mostacho as he thought, while the chop sat neglected in his fist. Then he roused himself and said, "I've met him before, but he don't remember that."

"*What*?"

"Yep. In New York, nigh on nine years ago, by my recollection. There was a deal of prattle going the rounds about Colonel Sefton . . . only what but he were not a colonel then. He was highly active in New York social circles, very wishful to better himself, for all that his family in Philadelphia were so bluenosed. He was chasing after a certain Miss Coffin, of the whaling and merchant lot."

Harriet paused. Then she said sharply, "Mr. Giles, you may pretend to be a mere poor roving printer, but my impression is that you are much more than that."

"Ah, a printer I am, and printer's devil, too, and typesetter, sales clerk, and editor also. I can write and be critic, at any acting affair, ma'am, and I can set up posters too."

"I think you write more than critical reviews, Mr. Giles."

"You are most perceptive, ma'am. There's a big interest back East in this here golden territory, publishers all keen to buy the stories that come out of here."

"I think you write even more than that, Mr. Giles, for I think you deal in gossip. What about this . . . Miss Coffin, in New York, for instance."

"Ah," he said, and rose from his seat, brushing his hands to flick off grease. "Miss Coffin married a much more likely man, and Sefton swore to make her regret it, but all he did was disappear . . . but I remember him."

Then he made to set off, and she said quickly, "Where are you going?"

"Why, to pack, ma'am, having replenished my belly and soothed my spirits. Don Manuel," said he, and pulled down his mouth, "has withdrawn his hospitality. His last words as he set off were a courtly adieu, which make it perfect unmistakable that he did not expect to see me on his return."

"But I thought you were my husband's guest?"

"Not at all, Mrs. Sefton. Chaffey was the one with the letter of introduction; Prenderwhite and myself were just bit-players, so to speak. It was a most gratifying surprise, to find my unknowing host so memorable. Tell me, do you think Don Manuel withdrew his hospitality because I disappointed him in some way?"

She snapped, "You speak as if you think my husband's dealings and Don Manuel are connected."

"Well, it do seem uncommon coincidental that my welcome should wear out so soon after refusing to purchase those shares . . . and you have been here a long time, I hear, Mrs. Sefton. Don Manuel is a most obliging neighbor, he is indeed."

She bit her lip at that, brooding that her own welcome here was certainly worn out for a stranger to see it so quickly. The humiliation of living where she was not wanted nagged again; she hated her husband, she thought resentfully, but hate him or not, she had a right to be the mistress in his home.

She said quickly, "The Vidrie men are coming back?"

"Yes, Mrs. Sefton, this very day."

And when they came back the situation in this house would take up just as it had before, for Don Manuel, certainly, would not allow her to travel without her husband's permission and an escort . . . and Mr. Giles, while insinuating in speech and unattractive in manner, was an escort, of a kind. She said, "And my husband?"

"Ah, that be a different matter. My impression was that he intended to stick with Chaffey and Prenderwhite as long as he was able, in the hope of altering their minds about those shares, and then, that done . . . or not done, as the case may be . . . journey back to his own rancho."

That settled it. "Mr. Giles, you will oblige me by delaying half an hour," she said firmly. "For I've determined to come with you."

She did not feel nervous about her decision until Don Roberto's fort came into view. The Vidrie women had been most unexcited about her decision to leave them so abruptly, which proved, Harriet thought, how truly her presence had become boring. The only anxious one was Ah Wong, who, as her servant, was forced to accompany her wherever she might go; Mr. Giles had seemed dourly amused. "I don't intend to go farther than Don Roberto's fort," he warned, and Harriet studied the thick walls of the fort as they plodded toward it.

"And after that?"

"Down river, somehow, to Sutter's."

"My husband did not persuade you that Sutter's Fort is dead?"

"Your husband, the Colonel, experienced little success in any of his persuasions last night."

"Sutter's was about under water the last I saw of it."

"Is that so?" And Mr. Giles appeared to meditate. He rode his horse like a sack, drawing his mule along on a lead string. The mule was a most morose-looking animal, and untidy withal: to Harriet's secret amusement, both animal and man looked remarkably alike.

Then he said, "I'll see Sutter's for myself, I reckon."

"You've heard other report, perhaps."

"All I know, ma'am, is that a large crowd of men was awaiting at Sonoma for passage up the Sacramento when the river goes down enough to allow it, and that I heard that a mighty crowd was waiting, too, at 'Frisco. And I can look at a chart, ma'am, and halfway understand it, and the situation of Sutter's Fort seems sufficient promising for men to want to drain it and settle it. So that, until my mind alters, is where I've concluded to set up my press."

Harriet looked at him thoughtfully. He and Don Roberto should have much in common, she mused, looking down the valley at the fort again, and froze.

There was a cavalcade of men and mules coming out of the gate. She could see the light spark off trappings and see, too, the flag flying on the corner bastion which showed that Don Roberto was home. At first glance she had thought the riders the Vidrie party but soon saw that they were not . . . so why did the hairs stand up with a chill on the back of her neck?

She reined in and stared, scarcely aware of Mr. Giles's inquisitive looks. The mule train looked tired; the animal's heads hung low, and their flanks were gray with the dust of heavy going, and yet it seemed that they were only just setting out on their journey. Then Harriet thought that the stop at the fort had perhaps been a brief one, for the mules to forage a little and drink water, while men ate, drank, conferred . . . about what? The men with that train were on horseback, riding flamboyantly like Californians. Harriet heard distant shouts and whooping and saw hats and lariats whirled, and she frowned as she nagged for that feeling of familiarity. Then, as the train labored up the hilly trail on the farther side of the bridge and the river, she suddenly knew those men. Her stomach clenched: they were the Murietas, taking the mules to . . . where, and carrying what?

They were gone, and she couldn't hear the shouting anymore. She slowly clicked her tongue and set her horse in motion again, and Ah Wong and Mr. Giles followed her along the track, through the entrance of the fort. Echoes rattled off the walls as the horses and one mule clattered in on the cobbles.

Harriet slid down slowly, and then looked warily around. The courtyard and stables were empty, but she could smell the manure and urine the mules had left behind. The shadow cast by the ugly block-shaped building in the middle was littered with straw and discarded papers and rags. The place was so neglected and shabby that she wondered if Don Roberto had gone with Frank Sefton or the Vidries . . . or the Murietas.

Then with a sudden clatter the door of the house opened, and Don Roberto's comic figure was revealed. He stared, rubbed his face, stared again, and cried out in shocked tones. "Mrs. Sefton! But your—your 'usband be gone, this whole hour back, and he didn't say you were coming."

"There was an alteration in plans," she said evenly. "I also want to speak with you . . . on a certain matter that concerns you."

If she had come alone or with Ah Wong he would not have let her in, she thought, but the presence of Mr. Giles made all the difference. Don Roberto grumpily led the way inside, and she, like the reporter, stared about with some awe at the empty spaces downstairs. "I ain't all primped up for callers," Don Roberto grumbled as he led the way upstairs to a bedroom–sitting room that was as full of furniture as the downstairs rooms were not. Huge carved sideboards leaned against each other, their mirrors all a-kilter, and large ornate chairs were stacked so tightly that Harriet had to lift her skirts to clamber over one of them to find a seat on another. There were carved wooden tables too, one with a huge tarnished tray that held an assortment of battered pitchers and rows of grimy tumblers. Harriet silently wondered how Don Roberto had contrived to get all this encumbrance to this far-flung place, and saw Mr. Giles looking about in wonderment too.

"One day I plan to turn my fort into a first-rate hotel, Mrs. Sefton."

"You do?"

"And will do it, when the alcalde business gives me time." Don Roberto bobbed about while Mr. Giles folded his frame onto a chair, and muttered peevishly, "Being alcalde ain't nobbut a theft of my time and industry, Mr. Giles, Mrs. Sefton. 'Tis a doleful business at the best. Gawd'n bless me, I'm all the time runnin' about, adjudicatin' crimes, hearing all the evidence, ensuring that the right reparation be made. 'Ere, take this," he said, and handed one tumbler to Harriet and another to Mr. Giles.

She took it absently, staring up at him as he griped. "You've not a notion 'ow hard it is, and no mistake, it ain't. Murder's bad, but claim jumpin' is the very devil, excuse me Mrs. Sefton." Harriet said nothing: the incredulous quality of Mr. Giles's rivetted attitude had registered, and she—like he—was staring at the contents of their tumblers.

They were both half-full of busy murky water. Mosquito larvae tumbled about in their dozens. Then, dimly, she heard Don Roberto say, "Just 'old it out, just a moment, excuse me." She held it out, numbly, and he produced a dark bottle and tipped a potion into it; then he did the same for the reporter.

The contents of both tumblers immediately became frantic, as the wrigglers turned simultaneous somersaults. Then, as one, they gave up the ship and sank to the bottom. Even more incredulously, Harriet saw Mr. Giles lift the glass, an eyebrow, and then take an appreciative swig. It did not seem to harm him. She returned her gaze to Don Roberto.

"Murder's bad, I admit it," Don Roberto was saying querulously. He looked about and then planted his fat rump on a chair. "But when you got a corpse, at least you've got a crime, motive, cause and effect, all lying there afore your eyes. But claim jumpin'! I know you must feel bad about it, but what else can I do but take time to think over the evidence?"

Harriet gaped in bewilderment. Then she echoed, "Feel bad?"

"Well, no doubt you feel some anger on behalf of your brother, for no doubt he rails enough, saying the claim were rightfully his, but how do I know that, when the tools and stakes was all throwed away?"

"Claim?" Her breath caught. "What claim?"

"Why, the claim at what they call *Hakluyt* Gully, the one right near to Dry Bones Gulch, the richest find thus far this season! You saw the gold go out, perhaps, on that muletrain bound for the bank at Pueblo San Marco. A most gratifyin' pile it was. We dug out twenty thousand."

She snapped, "*Did you say twenty thousand dollars*?"

"All from one little vein." The alcalde's tone was injured. He took a gulp of his drink and nodded at Mr. Giles, saying, "Perhaps you've heard of the system, sir, perhaps you have not. But when I get called in as alcalde to adjudicate on claim-jumpin' offenses, I hire my deputies to dig out all the gold and then stow it all safe in the village bank, till I feel certain sure that I know who rightfully owns it. It takes time, and we get a percentage, of course, but at least I know that justice be done . . . and 'ow many east-side judges can boast of that, eh?"

Mr. Giles's silence was more attentive than ever, but Harriet scarcely noticed that; her mind was taken up with that number. Twenty thousand . . . twenty thousand, the exact value of the shares that Sefton wanted to give her.

Sefton had taken the certificates away with him, no doubt, when he stole her book. Perhaps he had sold them already, to Chaffey or Prenderwhite. She said tensely, "That gold that the Murietas are taking into the bank came from my brother's claim . . . that someone jumped?"

"I don't say jumped, Mrs. Sefton, for I don't know that." Don Roberto took a moody gulp from the glass he had poured for himself, and muttered, "All the evidence says that there were no stakes nor tools on that claim, for they'd all been taken and throwed away."

"But surely the tools and stakes were there in the first place?" she snapped. "If men declare they were thrown away, then they declare also that those tools and stakes were there originally."

He went red and shouted, "Oh, very clever Mrs. Sefton, but dead bodies don't stake a claim, and in partic'lar bodies what were not even lying on that place . . . and the Indians who stole the tools ain't catched!"

"*What?*" Her vision went dark, and the room, most sickeningly, was swaying. She whispered, "What bodies . . . and what Indians?"

"Why, them Indians what invaded that ravine and massacred them two men! The folks at Dry Bones Gulch had just but learned that the *Hakluyt* men prospected there, and they all went to look, and found them two corpses."

She cried out in a kind of agony, "What corpses? For God's sake, tell me!"

"Two foremast hands. A Chilean and a Fayal man."

Pablo. Joseph Fayal. She said huskily, "Was anyone else hurt?"

"No, of course not, 'ow could they be? The way your brother tells it, the three of them was prospecting and turned up that rich find. So they claimed it and 'e went back off to fetch the rest of the men, leaving them two to work it. When he got back the murders had been done and the ravine was all taken up with diggin's."

She swallowed. Then she said icily, "And who was digging the *Hakluyt* claim? Who are the men who jumped it?"

"I don't know that it had been jumped!" he shouted, perfect puce in the face. Then, reluctantly, staring down into his tumbler, he added, "The men digging in that place were three of the Murieta brothers, the same ones who be my deputies, but that ain't nobbut more than a coincidence. They 'ad it staked all legal, Mrs. Sefton, and they 'ad naught to do with the foul murders. 'Twas the Indians did that foul deed."

Indians? She whispered tensely, "On what evidence?"

"It 'ad to be Indians what killed those men, for they'd been scalped!"

Scalped. She shut her eyes as the room swung again. *The administrators of Sonora and Chihuahua pay a bounty for scalps . . .*

Pablo and Joseph had both had Indian-black hair. She opened her eyes, trembling, and snapped, "How can you bear to hire men like the Murietas?"

"Because I 'ave to 'ave deputies, Mrs. Sefton, and it ain't no use not 'aving men who are tough and not squeamish; the Murietas serve my purpose and it ain't no business of your'n, ma'am." Then he shouted, "Why are you 'ere?"

"What?"

"I thought you'd seen your brother, or someone 'ad come out of Bedstead Gully now I 'ear it be open and Cap'n Dexter back there, but you knew naught of the gold, Mrs. Sefton, so why 'ave you come with these questions?"

She lifted her chin and said sharply, "I came to talk about that land I bought at Sutter's, Don Roberto. You recommended the purchase most highly; I bought the land on your advice. So why did you tell my husband about it, without first informing me?"

"What?" Then his eyes shifted, leaving hers. He shuffled on his seat and muttered, "I didn't know then that you were Mrs. Sefton. I didn't even know you were married. It was your deception what done it. You can't say fair for one moment that I were the one to blame. It embarrassed me most highly to find I'd gone and sold Colonel Sefton's land to his very own wife; don't think for an instant I were pleased. It made me look a proper fool, selling a man's land to 'is wife."

"It was Frank's . . . ?" It was so unbelievable that it was almost funny; she stared at him, fighting down hysterical laughter. Then she frowned and snapped, "I don't believe you."

"But 'tis the truth!" he yelped.

"My husband would never consent to own land in that place; he declares it worthless, and Mr. Giles will bear witness to that opinion."

The little eyes were sliding about, flitting over furniture and dust. Then he muttered, "Colonel Sefton did not get that land by purchase. It was collateral on a debt that Captain Sutter owed him, and the money never got paid back, so Colonel Sefton took the deed, as was 'is legal due."

Collateral. That word again. She had had the chance of twenty thousand shares in Sefton's bank . . . the exact same amount as the value of the confiscated *Hakluyt* gold. All she had to do was see Sefton again and graciously consent to sign his paper and accept those shares . . .

She stood up, trying hard to hide her haste. Don Roberto saw her to the courtyard; Mr. Giles did not bother. He was down to the dregs of his glass and declared he would try another before heading for Pueblo San Marco. Don Roberto appeared glad to be quit of her and even helped her mount her horse. Ah Wong was waiting, already mounted. Harriet led the way to the rancho-ward trail before she noted that the little Chinese was sweating with what looked more like abject fear than simple anxiety.

27 ❧   She watched the little Chinaman as they galloped along the
dales and crests en route from Don Roberto's fort to her
husband's rancho. Ah Wong rode far forward in his seat, the
way he always did, sitting over the withers with his thin knees
cocked sideways like a cricket, his pigtail pattering like a
buntline between the blue-covered shoulder blades. Harriet had
become fond of Ah Wong over the months, and not just
because he, too, had been politely incarcerated in the Vidrie
establishment. He was overanxious and overconscientious, but
she had found much pleasure in teaching him English, for he
was such an apt and eager pupil . . .and, more than that; she
had learned from him the strange enjoyments of Chinese
poetry.

    That poetry had taught her to look more closely at nature.
Because of Ah Wong she had learned to look at California: pale
spring sky, the misty horizons of late afternoon, the lines of
dark purple pines on the gold-grassed slopes, the ethereal

outlines of mountains. A skein of waterfowl flew high, flying
north to the Siberian summer; perhaps they were the same birds
she had watched last autumn in the Bay of San Francisco,
flying in the other direction. Five months, she thought, five
months of loss and heartbreak and shame and waiting; she had
changed—and so had California.

In ordered beauty, as the wild ducks fly
Note follows note in melody
The red-toothed plectrum plucks the strings
Lilylike fingers hold the lute
Delightfully, and in perfect accord, the new refrains
Set to new melodies, echo among old pillars . . .

Ah Wong's head did not turn, but she heard him whisper:
wan fu.

Wan fu: happiness thousandfold. She often wondered about
Ah Wong and his native land, for life, surely, must have been
hard there, for otherwise a man would not have to search for
wan fu in a string of ducks and a poem. Ah Wong had
described his scenery as a never-ending tapestry of patches,
centuries of landscape, made by generations of men and
women who grubbed endlessly in the dirt of Cathay to keep
that patchwork complete. Ah Wong had scrimped and saved
and then sold something valuable to make up what seemed a
pitiful sum of money to buy his way to San Francisco, the
golden promise of a younger, less patchworked land. She knew
how harsh that scrimping had been simply by looking at Ah
Wong's face: the shriveled little man she had thought was sixty
had proved to be thirty-two.

He had paid that money to Sefton and had bonded himself as
Sefton's servant for five long years. Harriet often wondered if
Ah Wong regretted that; looking at him now, and his increased
fear as they approached the rancho, she wondered if he would
have made that bargain if he had but known what lay ahead.
Night was falling, the shadows swooping over the hills to touch
them, evening mists rising from the river, and she heard Ah
Wong hissing to himself in a constant mutter of worry as he
jogged in his saddle. In the distance she could see the town, the
brig, the schooner moored at the far-off embarcadero of Pueblo
San Marco, and then night fell and she could see the river no
more. Then Ah Wong reined in, under a tree. The gate to the
rancho was a hundred feet ahead. Harriet reined in too, and

when she looked at Ah Wong inquiringly she could see the
gleam of sweat drops rolling down his cheek.

She said, "What's wrong?" He did not answer. In the fields
the goatsucker birds were calling, *Whip poor Willy . . .
work, poor Willy, weep . . .* but the house was dark and still.
The air was scented with growing grass and orange blossom.
Harriet tapped her heel on her horse's side, and the animal
moved forward reluctantly. Then, from ahead, she heard
whickering.

There were several horses, very quiet. She could hear the
clump as one lifted its hooves, and the inquiring snorting as
they scented her steed. She slid down from the saddle and led
her horse forward, round the corner of the garden to the path
that led to the courtyard door, and found the other horses
tethered together under a tree.

There were four of them, with California trappings, with
high pommels on the saddles and broad stirrups made of wood:
the Vidrie horses. She recognized them instantly. And
yet . . . and yet the house was so quiet. Then, stealthily despite herself, she opened the door and stole into the courtyard.

The fountain rippled almost silently, and the leaves of the
climbing plants whispered. Harriet stopped and listened . . .
to voices, male voices that echoed from the inside of the house.
They spoke in Spanish: the Vidries. She recognized the tones
but could not discern the words. There was the same feverish
excitement in their voices that she had heard in the past, around
the arena where the bull and bear battled for their sport. When
she heard a step beside her she whirled, her heart jerking, but
it was only Ah Wong, come into the courtyard to join her. She
began to speak . . . and heard his whine of utter fear.

She thought he was going to scream. His eyes bulged and his
mouth opened wide, but only that whine of abject terror came
out. His face in the faint light had gone as pasty as cheese, and
his mouth opened wider and wider, but all she heard was that
horrifying sound of superstitious fear. She stared at him in
fright and pity—and Sefton's hand shot out of the shadows and
gripped her arm.

She almost screamed then, herself, for she'd heard not a
sound to warn her he was there. Frank's fingers bit into her arm
as he snapped, "What the hell are you doing here?"

Harriet's mouth opened but nothing came out: horrifyingly,
her throat was too dry to allow her to speak. She stared

helplessly up into his round eyes, and Sefton shook her and said, "Who brought you here? Surely not Ah Wong?"

Ah Wong . . . Ah Wong had gone, as if he'd never come into the courtyard. Then, belatedly, she registered the sound of his running feet and realized that Ah Wong had run away into the depths of the house. Ah Wong . . . Harriet heard a giggle, another distinctively Chinese noise . . . Mei-mei's shrill teasing laughter. She had forgotten the pert depravity of the Chinese woman's laughter, and the sound of it now gave her the strength of fury.

Harriet snapped, " 'Twas not Ah Wong's fault that I came here, so please do not blame him. He merely obeyed my instructions."

"Your instructions? when he happens to be my servant?"

"And," she flashed, "I was escorted."

"Escorted?" She saw his head turn to the sounds of the Vidrie men and Mei-mei; she could feel his consternation, along with his anger. The fingers bit cruelly, and he hissed, "Escorted by whom?"

"The reporter. Mr. Giles." Her voice came out more unsteadily than she would have liked. She was afraid, she thought, and that made her more scared and angry than ever. "Surely—as your wife—I have the right to live in your house? And yet, Frank, you insist on leaving me, over and over again. I have come to sign your documents, take your shares. What more do you want, pray? *I've come to sign your goddamned papers*!"

She shouted it out, unaware for a moment that her voice had risen. Then she heard the abrupt horrified hush in the room where the Vidrie men had been giggling with Mei-mei. She saw Sefton turn his head, too, and heard him mutter, "Giles . . . the reporter, Giles."

Then, infinitesimally, silence, quickly broken by Sefton's sharp intake of breath. Then he pushed her, shoving her along. She fell into the room behind the screen. She had been there before, a long time ago and never had liked it, but she hadn't seen it like this. It was lit with lamps and joss-sticks . . . and the light fell weirdly on the open-mouthed faces of Don Manuel Vidrie, his brothers . . . his cousins . . .

And Mei-mei. The woman Mei-mei was sprawled on the great bed. She seemed awry, twisted, and then Harriet saw that the bandaged feet were tied to the two bottom bed-posts, tied with the loose ends of bandage so that the feet made a dark triangle, and Mei-mei's face floated in the apex of it. The light fell on the pale perfect face, and Harriet saw the hatred.

It was the same jealous hate she had glimpsed before, for her, Sefton's lawful wife. Harriet stared, uncomprehending, and Mei-mei slowly and gloatingly smiled.

The smile was as ancient as the malice it held. Harriet stood numbly, on the verge of sickness, and then felt Sefton's fingers tight on her arm. His hand jerked, dragging her out of the room, and then he shoved her up the passage, to her bedroom, the room that had been hers, and Sefton let her go so abruptly that she stumbled.

Everything looked just the same. The fireplace was as cold and empty, the furniture was as black and huge. The same quilts were on the same canvas-bottomed bed. Harriet caught her balance with a hand on a bedpost and then looked warily at Sefton.

Forebodingly, he was smiling. She said very quickly, "Please don't punish Ah Wong; it was not his fault," and the smile merely widened.

"I'm pleased you have obeyed me, my dear, and given more thought to my gift of the shares. Sleep well," he invited, his hand on the latch, "and we'll discuss the matter further, in the morning."

Then, before she could move or say a word, he was gone, and the door shut firmly behind him. The room was dark; she found a lamp, and lit it with trembling fingers. Then she slumped onto the side of the bed, looking around and wishing fervently she had not come. Now, at this distance, the Vidrie pueblo looked a most comfortable prison.

The Vidries . . . Outside she heard subdued voices, and then the sounds of horses being mounted and hastily galloped away. She didn't want to wonder what scene in the room by the screen she had interrupted; every time the thought came into her mind she pushed it away and concentrated on her own situation. When she at last lay down she dreamed uneasily, of Pablo and Joseph Fayal, and Jake Dexter. She woke once in the blackness of midnight and thought she heard Ah Wong sobbing, crying out. She got out of bed and rushed to the door, but the door was locked. She must have dreamed that too, for in the morning the door opened freely, held shut only by the latch.

Ah Wong brought her breakfast. He looked the same as always, his manner subdued. Colonel Sefton was not in, he said, but had gone over the river in the ferryboat to Pueblo San Marco. He had gone on bank business. Harriet grimly thought she knew what that business was. While she ate her breakfast she thought about the twenty thousand dollars' worth of *Hakluyt* gold that the Murietas had taken to Sefton's bank.

Then she dressed and moved about the house, listening to the waiting silence. The rooms were empty; there was no sign of Mei-mei. It was like her first morning at this place; she even had a horse, so she could ride about the rancho if she wished. There was nothing to stop her ordering her horse saddled up and then taking Ah Wong and riding to the Vidrie place . . . nothing except her memories of the Vidrie men's voices the night before. She couldn't go to Pueblo San Marco, for Sefton was there; Sefton had the ferryboat. She tried the door of Sefton's study, but it was locked; she wandered about and ate another meal and then, after waiting a long time in her room, she decided to try Sefton's study door again. She pressed on the latch, stealthily, and it opened so suddenly that she gasped. It swung wide, and Sefton, sitting at his desk, looked inquiringly up.

She said in that gasp, "I didn't hear you come back." Then she saw what he was reading, and cried, "That is my book!"

"Your book, my dear?" His voice was perfectly unstartled. "I must admit that when I first saw you with it, I assumed that it was a journal you kept yourself, perhaps dating from our meeting in New Zealand. . . . But now I see that it belongs to the brig *Hakluyt*. Perhaps you stole it, for it certainly is not yours."

"I did not steal it!" Then, more quietly, she said, "It was . . . loaned to me, by a friend."

"And that friend, no doubt, was Captain Dexter. Was he the man who kept this journal?"

She said very evenly, "He was not," and then pressed her lips shut.

"Then who, pray, was the keeper?" She did not reply but watched him pout. Then Sefton looked down, his smooth clean hands turning pages. "I have read it with much interest," he murmured. "Such scribbles, so tantalizing, such a preoccupation with gold. Your brother told me much about Captain Dexter, and the *Hakluyt* crew, and gold. . . . He said that before they sailed for Valparaíso they'd been treasure-hunting on Judas Island, digging there for gold."

She snapped, "That is scuttlebutt—gossip!—and Royal had no right to tell you about it; he wasn't even there!"

The blue eyes sharpened. "But you were, my dear?" he murmured. "And tell me, was that gold found?"

She paused and then shrugged. "There is no gold on Judas Island."

"But Judas Island does exist? Ah yes," he murmured, slyly watching her face. "I believe so indeed, even if so ornately hidden . . . for I believe, dear wife, having read this journal with such interest, that this chart—here—is of that certain island. Am I not right?"

Her skin crept. Sefton had always been clever, she remembered; she hid the chill, saying nothing, merely shrugging.

"And you have searched it, with Captain Dexter and the *Hakluyt* crew?"

"Many people have searched it, from the pirate Henry Morgan onwards. For all I know they found the gold and took it away, for there is surely no gold there now."

"Unless that gold is hidden, unless it is, truly, buried treasure. Do you think this book might hold the answer, to the puzzle of where that treasure is hidden?"

The hairs on her forearms were rising. She kept her voice even and said without inflexion, "No, I do not."

"No?" Then he was silent; she watched him set the book to one side and lay out a little piece of white paper. His face turned down as he scraped tobacco and twirled the paper into a tiny cigar; it was as if he had forgotten that she was in the room. Then he lit it and leaned back in his chair, studying her through the acrid puffs of smoke. "So you have reconsidered and come to sign the paper and take the shares," he said musingly. "Can it be that you could live no longer away from me?"

His tone was derisive. She snapped, "I couldn't give a damn if I never saw you again, Frank; marrying you was the most foolish act I have ever committed, but, yes, I have come to sign for those shares—and I will sign for them, on two conditions."

"What!" He looked thunderstruck, genuinely shocked. "You—my wife, a woman—you dare to set conditions on my gift?"

"Yes," she said curtly. "I'm persuaded that you are most anxious to get quit of those shares, Frank, though I'm completely at a loss for a reason. All I know is that you are desperate. On the other hand, I am not at all eager to sign any more of your papers, for I suffered so much from the consequences of signing the last set. But I will do so if you give me back that book and give me back the deed for the land at Sutter's."

He stared at her, his stare veiled, like a lizard's. She felt chilled again, momentarily aghast at her foolhardy courage, but she bit down the fear, keeping her own gaze level. Then he said slowly, "And who was it that persuaded you that I need to quit those shares, h'm?"

"My own sense . . . and the advice of Mr. Giles."

"Giles!" The sharp word was like a curse; for a moment she thought he was going to lunge out of his chair, but instead he hit the top of his desk with one flat hand, making a noise like an explosion. He snapped, "You're a fool!"

"Am I?" she demanded. "I know, too, that you have an obsessive need to get back to New York a rich and successful man, so men—and women—will say, 'There goes that wonderful rich adventurer,' and I know that while I have nothing to do with your plans, selling the bank off somehow has. So don't ask questions, Frank, or worry for my reasons, be satisfied instead that I am prepared to sign . . . just so long as I also get that book and that title to the land."

He stared at her, his eyes unblinking; she could hear his heavy breathing. Then all at once he shook his hand and swore: the little cigaretto had burned to the end. He stood then and stamped the little ember out. She flinched but stood her ground, and when he shouted, "And you're a fool to want that land at Sutter's!" she merely lifted her chin.

"I don't believe so, and neither does Don Roberto. I also know how you obtained that land that Don Roberto mistakenly sold to your very own wife. It was collateral on a bad debt. Well, Frank, I hope you do better on the monies you've advanced to men who've bought shares in your bank! I know now that you truly believe that the land is worthless, so giving the deed to me is hardly a condition at all."

"No?" He stared at her, while the silence dragged on. Then, so suddenly that she flinched, he laughed. "And what do you intend to do with this deed for this worthless bit of ground, pray?"

She said steadily, "I will give it to Captain Dexter, for his crew."

"And I'm not supposed to mind?" He laughed again, cruelly, and said, "And do you really believe that the good captain will want it . . . or will you sweeten the package somehow?"

"I don't know what you mean."

"Do you not? I think you do. I think you mean to escape me and live with this man, now that the trail to Bedstead Gully is open and the good captain can get out . . . I think you mean to commit adultery, my dear, I think you hope for divorce."

"How dare you say a thing like that!"

"But why not? Do it, my dear, do it," he urged, and scornfully laughed. "Do what you should have done in New Zealand when you found yourself alone, and go and live in sin. Go over the river, do, and take up residence on the brig *Hakluyt* or wherever else pleases your adulterous little nature, and then I will prove most kind, and sue you for divorce, and give you your heart's desire."

She whispered, "My God." For a moment she truly believed he'd gone mad. He was laughing but his eyes were veined with savage red, and she involuntarily fell back a step. Then, to her heartfelt relief, he turned and went back to the chair behind his desk.

He produced the paper, and somehow she controlled herself so that when she signed it her fingers were steady. Then she took the shares.

"And now the logbook," she said.

"Of course."

"And the deed."

"That, too." His tone made her shiver inside, for it was as full of pitying derision as his smile. He leaned back in his chair as she took the book, deed, and shares, tapping his teeth with the point of the knife he used to make his cigarettos, studying her blandly.

"And now?" he murmured.

And now. There was a pause in her mind, with nothing to fill it. She realized then that this was where her plans stopped, for her whole mind had been intent on making sure that she owned those shares in the bank.

Twenty thousand shares, with the *Hakluyt* gold as collateral. She would give everything to Jake Dexter . . . how? and when? *One step at a time*, she thought; like any actress she could improvise. "In the morning," she said calmly, "I will go into Pueblo San Marco and deposit all these things in a very safe place, Frank. I will deposit them in your bank."

And then? *One step at a time*, she thought, and nodded at Sefton. Then, deliberately, she stepped out of his study and along the passage to her room.

28 ⌒ Harriet was dreaming. She dreamed she heard horses and men moving about in the darkness outside of her window. She dreamed she heard a distant scream, and dreamed of Joseph Fayal and Pablo . . . or perhaps she did not dream, for she woke with a jolt, sweating with fear, and someone was in the room with her.

She lurched up in bed, her throat too dry to cry out. It was Ah Wong. He touched her shoulder with a shaking hand and whispered, "Come, please come, quickly."

"Wh-what?"

"Quick, I beg you do not talk. Please dress and come, quickly."

The whispered plea seemed jerked out of him; she could hear his teeth chattering with fear. She whispered, "Where?"

"Away."

She scrambled out of bed and grasped petticoats, gowns, shawls, and draped them all about her. It was as if she were a

316

child again, when her family had to leave their lodgings in a hurry, wearing as much as possible to save carrying it. Then she gripped the shares, the book, and the deed, and whispered again, "Where?"

Ah Wong said nothing. Instead he furtively opened the door and peered out into the passage.

The passageway was dark. He seemed to stand there forever, utterly still, listening. Then he moved, and she followed. She held her skirts tight to stop them rustling. Voices echoed outside, men speaking in Spanish, and she heard Ah Wong suck in a breath. She waited with him, her own heart bumping with fright, and then the voices moved on, in the garden. Ah Wong moved again, and Harriet followed him, through the bare kitchen and into the courtyard.

There were horses under a tree, but not the Vidries' horses. One snorted on an inquiring note, and she heard Ah Wong's faint whine of fear. He kept on moving, sidling through the night, past the tree, along a hedge to the pool of shadow under an oak. There was a loud voice in the house. Ah Wong froze. Harriet stilled too, and they . . . listened. For a terrible moment all Harriet could hear was the loud thump of her heart in her throat.

Then she heard the man again. He came out of the house by the same gate they'd used, and he walked to the horses. He took down a saddle bag. It bulked small but seemed heavy. He was smoking a cigar. The end glowed red when he puffed. Harriet saw his face. It was Joaquin Murieta.

He looked around, seemingly directly at her. Her breath was stifled in her throat. Then, after an endless time, he turned and went back into the house, and Ah Wong moved. Harriet followed the scuttling shape along another hedge to a barn and then into the barn's interior. A horse whickered and stamped, and then another, as Ah Wong led them out.

They were already saddled, with regular Californian saddles. Ah Wong had to help Harriet spring up, and then she had to haul her skirts around so she could ride astride. Then Ah Wong vaulted up into the other saddle. The sounds they made seemed as loud as thunder, but there was no crying out from the house. They walked the horses along the grass until the trail crested the first rise, and then they began to gallop.

Ah Wong led the way upriver, toward Don Roberto's fort and the trail to the Vidrie rancho. Did he think to escape to that latter place? Surely not, but Harriet had no chance to ask. Then

Ah Wong took a side path, and the going became rugged. Harriet's horse began to labor, but Ah Wong kept up the smart pace. He looked back every now and then, and Harriet could see his lips drawn back over the big teeth. She kept on looking over her shoulder herself, waiting for the shout of pursuit, but the miles went by and the night was silent, except for her panting and the snorting of the horses.

The edge of the night was paling to gray; dawn would be on them in not much more than an hour. Ah Wong galloped faster, faster, as if pursued by some oriental demon, and Harriet was hard put to it to keep up. Then, all at once, they were stumbling down a steep hill, and she could see the river, and she could see Don Roberto's fort. Then they reached the flat, and Ah Wong reined in his horse.

Harriet stopped. He said apologetically, "Mrs. Sefton, please dismount."

"Here?"

"I must return, with both horses, before . . . before it is seen that you are gone."

"But you can't go back!"

"I must." He would say no more, but he seemed so anxious that in the end she gave in and reluctantly slid down from her mount. He galloped off then without a word. Harriet stood and watched him until he and the horses were out of sight, over the top of the hill.

Then she turned slowly and walked to Don Roberto's fort. She thought, one step at a time. Her legs were stiff but her muscles loosened as she walked. She had her head down as she walked, worrying about Ah Wong. Would she ever see him again? Apprehensively, she doubted it. No one called out as she passed the big studded door in the wall of Don Roberto's fort, or watched her as she walked along the wall onto the path which crossed the bridge to the other side of the river. When she looked back she could see the first dawn breeze shake the flag on the corner bastion. She supposed that that meant Don Roberto was home, but the fort was so silent that she doubted that too. When she reached the fork in the trail she did not pause. She scarcely bothered to look at the route to Pueblo San Marco; instead she turned without hesitation onto the trail to the mines and Bedstead Gully.

The trail was easy to follow. The eager feet of hordes of miners had marked it plain already. Nevertheless the going was not easy; Harriet had not anticipated for a moment that the way would be so rough. However, she persevered . . . one step at a time. The sun rose; it was cold in the shadowed clefts where she had to stumble through icy rushing streams, and suffocatingly hot in the exposed ravines. Her shawl became alternately a curse and a blessing, and her layers of skirts a merciless encumbrance. She had to lift her petticoats high when she crossed the streams, and the weight of them unbalanced her.

Then, all at once, she found herself creeping along a cliff face. She looked down once and gasped, shutting her eyes and hanging onto the rock with tightly dug fingernails. If the wind gusted . . . She swallowed, opened her eyes, and sidled along with her face to the cliff, more quickly than ever, terrified of a sudden wind. Then instead of a gust, swallows came screaming out of their burrows in the stone and attacked her.

She screamed. They were beating at her hands and face. She scrabbled for finger holds and screamed again as nails tore loose. Claws slashed at her face and tangled in her hair, and wings beat madly. Pins dislodged, and her hair pulled loose; it stuck to the sweat on her cheeks and the tears of pain in her eyes. She sidled faster and faster, three-quarters blinded. The birds shrieked and flapped, and she put one foot on a ledge that gave way and she fell. She fell rolling, tumbling and screaming forever, down, hitting gravel each time she rolled. Then with a ghastly swoop she hit nothing and was falling through air, falling, falling, screaming with terror as she fell. Then—crash! She was caught by rough clutchings, bounced, crashed a little more, was caught, and bounced again. There was a vivid scent all about her . . . of pine. She was suspended in a giant pine.

The pine tree rustled; the world was full of the rustling of the rough tangy pine branches and her own loud weeping. Her cheeks were wet and sticky with tears and blood, and there was dust and pollen in her mouth, turning rapidly into mud on her tongue. Her hair hung, snaggled. Her shawl was dangling like an exotic bird from the branch four feet above her. It was a long time before she could stand, let alone climb, but after a long while her trembling eased, just enough. She climbed up, grasped the dangling corner, tugged at the shawl, heard it rip, and then with the shawl she tumbled down another few feet.

She managed to climb down the rest of the trunk. She staggered back from her savior pine, and it was not until she looked up, up, that she realized how miraculous that pine had been.

The cliff face reared above her forever. She couldn't bear to look at it. Instead she grimaced and turned and trudged on, down the valley, one step at a time. When she arrived at the next stream she knelt down and drank from it, thirstily. The water was icy, like best champagne. Then she stood up and marched on.

When she saw the people she stopped, amazed. There was a flat space at the side of the valley, about an acre in extent, and people lived there, Indians. They looked like the Indians who lived farther down the river, the ones she had seen from the deck of the schooner. Like those others, these were but women and children, and then she saw a few old men and . . . Davy. Davy Jones Locker. She stared for a long moment at the familiar figure, and then gathered her shawl about her and walked over toward him.

He was sitting on the ground by some women who were grinding some kind of flour and making flat cakes which they baked on flat stones. He was watching them, his every manner listless, not even giving the appearance of supervising their tedious task. The women were grinding the flour from acorns, Harriet saw with wondering pity; they took the acorns, blackened with roasting, and then ground them up with rocks and sand. Other women took the mixture of rough flour and sand and put it into bowls of water, so the sand fell to the bottom and the flour floated to the top. Then it was skimmed off, roughly slapped into shape, and baked. The smell was not appetizing. Harriet slowed as she neared them and said questioningly, "Davy?"

He took a long, long time to look up. When he did her nape crept, for his eyes were so uncomprehending. One of the women looked up and then came and stood close to him, her manner protective. She had a board on her back and a baby strapped into it. The little bright eyes looked at Harriet inquisitively, but the infant made no sound.

Harriet said, "Davy, what are you doing here?"

He frowned and said, "I live here, mistress."

Mistress. That shiver on the back of her neck again. Harriet looked about at the encampment. Like the river Indians, this tribe lived in huts that were fashioned from pits in the ground, the walls built up with dried mud, topped with a kind of thatch. That was all they seemed to have, the huts, the earthenware bowls and baskets, all that and the acorns.

She said, "Where is Captain Dexter? And why are you here?"

Two questions, she saw at once, were one too many, for Davy frowned so painfully. There was a movement beside her and Harriet jumped, but then she saw it was the woman with the baby, offering her a cake of the baked acorn flour. The other women had all drawn away and were gathered in a tight group, all eyeing her sideways; perhaps, Harriet mused, she was the first Englishwoman these Indian women had ever seen. She looked back at the one with the baby and found the cake offered even more insistently. Harriet didn't want to take it, for these people looked so poor; the corner she took for politeness and ate was gritty with sand and almost impossible to swallow.

Then Davy said, "At Bedstead Gully, that way."

He was pointing, farther up the trail to where the defile narrowed. She said, "Captain Dexter?"

"Yes," he said. "You go." He was smiling, politely. She stood a moment, uncertainly, and then she gave up and went. Within ten paces Davy and the Indian encampment were out of sight.

Time became meaningless. The sun rose to its zenith, and the ground under the trees was slippery with needles. At each stream she drank more water, but still there was sand in her mouth. She wondered what it must be like to live like that, in this land with its blatant promise of gold. Then the Indians, even, became meaningless; the world seemed empty. She knew that miners were invading these hills by the hundreds, but somehow they had been swallowed entire. Her thoughts drifted in circles as she trudged mechanically. She had the book, the share certificates, and the deed kept safe in a shawl with the corners tied to make a bag. She would give them to Jake, when she found him, and then . . . and then . . .

He would know what to do, surely. Then she found herself climbing. She slid down the steep other side on her seat, cushioned by her skirts. Then, stiffly, she stood up, and obstinately she trudged on. The trail led under trees, around loose outcrops, and then all at once she emerged from some trees, and Bedstead Gully lay before her.

It was green and very pleasant, overlooked by slopes of pines and oaks, and there was a stream running through the bottom of it. The valley was almost empty of men. Jake Dexter was standing in the middle of the stream, pouring pails of water over his head. He was fully dressed, and his clothes and hair

and beard were streaming. Harriet stopped short on the bank
in utter astonishment, and said, "What in heaven's name,
Jahaziel, are you doing?"

He lowered the bucket. He turned and looked at her. "My
God," he said. " 'Tis Harriet, and now I know I'm ill and
delirious." Then he looked down at the water he stood in and
clambered unsteadily out. He stalked over to her and stood
looking at her. Abner came running down from the hill,
hollering. Jake Dexter turned his head at the noise, and that
unbalanced him entirely. He sat down on the grass with a
sudden bump, and when Harriet touched his forehead it was
burning up with fever. He was very ill, she thought with a
lurch.

The thought that she might have struggled so, come so far,
just to see him die was terrifying. She said to Abner, "In God's
name, what is wrong with him?"

"C—Californian ague." Abner stuttered, and his eyes were
round with pity and horror as he looked at her tattered and
travel-stained condition. "The ague," he said, and she could
feel his fear. Jake sat there, slumped, and Harriet thought of the
tales she'd heard at the Vidrie place, of how the Californian
mountain fever had laid low so many. "I was sick too," said
Abner, " and Jonathan. Jonathan died," he added, and she
thought, *Oh dear God*, and then helped Abner get Jake up the
slope and into a neat little log house. "Davy was sick too, and
they all went away," Abner babbled. He sounded so young, so
profoundly relieved to have someone come to take over his
worries and fears . . . and Abner, Harriet thought in weary
anxiety, was two years or more older than she. "Cap'n Dexter
and Mr. Martin and Tib and Dan and Royal went, off to the
hills to dig a claim, a claim where Pablo and Joseph Fayal were
working, and they left us alone and Davy got sick and Jonathan
died and Davy went away, and then jest the cap'n come back,
he said he'd sent the rest to the brig. He came back, he said,
to fetch Davy and Jonathan and me, but Jonathan was layin'
there dead and buried, and Davy gone, and the cap'n were sick
hisself. And I didn't know what to do, Miss Gray!"

Oh dear God, Harriet thought; she could have wept but
helped Abner get Jake into dry clothes and into the bedroll that
was spread on a shelflike bunk built along one of the walls of
the hut. Jake said nothing and did little to help, but watched
Harriet feverishly, every second of the time.

"Davy went away," said Abner; his talk went in circles, as

if to echo the lonely circling of his mind these last solitary days. "He must've buried Jonathan, but then he went away."

"I saw him," Harriet said wearily. "At the Indian encampment. He seemed . . ."

"Brain fever," said Abner. His tone held ghoulish fascination. "The fever burned his brain all up, and now he thinks he's an Injun."

Poor Davy. Harriet looked with more foreboding than ever at Jake. His skin was hot and clammy, but he said, "How did you get here?"

"Walked."

"But why?"

She sighed, and then tried to smile. Her mouth was dry and sandy, and her smile was stiff. Her whole body felt stiff. Her voice came out as a croak, but she tried to say lightly, "Perhaps I thought you might be sick and trying to medicate yourself out of your dreadful book."

She watched him smile and shut his eyes. He looked like a desperate stranger with his beard. He said, "The same young Harriet. I think you came to argue." Then, as she watched, his face smoothed out. She was struck by awful apprehension that he might have fainted or died, but when she touched his face he was merely sound asleep. At that moment she envied him; she would have given her soul to sleep, but felt too weary even to sit down.

She looked about at the hut. It was a neat, clean place despite its small size and the bare earthen floor; it was kept all trim, mariner style. There was a hearth with a fire and a wire spit over it, and pots and pans hung from wire hooks. It had the well-worn air of a place much lived-in, with the smoke-smudged roof of a long cold winter. Abner said in the same worried monotone, "The cap'n, he said, when he come back, that Pablo and Joseph Fayal be all dead. They'd found a mine of gold off over them hills, and then others found it, and killed Pablo and Joseph for it. He said that mine be not for us. Is that right, Miss Gray?"

His face mutely begged her to tell him it was wrong. She sighed and said sadly, "I'm afraid that was right."

"Jonathan's dead," he said, and took her outside to show her the grave. Jonathan's name was written in charcoal on a board at the head. Harriet stared at it with sore dry eyes. This true-blue Yankee would never see his homeland again, she thought drearily, and wondered if his sweetheart . . . Mary-

Jane? . . . still waited. Jake was still asleep when she looked again in the cabin door, and to escape Abner's monotone she went upstream to bath and wash most of her dustiest clothes. She felt a little better afterward, but even more troubled in her mind about Jake's fever, for the water was so very cold.

Sun set behind the long purple mountains, and Abner cooked beans and flapjacks for supper while Harriet read the medical book. The guide held many suggestions for the treatment of agues and fevers, but she did not have gelsemium or aconite root, or even know what they looked like. There was quinine in the chest, almost all gone. Abner told her that Captain Dexter had boiled spruce twigs and added molasses to make a medicinal tea, so she made some. When Jake woke and tossed they gave him some tea, and then to Harriet's utter relief, both Abner and Jake went to sleep. She gratefully lay down with her shawls and a blanket and meant to think, but instead she fell into an instant slumber.

She was awakened by a voice. For a confused moment she thought it was Ah Wong, and she would have to start escaping again. Then she remembered where she was and recognized the voice as Jake's. She fell off her shelf and stumbled over to him. He seemed confused. He said, "Harriet?"

"Yes." She groped in the light of the embers and found the tea. Jake drank it thirstily, but when she took the cup away he held her other hand. His fingers were hot and dry, and he would not let go. Finally he set down the cup and sat on the floor by his bunk, her shawl wrapped about her shoulders, holding onto his hand all the time.

He mumbled, "I thought you were a dream."

"No, 'tis I, Harriet, myself, me, complete with bumps and bruises."

She heard the ghost of a chuckle. Then Jake was quiet. She thought he slept, but he would not let go of her hand, so she leaned her tired head against his side and drifted off herself.

In the night he whispered, "Why didn't you tell me you belonged to another man, Harriet?"

She could hear the slow bump of his heart and feel his warmth against her cheek. Her eyes were too heavy to open. *Because it would not have made any difference*, she thought, but did not say that. She whispered, "Because I didn't feel as if I did, Jahaziel." He said nothing. Perhaps, she thought, she had dreamed it. Then she went to sleep again and slept all the way through to a stiff and cramped morning.

Jake woke soon after. He was bright-eyed, but not with fever; the improvement was astounding. In fact, she mused wryly as she studied his face, he seemed to be in a great deal less pain than she was.

He ate ravenously and complained about the food with each and every mouthful. Then he asked that the cabin be made a little more tidy please. That made Abner bad-tempered, and he muttered balefully with every sweep of his broom. Harriet washed and thought moodily that neither of the men had asked her why she had come; perhaps they believed her jest and thought she really had thought Jake sick and had come with the express purpose of nursing him. When Abner announced that he'd decided to set off and find out what the others were a-doing on the brig, she greeted the news with pleasure. At least it would mean one less cross male under her feet, she thought tartly, and put up no argument.

However, she went with him as far as the place where the boulder had fallen. "Tell them to send a party," she said, for Jake might be right smart but was still not fit for the tramp to get out of this place. She was nervous, too, about the miners who inevitably would come here. Bedstead Gully was all worked out—or so Abner had told her—but prospective miners, she felt certain, were optimistic by nature.

She had wondered whether to give him the deed and share certificates for safekeeping, but the thought of the incoming miners had scotched that idea, for one lone sailor would be so easily robbed. At the place where they parted she hesitated and then said, "Abner, would you do me a favor?"

He said, "Yes," but his look was suspicious.

"Over the river from the brig there's a . . . rancho, and there is a Chinese servant there, a man, Ah Wong. I'm troubled in my mind about him. I wondered if a small party went over in the ferryboat and made inquiries . . ."

"I'll tell Chips about it," he said, but the tone was grudging. Then she stood and watched him go. He seemed much relieved, she thought, to be quit of the place and the responsibility of the captain, and no wonder, perhaps, for such doleful things had happened here. Then she wondered nervously if she should have kept her silence about Ah Wong, for she did not want Frank Sefton to find out that she was at Bedstead Gully.

For if he did hear that, he would derisively assume that she had taken his spiteful advice. Her head was down as she trudged slowly back to the cabin. There she would be alone with Jake . . . for the valley was so empty.

Jake was waiting for her and was as tetchy as ever. She had been gone too long; she had been too slow. The beauty of California surrounded them, roofed by pale spring sky; pines wafted pollen and tangy scent, and birds caroled in the oaks; the brook babbled as it ran through the holes that had been mined last season, and Jake grizzled and grumbled.

Then, mercifully, he slept, and smiled as he slept. Harriet surveyed him with weary fists propped on her hips where the apron was tied. She'd forgotten how much she loved him, she thought wryly, and went upstream to change and bathe. Then she washed the last of her dirty clothes. She trudged back to the hut with her mind all set to start preparing supper, but when she arrived Jake was awake and waiting again, and he demanded that she shave him.

His beard itched, he complained, and made him feel dirty. Harriet, feeling martryed, set to and boiled water. When she mixed the lather her fingers hurt where nails had torn and rocks had scraped off skin. She concentrated on the pain and her irritation, uncomfortably conscious of the weight of Jake's attention as he sat on a stool and watched her and waited. Outside, the shadows were growing long, the late afternoon cool in reminder of the winter just past. Birds gave long crying calls, unlike the bird chatter of daylight, and she could feel the weight, too, of their solitude and the watching mountains.

The sense of intimacy was almost unbearable. She honed the scissors on the neck of a bottle, and then studied the bushy brown beard, kneeling in front of Jake to do so. He frowned at her, impatient that she was taking so long, and only the a-kilter brows and the bright brown-green eyes were familiar. Otherwise he looked like a bear, which matched his mood, she thought wryly.

She leaned forward and clipped carefully. She could feel his breath on the back of her hand. The scissor handles bit into the sore cuts on her fingers, and she was glad when she'd removed enough to start the shave. She brushed on the lather, twirling the soap into fluffy peaks and valleys, and then she stood and went round behind him.

His head leaned back into her apron, heavy against her soft abdomen. It was years since she'd last shaved a man; that man had been her father, and shaving had not, she thought with a wry awareness, been like this. She scraped slowly, very carefully, afraid of cutting him. It felt . . . strange to see the familiar creases appear like magic as she stroked hair and soap away. His skin felt warm and supple, and he smelled familiar too, of soft leather and soap. She smoothed that skin carefully, with the tips of the fingers of her left hand, very gently, feeling her breath catch in her throat. She felt warm, as if something inside her were melting, and she wondered if he liked her touch, if he enjoyed the cushion that her body made for his head.

It was impossible to tell. He pulled frightful grimaces to straighten out his cheeks. Then, when she had finished and come round the front to inspect her work, he complained. She had taken too long, she had made his face stiff. She had forgotten how much she loved him, she mused, and bit back a wry chuckle. Instead she said, "Welcome back, Jake Dexter," and cupped his jaw in both hands and stopped his mouth with a kiss.

She felt the lurch inside him. Then he jerked back. It was like a blow in the face. Her stomach tautened, and she scrambled back before she knew she'd moved. She looked around quickly for an excuse to get out fast, grabbed the shaving bowl, and fled.

Her eyes stung; she had a stonelike pain inside her, but she refused, refused to betray how cruelly he had hurt her. She ran and emptied the bowl, fetched a bucket, went down to the stream for water, at a furious pace. Her face was reflected in streaks in the running stream. Rocks and pebbles tumbled and gleamed, and Harriet wondered how men could ever believe that stones like these held a promise of gold. Jake's voice echoed over and over in her mind: *I do not rob other men of their wives.* The echo was so loud she scarcely heard him calling her name, and when she did she ignored the summons. Supper was a strained and awkward affair, and when they each went to bed, they did so in silence.

The silence was just as miserable next morning. Jake was about better, but they scarcely noticed it. He tidied and dressed and washed and shaved himself without a word, without looking at Harriet. Harriet, her head bent so he could not see her face, got breakfast. When she fetched more wood for the fire he silently helped her, and when she poured coffee he took the mug without saying thanks. Then she went off, upstream, into the pines to do her washing.

Jake stood in the doorway, watching her go, watching the

slim form hungrily. He'd forgotten her beauty, the wry winsome smile, the tangled gold of her hair, the humor in the fine dark eyes. She'd changed, had become older, subdued, he thought. Then he thought, no, she was the same Harriet who had boarded his brig; she had the same waiflike look, the careful expression of a girl whom life had made a cynic. It had been the carefree Harriet he had remembered all these months, the girl who had laughed and teased him on the passage up the South American coast.

Reunion with her husband had changed her back to the way she'd been. Jake wondered where Sefton was, whether he knew that Harriet had come to the valley. He thought of the scratches on Harriet's arms and face, and the way her nails were torn and scraped; Harriet's appearance was witness to the ordeal of her journey to join him . . . but he'd welcomed her like a grudging miser, parsimonious with his welcome and his questions because he remembered her husband, all of the time. That kiss . . . that kiss had been just like the soft innocent caress that night in Valparaíso. Jake turned abruptly back into the cabin, for that kiss had reminded him, too, of the way he'd felt ever since.

Then he stood still, looking around, at a loss for how to fill his time. The cabin was tidy, the way he liked things, the way he liked his life. Something tiny gleamed on the floor. He bent and picked it up. It was one of Harriet's hairpins. Even here, he thought miserably, he was collecting her pins. He turned it over and over in his fingers, looking at it, such a simple thing to mean so much, a mere scrap of wire that would stop in her hair so much more easily if someone put a crimp in it. Then he put it in his pea-jacket pocket, along with all the other pins that he'd collected.

Her shawl was in a corner, crumpled; Harriet, he mused, was not tidy. He picked it up to fold it and found that it had been tied by the corners into a bag, which held something hard and rectangular. He hesitated no more than a moment, and then he pulled open the knots.

Old Rochester's book fell out. Jake opened it, greedily, for it was so long since he'd seen it. It fell open naturally at the page with the map. The light from the door fell across it, lighting up scratches. Jake cursed softly, anger rising. Someone had made a tracing of the map, he was sure of it, and he was sure too, illogically, that it had been Harriet's husband who had traced it. Harriet had betrayed the unsolved secret of

the Panamanian gold. Then he looked at the documents that
had been in the bag with the book, and the fury became savage.

The deed to the land at Sutter's, no doubt sent back
contemptuously because Jake had neglected to cash that note
for one thousand; share certificates, shares in Sefton's Bank for
Miners . . . to the exact same amount of the gold that had
been stolen from the *Hakluyt* men and stowed in Sefton's bank.
The taunt was obvious . . . and unbearable. Jake dropped the
papers as if they stung him and ran off after Harriet, stumbling
in his furious rush.

Harriet was out of sight, but he knew which way she'd gone.
He stumbled all the time but did not pause to think that he
stumbled because he was feverish. The ground was rifted with
holes, ferns, and grasses springing up to hide them now the
miners were so long gone, and that was reason enough for
stumbling. Then Jake was in the trees, shoving through
undergrowth as if in a nightmare. He swore as he shoved his
way through, only faintly aware that he had fumbled off the
clearer path. It was like a delirium: a briar swiped at his eyes,
fuelling his rage. He shouted Harriet's name, feverishly,
"Harriet!"—and heard her answering shriek of fear.

Then, the roar of a bear. A grizzly, *so close*. Oh God, such
a terrible snorting roar, unmistakably hungry. Jake's gun was
back at the hut. He began to run, not back but forward,
crashing through the thicket. Branches sprang into his face,
snarling at his clothes, and then he burst into a clearing. And
saw the bear.

It was huge. It filled his vision. It reared on its hind legs on
the top of a great boulder like the nightmare bear of five
months ago; it bellowed, a stinking roar. Its shaggy hide hung
in rank folds about its shape, and the light struck on the huge
claws and jagged teeth. Harriet was standing directly below the
beast. She was facing the bear, her back against a rock, both
arms spread out like a sacrifice.

Jake shouted, "Run!" His cry was hoarse, feeble even in his
own ears, and his legs felt heavy. He seemed unnaturally weak,
held down by nightmare. His legs were bogged down as he
tried to run, and Harriet seemed deaf, or paralyzed. Jake hurled
himself forward, desperately, glimpsed the bear brace its legs
and plunge. Then his fingers reached Harriet, and he gripped
her, desperately, and bore her with him in a crushing fall, over
and over and into the edge of the undergrowth.

The bear roared in pursuit, swiping at rocks and branches.

Jake scrabbled up to his feet, hauled Harriet up with him, shoved her into a stumbling run. She ran zigzag, her hair flying out, seeming as dazed as the way he felt. The bear snorted at Jake's heels. Harriet turned her head and screamed. Jake saw the terror in her eyes. Then she stumbled, and fell headlong . . . and disappeared. Into a hole in the ground. Ferns parted and she was gone with scarcely a noise. Jake roared, "Oh, dear God, oh, Jehovah . . ." and fell after her. His boots shot out from under him. He fell in a series of crashes. His legs and shoulders hit stones, ferns, bracken, dirt, while ferns sprang back over his head, hiding the top of this endless tunnel. The bear bellowed . . . so close, right above. Jake rolled over frantically, onto his back as his fall crashed on, and saw the bear's shadow. Right overhead. He smelled the rank breath and the stinking roar, and he heard the crash of the bear's headlong progress . . . and then, all at once, the bear had gone, and Jake's fall stopped when he thumped onto something soft, that wriggled.

The bear had gone; it had vaulted the top of this hole in the ground and kept on going. Jake knew that somehow they had been saved; he shook his head dazedly, and then rolled over again. The light filtered green and pale gold into this cleft in the scenery, and the light illuminated Harriet's pale and furious face.

He was on top of her. He lifted himself and listened to the thud of his pulse. He said huskily, "Oh, Hat, are you hurt?"

"Of course I'm not hurt!" Her voice in his ear was loud, frightened and furious. She was breathing fast; her breasts pressed against him, and she said angrily, "And don't call me Hat. I hate it." He began to move away from her, and she grabbed him.

"What's wrong?"

"Nothing. Everything. I don't know what to do," she said, so he kissed her.

Her mouth was open, panting, moist. He could feel her heat. She wanted him, he was sure of it. Harriet was trembling so he held her tight, hugging her close while his hands moved, faster, more greedily, pulling away fabric, searching, cupping. He thought he heard her cry of protest, so he kissed her again with mindless hunger, thrusting his tongue in her mouth. His hands moved and petticoats rustled like desperate leaves. Then her clothes were all up in a heap. He was on top of her, squirming between long endlessly beautiful legs, such tender flesh. Another cry, another mouth-stopping kiss, and the blood was pounding in his chest, hammering in his ears so that all he could hear was his own pounding need. He thrust, missing, and then with a jolt of sensation so brilliant with delight that it hurt like a pain, he found his mark and entered the tight hot flesh, thrusting, thrusting forever.

Then he was stopped, buried to the hilt. *Oh, Jehovah, such exquisite vanquishment.* Jake stilled, shivering, lost in pleasure, his entire being concentrated in the damp heat where their bodies merged, where he possessed Harriet. He kissed her and her cheeks were wet, so he kissed and licked them, nibbling at the salty tracks. Then mounting pleasure necessitated another thrust, the slow suspense of drawing out and then the triumphant lunge. If she had cried out, he would not have heard it; if she had been dying, he would not have been able to stop. The delight was unendurable; he yelled out wildly. One last thrust, too soon, soon . . . and he foundered in unstoppable crisis, spending forever and ever.

Then, slowly, he came to his senses. Harriet lay still beneath him, as still as death, her eyes shut. Her face was so white and shocked that he could see the pink of the scar on her cheek and the more recent, redder, scratches. Jake moved back and said numbly, "Oh, God."

"Please . . ."

"That was despicable." He rolled away, sat up, and stared bleakly up the green cleft in the ground, thinking one word, over and over, hating himself, looking miserably up at the placid blue sky. An eagle floated in the mile-high blue, and at that awful moment Jake envied the bird. He said woodenly, "I have no excuse, for I know you are married."

"Please don't blame yourself." Her voice was bitter. "My marriage has been dead for quite eighteen months; it died the night of our wedding."

Oh, God, he thought. He watched her as she moved about, arranging her crumpled clothing. She moved stiffly, as if her body hurt. Even wounded she was beautiful, so beautiful that he didn't believe her. He said sharply, "Perhaps your husband would say different."

For the first time she looked at his face. She frowned and said, "What do you mean?"

"Perhaps Sefton still wants you."

He could hear the black jealousy in his voice, the rage and pain that he'd lived with for so many months. Then he saw

Harriet's eyes widen, incredulously. "I'll tell you how much he wants me," she spat. "He has spurned me since that first day at Sutter's; he has a mistress who can do everything I can and entertain his friends as well. He sent me off to live with others . . . for more than four months. Then when I returned to his house he bid me leave and told me, further, to go and live in sin. Then, he informed me, he might do me a favor and sue me for divorce."

Jake shouted savagely, "And is that why you came to this gully? Did you come to seduce me?"

Then, with a sick lurch, he realized what he had said and wished he had cut his tongue out before asking that question. Then he hoped, with fierce grief, that she would lie or refuse to answer. He stared up at the pallor of her face in silent entreaty and saw her eyes go shiny with pain.

Then she said very clearly, "Yes, you are exactly the person he had in mind, and I, like the fool I am, thought that you might want me on those terms."

Jake flinched. He said bitterly, "And is that why he sent those shares along with you . . . and that deed to the land?"

Harriet stared. She said, her tone bewildered, "But he didn't send then along, I brought them of my own accord. How did you find them, Jake? Were you looking through my things?"

He did not reply; he couldn't. He numbly watched as Harriet brushed herself down with sharp angry movements. "If you found them, Jake, why didn't you look at those documents properly while you were at it, and see that my name is on each and every one? Those shares are mine, Jake. They were gifts to me, from Frank, and I signed for them. I had sworn never to sign anything of his ever again, but when I heard about the *Hakluyt* gold . . . Oh, goddammit," she said. Her voice was weary, and she muttered, "And no doubt you don't want the deed to the land either, and the logbook was yours to start with. Frank shamed me when he informed me that I would have to sweeten the gift with the favor of my body to make the gift acceptable, but now I know he was right."

She was crying, he thought, but she turned her back before he could be sure he'd seen the tears. He watched her numbly as she scrambled up the tunnel to the light; he tried to call her back, but his tongue was too dry to work. Then Harriet was gone. He knew when she reached the level ground, for he heard her begin to run.

He followed her slowly, marshaling words into arguments in

his mind so that he'd know what to say when he arrived at the hut. The trees rustled about him, but he gave no thought to the bear. He wondered what Harriet would be doing when he arrived: it would be easier, he thought, if she were grimly setting about domestic tasks, because they could then go back to the hostile, awkward silence . . . but it would be so much better if she were weeping, for perhaps then he could find it in himself to give her comfort.

He was prepared to find her disconsolate, he was prepared to find her angry. What he was not prepared for was to find the hut deserted. He looked about incredulously, and all Harriet's clothes were gone. The cabin was as clean and tidy as if she'd never come. He swore, in a mutter and then loudly, and launched himself into a run.

He caught up with her on the path to where the boulder had fallen; she had gotten so far in such a short time. She was wearing all her clothes and looked as bulky as the night he'd first seen her. She was walking doggedly, with determined pace.

He ran up beside her. She turned her face away and kept on walking so he ran round her and stopped in her path. She stopped. He said grimly, "Where the devil are you going?"

"To Don Roberto's fort, for a start."

"Why Don Roberto?"

"I don't need a reason. As I said," she said wryly, " 'tis a start."

"But the trail—"

"I've walked that trail before, Jake, and survived it."

So she had. He thought about her torn nails and the scratches on her arms and face, and loathed himself. He shouted, "You're not bloody well leaving me, Harriet—" and saw the party come into sight at the far end of the track. There was Abner at the front, Tib and Dan, and Royal. Then Jake felt Harriet push past him. She ran to her brother, stopped him, clung to him. Jake arrived more slowly, in time to see Royal hold Harriet with one arm about her shoulders and hear him say, blankly, "Swamp it, Hat, what the devil are you doing here? Sefton told me you were stopping with the Vidries."

"No," she said without expression. "I left them."

"And came here?"

"Yes." Harriet paused, and Royal stared first at her and then at Jake. He still had his arm about his sister's shoulders, and the stare became challenging. Jake made no movement; he was standing with his legs braced, tensed, ready . . . for what? But she merely said again, "Yes."

Royal snapped, "But what about your husband, Hat? Surely you ain't left him?"

Again, she paused. Then she said somberly, "I think the better word would be *escaped*."

Jake's belly cramped. Royal said, "For God's sake, Hat!" She said nothing. Then her brother said slowly, "We . . . were worried about you; we discussed you much; we had begun to wonder about that business in New Zealand, how you'd been alone since Father was killed." Then he said more sharply, "You're shivering, Hat. Are you well?"

She didn't answer. Jake watched her turn her head, and then their eyes meshed for an endless moment. Then she said idly, "Oh, it was naught but a bear, Royal, a bear that chased me."

"What!" Royal shouted the word, and Tib and Dan and Abner had their fists on their pistols, their eyes searching the hilltops in instant wary inspection. Royal said, "Hat, you seem so strange; are you hurt?"

"I'm fine. Jake chased the bear away."

Jake shifted uneasily and became uncomfortably aware that Tib and Dan and Abner were regarding him with expressions of suddenly increased respect. Royal's expression, by contrast, was brooding, almost suspicious. Then Harriet said quickly, "Royal, when did you see Frank?"

"Three days ago, in Pueblo San Marco."

"Three days! But . . ."

"And I didn't have much chance to talk. He was busy enough, with bank business, in and out of his vaults with his ledgers in his hand, as busy as a squirrel in autumn. My God, though," Royal went on, "the whole town is all busy and alive-oh! God's thunder, Jake, you just wait till you see it." His voice was as animated as if he'd never lost the richest claim thus far this season. "The town's as full as a boot with prospective miners; men are paying small fortunes to come up river from 'Frisco, and then they lose even larger fortunes to the crimps and taps and gamblers of Pueblo San Marco. The town is bulging with men with naught to do but drink and fight and gamble, all a-hunt for a grubstake and entertainment. I tell you, Jake, this California gold rush is fated to be the greatest adventure yet; 'tis the Crusades all over again, but without the restriction of piety."

And without the restriction of law, Jake thought suddenly; he frowned and said swiftly, "How do they fare on the brig?"

"Oh, good Lord, Cap'n," said Tib, and winked and poked a cheerful finger up at the sky. "We may've lost our vein of gold, wasted a winter and lost good men too, but good Lord, sir, how they make up for that on the brig."

"Aye," said Dan, and shook his head. "A fortune, they're reaping, an ever-livin' fortune, and in the merriest manner possible."

Dire forebodings took root in Jake's mind, growing with every ebulliant word. My God, he thought, and said sharply, "They make this money in the boarding business?"

"No, they don't, sir, and that be the wonder of it!" cried Abner. He looked as uplifted as the other men. "They don't need boarders, sir, for they have this café-restaurant; Valentine and Crotchet won it at a game of chance, and it has taken all their efforts since, for that little business be so booming."

29 ❧　　　The whole of Pueblo San Marco
was, it seemed, crowded into the
gambling house. The evening was chill but the restaurant was
remarkable hot, and yet more and more kept on coming. Some
played, many watched, and the atmosphere of anticipation was
palpable. Valentine kept on glancing at Crotchet, but Crotchet
was as quietly affable as ever . . . and then Abrigo came in.

The fat Californian looked the same as he had the night
they'd won this place. He even seemed to be wearing the same
grimy damp shirt. His fat face was as expressionless as a
pudding. He nodded to those who spoke to him but never
smiled, never frowned, and said very little. He looked around
and breathed heavily as he watched the play, but he did not
play for quite an hour.

Then he played at Valentine's table, but his luck was
indifferent. He bet on black all the time, and then just on
clubs; the quick way, Valentine thought, to lose all his
money . . . but slowly, slowly, Abrigo's luck turned. Clubs,

clubs . . . the gate turned up clubs three times in a row, and Abrigo's mountain of winnings rivaled the mountain in the middle of the table. Valentine surveyed the two heaps of gold thoughtfully, and then he sent for pisco.

"Pisco!" He snapped his fingers, and one of the Californian women who served the meals came with the bottle. Abrigo merely nodded and drained the little glass. Then he bet the lot, on spades, and won.

His pile of dust and nuggets glittered with little coin landslides on the slopes. The crowd pressed close, whispering, craning to see, but Abrigo paid no attention. Mr. Giles was there, a notebook in the crook of his left arm while his right hand briskly wielded a pencil, but Abrigo merely took off his left boot and shoveled in the golden hill. Then he limped over to Crotchet's table and plonked the boot down on it.

Crotchet was waiting, his hands in his pockets, standing easy, whistling a little. The whole crowd moved with Abrigo, and Crotchet smiled at them all tranquilly. His fingers gently took the forty card pack. "*Buenas tardes!*" he said. "I thank you for the pleasure of your custom, señor!" Abrigo inclined his head, and then breathing heavily, he set his paunch against the edge of the table. His little moist eyes watched the cards and Crotchet's fingers as they shuffled.

Despite the boot, however, Abrigo played as cautiously as if he were down to his last three ounces. Crotchet nodded each time the coins or dust were squeezed reluctantly by fat fingers onto the chosen places, and dealt the cards with equal care, like moths. Then Abrigo began to win again, slowly, betting all the time on black.

Crotchet could not recollect any time in his gambling experience when the gate had turned up spades or clubs so often. Soon, he gambled, the deal would turn up red, and Abrigo's luck would turn up too, but as relentlessly as time the gold and the coins and the nuggets shifted, the profits of weeks of gambling and restauranting, all moving as if by magnetism toward Abrigo's boot. The pile rose high and equalled the bank right easily, and Abrigo expressionlessly took off his other boot, shoveled his pile into it, and set both boots beside each other.

"I challenge," he said, "for the tap."

"I see," said Crotchet. Then he listened to the babble that ran around the room and felt the excitement in the air. All of Pueblo San Marco, he mused, had waited for this moment. The men in the hills who had passed through here would say to others as they arrived, how goes it between Crotchet and Abrigo now . . . ? And even those who were digging a fortune would rue it that they were not here tonight.

"The bank," he said regretfully, "is about bust, suh."

"But I challenge for this fine establishment, señor."

"So I thought," sighed Crotchet. "So I thought."

"You refuse?"

"Of course not." Then Crotchet whistled a line from "Yankee Doodle." He surveyed the table with his head a little tilted, flashed a glance at Abrigo, and dealt four cards, two from the bottom, two from the top. They floated with flair and style, each to its proper place, and every man in the room rose on tiptoes to see their nature.

The two of hearts, in the bottom layout, the seven of clubs beside it; the three of hearts in the upper layout, along with the seven of diamonds. "No tiny faces smiling," hummed Crotchet; and only one black, he thought. Abrigo wheezed and grasped his boots, and everyone silenced instantum, riven with suspense.

The fat man deliberated . . . deliberated forever, while all the time Crotchet waited, holding the pack, waiting for Abrigo to place his bet on that one black card. Then, grunting, Abrigo placed one boot by the two of hearts, and the other by her sister three.

Everything bet, on just one suit. The air was hushed and steamy. Crotchet poised his fingers, ready to deal the gate, and Abrigo grunted.

"I deal the card, Señor," he said.

"Certainly, suh!" Some of the crowd had climbed on stools to see better. Abrigo's fat fingers received the pack with apparent indifference. However, once in his hands he fondled them, as a lover fondles his mistress. Everyone knew Abrigo's magic with a deck. He could pick and deal at will, it was whispered, and those plump awkward fingers could move invisibly, like fluttering wings in the night.

Crotchet's eyes, however, were very sharp, his concentration merciless. He whistled insouciantly, but the frivolity meant naught. Abrigo's hands moved, slowly, and Crotchet watched a droplet of sweat begin to run down the fat man's nose.

It glistened like oil . . . and the fingers paused, bent like caterpillars . . .

And the door crashed wide. A man hollered, "Fire, fire, Colonel Sefton's house burned all down, nothin' but ashes on his rancho! The Colonel's dead and gone, a burned-up corpse, with the corpse of his wife beside him!"

. . . and Abrigo dealt the gate. Crotchet's eyes had shifted for the tiniest instant, drawn by the uproar, and in that infinitesimal pause Abrigo had dealt the gate.

It was the knave of hearts. The saucy fellow was riding a roan and white horse, and his grin was evil. "H'm!" said Crotchet.

"H'm!" said Abrigo. "*Lindo el overo rosao, sí?*"

Crotchet paused. Then he began to laugh; he couldn't help it. The steed the jack was riding was a pretty mare indeed in her roan and white. The only pity was that the crowd, too, had been distracted, and had missed that melodramatic drop. "Thank you, señor," he said. "A brave gamble indeed! And I wish you good fortune with this fine place. May you keep it longer than I did, suh!"

"I will," said Abrigo, and for the first time in Californian history, the people of Pueblo San Marco heard Abrigo laugh.

Sefton's house had burned down more thoroughly than Harriet would have thought possible. Even the most massive adobe walls had collapsed with the heat and lay like blackened sand dunes. Rafters had fallen helter-skelter, piled on top of one another and crusted with shining charcoal. The rest was rubble and ashes, well raked over. She could see tracks in the black crumbling dust where men had scavenged for anything worth the looting.

There was nothing for her here. She turned to Mr. Giles and said angrily, "Why did you want me to see this?"

The reporter was standing in his customary slouch, studying the ruins with a straw in his mouth, nibbling at that straw like a rodent, so that his mostachos revolved in bucolic fashion. "Why," he said, "perhaps I wanted your thoughts on the subject. After all," he pointed out, "'twas your husband, the colonel, what lost his life in this mess. How do you feel about that?"

How did she feel? Harriet glanced away with dislike, angered by the way he'd put the question. So Frank was dead, and she was a widow . . . a widow. It sounded so strange. She didn't feel like a widow, but she hadn't felt like a married woman, either. Instead of answering she snapped, "No doubt you want my feelings for your story."

"Story, ma'am?"

"The story you're sending back East . . . and don't pretend there isn't one."

"Wa-al, of course there be one, Mrs. Sefton, for was not the colonel a prominent figure? And, after all, for quite a while people thought that you had expired in this fire as well. What do you think of that, huh?"

His tone was sardonic. She said curtly, "I feel astonished, if that holds interest, astonished that it took so many days for the tragedy to be reported. Why did no one see the house burning? It must have gone up like a torch."

"That's true," he ruminated, mumbling at his straw. "Mind you, ma'am, and beg to differ, those adobe walls were mighty thick. The fire could have smouldered for hours without no one noticing, like a baker's oven inside but without apparent light and heat."

That could well be so, Harriet thought, and winced. The chief clerk of Sefton's bank had had just one thing for her: the ring that Frank had always worn. It was a half-melted lump, silent testimony to the heat of the blaze. It had been taken off the corpse; perhaps the coroner had had to chip it off the bone.

She grimaced and then saw that Mr. Giles was watching her closely. "You could've been the other victim of the drama," he said.

Harriet shifted uneasily, and said, "Perhaps." The night that Ah Wong had helped her escape was vivid in her mind. She had escaped the very night that this house had burned down.

"And I do wonder about the identity."

"What?"

"Of the other woman, the one what burned to death beside your husband in your very own bed."

Harriet's diaphragm clenched with the shock. She cried, "How do you know where they died?"

"Ah, Mrs. Sefton, I know where to ask questions, and how to find answers. It was your bed and your bedroom, and the corpse lay blackened by the corpse of your husband, so folks all assumed that the body were your'n." Harriet stared at him, swallowing, humiliated rage rising inside her, and felt the reporter take her elbow.

He led her to the oak tree where the Murietas had tethered

their horses that night. There was a broad raked mound of dirt there now, with two boards at the head.

One board informed her that here lay the remains of one Colonel Francis Sefton. He had belonged to Philadelphia and he had been forty-two years old at the time of his death. So this was the end of Frank, she thought, the miserable end of his devious dealings. All he had wanted was to arrive back in New York with immense riches, to make one woman regret her rejection of his suit . . . and what had he got? This grave.

The other board was blank. "Folks do say," said Mr. Giles insinuatingly, "that your husband, the colonel, had a Chinese mistress."

"He had a Chinese ward," she snapped.

"And the feet of the second skeleton were all twisted up, like bird claws."

Harriet gazed at the reporter, feeling sick; his head was tilted, so that he looked somewhat like a bird himself. So the whole of the Feather River region knew that Sefton had spurned his wife and kept a doxy, and now the whole eastern seaboard of the United States was due to learn that as well. She said sharply, "Who told you that; was it Don Roberto?"

"I don't divulge my sources, ma'am."

"Do you not? Then where is he now?"

"Who knows, Mrs. Sefton, who knows?" The reporter emitted a single snort of sardonic laughter and then said, "No sooner had he signed the death certificate and looked for his fee than he skipped, ma'am, and who can blame him? He scampered off for the hills and no doubt over the border to Mexico, with a posse of disappointed gold miners all baying at his heels, crying out for their gold."

The gold, the vanished gold. No one wanted to find that gold more desperately than Harriet. The bank had been the first place she called when she'd arrived in Pueblo San Marco that morning; she had shoved her way through the shouting mob outside the bank doors, in company with her brother, Royal, but all she had found were harried, agitated bank clerks. All that gold that the bank had held, the gold that had been confiscated from God alone knew how many disputed claims had disappeared.

Royal had stormed into the vaults and found the vaults broomed clean. Jake Dexter had arrived and demanded to inspect the ledgers. Then Harriet, bewildered, had found Mr. Giles beside her. She looked at him now, turned on her heel, and set off decisively for the path to the ferryboat. Then she heard the reporter's steps as he roused himself from contemplation and slouched along to join her.

She said, "My brother told me that he saw Sefton the day following the one when you and I rode to Don Roberto's fort. As you know I came on to this place, but Frank led Royal to believe that I was still with the Vidries. Can you think of any reason why he would have lied?"

Mr. Giles was silent. Then he sniffed liquidly at his nose and brushed his damp mostachos. "No, ma'am," he said then. "That I cannot guess."

"Perhaps Royal was mistaken. He said that Frank was busy in his bank, too busy to talk, preoccupied with his ledgers."

"Yep," said Mr. Giles.

"What? You saw it too?"

"That I did, and I never saw your husband, the colonel, thereafter."

"What about Ah Wong? You remember Ah Wong, my servant. Have you seen him?"

"No, ma'am, that I have not."

"Poor Ah Wong," she said and shivered, remembering how frightened poor Ah Wong had been, how she'd dreamed she'd heard him crying and sobbing in the night. She wondered then if it had truly been a dream, whether Sefton had been punishing the little man for bringing her to this place; and she wondered, too, if she would have been that second corpse in the bed if Ah Wong had not helped her to run away.

She said angrily, "What was Sefton doing all that day in the bank?"

"But you know that, ma'am, for you can work it out for yourself. I recollect quite plain how we both did wonder about those shares your husband, the colonel, was so anxious to sell . . . and we wondered, too, why he was so strangely willing to give men credit for the purchase . . . with the shares in the bank as collateral."

The last sentence held more insinuating meaning than all the other words put together. Harriet glanced sideways at the slouching figure, dislike mounting inside her. She, too, remembered the discussion, clearly, but the way she remembered it the suspicions had all belonged to Mr. Giles.

She said tersely, "So?"

"So on that day he was converting all those loans he'd made, declaring the debts all bad. With one stroke of his pen he was taking back those loans with the gold that had been collateral. In a word, ma'am, your husband, the colonel, was collecting on unpaid debts."

The reporter nodded to himself, but apparently not with smugness at his irrefutable logic; he merely looked world-weary, as if this kind of confidence trick happened every day. And no doubt it did, Harriet thought, and then thought further, wearily, that the number of women who had fallen for two such tricks in a row must be small.

She'd been a fool, a double fool; like the men who'd bought shares in Sefton's bank and taken out mortgages to do it, she should have taken legal advice. The only legal advice available, however, was now running off in the hills. She said, "Was Don Roberto in on the scheme, or was he gulled like everyone else?"

"Who knows, Mrs. Sefton, who knows?" Mr. Giles silenced a little, in one of his meaningful pauses. Then, his voice pensive, he murmured, "That was a powerful lot of gold for one man to run off with."

It took the space of a breath to see his hidden meaning. She cried, "You think Don Roberto stole that gold?"

"Not without help, he couldn't."

Perhaps not, there being such a pile of gold . . . but Don Roberto had had six deputies, she suddenly thought. She stopped and stared at Mr. Giles in growing speculation, and he nodded and said, "D'you want to know what I think, ma'am?"

"Knowing you as I do," Harriet said tartly, "I'm certain that you have formulated at least one theory."

"Ah, Mrs. Sefton, you know me well." He snorted with cynical mirth and said nonchalantly, "I think the men who stole that gold also murdered your husband and his mistress, either on purpose or accidentally, when they set that house on fire."

She gasped, "Murder?"

"Yep. What could be a neater motive than all that confiscated gold?"

"But no one has suggested that the house was deliberately fired."

"Have they not? Wa-al, ma'am, I suggest it now, for it would provide yet another reason for the long delay in reporting the blaze. After all, if folks what saw it also knew that it had been set afire on purpose, then their own good sense would advise them to keep shut about it for a while."

She said, "My God." She set off agitatedly for the ferryboat.

The night she had escaped was vivid in her mind; she heard Ah Wong's terror again and saw Joaquin Murieta under that tree; she remembered the red light of his cigar. Joaquin Murieta . . . the Murietas. Don Roberto's deputies. All at once she was tragically certain that poor little Ah Wong was dead.

Then Mr. Giles said, "And where are you headed, Mrs. Sefton, that you appear so much in a rush?"

"To the brig," she said shortly.

"The brig *Hakluyt*?"

His tone held curiosity. She didn't look at him. She said shortly, "I have to attend a meeting."

30 ❧ When Harriet arrived at the brig the late afternoon shadows were growing very long, and for some moments she thought that the meeting was over or postponed, for the decks of the old brig were deserted. Then she heard voices through the skylight and realized that the meeting was being held in the main mess cabin below.

Those voices were loud with anger. She walked down the companionway slowly, feeling her way down the dim familiar steps. The old brig smelled . . . and felt and looked the same, and yet so much was different. When she quietly opened the door at the bottom, the cabin seemed smaller than before, because of the crowd of men and the anger they emanated.

And yet, she thought, watching all the faces turn to stare at her, the crew of the brig had been so diminished. Pablo was gone, Joseph Fayal, Jonathan, and poor Davy was still living on the Indian plantation. Tib and Dan had been left back at Bedstead Gully to look after the hut, the claim and the llamas . . . and yet the men here seemed diminished too, somehow dwindled to meanness.

They all watched her as she came in, but no one smiled, and no one said a word of welcome. Old Chips, Sails, Cookie, Bodfish, were seated at the table with Mr. Martin, and the four old men seemed much older than before. The steerage door was open, and in its frame stood Valentine, Crotchet, Royal, and Bill. Bill had grown amazingly, and perhaps, she thought, this was why Valentine and Crotchet seemed so much smaller, their flamboyance shrunk, perhaps, by their spectacular loss of the café-restaurant. Even Crotchet's courtliness had gone. Harriet winced inside but met all the stares calmly. Then she was aware of only one man: Jake. He was seated in his chair at the end of the table, and he watched her intently, concentratedly, all of the time, even when the others lost interest and stopped their staring.

Harriet said nothing to fill the awkward silence. She sat down quietly when Mr. Martin shifted along the bench to give her room. Then she folded her hands and put them on the tabletop and contemplated them silently, still heavily conscious of Jake Dexter's gaze.

Abijah Roe's voice was the first to fill the awful pause. He said loudly, "But it jest ain't possible that we've gained nothing."

Harriet looked at him. Abijah was sitting in the pantry doorway, perched like a peevish secretary bird on a stool. Jake said evenly, "Nonetheless, that is exactly the case. We are no better off than we were when we weighed anchor at Judas Island."

"But that ain't right!" cried Bill. His voice was breaking, hoarse and shrill by turns. "Sir, we was about the first to get to California, why we came more'n five months a-fore the real rush. They tol't us in Tombez that the gold lay about in great lumps, so that the first men to arrive would get the most . . . so how come we got nuffin'?"

"Aye," grumbled several voices. Hoary heads and young ones too were nodding. Cookie said, "How can it be, sir, that our luck is so awful?"

"We did find a rich vein," Jake pointed out.

"Aye, sir . . . and what happened next? We lost it!"

"That was bad luck, I agree."

All the heads nodded again. Then Abijah snapped, " 'Twas his fault that we lost it, so was it his bad luck—or our'n?"

The nasty sentence was heavy with meaning, and when Harriet turned her head to frown at the old man she saw his bony fingers pointed sharp at Royal's chest. Abijah said then, "It were our bad luck, sir, that he were in our party, for he neglected to stake the claim proper."

"I bloody well did stake it properly!"

Royal's voice was a roar, and a chair went crashing. Harriet flinched; the blatant anger battered her. She felt on the verge of tears, every nerve in her body stretched and quivering. Abijah shouted, " 'Tis their fault!"

Jake was frowning. He said slowly, "I don't know what you mean."

"Everything's gone wrong since them Grays came onto our brig. *She* comes on board, and persuades us right devious to sail to Valparaíso, and then we pick up *him* and get all chased out of the place, sir."

Jake snapped, "Now just you wait one moment."

"But he's right, sir," said old Chips. He sniffed and pulled his bottom lip. "We dassent show our faces in that port again."

Jake said coldly, "Let me be the judge of that."

"But 'tis strange, sir," said Cookie. "He told us, excuse me sir, that there were alpaca up the Tombez, beasts which would make us an ever livin' fortune. And were there beasts? No, there were not. So we come to California. He told us that gold lay all about here, and he found a vein of it hisself. But do we profit? No, we do not. Somehow that gold gets fust of all confiscated, and then it gets all stolen."

Jake snapped, "Many people were cheated."

"But it were her husband, sir," said Abijah Roe's spiteful voice. "It were her husband's bank, and they told me in town that she be the largest shareowner, now that her husband be dead. 'Tis her responsibility, and she belongs to our very own company, but do we have our gold? No, we don't."

Harriet was beginning to shake. She stared at her hands, and they were tensely spread on the tabletop, the knuckles blue-white as she gathered strength to hurtle out of her seat. She was scared to blink, lest she shame herself by crying, and scared to stand, for she thought she might faint. Then she heard old Chips clear his throat awkwardly, and say, "I don't like to say it, sir, but I must admit I do agree. We made our pile surely here, but they both went and lost it."

"*You* made the pile?" Royal demanded in a roar. He was scarlet in the face. "I was in the party that found that gold, and not you . . . you . . . you scapegoat-hunting bastards! I staked that claim properly and left two of your men to look after it, and it was not my fault that the claim got jumped; and as sure as old Scratch it was not my fault, either, that you fools who were left here to look after the brig sank everything and lost it in a common little gambling house!"

There was instant uproar, punctuated by Abijah screaming nastily, "That's it, sir, that's it . . . the devil himself! It was the devil who enticed us to invest in that café-restaurant, for were we not profiting from the devil's tickets in the devil's drawing room itself? The devil came on board when Miss Gray boarded us that night, for the devil loves a ship that carries a woman, for that vessel is then doomed to be allus unlucky!"

Harriet's heart lurched. Then Jake's hand shot out and gripped her wrist. His touch galvanized her at last; as if she'd been burned she snatched her hand away and scrambled up from the bench. Then she ran the short steps to Royal and stood close by him. Royal didn't seem to notice but roared, "Ignorant sailor superstition!"

Jake shouted, "Silence!" His face was dark, the lopsided eyebrows curled right down with fury. He snapped, "Quiet," and gradually all the gape-mouthed faces were focused on him. Harriet stared at him tautly, trembling with anger, thinking that she now knew the reason for the gift of the shares. Her husband's intention, she mused bitterly, had been to leave her the scapegoat while he ran off with the gold. She waited for Jake to tell his men that she had accepted the shares in an attempt to compensate the *Hakluyt* men for the loss of their gold, she waited to hear him say that she'd risked much and walked a long rough trail to do it.

Instead, she heard him say in matter-of-fact tones, "This matter is not on the agenda. You are all out of order. The purpose of this meeting is to make up our minds what to do next."

"In that case," she snapped, "it is no doubt in order for me to announce that I wish to quit this company and this brig."

Silence, utter silence. The men all stared at her, and then she saw the stares waver, as they looked away restlessly, checking each others' faces for reaction. Only Abijah smirked, and she snapped, "You look pleased, Mr. Roe, and so you should be, though you might miss me, on occasions, for 'tis so convenient to have a woman around to blame when things go badly."

Even his stare fell away then, and old Sails said unhappily, "But der woman, alone, in a place like dis . . ."

Royal snapped, "I tender my resignation as well."

Good, Harriet thought; she felt warm inside with relief, for Royal was so unpredictable, so unreliable, so apt to go his own merry way. In her relief she unconsciously sought Jake's eyes . . . and tensed again, in response to the utter tension in his face.

However, his voice was emotionless as he said, "And what, pray, will you do?"

She lifted her chin. "I have the deed to the land at Sutter's, and I don't believe that anyone will dispute my ownership, for I am a widow now, with my own legal signature."

He said sharply, "But you borrowed money to buy it."

"I know that, but the hundred dollars payment for relinquishing our shares in the *Hakluyt* Company will be a start, and—"

"The *Hakluyt* Company is insolvent, madam . . . or perhaps you arrived too late to understand that. The company is in no position to pay anything out on shares."

"Then I will borrow the money to pay the men back."

"And what will you do with the land, pray?"

"Exactly what I intended when I bought it. I will seek investment from others, and build a theater."

"You seem to think that finding men with money to invest in such a scheme will be easy."

"I'm sure it will be," she said, and nodded with the perfect certainty she felt. There were merchants in the dozens just along the street, she knew, all making so much money they did not know what to do with the dust, there was so much of it. She gazed at Jake and saw his eyes narrow, and then she heard old Chips clear his voice.

"Miss Gray," he said awkwardly, "you don't owe us what we loaned you, not now, for Cap'n Dexter paid us all back. But I've still got that private cash, and if you need to borrow—"

"Me too," said Bodfish. He seemed very glum, his long face longer than ever. Several of the others were nodding; the old men of the *Hakluyt*, Harriet observed with disbelief, were feeling thoroughly ashamed of themselves. It was as if they had only just realized that the loss of the gold had impoverished her too.

Then Jake said curtly, "None of that is necessary. There is

no need for Mrs. Sefton to pay me back. I will retain my interest in the business."

"That," she flashed, "will not be necessary." She saw his face darken, and added, "After all, you may well be back in the hills when we make our fortune at the theater . . . and how will I find you then, to pay you back?"

"That," he snapped, "is out of order, for we still have not decided what the company does next."

She frowned, and said, "But surely you go off prospecting again?"

"I have no relish for the business," he said curtly, and to Harriet's consternation she heard grumbles of agreement all about the cabin. Even Valentine and Crotchet looked reluctant; the only one who seemed peeved at the prospect of not going to the mines was Bill.

Harriet gazed about at all the faces and felt obscurely frightened. Why? Then, apprehensively, she realized that she couldn't bear the thought that the brig might quit California . . . because of Jake Dexter. She swallowed and said in a low voice, "Where will you all go then?"

There was a long silence. Jake had tipped his chair around so that he faced her squarely, and she was very conscious of him watching her, his eyes still narrow and veiled. Then Bodfish said in a tentative voice, "There would be a great profit in fetching recruits from the Sandwich Islands to trade in California. In Lahaina potatoes can be procured for nine dollars a barrel at this season, and we could sell them here for ninety."

"Good idea," said old Chips, but no one looked enthusiastic.

Bodfish muttered then, "Mind you, even at nine dollars potatoes are high; if we waited two months till the northern whaling season starts and the whalemen have finished reprovisioning, then the price of potatoes will get much lower."

Would the price drop? Harriet doubted it; the California trade, she thought, would keep the prices high. However, she said nothing. Then old Chips blew reflective smoke toward the skylight and said, "We'd be able to take on more if we rid ourselves of that half cargo of lumber we still have with us. There are all those trade goods too, calico and such. What d'you reckon, Cap'n, about that?"

Jake's voice, still, was expressionless. He rocked his chair back on two legs and said, "Why don't you tell me what you think, Chips?"

"Wa-al, Cap'n, I were thinking that a real nice way to use that timber and cloth would be to build a theater, jest to git Miss Gray and Royal a-going, so to speak."

Silence. Harriet held her breath. She stared at Jake, wondering . . . wondering why she had an obscure feeling that this scene had been stage-managed. She could tell nothing from his face; he merely seemed lost in thought. Then all at once he sat straight, setting his chair back on four legs. "Why not?" he said idly, and as quickly as that the affair was decided. He gave out brief orders for Abner to go back to the gully to fetch Tib and Dan and the llamas, and orders to get the brig water-worthy again, for the passage down river to Sutter's.

Then the men quit the cabin, in bunches, most of them via the steerage door. Royal sloped off to the fo'c'sle, his expression sardonic and somewhat amused. Harriet waited, and then all at once she and Jake were alone. She watched the steerage door close, and then, slowly, she turned and met his waiting gaze. Her breath was a little erratic; they had not been alone since that . . . since that time in Bedstead Gully. She had avoided his company, even during the night the party had spent at Don Roberto's fort.

He said calmly, "Harriet."

"Yes. I want . . . I wish to ask a favor."

"What? Another one?"

She felt herself flush, and said angrily, "This is not on my own behalf, I assure you."

Then she stopped and watched him slowly unfold himself from the chair. He stood over her, much to her exasperation, and lifted his a-kilter eyebrows when she still did not speak, and said in prompting fashion, "Well, Harriet?"

" 'Tis Davy. I'm troubled about him, in my mind."

He frowned and said curtly, "So am I, but there is very little I can do about it."

"I know he'll refuse to leave the Indian camp, but I wondered if . . . if there were any spare provisions at all, if some could be sent along. They live on acorn-meal cakes. I've tasted one, and they are dreadful. There won't be much game, for the miners shoot it all, and so . . ."

"Consider it done."

The sentence was so abrupt that she felt taken aback and angry with it. She said sharply, "Thank you," and turned to the companionway door. Then, so abruptly that she jumped, he was beside her, his hand on the door, holding it shut.

He said tersely, "And where the hell do you think you're going?"

"On shore, of course. Where else?"

"I didn't hear the company accept your resignation."

"That makes no difference. I'm not stopping on the brig."

She stared up at him defiantly; he was close, too close. She could smell his soap and leather scent, and feel his warmth, and the tight anger inside him. She snapped, "If you wonder where I'll spend the night then set your mind at rest. Mr. Giles has agreed to find me a place to board."

"Giles?" His brows snapped down; he seemed instantly furious. Then the brows lifted and he muttered, "The reporter." Then more clearly, perfectly businesslike, he said, "I'll send a message, for you stop here," and his hand turned her and guided her inexorably to the door of the stateroom where she'd lived all the time she'd been on the brig.

Shock took her as far as the door, but when he reached out one hand and opened it, she stopped dead and snapped, "I do not stop here!"

"Yes, you do," he said with perfect certainty. Then he swung her round and kissed her hard, with something more than anger in the kiss. She lurched away and sat with an undignified little bump on the edge of the freshly made up berth. Jake Dexter grinned tightly, and then she watched the door slam shut.

She was alone. After a long moment she stopped shaking. Then she reached up and pulled the latch string through to her side of the door.

It took Harriet a long time to fall asleep. She was angry and hungry, and the brig felt too strange. It lay unnaturally still, what with the topmasts down and being moored so tight, and there was a constant hubbub from the town as well, as men roistered away the night hours. Then, when she slept, she had nightmares. She dreamed of the Murietas and Don Roberto, galloping off for Mexico . . . for, after all, the alcalde was a citizen of that land . . . and Ah Wong, and poor Davy, at the Indian camp.

Davy slept too. He was asleep when the horsemen thundered in from the night. He was stretched out on a blanket in the shelter of his house, and his wife lay asleep beside him. The baby slept too, in the cradle board that was slung on a post.

The baby never cried. Davy often wondered about that, in the daytime. On the plantation in Guiana babies and children cried all the time, even though they had so much affection and care. Indian babies, it seemed, had enough care but no affection, and yet they never cried. They were trained not to cry, he understood in the end, for crying babies attracted animals and enemies. If a baby cried he was taken outside where his board was slung from a distant tree branch for the night. Then if the babe still lived in the morning, he had learned not to make any sound . . . so Davy's baby made no noise to wake Davy and warn him of the danger.

Davy woke with a lurch, with a howl of fear, to a nightmare hell of shots and shrieking, the pounding of hooves and the desperate sound of running feet, and the swish and crunch as clubs and hatchets swung. Davy sprung up, shaking with uncomprehending terror, and the hide that made the door of his house was torn to one side.

The red glare of flames, a vicious silhouette, fire shining on the wet gleam of an ax blade, and behind that . . . the crying out of women, and the shadows of people—Davy's people!—fleeing in horror and panic. Children, old men, horses rearing and screaming as riders clubbed the fleeing helpless. At that nightmare moment Davy cringed, weeping, whimpering, and couldn't understand who he was or what he should do, and he cried out, terrified, "Oh, Cap'n Dexter, help me!"

And the man in the doorway laughed, and swung his ax.

31 ∾

In the morning Bodfish came for Jake, to ascertain which provisions should be sent along with Abner for Davy and the Indians. Jake rubbed his forehead where the headache nagged, and then nodded and went into the hold with the steward.

It was gloomy belowdecks, but noisy enough, for the men were pulling apart the berths for the planks. They were readying the timber for the building of the theater, while the younger ones abovedecks were restoring the masts, yards, and all the running rigging. The hold was a kettle of noise, and Jake watched as floor planks were brought up to reveal what was left of the stores.

Then his lips pressed together, grimly. There were but four barrels of salt meat left, and even fewer bags of flour. The rice had gone, and the beans, all cooked and sold to the patrons of the café-restaurant, and then the profits all wasted. However, Jake said nothing; it was too late for remonstrance. Scolding would achieve nothing but a further fraying of tempers.

Then he saw that Bodfish was peering up at him sideways, over his bent shoulder. The old steward's expression was anxious. He said, "Cap'n, how much do you think we can afford to send?"

Jake paused, remembering the Indian encampment the first time he'd seen it. In his mind he could smell the stink of the burning corpse, and he thought of the food Davy had given the woman, and he remembered how she had burned it. Four barrels, and barrels of salt meat cost a hundred dollars each here, perhaps more, for he remembered the fine quality of the pork the Ecuadoreans had brought to the brig at Tombez. It would take a week to get the brig water-worthy, and then God alone knew how long to build Harriet's theater. He bit down a sigh and said crisply, "One. A hundred pounds of meat should last them a while."

Bodfish nodded. His expression held some approval. Then he said tentatively, "Which one?"

Which one? Jake, surprised, turned his head to study the old face. Did it matter? Then he looked at the barrels again, and paused.

They all looked the same. An arrow of dusty light fell over his shoulder and illuminated a dusty arrowhead mark in the side of one of the casks. Jake remembered that barrel, and he remembered that hot, late afternoon by the sugarcane field when these casks of salt pork had been delivered. One of the men had flung a knife, one of the Murietas . . . he had flung a knife and he had said . . .

Jake said, "That one," and then turned away and forgot about it. He went up on deck and then strode over the plank to the cobbled embarcadero, setting his mind to the next problem. Harriet's favor was not that easy, he thought wryly . . . Harriet. He had dreamed about her through the night, constantly, waking in a sweat of passion . . . Harriet.

As was his experience on this Pacific coastline, the embarcadero was also the main street of Pueblo San Marco, suffocatingly thronged with people, almost all of them men. Many of them had just come upriver, some fresh from a four-month Cape Horn passage; others were seasoned men, with the experience of a summer in the hills already. However, they all looked alike, all dressed the same, in stained and torn trousers, and tight boots that went all the way to the knee. They had checkered woollen shirts and sashes and scarves to match, and they wore wide-brimmed leather Californian hats with a plaited cord around the brim, but the most of them spoke United States American.

Colonel Mason's report had done its work well, Jake sardonically mused. No one would mistake this territory as Mexican now. The Californian traders and gamblers had all learned United States American in a hurry, and why not? For the traders and gamblers were making small fortunes out of these men with each day that went by. The touts stood in doorways hollering for customers, and some swung bells to add to the din.

> "Come 'n see the real fandango, come 'n see the Spanish wimmen dance!"
>
> "Boots, boots, best minin' boots, twen'y dollar, double-cleated, yer'll cuss yerself if'n you pass 'em by."
>
> "Mule train, mule train ter Don Roberto's fort, gateway to the mines, sign up, ten cents a pound fer yer baggage, fifteen dollars fer the ride."

Jake sighed; the llamas, he thought dourly, were at the wrong end of the trail. He paid ten dollars for the cask of salt meat to be carried to the fort, and then watched the train and Abner trudge off. Abner could walk, not ride, and when he arrived at Don Roberto's fort he would have to improvise. The best he could do, no doubt, Jake mused, was to leave the cask at the fort and then take it to Davy later, when he'd collected Dan and Tib and the llamas.

When Jake returned to the brig he had to push through a group of men all a-gaup at the sight of a small Italian with a barrel-organ and a performing monkey; it was as if they had never seen a Savoyard before. Then, another crowd, gathered about an itinerant artist as he sketched the scene in the street. As Jake pushed through he noticed with wry humor that the men were paying five dollars apiece to have their faces drawn in with the rest of the scene on the canvas. Then the artist auctioned the finished sketch and got quit of it for a further fifteen. This indeed was the essence of entrepreneurial California, Jake thought dryly. Harriet's theater would perhaps do equally well . . . Harriet.

When he arrived back at the brig he found that Valentine and Crotchet were auctioning off the mining tools that his party had brought back for equally astounding prices. One hundred and fifty dollars for a battered old cradle that had cost less than seven to make! The boys were staging their auction on the embarcadero, and Harriet was on deck, leaning on the starboard rail, watching the fun.

For some moments as Jake strode toward her she seemed unaware of his impending arrival. He slowed, studying her form, the curve of her cheek as she rested her chin on her arm, the posture that outlined the long sweet waist in the small of her back so acutely. He wanted to swallow but his chest felt too full. He couldn't help watching her; it was as if he was intent on storing up every detail of her for recollection afterward: the tousled gold hair, her ears, the way the short hairs curled at the nape of her neck, the roundness of her smooth upper arms in the short-sleeved dress, the way her lower arms tapered to wrists so narrow that he could encircle one with thumb and finger. A New England woman would never wear a gown that showed arms, shoulders, and the upper swell of breasts to such advantage.

Those delicate white shoulders . . . She straightened; she had seen him. Their eyes met briefly and he saw her waver. Then she turned and went below . . . Harriet. She could have been his; she had been a widow even then. If only, if only he had waited.

Jake strode deliberately onto the deck. There was much to do if the brig was to be made water-worthy within a week.

A week. It was March, the season of the upriver wind was upon them. The sky was pale and the air crisp, with the promise in the mornings of afternoon heat. Behind the terraced streets of Pueblo San Marco the purple mountains were tipped with white, but the townspeople wore cotton clothing. Harriet spent much of her time on deck, but said very little to any of the men. She scarcely even spoke to Royal. Jake wondered often what she was thinking as she watched the men restore the rigging. He thought she watched him but was never sure of it. He certainly watched her. At times with the sun on her hair she was so beautiful he forgot to breathe, and if she brushed against him his heart stopped too. He worked hard on the refitting of the brig; he had never worked harder in his life. Then, all at once, the brig was ready, and Abner and Tib and Dan had not come back.

He mulled over the problem at supper, and thought he would leave a message and order weigh anchor nevertheless. The three men were perfectly capable of joining the brig at Sutter's.

Then, as he drank his coffee, he heard the cries from the embarcadero.

Abner's face was a pale blob in the dim evening light. Dan and Tib were there too, with one llama and a mule. There was a body lying across the mule's saddle. It was Davy. The bandages about his head were pale in the evening too. The men all clustered around, sucking in breaths of horror and pity. He had had to exchange two of the llamas for the mule, Abner wearily explained, for the llamas had all refused to carry the burden of a man. The other llama had run away; perhaps it would return to Don Roberto's fort sometime.

They carried the unconscious body down the steerage ladder, lowering Davy carefully. Then they put him in the second mate's stateroom, hastily vacated by Mr. Martin. Jake took one look by the light of the lamp, winced, and then asked for hot water, his medical chest, and his book. Davy was unconscious, mercifully, for the head wounds were ghastly. It seemed impossible that he still lived.

Jake sensed Harriet come in before he heard the rustle of her skirts. Then he said quickly, "Don't look," but too late; he heard her swift gasp. She didn't go but handed him clean rags and rinsed them in hot water as he handed them back, calling out for more hot water as she did it.

He'd forgotten her courage but was grateful for it. He said to Abner, "What happened?"

"I found him . . . thus." The boy's exhausted voice was ragged with strain. "He was the only one that lived, the rest . . . the rest were all slaughtered. Scalped. They were all scalped, women, children, babies."

"Scalped!" This was Harriet's voice, a sibilant whisper. She, like Jake, looked quickly back at Davy's wounded head. His peppercorn scalp, while slashed and tattered, was still there. Then Harriet whispered again, "The administrators of Chihuahua and Sonora pay a bounty for the scalps of Indians."

"*What*?" Jake broke off his grisly task, staring at her, horrified. "Who the devil told you that?"

"Sefton. The bounty is two hundred dollars for the scalp of a warrior, but only one hundred for that of an Indian woman."

Jake said, "Christ." He had taken a bottle of oil of turpentine out of his chest and was warming it over a lamp, but he watched her face as he held the bottle, and his hand shook, just a little.

Harriet nodded. She was very pale. Then she looked down

at the long clean rags she was laying out and said tautly, "At the time I remarked that the system begged deception, for how would the Mexican administrators tell one from the other?"

Jake swallowed; he felt sick. Then, slowly and evenly, he poured the warm liquid oil onto the cloths. The oil would prevent the bandages from sticking to the ghastly wound in Davy's skull, and work against putrefaction as well, he hoped. Then, carefully, he began to dress the poor damaged head. Charlie Martin, his features stiff with horror, held the head up while Jake wound bandages, and Harriet handed over more rags as Jake came to the end of each one.

Then it was done. Davy's head was lowered gently back to the pillow, and Jake looked down at him. The black man was deeply unconscious, snoring on a choking note, his eyes not fully shut so that Jake could see the rolled up whites. He doubted that Davy would last the night; it was a miracle that he'd survived not only the attack but also the journey from the encampment.

Harriet had her head bent as she gathered up the filthy rags and the wet ones that had been used to clean the wound. Charlie left the stateroom with all the haste of fervent relief, and momentarily she and Jake were alone. Jake looked down at her; he wanted to touch her, but couldn't. Instead he said carefully, "Do you know something that I should know, Harriet?"

She was silent so long he thought she hadn't heard or had decided not to answer. Then she said, "Chihuahua is part of Mexico, is it not?"

"So I believe." He kept his voice casual but wondered what made that fact seem so significant.

"I thought so." Another pause. Then: "Mr. Giles told me that Don Roberto ran for the hills and Mexico when the men who'd lost their gold from Sefton's bank started baying for their money."

"Yes." Jake had heard that, too.

"And the Murietas . . . they were his deputies . . . and they also were the ones who jumped Royal's claim when Pablo and Joseph were murdered, were they not?"

Jake frowned. Then he heard his own involuntary intake of breath. He said, "Harriet, what the devil are you saying?"

She sighed and picked up the last of the rags and put them in the basin. Then she grasped the bowl. "I just don't know," she said. "I can only guess, and I don't even want to do that."

Then, while Jake was still grappling with hidden meanings, she left the room.

He looked about, frowning, and turned down the lamp. Davy was snoring, but Jake left the dim light, for the men would take turns to sit with him all night—or until he died.

Davy survived the night; he was still snoring in the morning. There was no point in hanging about there at Pueblo San Marco, so Jake ordered the anchor weighed, and the brig set sail for Sutter's.

The oaks that stood along the river still grew thickly, but the grassy banks were unfamiliar, bristling with the slender stems of oak seedlings. The Indians who usually harvested the acorns in fall had been driven away or had gone of their own accord into the mines. Jake saw one elk where there had been bounding herds; no doubt they, too, had taken for the hills. Waterfowl had become exceeding scarce, but in their places the river was breasted by accumulating fleets of little boats.

There were whaleboats aplenty, under sail or pulled by clumsy young oarsmen, elegant gigs, and awkward dinghies, all moving upstream on the way to the mines, all full to the gunwales with boys all dressed up like miners, their faces shiny and a-gaup with all this exciting adventure. Jake could hear the *Hakluyt* crew laughing about them; oh, they said, this gold-rush business was a wonderful lark . . . until the seven-thousandth bucket of profitless dirt had been panned. Jake himself wondered where all these boats had come from, surely not 'Frisco, for San Pueblo Bay was a deal too rough for craft like this, or even Sonoma. They must have put out from Sutter's, he decided, and thought that the Embarcadero might look a little different from the last time he'd seen it.

Then the men in the hamper all called out as one, in wonder. Jake climbed the main shrouds swiftly, hauled himself over the top, and stood shading his eyes to look at Sutter's and the Embarcadero . . . and that Embarcadero had become the front street of a most strange town. A calico city! Where the three lieutenants had marked out straight streets, there were now ragged lines of calico houses.

Houses made of cloth, of blue cloth or white cloth or even in fancy colors, all tacked onto wooden frames. There were tents too, in abundance, clustered like toadstools under huge trees: round tents, square tents, tents made of old shirts pinned over heaps of branches. The whole area was awash with mud but was even fuller of men. Hammers banged and saws grated, and men shouted as more houses went up, and all the shouting was in United States American. Masts of large vessels lined the Embarcadero, and the river was full of boats. Charlie Martin was roaring about, hollering orders as the brig eased toward a mooring; Jake braced himself to drop down from the mast— and then he recognized the schooner.

The vessel was moored in the same space at the Embarcadero that it had been in the fall. Sefton's schooner. How had he forgotten it? Jake cursed softly and slid down a backstay to deck. The instant the gangplank dropped and joined the brig to the mud of the town, he led a gang on board of the schooner. His last glimpse of the brig was Harriet's face as she watched him over the rail. She was nibbling the tip of one worried finger, in the expression he knew so well.

There were men lounging about the decks of the schooner, but he soon found they had no right to be there: they backed off in haste the moment he began to ask questions. There was no one belowdecks at all. Jake glanced around at varnished walls and varnished benches set out in the holds. Then he issued orders, and his men searched the vessel from tops to bilges. They found nothing, naught but an air of neglect. Jake, grim-faced, returned to the brig. It took ten more minutes for him to realize that Harriet had gone. She had disappeared.

Bodfish was sitting with comatose Davy and had not seen Harriet for a half hour. Jake found Royal and snapped, "Where is your sister?"

Royal looked about vaguely and shrugged. Then he said idly, "Perhaps she's gone off to view the land she so unwisely bought."

That seemed very possible. Jake said urgently, "Where is it?" and Royal led the way down the gangplank. He looked about, scratched his head, and then turned right. Jake followed him.

Calico city was crowded. The broad expanse of mud called Front Street was thronged with men. Royal and then Jake had to dodge teams of horses and oxen, mutinous mules and galloping riders, dogs that yapped at Jake's heels. There were hand-lettered signs everywhere. propped up against trestles and calico walls . . . Saloon . . . Tavern . . . Good News for Miners . . . Café Francais . . . Italian Confectioners . . . Saloon . . . Tavern . . . Saloon. Trestles and tents held boots, saddles, gold-washing equipment, mining shirts, bottles and medicine chests. Nothing looked familiar; everything looked strange. Then Bill the boy came hurtling out from behind a dray, hollering. "Cap'n, Cap'n."

He seemed blinded by his rush. Jake grabbed him as he flew by and said, "What is it?"

"Miss Gray, Miss . . . She run off, sir, off after a China-man. She hollered out, 'Ah Wong!' And then she run off."

Ah Wong. The name meant nothing to Jake. He snapped, "Which way?" and Bill whirled about and dashed off into the crowd again. He moved like a ferret. Jake was hard put to keep up with him, and when he looked over his shoulder Royal was out of sight.

Then Bill's fleeing feet led the way up the long trail to the fort. It was as crowded as Front Street. The boughs of felled trees lay all about, and Jake had to vault them in his run. Touts stepped forward and jangled little bells in his face, and he swore at them for their trouble. Then the crowd at last thinned out, going into the entrance of the fort, and Jake saw Bill dash past the entrance and onward, up the track to the adobe barracks.

In contrast to the Embarcadero, the barracks seemed much emptier than the last time Jake had seen them. The stout high fence of the semicircular corral appeared to house no horses, and the long balcony that overlooked the corral was empty. There was no sign of Harriet on the path that wound past the corral fence, and very few men. Then Jake saw a familiar burly shape, wearing uniform, marching down the path toward him. Bill whirled and came racing back, but Jake stopped still.

It was Captain Mervine. Oddly, perhaps because he had been thinking how American this place had become, Jake felt no surprise. Mervine, he noted, was not surprised either. Instead he marched right up to Jake and barked, "And what do you think of it all, Captain Dexter? Ain't it all amazin'? Ain't it all a monument to American drive and energy? Tarnation, Captain, I would not have believed it if I had not viewed it myself. I arrived with a small force, after deserters, you understand, two weeks back. This place were deserted then, naught but a few wayfarers at the fort, and what do you see now, huh?"

Jake said swiftly, "Have you seen Mrs. Sefton?"

"Mrs. . . . *who*?"

"Miss Gray."

"Two ladies, are there? Right uncommon, in these parts!"

The captain broke off to enjoy a chuckle, and then said, "No, I can't say I've seen neither."

"I was told she came this way, after a Chinaman."

"A Chinaman? That explains it," said Mervine with mysterious disapproval. "Come and have a look for yourself," he bid, and turned to march back in the direction from where he'd come. It was the right direction, so Jake followed him. Then he heard Mervine grumble, "'Tis a scandal, and stripe me if it ain't."

It was as if the intervening months since their last conversation hadn't happened. Jake said cautiously. "It is?"

"Yes, Captain, and never a truer word did I speak. I brought a small force only, caught some deserters, had to send 'em back with some of my men to San Francisco, to the frigate. And you know why? Because the barracks have been taken over, Captain, army quarters have all been requisitioned by the cooks and restaurateurs."

"It was used as a hotel the last time I was here, in the fall."

"And now it's full of Chinese coolies, sir, all brought in as indentured labor by the rancheros and the restaurant-keepers! And what d'you think of that, huh?" Mervine stopped and waved an arm at the corral; they were near the entrance of the building, and the stout, high wooden fence rose up on Jake's left side. Ahead was the entrance to the barracks, and above the entrance and the corral, the balcony. There were two sullen characters standing at the entrance. Jake looked about distractedly, and then heard Mervine say, "Did you say Sefton? You can't mean Colonel Frank Sefton, for he ain't got a wife. He's a settler here, done right well, believe me."

Jake paused. Then he said carefully, "You know him?"

"Of course I do! Met him twice, at least."

"That schooner moored down at the Embarcadero was his."

Mervine stared. Then he tut-tutted. "Dearie me," he said. "That was the vessel where I found the deserters. Found them lounged all about belowdecks, as easy as if they had crystal-clear consciences. I sent 'em back to the frigate as I said, but I'd thought better of Sefton than that he employed runaway men."

"Did they have any gold in their possession when you arrested them?"

"Gold?" Mervine stared again, and then guffawed. "Nope. They didn't look the lucky sort to me. Worse luck for the United States government too, for I would've confiscated it if they'd had any." Then he said, "Who is this Mrs. Sefton you asked after?"

Jake was glancing all about; his hands in his pockets were clenched with his tension. There was no sign of Harriet, but he could hear hints of strange sounds from inside the barracks, a kind of chanting, and his nape crawled with a sense of danger. There was a smell in the air, of violence and death, mingled strangely with the smell of burning tobacco.

Mervine was staring at him, repeating the question. Jake said reluctantly, "Mrs. Sefton is Colonel Sefton's widow."

"What? He's dead? My God," said Mervine. He seemed very shocked. "Truly, in the midst of life we are in death. Has he been dead long?"

"He died about three weeks ago, when his house burned down with him in it."

"My God. Where is he buried?"

"What?" Jake stared, wondering at the question. Then he shrugged and said, "He's buried on his rancho, I think." Then his voice faded, as he glimpsed movement from within the corral. He could see the shape of the well and its little roof, and beside it, on the brown ground, something dark brown moved . . .

"But that's a scandal," Mervine expostulated. "We'll have to fix that; he came from a most prominent Philadelphia family!"

Jake hardly heard him; his attention was riveted. He said, "My God," as the bear stood up, and had to fight the urge to flinch back despite the stoutness of the fence. He said, "What the hell is *that* doing here?"

"Terrible, ain't it," said Mervine.

"My God, yes," said Jake fervently. The beast was huge; he could see the long claws and smell the rank fur. It was like the bear that had menaced Harriet . . . Harriet. He said violently, "Why don't you shoot it?"

"'Cause it ain't mine to shoot," Mervine said crossly. "It was here when I came, we couldn't even quarter our horses here, let alone ourselves. The barracks' full of coolies, and the corral's full of bear. Those men, there, they captured him and brought him here, and only Providence knows how they did it. They put that there bear there and went and lodged at the fort."

The two men he indicated were mountainmen, judging by their surly looks and the fringes down the seams of their dirty shirts and trousers. They leaned each one against one side of the entrance, and they had longbarreled Kentucky rifles, longer even than themselves, which leaned against them. "They say they'll get good money for that bear when they sell him," Mervine moodily said. "Providence knows how they'll get him there, but they said they'll sell him to Don Manuel Vidrie, who . . ."

Jake had stopped listening. Harriet ran out onto the balcony so precipitately that for a ghastly second Jake thought she was going to topple into the corral with the bear.

She caught herself with both hands on the rail, but in imagination he saw her fall, heard her scream, heard the crunch of terrible jaws. He cursed and shoved past Mervine, past the mountainmen and through the entrance, and then through a doorway into a room.

The room was full of Chinese coolies. They were seated about rough pine tables, and they were playing a game. Jake heard clapping, and weird syllables cried out, "Aie, aie, san, sze!" The yellow sun slanted in the long, barred window and lit smooth faces, lips drawn back as the men called out their words. "Aie, sze . . . san!" they cried. It was like some ancient incantation; Jake's mind was full of incoherent pictures, of frigid eastern deserts, and the tough little horses warriors like these had ridden. Then the sounds in this room stopped as all the men saw him; all the faces turned. In a further room the sounds went on, and Jake set himself into a run again, toward the gaming noises that were still obliviously loud.

He called out Harriet's name as he ran. Then he found stairs, winding up a bastion. He dashed up, round and round, up, and then he spun out onto the balcony, to lurch up at the rail with his momentum, just as Harriet had done.

He caught himself. The bear looked up; he could see the teeth in the snarl and smell the stench of its breath. Harriet was standing still, looking at him, wide eyed. Then he heard her fast breathing. She gasped, "I saw him. I saw Ah Wong. He was terrified, Jake. He shouted out to me to run away, and then he ran away himself. I thought he was dead but . . . I followed him. I'm sure I didn't lose him. I'm sure he came here, but those men down there, they just stared and wouldn't understand me, and then they went back to their gaming . . ."

Jake stopped listening. He took two steps and gripped her by the upper arms and said harshly, "Don't you ever do that again."

She flinched; then he saw anger in her eyes. She snapped, "I beg your pardon?"

"Don't ever give me a fright like that again. You're a member of our company, and you live on the brig, which means, Harriet, that you do not leave the brig without telling me your destination."

"And I suppose that means that I must have your permission too?"

"Yes!"

She paused. Then she said icily, "I see." He could feel the stiff rejection in her shoulders, and slowly he let go, and his hands dropped. She turned, and with head high, with sublime dignity, she walked through a doorway and through an upper room to the stairs. Jake followed her. The Chinese men here, as in the lower room, had been playing their game. They were watching in open-mouthed silence, their lips drawn back uneasily to show their big white teeth.

Mervine said, thunderstruck, "Miss Gray!"

"Yes," said Harriet. She inclined her head, graciously. Then Jake saw Royal come up the track, having evidently found them at last. As he watched, Harriet took three quick steps to stand close by her brother, her hand tucked into the crook of his arm.

He looked away. There was a feeling like grief inside him.

32 ⟋⟍ Harriet went to live at the fort.
She borrowed money from
Bodfish and rented a bed in the same room on the second level
of Sutter's house that she'd slept in last fall. It was the same
bed too, and apparently had the same corn-shuck mattress.
There was the same loud angry commotion, too, from the men
who lodged in the attics above. Those who slept snored just the
same; it was as if time had rolled back, and Harriet felt no
surprise whatsoever when Mrs. Marchant bounced into the
room.

Mrs. Marchant, however, looked astounded. "Miss Gray!"
she cried, and threw out her arms. "Welcome to Sacramento
City!"

The Embarcadero, it seemed, had grown a new name, along
with its uprush of tents. Despite the change Harriet found that
the dining room in the compound looked just the same and
served the same food to similar men who ate with silent

voracity. The same sweating Chinese cooks carried huge platters of meat and molasses in saucers, and Mr. King was every ounce as complacent as before.

His hotel, he informed her at the top of his voice, was a-building. He barely paused to offer half-hearted condolences on the loss of a husband before he ran on at length about plans and prices. "I must confess," he confided in a bellow, "that without a word of a lie my business sense is renowned as infallible. Bricks cost forty-five dollars per thousand here, and yet I pay without complaint, for I have great faith in the future of this here Sacramento City, Miss Gray! A veranda, with a balcony on the second storey, I've planned, and saloons below, billiard table, dining room, an omnibus apartment for second-class guests, and, above, staterooms!" And bathrooms, with long baths, Harriet remembered. "But long baths be a scarce commodity here," Mr. King mourned. "In fact I must confess it, I ain't been able to buy a single one."

Then, with scarcely a pause, he asked her about her plot of Sacramento City ground. "I hear you paid but one thou' for that," he said, insinuating. Harriet's lips pressed together with annoyance, but then she realized that Mrs. Marchant must have told him the price. When Mr. King politely offered to escort her to the brig she accepted, for she had promised to sit with Davy.

When they set out the path to the Embarcadero seemed more crowded than ever. Some men were hard at it, building a corral for mules, making it the easy way, with half-tanned hides stretched out on wires for fences. Mules were arriving in plenty, she learned, brought in by the men who'd come overland to this new land, men who'd arrived so impoverished that they were forced to sell their pack beasts for a grubstake. The mule traders fattened them, and then sold them to the prospectors at high profit: this, she mused, was but another of the multitudinous ways of making a pile out of California.

It was all part of the general ruckus, a most battering kind of scene to watch. The big trees at the Embarcadero made the scene prettier than it deserved to be, and had other uses as well. Men hung their bags in the branches, and there, apparently, the bags hanging like gross fruits were as safe from robbers as they were from trampling boots and hooves. Then Harriet found out at least part of the reason for Mr. King's gallant company: he wanted to show her the beginnings of his hotel, as proud as any prospective new father.

"Spiles," said he, beaming, and foundations, certainly, there were. Many of them were the stumps of the trees that had been felled to make room for the structure. Harriet mused, privately, that in Mr. King's place she would have made those foundations about twelve feet higher, to avoid the floods, but she kept that opinion to herself.

Then, slowly, she noted that Mr. King was eyeing the piece of land she had bought and was breathing rather heavily. "Tell you what," said he, "I'll give you two thou' for it."

"What!" She stared, amazed, quite certain she'd not heard a-right. Then, even more amazingly, he winked and nudged her with a meaty elbow, all in most conspiratorial manner.

"Or p'raps," he said, and winked again, "I should convey my offer to Captain Dexter." Harriet glared, tilting her chin, but the gesture was wasted, she saw, for the shrewd little eyes had focused past her. Before she turned her head she knew that Jake Dexter had joined them.

She moved slowly, meeting his narrow stare. His expression was bleak, and he said, "Harriet."

"Captain Dexter. Is Davy . . . ?"

"Davy is alive. Davy is the same. He—"

Mr. King bellowed, "Captain Dexter, I'm right glad to see you!"

"You are?"

If Mr. King noticed that the tone was abrupt, he certainly didn't seem to let it worry him. He beamed on as readily and boomed just as loudly, "I've been making this little gal an offer, sir, but she don't pay attention, and I can guess the reason for that, I can. Three!" he hollered. "Three thousand I'll give you, for that bit of ground." Harriet stared at him, incredulously hot in the cheeks, and saw the stout Yankee give Jake one of his heavy meaningful nudges, saying in what perhaps he thought of as a conspiratorial mutter, "Beautiful woman, lovely."

Harriet didn't dare look at Jake but was aware all the same that he'd pushed back his hat, and that his eyebrows were extremely lopsided. He said very neutrally, "Yes."

"A woman is worth her weight in rubies, I allus say."

"Or gold dust," said Jake dryly.

" 'Tis the prime disadvantage to this Sacramento City, the mournful lack of women. A widder here is not a widder long. 'Tis the washing, you know."

"The . . . ?"

"The laundry. The merchants in 'Frisco were paying one dollar a piece to have their washing done when we were there this last winter, one dollar! Can you credit that, sir? Many a men who has failed to wash out a fortune at the diggin's has found that his wife has washed a fortune for them both." Mr. King laughed immoderately at his little jest and then said, "Four thou'."

"I beg your pardon?"

"For that land. A four-fold profit. Why not grab it?"

"I'll think about it. Who knows what it will be worth if I wait a week or even one hour?"

"But can you afford to wait, Captain? Surely you don't intend to build! Do you know how much this building will cost me? One hundred thou' and not a cent less. I don't do things by halves, I don't. Tell you what, I'll give you five."

Jake was silent. Harriet gazed at him, willing him to take the offer and accept the cash. At least then the *Hakluyt* Company would take a little profit from California, she thought, and Jake turned his head a little.

Their eyes met, and she thought how bleakly tired he looked. Then he said shortly, "No."

"No?" Mr. King echoed in tones of great astonishment. "You say no, and don't even give yourself the time to ponder? Reconsider, Captain, reconsider!"

Mr. King, thought Harriet, seemed on the very verge of an apoplectic fit. She gazed at Jake but he merely shook his head. "No," he said tightly. "I am determined to build a theater."

When Harriet arrived on the brig he was waiting for her. She hid apprehension with tilted chin and tried to whisk past him on her way to the stairs, but his hand came out and stopped her, the grip not hard but firm.

His voice was harder. He snapped, "Who the hell is Ah Wong?"

She wondered if he had asked about but then realized that no one on the brig would know the little Chinaman. She said quietly, "He was my servant."

"What?" He looked taken aback. "At Sefton's rancho?"

"No. As I told you, Sefton sent me away, the very day that the brig arrived in Pueblo San Marco. I don't know his reasons, Jake, but he may well have been making sure that I did not get in touch with you, or my brother. He sent me to live with the Vidries, and sent Ah Wong along with me."

He was frowning; his hand dropped away from her and he stepped back one pace to study her. Then he said, "Why?"

"Who knows? I didn't have much chance to ask my husband," she said bitterly. "I only saw him three or four times after that, and there were usually other people present."

Jake paused then, a very long moment, but she knew he would stop her if she tried to go. The shadow of his hat was very dark, his face in the shade of it, and she wondered what he was thinking. Then he said abruptly, "I wish you had not gone to live at the fort."

" 'Tis better that I do."

"I think it's safer that you stop here."

"What?" She gasped. "What do you mean?"

"You said Ah Wong . . . you said he told you to run away."

"Perhaps it was not he," she said uneasily, but at the time she had been so certain. She had known Ah Wong so very well; for months he had been her only friend. She said, "There were so many Chinese men in the barracks . . ." She worried about it constantly, wondering if she had been confused, for surely she had searched every room in her rush through the barracks.

In the middle of the night, tossing wakefully, she had felt a harrowing certainty that she had not seen all the rooms. They had been so crowded, the men all so strange, and she had been so flustered, trying to make them understand.

Jake was watching her intently. He said in that abrupt tone, "I don't think you've told me everything, Harriet. What are you holding back?"

"Nothing," she said. Nothing, she thought, save the fact that Ah Wong had helped her run away.

"I want you to come back to the brig."

"Well, I won't. While I'm gone Mr. Martin has a stateroom; it is only fair to him."

"That has nothing to do with it, and you know it. Charlie doesn't care where he sleeps."

"How do you know?" she said angrily. "And don't worry about the cost, either, for I've paid for my lodgings."

"And that has nothing to do with it, either!" he shouted. Then, visibly, he controlled himself, saying in a low tight voice, "I know you borrowed the money, and 'tis you who does not need to worry, for I've paid Bodfish back."

"How dare you," she snapped, and flounced down the stairs. He made no attempt to go after her.

"You're going to build a theater?" Mrs. Marchant demanded that evening. Harriet surveyed her wearily. She had spent the day sitting with Davy, putting warm bottles to his feet and cool cloths to the nape of his neck, feeding him soup and soothing potions that Jake Dexter had mixed. Davy had muttered a lot, and tossed and turned; he'd seemed feverish, but for the first time Harriet allowed herself to feel some hope for his recovery.

Jake Dexter had escorted her back to the fort, in aggressive silence. She had coped by pretending that he wasn't there, but had been the more aware of him because of that. Now she heard Mrs. Marchant confide in a hushed whisper that, "My epic drama, Miss Gray, be about complete," and wondered what the devil the woman was talking about.

Then she remembered; it seemed so long ago, but she remembered the vivacious chat about young miners a-bringing their wives. Or perhaps it had been but one young miner, and one wife . . .

If Mrs. Marchant noticed Harriet's vagueness, she certainly didn't seem to let it worry her. "My poem begins with the courtship, Miss Gray, so wonderfully adaptable for the stage. I've named my heroine Malvina. *'Malvina was fair and of a tender heart,'* runs the first line of my poem."

"It does?" said Harriet rather helplessly. Men in the attics above the ceiling were shoving and cursing. By the sounds of it there were ten too many, and they were fighting each other for room. Harriet expected to hear the firing of pistols at any moment, but Mrs. Marchant did not seem to think this accompaniment inappropriate for her retelling of her romantic saga, no matter how the planks rattled.

"And the hero is named Jed. Malvina prized his noble spirit, so full of loving notions!"

"Merciful heavens, did she?"

"Then the next scene shows the happy nuptials. Then—his fatal announcement, that he be off to the land of gold, that wondrous coast, Miss Gray! Malvina cries, 'No, ah, woe, no!' But does he pay a blind bit of notice?"

Harriet, sitting on the edge of her bed, was fighting half-hysterical mirth, but the poetess did not even seem to notice that, so lost was she in her poesy, standing poised with her hands clasped before her ample breast. "I don't suppose he does," Harriet admitted at length.

"And you're right, Miss Gray! So . . . Malvina declares her intention to go with him, she speaks with hard purpose, there are scenes of great emotion, and then she braves the pitching deck and the pirate-ridden Carib sea, to disembark at Aspinwall. . . . Once more upon the land, o'er the appalling wilds of Panama, that place of skulls, they took their pilgrim way! Then, 'Frisco, then, Sacramento City, then, the diggin's, Miss Gray; Malvina expires, with great passion, leaving a helpless babe and grieving swain. Jed toils on, digs his pile, makes his way home with his son, while Malvina's smiling ghost looks on, a most happy apparition, for love conquers all, Miss Gray!"

"Does it?" Harriet said wryly, but that, she saw at once, was not the response the poetess wanted.

"Tell me what you think," Mrs. Marchant begged. "Do you think it could do the stage; do you think it possible? You are an actress, so pray be truthful and honest."

Harriet paused. Then she said, with perfect honesty, "In this place and at this time, I think it would make a great deal of money."

"Ah wonderful!" cried Mrs. Marchant. She seemed uplifted. "I beg you a favor, Miss Gray."

"Yes?" said Harriet. She waited in some suspense.

"Please, Miss Gray, convey that same opinion to Mr. King."

To Harriet's surprise Royal was waiting for her outside the eating room next morning. He gave no reason for being there, but laughed when she told him the story on the way to the brig. Then he said, "And what did King say?"

"Oh, he agreed! His business sense, you see, is infallible even when he confesses it himself. He ventured the opinion that minstrels would do even better."

"He could well be right," Royal said. They were walking past the mule corral; there were horses in there, Harriet noted, and she thought that the corral at the barracks must still be full of bear. "White men in black face," Royal said angrily. As usual he was inconsiderate, walking in long steps so she had to trot, not measuring his pace to hers. "Americans," he exclaimed.

"Yes," she said, not paying attention; she knew his views on the subject full well. "The point is," she said, "that Mr. King is equable to the idea of theatrical manager; he seems to have funds aplenty to waste. And if he does, there will be need for actors . . ."

"Yes?" said Royal. The look he bent on her was not enthusiastic in the slightest. After that he was silent, brooding, it seemed, and Harriet put her mind to wondering how Davy would be when she arrived on the brig.

He was better in body, very much better. Then, next morning, when she arrived on the brig he was not in his berth. She was gripped by panic; she was certain he'd died, and she ran out into the cabin, calling for Jake. He came quickly, frowning, and searched the steerage and fo'c'sle while she went on deck. She was the one who found Davy; he had got himself up and somehow half dressed, and he was sitting on the fore hatch in a patch of sun, crooning to himself. Harriet stopped short and felt Jake come up beside her.

They were alone; the *Hakluyt* men were all at work on the theatrical site. Harriet had the most of her attention on the invalid but then slowly became aware of Jake's pensive regard. She had called out his name without thinking, she thought uneasily, and swallowed, staring deliberately at Davy. She said in a matter-of-fact voice, "Do you think he's getting better?"

"I doubt if his mind will heal, but the sun and air won't hurt him." Still he watched her. Then he said roughly, "Royal tells me that you think to accept an offer of employment with Jed King."

"Yes!" she snapped. To posture for the miners, she thought, and she looked about wildly and said, "Why don't you take that schooner?"

"*What?*"

"It was Sefton's, but you know that. And I know you found none of the lost gold on it . . . the *Hakluyt* gold. So why not claim the schooner? I'm the widow, you could say it's mine and . . . and it is my present to you, to make up for your losses in California."

He shouted, "I want nothing that was Sefton's!"

"I know," she said bitterly, and turned and went below.

After that Davy was up and about most of the day. He recovered his strength visibly, but as Jake had predicted, his mind did not mend. His eyes were open, but at times he walked into obstacles that at other time he avoided like any other man. At times he tried to talk, but all he achieved were agonized grunts, as he tried, it seemed, to tell her about what had happened to his tribe on that awful night. He seemed happiest when he was watching the theater a-building, so Harriet perforce spent much time watching too.

Watching Jake. The weather was warm, and the men rolled up their sleeves as they worked. When Jake took off his leather weskit there was a damp patch on his shirt between the broad shoulder blades. He had kept clean-shaven, so that the creases in his face tanned again, the way Harriet remembered him. Did he know that she watched him? He certainly worked very hard, she thought. The theater might be made of lath and calico, Sacramento City style, but it was honor-built just the same, built with care and loving attention. It was a big task, for Royal's design had called for a building quite one hundred feet in depth by nearly sixty wide. It had seating for up to three hundred men, with a stage a full two feet above the auditorium, built of solid wood. There was a tumble-home at the front of the stage, sailor-style to shelter the whale-oil lamps, and all kinds of other similar detail. The building went up fast but could have gone up even faster, and sometimes Harriet wondered, secretly, if Jake Dexter were deliberately wasting time. It was as if he were waiting, but for what . . . ?

She refused to allow herself to ask him. Sometimes Jake was the man who escorted her back to the fort, and occasionally he was the one she found waiting when she came out from breakfast. There was a kind of bleak patience in his eyes, she thought, but found it impossible to ask why. They seldom talked at all.

There was always someone to escort her; she never walked that path alone. Usually it was one of the *Hakluyt* men, though sometimes it was Captain Mervine or Mr. King on his way to oversee his hotel. It was no problem holding conversation with either of these men. All she had to do was listen. Captain Mervine ranted on about the bear in the corral and the coolies in the barracks and the necessity to send another officer of the law for this place when he'd been recalled to the frigate, and Mr. King talked on and on about his theatrical ambitions, and his ambitions for his hotel.

Both ambitions sounded exactly the same; Harriet had much trouble to tell at times exactly which was the topic of talk. "Chandeliers," he said, and she merely listened cautiously, and, "I'll build one to accommodate two thousand men!" he cried. She was certain that time that he was talking about his hotel, but no, he was envisaging an entertainment hall. His knowledge of theatrical management would have filled the head of a pin, she mused, but his intentions were certainly lavish. He talked of gilded ceilings and velvet upholstery and baroque drop curtains with marvelous ease. The thought that such ornate surroundings would prove somewhat inappropriate for the staging of poetic dramas of the kind his ladylove composed never seemed to cross his mind. He was negotiating to hire the theater and had already hired Harriet and Royal to play the two stars, and was in the process of hiring a backstage crew.

Then, suddenly, her walks became changed in nature, for Davy himself was strong enough to be her escort. He was straight and strong again, even if his mind was feeble. His loyalty was remarkable; he followed her everywhere, and Harriet found him waiting each morning when she came out from breakfast. She felt uneasy about it, for she often wondered if Davy really knew her, or if he'd confused her with someone else, for he sometimes called her *mistress*. He often crooned to himself, as if he were back on that plantation in Guiana, and Harriet felt uncomfortable about that too.

But then, all at once, the theater was about complete, and the impending departure of the brig filled her mind instead. She couldn't sleep. She told herself angrily that she would do much better when the brig was finally gone and she could put the *Hakluyt* out of her mind. She spent evening hours at the window of her room in Sutter's house, staring unfocused. She could see the barracks from there, and the balcony and the top of the fence of the corral, but she never really looked, even though Captain Mervine still complained about it. Captain Mervine had been recalled and would be returning to Sausalito very soon; he declared himself disappointed that he would not be in Sacramento City to view the first performance of the great epic *The California Miner*, but Harriet scarcely listened. It would all come right, she told herself furiously, once the brig had sailed; she would be able to go back to taking life one step at a time.

Then, next morning, Royal was there as well as Davy to escort her to the brig, and when they walked out onto the path and Harriet looked across tent city to the Embarcadero, the old brig *Hakluyt* had her sails out, her canvas all loose on the masts.

Panic gripped her; she couldn't think, she couldn't move, she couldn't *breathe*. Then she cried, "No—oh, no!" and began to run. Davy grunted with fright, and Royal's hand lunged out and stopped her.

She was weeping wildly; she barely saw his face. Then he shook her, not at all gently, and shouted, "Harriet, what's wrong, for God's sake?"

"The brig, she's . . . she's . . ."

Royal peered at her. Her eyes cleared enough to see him hunch his shoulders as he peered into her face from her level. Then he said with eloquent disgust, "Oh, for God's sake, Hat, 'tis only the canvas out drying."

"Drying? What . . . ?" Then she realized what a fool she'd made of herself. She knew that canvas had to be hung out every now and then, or else like household linen it went moldy, of course she knew that. She straightened her shoulders, gathered the shreds of her dignity about her, said haughtily, "I'm sorry," and began to walk.

Royal's hand stopped her yet again. He said brusquely, "When will you stop this performance, Hat? You're sending the man to the end of his tether."

"I don't know what you're talking about."

"Yes, you do. He loves you, Hat. He loves you."

Something jerked inside her. She pressed her lips together and said curtly, "I don't inspire that emotion in men, Royal."

"What utter poppycock! Just because Sefton treated you so shabbily . . ."

"So you admit now that he did treat me badly?"

"I know that he cheated you; I know he cheated Father. 'Twas Jake made me see it, how we'd all fallen for that confidence trick when Sefton gave you all that land. Jake believed you in danger, Hat; he worried a-constant when we were dug in over winter."

Her heart jumped again, in horror. "In danger?" she cried. "How did he guess that?"

Royal stared. Then his eyes narrowed. Men shoved all about, and a horseman thundered past, riding breakneck in the infamous Californian fashion, but Royal paid attention to none of it.

Then he said flatly, "So you were in danger."

"Yes!" Then Harriet wavered. She looked about, her arms folded tightly, clutching her elbows in her hands. Then she muttered, "I . . . might have been in danger. Ah Wong made me run away, the night that Sefton's house burned down; he came to my bedroom and helped me escape."

Royal was silent. Then he snapped, "Have you told Jake this?" She looked away but did not have time to prevaricate, for he roared, "For God's sake, stupid wench, I don't believe you have."

"I don't see why I should . . ."

"Of course you should; it makes all the difference. Swamp it, Hat, when I think how he wondered and worried, about you and the way Father was killed . . ."

She gasped, shocked, "But that has nothing to do with it!"

"Hasn't it?" His voice was somber. "That accident was a piece of luck, then, for Sefton."

Harriet whispered, "Oh, my God. Oh, surely not, not murder, not Sefton."

" 'Tis possible. Think about it."

Harriet did think about it. She didn't want to, but it haunted her day and night. Had Sefton killed her father? She remembered trudging head down when she'd gone to her father's hotel and found him gone out. She remembered hearing the shouts, the people all about saying how a man was dead, had been killed, had been knocked down by a horseman, had fallen under carriage wheels . . . Then she remembered the shock and the waiting, waiting for Sefton to come.

Frank Sefton never came. He had been sailing out of the harbor on his way to Canton. Was it possible that Frank Sefton had had the time to commit murder? Harriet wondered fiercely if that ship had weighed anchor just late enough . . . just in time for a horseman to hurry on board and claim his cabin. He had deliberately left her without a penny in the world. Had Frank Sefton deliberately left her without a friend as well?

It fitted . . . it fitted, for he had done about the same when he'd given her those shares in his bank, leaving her the scapegoat of his actions. But if he'd done that, Harriet mused apprehensively, Sefton had certainly intended to quit California with all that confiscated gold. Again, Sefton would have succeeded in leaving her bereft . . . but Sefton had died, instead.

Then, two days later, the theater was finished, and Jake Dexter put on a party to celebrate. Half of inquisitive Sacramento City came. Jake provided brandy in barrels and savory food on paper plates: it was a long time since Harriet had seen him so good-humored. She watched in disbelief as the eatables were rushed; she even saw men gnawing hungrily at the plates, and, "Oh-h-h," yodeled Royal, more than a trifle drunk.

The axes all go clack, and the hammers bang like hell
To build a wooden frame for a canvas drilling shell.
There's only but one door for the folks to come in,
But she's a damn fine theater—for the shape that she's in!

"A wonderful theater," boomed Mr. King. The banging of
the hammers was all happening backstage, where men he had
hired were making stage scenery, and Mr. King was wearing a
top hat in honor of the occasion. Harriet felt ebulliant herself,
for she'd just accomplished a piece of business. She had hired
out the theater to Mr. King.

It had been strange, to find that her signature was valid
again. Because of her widowhood she was able to hire the
theater out, at the most favorable price of forty ounces of dust,
forty ounces of gold per night, eighteen carat pure, plus ten
percent of the takings. The money would go to Jake; she would
make sure of that, though she was not at all sure how she could
do it, but it was a weird intoxication to have a lawful presence
again.

"How much be she worth to you?" jovial Mr. King shouted.
She saw then that he was shouting at Jake Dexter, and saw,
further, that Jake's lopsided brows were the most a-kilter she
had ever seen them.

"Why?" he countered. "Does an eye for cost and profit
come compulsory with Californian citizenship?"

"Of course it do, sir!"

"Then I wonder why I asked." Then Jake, wryly, began to
figure out loud. "Calico . . . hmm, that is surely one thing,
for we used such a deal of it here, and calico costs more than
fifty dollars per bale here, and at fifty-five yards to the
bale . . . And then, the lumber, reckoned at six hundred
dollars per thousand feet . . . and roofing iron! Roofing iron
costs six dollars per square foot! Then, the labor, at an ounce
per day per man . . ."

Harriet watched him incredulously, and his gaze turned to
her, and for the first time in so long, she saw bright amusement
in his eyes. "Seventy-five thousand dollars," he said.

Men whistled, all about, and shook their heads in wonder.
They all tipped their wise heads to study the roof with renewed
respect, and Harriet thought dryly that the value placed on
possessions here certainly marked the respect for a man.
"Wonderful," said Mr. King.

"A monument to American energy and initiative," said

Captain Mervine, and everyone looked at him. He was wearing regimentals and braid; this was his last call, for he was off to 'Frisco and the frigate. He nodded most pompous, his every manner of the most approving. The men about all nodded in time, except Jake. And Royal, she noted.

Royal's expression was cynical, almost brooding. "American energy and initiative," he muttered. "Why don't you go and put a gold American eagle on it?" he sarcastically demanded.

And they took him quite seriously and did.

It was late, and dark, when Harriet set off for the fort. She had delayed leaving the festivities . . . why? Then she realized that she had unconsciously waited for someone to tell her when the brig would sail. There was no reason for the *Hakluyt* to stop here now. The commotion of Sacramento City bustled on despite the dark. Gambling games were set up on wagon trays, and restaurants were set up under canvas, with humble Chinese cooks working at open braziers. Wherever a lamp was set up in a tent, that tent immediately became transparent, so that she could watch the occupants in silhouette. She could hear the men in those fabric houses talking, too; everyone spoke so loudly, in California. There was something about this land that made everything bigger, more blatant, more lucid.

Then all at once it was quiet. Outside the immediate Embarcadero the tents were all dark and quiet, for most men needed their exhausted sleep. It was beginning to mist with rain, a dank mist that smelled colder than it felt. The path she trod was full of shadows, and then she smelled manure and horse sweat, and the path was even darker.

Then she heard the snuffling and whickering of animals, and realized she was walking abreast of the mule corral, the one that was fenced with hides. It was the shadow of the hides that made this part of the walk so dark, and the smell of them that made most of the stench. She could hear mules shift at their hobble ropes . . . but naught else. The nape of her neck shivered. She stopped and called out, "Davy."

Her voice came out more tremulous than she had intended. She tried again, but still there was no reply. Clouds silently flickered across the moon, and in the distance she could see the shape of the fort and, beyond that, of the barracks. There were very few lights.

She moved again, carefully, brushing the damp stinking hides with the back of one hand. The path was treacherous in the dark, full of potholes, those holes filled with dust and worse. Then she saw men, galloping, men on horses up the track from beyond the fort, men with serapes flying against the shape of the fort and the barracks and the moon, galloping full force in the Californian style, galloping toward her.

Harriet froze, abruptly terrified. She shrank back against the fence, but the hides gave poor protection. She heard the agitated calling of mules and the screams of horses and the wild triumphant shouting of the horsemen. Then—a shot. It blasted the night, right by her ear. She lurched back, crying out, and there was another shot. Something slapped viciously into the hide by her head. Then a scream from inside the mule corral, and a terrified threshing of hooves.

Harriet screamed, men shouted, screamed. A man galloped close to her, his horse reared, screaming, and hooves struck the air by her face. She saw—a hatchet, swinging. She saw the billow of a flying serape, and then . . . Davy. Davy came running.

Davy. He was *howling*. The mules were lending a ghastly chorus as they bucked and tried to break free from their ropes and run. Davy ran . . . not for the rearing horse, not the man. *He hit her*. Harriet felt the flail of his arm. Then she fell, screaming, plunging through the fence as wires snapped and bent. Loose wire scratched her, reaching with stinging claws for her eyes. She rolled over and over among the plunging hooves of the terrified mules.

Screaming. A shot—another shot. A mule screamed, fell with a crash, dragging others with it. Harriet blindly plunged to her feet and fell again instantly, tripped by whipping picket ropes. Shouts in the distance, the horsemen shouting to each other, in Spanish, shouting in panic, some kind of superstitious terror, Davy howling, and then the galloping of hooves as the horsemen fled. Harriet panted, her mouth open as she sobbed with terror. She was rolled up against one of the mules, and blood was pumping out all over her. Then, at last, she was able to lurch to her feet.

She heard steps running toward her, a familiar voice shouting. She put out her hands, touched the wet trembling hides of mules, stumbled over ropes, and then . . . rough arms holding her, pulling her up against a laboring chest, Jake, Jake's voice, hoarse with fear, Jake, Jahaziel. Then she fainted.

*   *   *

When she opened her eyes she was lying on the transom sofa in the brig. Home . . . she was home. She tried to sit up but found she was naked, wrapped only in a blanket. Then she forgot even about that, for she thought she was going to vomit. A bowl was held out, but the sickness passed, and when she saw who held the bowl, she was glad that it did.

Jake. There was blood on his shirt, and then she saw her discarded clothes, all dank with the dark blood of the dying mules. Bodfish tapped on the door and came in, and Harriet held the blanket tightly. He was carrying a steaming bucket, and she saw then that there was a bath on the floor, and he was filling it.

The bath was a cask. Of course, she thought dazedly; there were no long baths to be obtained in California. Bodfish went out. Jake was watching her. He said wryly, "You're not hurt. I can't believe it, but you're not hurt."

She thought about that but decided she felt bruised and dazed and sick enough, and concluded to treat this with the contempt it deserved. She said huskily, "Davy . . . ?"

"He's gone, after those men who attacked you. He must have taken a horse from the corral, and we think he has a gun, a rifle. One of Sutter's Indian workers will track him, in the morning; we'll make up a posse from the brig."

Too late, but too late already, she thought; she was certain that Davy was dead. She remembered the way the horsemen had cried out when they'd seen him, the note of superstitious terror, and shuddered. She tried to sit up, but Jake stopped her. He had a glass of amber fluid in his hand. She said shakily, "What is that?"

"Don't ask."

It was brandy. Her teeth chattered against the rim of the glass and he had to hold it for her. The first mouthful tasted dreadful and the second even worse. Then it got better. No doubt, she thought, the numbness of her mouth helped. Then the brandy felt like a scorch in her stomach; then the warmth spread, and all her muscles felt warm and soft. Only her mind was tense, and she wanted to tell Jake, over and over, how the men had attacked her, how they had galloped, how scared she had been, how Davy had screamed and the mules had screamed and died and bled. It seemed impossible to stop. Jake sat at the foot of the sofa and listened quietly, saying yes, now and then. He seemed to understand that she felt this compulsion to tell him about it, over and over again.

She said, "Those men . . . they were the Murietas."

"Are you sure?" But he did not seem surprised.

"They—they chose me deliberately as their target; they knew I would be there on the path. How, Jake, how? They would have killed me if Davy had not come. Then, when he did, they sounded so terrified, as if they thought Davy an apparition—from the grave. I think they were the men who slaughtered his tribe and sold their scalps, the way they killed poor Pablo and Joseph, but why kill me? My hair is not black."

She saw Jake shut his eyes momentarily, in a wince. Then she realized he was rubbing her feet, and had been rubbing her feet for some time. Her feet felt cold and then they tingled and she realized he was rubbing them with brandy. The fumes rose gently while his long fingers rubbed and moulded her toes. She said on an inquiring note, "Jake?"

His fingers stopped. "You must know something, or have seen something that you don't remember as important, but which is more valuable to them than your life. Can you imagine what it might be?"

She thought about it; it was hard to think. She said, "No."

He said, "Why didn't you tell me when you came to me at Bedstead Gully that you'd come because you needed me, because you were in danger?"

So he'd been talking to Royal, she thought, and remembered Royal had exclaimed that knowing that made all the difference. Perhaps he had even been talking to Mr. Giles. Why hadn't she confided in Jake at the time? There had been plenty of reasons then, but she couldn't think of them now.

She said softly, "I'm sorry." Jake had a little bottle and was tipping a heavier fluid into his palm. It was a kind of oil; he rubbed his palms together and then took her feet again, one at a time, working up her ankles, smoothing up to her calves. She remembered how he had asked her if she'd come to Bedstead Gully to seduce him, and she had said, yes, for that, too, was part of the truth. His hands moved, up, up; her limbs felt heavy, heavy like her eyes.

There was a strange kind of shivering inside her, deep, like a fluttering of responsive nerves. Jake's hands worked around the tight calves; he was seducing her, she thought, and gasped with the beginning of panic, "What—what is that?"

"Turtle oil."

"My God." she couldn't believe it. "You call that medication?"

"Yes."

"Do you know what Royal says about Americans?"

"I've heard a-plenty of Royal on the topic, but this might be a new one. Try me," he invited, and stood up.

She watched him. He seemed to tower over her. "He says that Americans love to medicate; they'll medicate anything, man, woman, or beast, even if the patient has to be tied down to do it."

He laughed. "No, I hadn't heard that one," said he, and stooped, picked her up, shook her free of the blanket, and dropped her in the steaming tub. She shrieked with shock and outrage. The water was hot, and her skin prickled with the delicious sensation, her nipples stood out. She was kneeling in the cask, and suds bobbed about her breasts.

He stood with his hands propped on his belt, his head a little to one side, watching her. She said, "Don't look," and sank lower.

"Why not? For you are extraordinarily beautiful, Harriet Gray. You've all growed up, as they say."

"I don't know what you mean."

"You must be nineteen by now, surely."

She looked at the lapping water, she looked at her hands, idly dabbing, making little waves so her white form looked wavery. Then she said, reluctantly, "No."

"You're still eighteen? Oh, Jehovah." He looked about then, sat down on the sofa, and made himself comfortable, she saw with some sense of unreality. He had one ankle propped on the other casual knee, and he had a brandy glass in his hand. He sipped every now and then and watched her, all the time, perfectly openly, with open appreciation.

It felt strange, part of the brandy she could smell and still taste. Tiny pools of brandy and turtle oil were rising up from her ankles and calves, making little rainbows on the surface of the water; the steam from the water mingled with the brandy tendrils in her head.

He said, "You've been less than honest with me, Harriet. Why have you been so reluctant to tell me about yourself?"

He was talking about the way she'd hidden her marriage, she thought, but the thought was as hazy as the brandy and the steam. She was trying to ignore the snatch in her breathing that the brandy fumes caused, that and the strange softness inside

her. It was the massage, she told herself; the rubbing of her
limbs had made her body weak. The brandy-scented air and the
warm water were soporific; she didn't notice Jake when he
moved, not until he was suddenly standing over her.

She gasped with shock and then gasped again when he bent
and hauled her out of the tub. He lifted her fast, in a
breath-snatching swoop, and before she could move or say a
word she was bundled up in a large dry towel.

He dried her down, as gently and competently as he'd
rubbed her feet and legs. She didn't dare move; she was
scared of what would happen if she did. As soon as he had
finished she looked about wildly for her shift, but once again
he moved too fast. Within one panicked heartbeat she was
bundled up again, in a white cotton blanket, and he was
carrying her as impersonally as a bale of cotton.

She shrieked, "Jahaziel!"

"Don't call me that," he said as he carried her into his
stateroom and dumped her on his bed.

The bed was an extended berth, with a wooden lip to hold
the mattress in place. It was made up with blankets and clean
linen. Harriet squirmed onto hands and knees, shuffled round
and snapped, "What the hell do you think you're doing?"

"Tut," he said, and grinned.

"You can't keep me here."

"No?"

"I want to go back to my room in the fort. Mrs. Marchant—"

He interrupted, as calm as a clock. "You can go to the fort
in the morning. Bodfish will escort you. Then you can collect
your things."

"I'm not one of your crew, Jake Dexter; you can't order me
around."

"Nevertheless, you have no choice. You stop here."

"Then I'll stop in my old stateroom."

"And sneak away the instant the coast is clear? I don't trust
you one inch, Harriet Gray . . . and, what's more, I don't
like to turn poor Charlie out of his room once again."

He had the sauce to grin. Harriet glared at him. Everything
inside her seemed to be fluttering, quivering expectation
warring with panic. He sat on the edge of the berth and took off
his boots and then his pants, saying in a matter-of-fact voice,
"You've given me too many frights, Harriet; I've had more
frights than one man deserves. So, sweet obstinate, you stop
here, and you sleep in this bed so I'm sure that you do."

She said nothing; her mouth was too dry. When he swung his legs up she flinched, and when he lay back beside her she crouched away from him, cringing against the bulkhead. He frowned; she knew he was angry, and she shivered so her teeth chattered when he took her into his arms. She tried to wrench free but he held her firmly, though gently. He said softly, "You're safe. I won't hurt you, I promise. I just want to make sure that you don't come to more harm."

She lay stiffly. His arms were around her. Then she felt his hand smooth her hair, cupping her head, tucking her under the jut of his chin. There was a single lamp, burning very low. It threw big wavering shadows. She felt Jake soothe her, his big hand moving rhythmically over her head, and then, wrackingly, with no idea of the reason, she began to cry.

She trembled wildly with the weeping and clung to him. She said, "Why? Why did Sefton treat me so? I was so . . . trusting. I was trusting then, just a silly frivolous goose of a girl. I was so happy, before he took away my trust."

Jake said nothing for a long, long interval. He smoothed her hair. Then the episodes of wild sobbing became fewer and shorter, and she was silent, shaking every now and then. She could hear the slow, heavy thud of Jake's heart under her ear. She felt Jake shift, making them both more comfortable. Safe . . . she felt safe.

"And now," he said softly, "tell me about the night Ah Wong helped you to escape."

And she told him. It was a wonderful relief.

She woke in the night. The lamp still burned, very low, and she had no idea where she was. All she knew was that her body was stiff with bruising, but that otherwise she was snug and warm and there was an insect whining around her nose. It was one of the voracious Sacramento mosquitoes. She lifted a groggy arm and swiped. The mosquito danced sideways, but her hand kept on going . . .

And hit a warm bristly cheek rather hard. The blankets heaved abruptly, and she found Jake Dexter scowling down at her. She had forgotten she was in his bed, and that struck her as so very funny that she had to hiccup to hold back laughter.

He looked fully as tetchy as he had at Bedstead Gully. He said, "What did you do that for?"

"I'm sorry. I—I forgot where I was."

"You forgot yourself entirely, madam! When you were the medic and I was the patient, I did not haul off and hit you."

"What?" For a delirious moment it made no sense. Then, helplessly, she began to laugh. She trembled with impenitent mirth, laughing up at him in the shadowy night, and he made an exasperated sound and kissed her.

The night instantly narrowed . . . to his touch, the blankets thrust aside, his weight, the prickling heavy, warm chest. She clung to him desperately, the laughter quite gone and a terrible craving in its place. Jake seemed dazed; she could feel him trembling. Her breasts were hot and tight, thrusting into his hands, thrusting into his mouth when he kissed and nuzzled. She could feel his hard arousal and the fluid hollowing inside herself. His hand moved down the arch at the back of her waist to her buttocks, spreading, lifting, so she arched and spread for him; he hovered above her, his tongue nudged and then thrust at her mouth . . .

And she tore her face away and cried, "No! Oh, please, no!"

He froze. She lay with her eyes shut, pain inside her, and his voice said, "Oh, God, I'm sorry, oh, *goddammit*!"

She could feel his tautness, like an overstretched wire. She said, "Jahaziel . . ." Then she stopped. If he said, "Don't call me that," she knew she'd die. She whispered. "I'm sorry."

He said, "Oh, God," again. "I asked you to trust me, and . . ." He moved. He was sitting on the edge of the berth; when she sat up too he had his back to her, his head in his hands.

"I've been so . . . so patient . . . I love you so much Harriet, I can't seem to think straight. I know all the time you're in danger but can't think why. 'Tis a feeling in the guts, a certainty in my bones that my brain can't work out, and . . . I let you go to the fort because I thought it might help. I stopped as long in this city as my pride would let me, but all that happened is that you damn-near got killed, and now I've done *this*."

She hardly heard him. Her mind was full of just one word, the ringing sound of love. He loved her; he really did. Royal had not been mistaken. She said shyly, "All I ever wanted was to be your mistress, Jake."

"And can I be blamed for wanting so much more? What do you want, Harriet? to stop here and act in King's productions while I take myself and the brig out of your life?"

She sat silent, her lips parted. She held the blanket up to her neck. Jake turned and gave her one restless look. "Of course you do," he bleakly answered himself. He stood up. "I'll go sleep on the sofa," he said, and she watched him stride to the transom door.

He had his hand on the latch before she found her voice. Then she had to say his name twice before he turned.

She gazed at him. She had dropped the blanket. Her white body was luminous in the low golden light. "Jake," she said softly. "Please come back."

"What?" He stood rigid. Then he shook his head as if to clear it. "Are you sure?"

Sure? She had never been so certain in her life. "Of course I'm bloody sure," she said.

33 ❧ By the time the *Hakluyt* men had done breakfast there was a large posse already collected on the Embarcadero. The attack on Miss Gray had provoked public outrage. Women were scarce enough in this territory, the spokesmen loudly declared, without Mexican desperadoes frightening them away. Even Mr. Giles was there. He was aboard a mule, his legs dangling unbeautifully on either side of the saddle. No doubt, Jake mused, he was after a story. Mr. Giles's stories, he'd heard, were making the headlines back east already.

It was difficult deciding whom to take from the brig. Now that the Murietas were on the run he did not feel the same alarm for Harriet, but several of the men wanted to hire themselves out to Mr. King on a temporary basis. Mr. King was paying craftsmen well, for his scenery was far from complete. In the end Jake decided to take Tib and Dan only. "Why go yourself, then?" Harriet said angrily.

"Because I must." It was a personal vendetta, but Jake

didn't tell her that. Instead he watched her, this flushed and vivid Harriet. She was dressed in bits and fragments of a shift and shawls and an old skirt, simply because most of her clothes were lost, or burned, or soaking to drain off mule blood. He lusted after her even as he looked at her, he thought wryly, and here she was just warm from his bed. Would he ever get enough of her? He doubted it, and kissed her hard.

"I'm coming with you," she said.

"Like Malvina?"

"Why not?" she countered.

"I haven't time to say all the reasons. Stop here, be good, learn your part so you won't let us down on the night."

"I know it already," said she haughtily. "We Grays are famous throughout the circuit as fast studies." Jake laughed. "Don't go; how long will you be?" she said all in one breath. He didn't know. He kissed her again, and after much shouting and shuffling and last-minute changes the posse from Sacramento City finally left.

Sutter's Indian tracker wore the usual California costume of denim pants and checkered shirt and knee-high boots, but his fierce ancestry spoke in his bronzed high cheekbones and the snaky disorder of his hair. He spoke little but set a fast pace on a pony, and as the day wore on more and more of the less fit men dropped back. For a long time even Jake could see the trail the Murietas had followed, heading east, along the river valley with almost no deviation. It was as if the Murietas had known exactly where they were going, as if they were heading fast for some hideout. Then it was evening, the long evening of summer. The foothills were blue and mauve and full of gullies, and the tracks were almost twenty-four hours old. The Indian's pace slowed, he leaned far out from his horse to scan the ground, and then he stopped. Without more than a grunt he let them all know that it was time to make camp. Then he lit a tree, California style. He chose the right size tree for the number of hours they needed a fire, about three feet through at the base and growing in the right direction, so that it would fall away from the camp. Lighting it was easy: he frayed the bark with his tomahawk and then applied a spark. Within moments the tree was glowing like a candle, sending out heat like a hearth. When the men woke in the morning the tree was about through, with just enough left to safely make coffee. Then, as they galloped away, the tree finally fell with a crash.

Again, north, winding north, following the windings of the

Feather River. The Indian rode slowly, slowly, dismounting now and then to sniff and peer. Jake sat easy in his saddle, watching him. Much farther, he thought, and they'd be in Pueblo San Marco. The trail scratched past rocks and thickets, only faintly discernible. It was midmorning, hot, silent. The air smelled of dust and firs. The posse had long since quieted, so that the only sounds they made were the hesitant clop of hooves, and the thin rattle of harness. Once they started up a wood fowl, and some of the men swore with the fright. The Indian stopped at each bend in the path, looking at the ground, straightening, sniffing at the air. There was an intangible sense of ambush, and the Indian stopped and dismounted.

The bunch of men stopped. Jake was to one side, near the front. His hat was tipped forward, so the hard shadow guarded his eyes. Horses snuffled and stamped, and the Indian ran forward in a crouching posture. Men shifted in their saddles, some reaching to their guns, easing pistols out of their belts and holsters. There was muttering from some, shushed by others. Tension mounted, surely, surely; Jake felt braced for the first shout, the first shot—and the Indian stood straight and walked forward, openly.

Jake tapped the reins so his horse moved again. He was the first to follow the Indian. At the next bend in the path he found the view abruptly opened out, down a steep slope to a gully below. In the gully floor a heap of ashes remained where a campfire had burned, clearly discernible—as visible as the bodies that lay on the grass around it.

Five bodies. Jake counted them as his horse slid and scrabbled down the gravel slope. He heard the others following; Dan Kemp was swearing as he struggled to keep in his saddle. Giles came last, still on his mule, sidling in clumsy fashion. Most of the bodies were lying facedown. Men tipped them over with the toe of a boot. Murietas . . . all Murietas. Not Joaquin, and no sign of Davy. All five Murietas had been shot in the head, with one bullet each.

Had Davy been that good a marksman? The Indian showed Jake and Giles the place on the slope where Davy had been while he shot at those men. Tiny piles like ash, little bits of paper, scuffing marks where he'd braced his feet. The place overlooked the camp but could not be seen from below. The Murietas had chosen unwisely when they'd made their camp in this spot. Perhaps, Jake mused grimly, they'd been driven by panic past the edge of alertness, while Davy . . . Davy had

had the strength of a rage for revenge. The Indian showed them, too, the marks that Joaquin had made when he escaped, and that Davy had made when he followed. Jake thoughtfully tipped back his hat, looking at the hills, the trees and mountaintops, the familiar edge to the sky.

They were past Pueblo San Marco, he estimated, and in the foothills beyond the town. The trail led upriver still, and he knew in his gut where it went.

Some of the farsighted men had brought along shovels. The party took turns digging holes. They buried the bodies while deciding what to do next. Most of the men were for turning back. They didn't want to catch the black man; they considered he had done Sacramento City a favor. The one loose desperado would not be much of a menace for a bit, and if he surfaced again, why, they sure could take care of that. Most of them made up their minds to go back right away; then the rest of them abruptly recollected urgent business and went off too.

The Indian followed them, without a word to anyone. The gully all at once seemed very empty. The sounds of the posse's retreat faded, and then the air was almost silent, without even birdsong to give the afternoon substance. It was hot. The sun bounced back off the pale rocks that stood out on the slopes, but Jake shivered. The sense of ambush was with him again, as if someone watched, and waited. Watched . . . down the barrel of a rifle, he thought, and worked tense muscles under his shirt, moving his shoulders as he stared around. He thought of Joaquin Murieta . . . and Davy, avenging Davy, who had most certainly gone mad. Tib's uneasy voice said. "Cap'n?"

Jake roused himself and turned. Both Tib and Dan were back on their horses. Jake pointed his chin at the track the Indian had indicated, and said, "That joins up with the trail to Don Roberto's fort."

Both men stared at him, and he realized then that they had expected to follow the posse to the brig. Then Tib said tentatively, "You think the Murieta and Davy have gone to that fort?"

"I'm sure the Murietas were heading there. 'Tis a chance . . . and we must find Davy."

"Yes," said Tib. His voice sounded reluctant. Dan Kemp was staring all about, looking at the slopes above the gully. Jake looked too. There was a buzzard floating high in the sky, perhaps cheated of his feast. Jake's neck crept again. He said nothing, but mounted his horse and led the way, climbing up out of the gully. Within a half-hundred yards the scene of the shooting was out of sight.

The trail was narrow, so they had to ride in Indian file, hemmed in by pines and rocks. Then Jake heard Dan's voice from the rear, "Cap'n, do you git the feeling we're bein' followed?"

"Yes," said Jake. He reined in. Then he heard the rattle of stones. He looked at the skyline again—out of habit, he told himself—and back at the track. A mule came plodding up around the bend. Giles was sitting astride the saddle, as elegant as a quarter-full sack of potatoes. Oddly, he too was looking around. Then he saw Jake and lifted his hat. Giles, Jake mused with irritation, was still after his story. He said nothing but set his horse into motion again, heading surely up the trail.

Silence, and heat. The afternoon wore on. Jake led the way surely, knowing almost exactly where he was. Nevertheless it was a relief to find they were on the familiar trail to the fort. Here, there were abundant signs of other people. The path had been smoothed and widened by hundreds of trampling feet and hooves, and mule and horse manure lay about, some relatively fresh and moist, other droppings dried to straw.

However, they did not encounter other men until they were nearly up to the fort. It was late evening, almost night, and Jake heard the rattle of the bells the mules wore before he saw the mule train. The beasts were heavily laden. Men trudged alongside the mules, the miners bright-eyed and bushy-tailed, the mule skinners scruffy, weathered and taciturn. Jake was silent himself. He had expected the fort to be about empty and realized now how illogical that expectation had been. As the party straggled through the entrance he began to feel doubts that Davy or Joaquin Murieta would be there, and when he saw the lights in the windows he didn't believe it at all. He reined in his horse in the cobbled courtyard and looked wearily about. Dan and Tib and Giles joined him. "Well, Cap'n?" said Tib.

"Yes," said Jake. He dismounted and led his horse to the stables, looking about. For the first time he saw the flag flying from the one bastion. It was too dark to see what kind of flag it was. Then he saw the animal in the stables. "Jehovah," he said, and began to laugh.

It was a llama, the last llama. The other had been sold as a curiosity—at a good price, he remembered. Perhaps there would be some profit in this venture after all; perhaps he hadn't entirely wasted his time in coming to the fort.

Then, abruptly, the significance of that flag dawned on him. It must have been his unconscious that had warned him, he thought, for when he turned, Don Roberto was coming across the courtyard. Jake said softly, "My God."

The alcalde's trotting footsteps had been hidden by the general ruckus as the mule train left. The mule skinners, Jake saw then, too shrewd to pay Don Roberto's price for stabling, had set up their own camp by the river. By the time they had gone Don Roberto had arrived, and Jake said softly, "Well, well, and what are you doing in these parts, sir?"

"I could ask the same of you, Captain Dexter." The alcalde's voice was peevish, and as he looked querulously about, that tone became shrill, almost hysterical. "You!" he shouted. "You, you lying bastard, how dare you come 'ere!"

Jake shoved his hat back in amazement and saw that Don Roberto was shoving a trembling forefinger at Giles's chest. "Muckraking reporters!" he hollered. "You've been printin' lies, you 'ave. Even in Mexico my reputation 'as been savaged, and all on account of your lies!"

"Lies?" Mr. Giles echoed. He smirked. Then he insouciantly slid down from his mule. This kind of gobbling confrontation, his attitude seemed to say, was an everyday experience for him. "May I take it that you're no longer persona grata with the Mexican authorities?" asked he. "Tell me, sir, have the folks in these parts all given up a-pestering you for their confiscated gold?"

With each question Don Roberto went more red in the face, hollering, "Git out, git out!"

With every word, too, the seekers after gold were gathering more closely, their faces all a-gaup with curiosity. "Have you got the gold here, Don Roberto?" Jake asked sharply. "Did you and your deputies steal the gold and then set fire to Sefton's rancho house before you came here, to bury the gold and hide it?"

"Lies!" bawled Don Roberto. "Lies!"

"Then why don't I ask all these gentlemen what they think? Perhaps if we discussed it here, they might take it into their heads to dig up this yard and haul up the planks of all your floors."

Then Jake waited, hat pushed back, his hands on his belt. He watched the alcalde's mouth slowly close, and then the little eyes flick all about as the sense of this got through to him. Don Roberto jerked his head and set off inside. Jake followed him through the first room to the billiard room. He stopped by the table, looking about. A fire had been lit in both lower rooms despite the warmth, and the shadows danced weirdly. In the far corner the stairs rose to the upper floor and Don Roberto's quarters, and a draft corkscrewed down them, setting the fire to twisting. He felt very tense, on the threshold of discovery, and the sense of someone spying chilled the back of his neck again. He took off his hat and put it on the table, and when Tib and Dan came in he bid them check the room upstairs.

They went up quickly, in a nervous rattle of boots, and then Jake could hear them treading back and forth in the ceiling, and the shifting of heavy bits of furniture. Don Roberto shouted, "What the hell . . . ?" Giles came in, and the door was slammed shut in the faces of all the other lodgers. Giles looked about, and then arranged himself on the edge of the table, his legs dangling idly.

Tib and then Dan came back. They shook their heads at Jake. He turned to the alcalde and snapped, "Where is Joaquin Murieta?"

"*What?*"

Don Roberto sounded genuinely astounded. Jake said carefully, "Have you see my crewman Davy Jones Locker?"

"Nivver 'eard of 'im."

"But it must have been you who sent the Murietas to Sacramento City!"

"How could I, when I ain't nivver 'eard of that place, neither."

Jake paused. If the alcalde had not heard of Sacramento City, he thought, then it was obvious that Don Roberto had only just arrived back from Mexico. He said slowly, "Do you mean to suggest that the Murietas came to Sacramento City and attacked Harriet of their own accord?"

"Harriet?"

Jake said, "Miss Gray." Never would he call her *Mrs. Sefton* again; he had vowed it. However, Don Roberto recognized the name, for he jerkily nodded. He did not seem surprised, either, that Harriet had not died in that fire; but then, Jake thought, the alcalde had acted coroner in that affair. He said, "Sacramento City is Sutter's, the Embarcadero. 'Tis a new name."

"Is it?" said Don Roberto with no apparent interest. "Well, that don't make no difference, for I didn't send my deputies there, for whatever reason, for I don't 'ave no deputies, anyways."

"That's true." Jake's tone was dry. "Or, if any, you have but one. What I want to know is why the Murietas were heading here when Davy Jones Locker shot five of them dead."

He saw Don Roberto flinch. The red face was paling, he thought, or perhaps it was the dancing reflection of the yellow fire. Then the alcalde said hoarsely, "Here . . . ?"

Giles said in his insinuating voice, "Were they coming here to dig up their gold, Don Roberto?"

"No! There—there ain't none. I sent it to Sefton's bank, true, but I had no hand in the stealin' of it."

"Then why were they coming?" Jake shouted. "Were they coming to settle accounts with you?"

"No! No . . . !" The eyes were sliding all about, hunting the dark corners of the cavernous room; Don Roberto's fear was blatant. He whispered, "Dead . . . five dead, oh gawd'n bless me . . . Was Joaquin the one who escaped?"

"Unless Davy shot him down farther along the trail to this fort," Jake snapped. "Unless he lagged behind and has been captured by the posse."

"P-posse?"

"From Sacramento City, assembled to capture the men who attacked Miss Gray, Don Roberto!"

"But . . . but why would the Murietas do that . . . why . . . ?"

Don Roberto's terror was more apparent with every second and every word: Why? Surely, Jake thought, frowning, surely not because of Davy; Don Roberto seemed almost uninterested in the man who'd shot down five of his fellow conspirators. He said tightly, "I can think of no other reason for their presence in the town, for they most surely attacked Harriet. You're not going to suggest that they came in all innocence, perhaps to collect the schooner and bring the vessel back to Pueblo San Marco?"

Don Roberto screamed, "The what?"

"Sefton's schooner," Jake said, puzzled. "The schooner was left moored at the Embarcadero."

"Oh, my gawd." The little eyes shut, as if to shut out nightmare. The alcalde's teeth were chattering. "'Ow . . . 'ow long 'as she been there?"

"Since the beginning of March, if not before."

"March? And—and Mrs. Sefton is there? Oh, my gawd," the shaking voice muttered. "Oh, my gawd, I'm dead."

Jake's belly cramped with abrupt fear; his mind was stuck on Harriet's name. Harriet . . . and the schooner? It made no sense, they could not be linked, but he felt an overwhelming urge to run outside and into the saddle, and gallop all night to get back to Harriet. Don Roberto's face had turned as white as cheese. Then all at once, before Jake could stop him, the alcalde fled. Jake could hear the sobbing whine of the fat man's breath, and then Don Roberto darted up the stairs and slammed the door at the head. Then the bolt shot, with rusty emphasis.

Some hours later Jake was wakened by the yapping of dogs. It sounded as if there was a disturbance in the stables. He had set watches to guard the stairs and the door, but when he opened one eye he could see Tib slumped asleep. Don Roberto was stealing down the stairs. Jake lay still, watching him surreptitiously.

Perhaps the alcalde was taking this chance to escape—or perhaps he was meeting someone in the stables. When the stealthy silhouette slipped through the door Jake picked up his rifle and quietly followed. Outside, the courtyard was full of moonlight and cool. He watched Don Roberto cross the cobbles and go into the stables. The dogs still barked from beyond the walls of the fort, and horses shuffled nervously. There was a smell of blood . . . of blood, and then he heard Don Roberto cry out.

Jake called out and ran. He had his gun leveled at his hip. He glimpsed the alcalde crouched by a cask, a cask, the kind used for . . . salt pork, and then he sensed the swift movement behind him. Then, agony in his head, whirling him into blackness, and like a dream, the echo of a shot.

34 ⟬⟭ Harriet was sitting in the transom cabin of the brig when Bodfish tapped on the door. She had, it seemed, a visitor, a man who had asked for her by name. She bid Bodfish bring him in with most lively curiosity, but the man who arrived was a complete stranger.

He was wearing regimentals, and he introduced himself as Dr. Stirling. "From the frigate *Savannah*," he said.

"Captain Mervine sent you?"

"Yes, indeed," he said. Harriet offered him coffee. Dr. Stirling was a tall, thin, dry-boned fellow with a peevish high-nosed face. It did not surprise her in the slightest to find he was from Philadelphia and had, what's more, once known her late husband.

"He belongs to a most highly rated family," he said.

"So I heard," she said.

"And he belonged to the United States forces, Mrs. Sefton!"

"I understood he was a colonel," she agreed.

"On both counts, Mrs. Sefton, his burial was quite unac-
ceptable."

She gazed at him silently, perfectly perplexed, remembering
the hasty double grave under the oak tree. "I had naught to do
with it, sir," she said at length. "But he was buried on his
property, on his rancho, so I thought it quite in order . . . ?"
But was the rancho his property, she wondered, and should he
have been in more hallowed ground? The chief clerk at the
bank had not seemed to think that as Sefton's widow she owned
anything, except the half-melted ring.

"So what do you want of me, Dr. Stirling?" she said
politely.

"Why, ma'am, merely the exact information of the position
of his grave. You say his rancho was over the river, the Feather
River, on the opposite bank to the town of Pueblo San Marco?"

"That's right. Why, do you want to put a headstone there, or
something?"

"Certainly not, Mrs. Sefton! The officers of the United
States forces merit much better than that, particularly men of
the . . . ahemm . . . social standing of Colonel Francis
Sefton. No, Mrs. Sefton, I have come to fetch the corpse! I
have a metal coffin in my baggage, and I intend to proceed
directly to the grave and disinter the body and send it in decent
order to the grieving parents, brothers, and sisters back East, in
Philadelphia." He didn't seem to notice Harriet's incredulous
look, but busied himself with an official-seeming paper instead. "So, Mrs. Sefton, if you would just sign here . . . and
here, giving permission . . ." She read it carefully, then
signed. "Thank you!" he said, and briskly rose and took his
leave. She saw him to the rail. A pinnace from the frigate was
waiting at the Embarcadero, and Dr. Stirling did indeed have a
coffin with him, she incredulously observed. The metal sides
of it sparkled brightly in the sun.

Then he was off. Harriet watched him go and wondered
what he would think when he saw that the grave was a double
one.

At noon on the second day after that the posse from Pueblo
San Marco brought in Jake Dexter. Harriet heard the shouting
and commotion and ran up onto deck with her heart jumping.
It was like the day that her father had been killed. The shouts
were the same; there was the same air of calamity.

Jake was coming up Front Street. He was sitting on his horse
with his hands tied behind his back, and Joaquin Murieta was

leading the horse by the bridle. The Ecuadorean was filthy, stubbled, and stained. The wormlike *mostacho* writhed with his gray-faced smirk. Harriet stopped frozen, distraught, unbelieving. Jake did not even seem to see her. He had lost his hat, so Harriet could see the grimy bandage around his head. She cried, "Oh, my God, Jake, what has happened?" He did not seem to hear, and someone else answered for him.

He had been arrested for the murder of Don Roberto Ross. Joaquin was the witness; it had been he who raised the alarm. The posse from the fort had brought Jake to Sacramento City for his trial. Tib and Dan had insisted on it, for Sacramento City was the place, in the meantime at least, where Captain Dexter belonged.

The trial was held that very afternoon. Because of public interest it was held in the compound of Sutter's Fort. A rough pine table was dragged out of the eating room and into the sun, so that the true filthy and greasy state of it could be seen. Jake sat on a stool under a tree, and a noose hung from a stout branch of that tree in readiness for a verdict of guilty. Joaquin Murieta stood guard over him, and Harriet and the *Hakluyt* men were not allowed to approach him. Tib and Dan and Mr. Giles stood over to one side as witnesses, and Harriet sat tensely by Royal in the front row of the audience.

It was like a feverish nightmare, perfectly unreal. The smells were too sharp, the light too bright, the colors too brilliant, the shouting and laughter too loud. It was like a festive occasion. Royal sat with Harriet and muttered on about Americans, but nevertheless she felt alone, unutterably alien. Where was the decorum of English courts; where was the etiquette of justice? Certainly not here, she thought in sick bewilderment. There was a jury of eight men, headed by an old man in a yellow scratch wig and a blue coat with tarnished brass buttons. None of the jury were known to her, for they either came from the upper Feather River or were old Californian frontiersmen. Two of them had once been ship masters, she was told, but they looked no more respectable than the others. There were barrels of brandy on the table, and members of the audience as well as the jurymen helped themselves freely. Other men chewed tobacco as they talked and joked and spat. The beaten earth of the compound was becoming plentifully slimed with tobacco gobs, and the commotion growing apace.

Then the old man in the wig said, "Wa-al, Cap'n Dexter,

you be in this here place to answer to the charge of murder, how do you plead guilty or not guilty," all in one breath.

The pause seemed endless. Harriet waited tensely. Then at last Jake shook his head and muttered, "Not guilty."

Joaquin Murieta laughed, loudly. "Not guilty?" cried a voice from the audience. "Yer be a fool, Cap'n, a fool! Why not jest say you shot the alcalde a-cause you found him a-rustlin' yer llama beast? That'll git yer off, sure as eggs!"

"Because it wasn't Don Roberto who had killed my llama!" Jake shouted. Harriet jumped with shock to hear him shout so loudly, and the men in the crowd silenced in surprise too. "The llama was mine, it belonged to the brig," Jake said angrily. "It had run away during a trek from the mines. I'd forgotten about it, was as surprised as anyone to see it there in the stables at the alcalde's fort, but it was not Don Roberto who killed and butchered the animal! It couldn't be. He arrived in the stables only a moment before I did."

"Fool!" cried the voice in the audience again. "Why tell 'em that, huh? That be yer best excuse for shooting the alcalde!"

"But I didn't shoot him," said Jake furiously, and the head juryman shook his head and spat.

"We ain't established that yet," he said severely.

Jake paused. Harriet watched him tensely. Then he said evenly, "Nevertheless, I did not. And Don Roberto did not slaughter that llama. Joaquin Murieta did."

Immediate uproar. Everyone stared at Joaquin Murieta and talked about it in a babel of commotion. Then the head juryman took off a boot and hammered on the table. "Wa-al, sir," he said to Joaquin, "is that the truth?"

Joaquin shrugged.

"Be that yep or nay?"

"I needed the meat. The llama belonged to the alcalde, and I was his deputy."

Harriet swallowed. Involuntarily, she wondered what llama meat tasted like. Mutton, she supposed, with that odd, detached corner of her mind.

The juryman seemed much diverted by this development. He grinned widely and said to Jake, "Then why didn't you kill him, instead of the alcalde?" Harriet saw Jake's mouth open, but he didn't have a chance for rejoinder, for the rest of the jury and most of the crowd thought this a most capital joke; they all laughed uproariously, and one of the jurymen pounded the top of the table in time to his merriment.

Then, at last, there was some semblance of formality. Harriet listened intently as men described how Jake had gone out with the posse from Sacramento City, the tracking of the desperadoes, the gully, the discovery of the five murdered men. Everyone stared at Joaquin Murieta then, and he sneered back proudly, strutting, vowing retribution. Men in the crowd called out corroborative details, and the jurymen paid as much attention to this evidence as the rest.

"Then," said Jake, "I concluded to press on, and follow the trail to the fort."

"After your man Davy, the murderer of those men?"

"Yes."

"And your two crewmen went too?"

"And Giles," said Jake expressionlessly.

Mr. Giles confirmed what Jake had said. "Why did you go?" said the questioner.

"Perhaps I was interested. Call me intrigued, if you like."

"And why should I call you that, huh? I don't even want to call you Giles."

This was the signal for another round of uproarious laughter. Mr. Giles waited and then said in his offhand way, "You can say I wanted to view this Davy, that I wished to view the man who'd dispatched five desperate men so uncommon neat. All single shots, in the head. A fine marksman, don't you agree?"

"Do I have to?" queried the juryman.

More merriment. Mr. Giles merely looked world-weary. Then he said, "You can say, too, if you want, that I wanted to learn more of the fort's owner. Don Roberto was the cause of much heartrending in this here province, on account of jumped claims and the like, sir, on account of confiscated gold, and then on account of the mysterious loss of all the gold and much else. Rumor had told me that Don Roberto had run off to the hills on account of so many men wanting to see the color of his guts, sir. I'd heard too that he'd run all the way to Mexico. Imagine my astonishment to see the man at home!"

"From what I heared he was plumb thunderstruck too," someone in the audience hollered. "And from what I heared he flew at you like a hog at his dinner. I reckon you be the man what killed 'im!"

"That's a point," said the head juryman in thoughtful style. He picked his teeth with a knife, staring at the reporter all the time. "Did you shoot Don Roberto?"

"I did not. I ain't no kind of marksman."

Harriet's heart jumped; the statement seemed oddly meaningful. She saw Jake frowning too. "It don't take no marksman to shoot a man from the length of a rifle barrel," the juryman said.

"That, indeed, is true, if Don Roberto were shot from close up."

The insinuating tone got through to the jury then, Harriet saw, for they were all staring at Mr. Giles and frowning in painful thought. Then one said, "You reckon the same man what shot all them deputies was after the alcalde as well?"

"Seems logical," said Mr. Giles in his insouciant fashion. He shrugged, and looked at the sky.

"And this here Davy, he be a good shot?"

Silence. Jake was sitting very still. Harriet waited tensely. She didn't want to remember how Davy walked into obstacles as if he didn't see them, but she did. Had he been a marksman before his accident and illness? Somehow she doubted it; slaves had very little opportunity to practice with guns, she was certain.

Then Tib Greene said heartily, "Why, good Lord, sir, but Davy were famous for his shootin'."

"He was?"

"Aye, indeed!" And, one by one, the *Hakluyt* men testified to Davy's famous prowess with a rifle. Their broad grins were guileless. Harriet saw Jake shift uneasily. She had her arms folded tightly, as she willed Jake not to speak. She saw him open his mouth—and Mr. Giles said thoughtfully, "Maybe good marksmanship don't come into it."

Jake shut his mouth. Everyone gaped at the reporter, including, Harriet saw, every man on the jury. Then the old man in the wig snapped irritably, "What plagues your mind now, sir?"

"Why, naught but the thought of all the men who lost their gold on account of Don Roberto's trick with the legal confiscation. The way I see it, half of the men on the placer wanted to shoot Don Roberto."

"And how much gold did he steal from you, Giles?"

"Why none, sir, none, on account of the fact that I've never had any. Nor was I one of his fellow tricksters."

"What the tarnation do you mean?"

Mr. Giles paused. Harriet saw him look about in conspiratorial fashion; he even lowered his voice, or gave the appearance of doing so, though she still could hear his words. He said, "This here affair be uncommon interesting, sir, it intrigues me greatly, sir, I must confess it. The way I see it, there was a gang of seven, headed by an eighth, all with a fine trick to worm men out of their gold. First there was the alcalde, who couldn't make up his mind. Then there were the six deputies, who dug up all that confiscated gold, and carried it off to the bank. Then there was the banker, who by yet another trick claimed it, and then somehow all that gold disappeared. And what is most interesting of all, sir, is that only one man of that gang of eight still lives."

Silence, utter, blank, bewildered silence. Then Joaquin screamed, "I was there, yes, in the stables, making the llama into meat, yes, I saw it, the alcalde fall dead, I catched the cap'n, I, yes, hit him, senseless, arrested him, he did it!"

Jake roared, "But I had no motive! Why should I kill the alcalde?"

"Because of the cask!" Joaquin shrieked. "Because he found what was in the cask, your cask, he broke it open!"

The cask. What did he mean? Harriet was shivering, the crowd all a-gaup. Joaquin Murieta whirled around and grabbed a canvas sack from the ground behind him. He gripped it, heaved, hauled the dripping sack to the jurymen's table. Then he stood in front of the bench, holding out the bag, jerking with his hands so the contents rolled about inside.

Silence. The jurymen all looked at each other. Then the head one stood slowly and leaned across the table to peer into the open mouth of the bag. Then he said, "Oh, holy Jesus," and sat down again with a bump. Then he took a fast gulp of brandy.

As Harriet watched, the other jurymen did the same; they leaned, they looked, and sat back abruptly. Men in the crowd were hollering, "What is it? Show us. We wanter see too," but the jurymen ignored them. The old man in the wig said to Jake, "Do you know what's in that there bag?"

"Yes," said Jake grimly. "However, the first time I saw the contents of that cask was when I came to my senses after the murder had been done."

"What did you think it held, huh?"

"I thought it held salt pork. At Tombez we took on provisions to bring to California, and that cask was one of many. We bought casks of salt pork and beef, and one such cask on inspection proved to hold pigs' heads and trotters. This cask slipped by the inspection. Evidently it is a ghastly jest."

The crowd was growing rowdy and restive, scenting drama and feeling cheated. The cries of, "Show us, show us," were turning into a chant. The head juryman nodded at Jake and said, "Tell 'em what that cask held."

Jake paused. Then he said grimly, "Heads, and feet. The heads and feet of men. Pickled."

"And do you recognize any of 'em?"

"Only one. He . . . was Honest Mill Mason, or that is what he called himself. He was the one who told us about the discovery of gold in this territory. He went off to his plantation to slaughter pigs and cattle, to salt them down and buy his passage with the proceeds. Some other men went with him. I never saw them again."

Babel. Never had a crowd tasted such sensation. One voice hollered, "What d'yer reckon happened to the bodies?" Harriet swallowed on sickness. Jake was grim and pale, and Joaquin strutted, like a rooster. The head juryman shouted, "Cap'n, why don't I ask you why you shot Don Roberto?"

Jake paused. The shadow of the hanging noose was on his forehead. Then he snapped, "Why don't you ask who sold me that particular cask of so-called salt pork?"

"Wa-al, sir?"

"For it was Joaquin Murieta . . . and his brothers."

Joaquin screamed, "He lies, yes, he lies! The desperate man, he lies to save his skin!"

"Then why, señor," said Jake slowly, every syllable audible in the dusty tense air, "why did you butcher the llama, if you were so desperate for meat? The cask was there, a cask of good salt pork, so why didn't you open it instead? Was it because you knew all the time what it held?"

Dead silence. Then an outcry as men saw the logic of this. It was obvious, Harriet thought, that this American crowd preferred a Spanish-American scapegoat if they could get one. Joaquin Murieta stared about wildly, his arms hanging by his sides, spittle on his lips. Men began to throw stones and dirt and bits of rubbish at him. One piece hit the noose and set it swinging; there was a scent of lynch-justice in the air. Joaquin whined with fear and fury; Harriet heard the noise that he made. Then he was whirling, running, bounding into the saddle of his horse. The animal reared and screamed, and then bolted for the fort entrance. Men scattered; some were for forming a posse and going after him, but the fascination of the trial brought them back.

The jury conferred for quite two hours while the shadows grew long, but still the crowd waited. Men were placing bets on the outcome. Jake sat on his stool and watched them all expressionlessly. The shape of the noose was lost in the shadows above his head. When the old man of the jury at last emerged, Harriet's arms were stiff from being folded so tightly so long. The old man was still wearing his blue coat, but instead of his wig he wore a hat.

He waited till the shouting for a verdict had stopped, and then he spat to one side and said, "The jury be a hung one."

Hung. Harriet's heart lurched at the word. Then, slowly, she realized that it meant that the jury was equally divided in its opinion. "If'n the murder of the alcalde and the shootin' of the deputies were all one and the same, then it can't be Joaquin, for even a Mexican don't shoot off all his kin at once. If them Murietas were shot by the black man Davy, then Cap'n Dexter be responsible for him, for he be one of his men. Four of us reckon he shot the alcalde, four reckon it was Joaquin. So," said the old man and spat again, "we've made up our minds California fashion. You've twenty-four hours to pack up your affairs and get quit of this place. If you're still here this time tomorrow, Cap'n, then we'll stretch your neck and no debatin' about it. That's what you've got—twenty-four hours."

35 ⟋⟍   Twenty-four hours. Harriet couldn't believe the injustice of the verdict. "It isn't fair," she insisted, but the men in the crowd had seemed happy with the outcome. Or perhaps, she thought, they had dispersed so fast simply because it had fallen dark and their bellies were empty.

Jake had said very little and had eaten like a starving man. Now it was as if time had rolled back. The same steaming cask of hot water was set up in the transom cabin of the brig, and the same low lamplight illuminated the early night. Jake was in the tub, and Harriet, behind him, inspected his head. She was wearing a shift, and nothing else.

He winced as she washed his hair, but the wound was not nearly as bad as she'd feared. Only about an inch of skin had been split, and the contusion was almost all down. As far as she could tell, there was no fracture. Jake's dazed condition, she thought, must have been due to shock, and the long ride in the sun.

She shaved the patch of hair, gently, and applied simple ointment according to his instructions and the book. Then Jake insisted that she shave his face. "Why?" she asked. He leaned his head back against her bosom as she lathered his cheeks.

The lather moved in time to the wryness of his eyebrows. "So I'll make a beautiful corpse?"

"Don't even say it!" she hissed. She stroked with the long razor gently, gently; it was like that day in Bedstead Gully. The brig was silent. The men still on board, she guessed, were in the fo'c'sle listening to Tib and Dan. Royal with some others was in the theater, working to fix last-minute urgencies.

Utter quiet; just the slow scrape of blade on soaped skin. Then he said, "I don't want to run away, Harriet."

"But you must!"

"If I go, 'tis a confession of guilt, and I know I did not kill Don Roberto."

"If you stay, 'tis a confession of guilt. You heard the verdict."

He was silent. Harriet paused to make sure her hands did not tremble and then finished the last of the job. She took up a towel and moved round to face him, wiped his face, and then bent to kiss him, saying, "You must go."

Instead of replying he grabbed her. She gasped with shock; then with a splash she was in the tub with him. "No . . . you mustn't!" He was kissing her; he touched her, drawing down the wide square neck of her chemise. She had landed on her feet, and he pulled her down so she was kneeling too, facing him, pressed against his warm, hard torso, pressed against him with his hands at her waist.

She cried, "Jake, you're mad!" and didn't know whether to laugh or be angry. Because of the steam, her hair was falling out of its pins and her skin prickled all over in a shivering wave with the exquisite heat. Jake was kissing her as if he would never have the chance to kiss her again, leaning over her so that water slopped onto the floor. She thought they would tip the tub over, and shrieked; she had to cling to him instead of pushing him away, so fearful was she for their equilibrium.

The mischief of the man! "For the sake of merciful heavens," she said when he gave her the chance. "Your head . . ." she cried. Later she said, "You'll hurt . . ." but the chances fled by as his hands cupped her face and he kissed her. She was terrified that he would hurt himself, that his movements would open the wound, that he'd fall victim to brain fever, that . . . "No, you idiot, no," she said, half laughing, half pleading, and he was making slow, relentless work of hauling up her chemise. The wet fabric clung to her thighs, hips, higher . . . "Jake, you must not!"

But all he whispered was, "Oh, Jehovah, dear heart, how I've missed you." All she could do was give in with a shuddering sigh. She was his.

She was his, except that possession was resisted by the pressure of the water. Jake swore and laughed, heaving her out of the tub. He made love in a slow progression that dripped water from tub to sofa to stateroom to bed; she was drenched with his love, inside and out. He made love with utter concentration, as if he would never have the chance again; she could hear his rough gasping, the thud of his heart in his chest. Then with a husky cry he grasped her buttocks tightly, fetching her at the same instant he spent, throbbing forever and ever.

Then, after a timeless interval, moist and lax, they lay quiet. It was almost dark. The one low lamp had been left behind, in the transom.

Jake said quietly, "I'm not running away."

"But you can't stop on the brig and wait for them to hang you!"

He shifted, and she thought he smiled. He said, "I want to clear my name, and to do that I must find Davy. He's the only one who knows what really happened. There is so much yet unexplained."

She held his hand, holding on tightly. At least, she thought, if he was off after Davy, the posse and the jurymen would think he'd obeyed the verdict. She said, "I'll come with you."

"What?" Then he chuckled. "No, sweet obstinate," he said. "You have other commitments."

Then he fell asleep. He slept like a dead man. Harriet lay with open eyes a very long time, thinking, holding onto him. Then she slept, and when she woke Jake was gone.

Charlie Martin told her that Jake had ridden inland, following the same trail that the posse had taken all those days ago. With him were Dan and Tib and the same Indian who had tracked the Murietas as far as the gully where five of them had been shot. Royal had the same gang helping him at the theater where all was frantic in preparation for the premiere that night, and the rest of the *Hakluyt* men were on board of the schooner. Harriet, when she went on the deck of the brig, could hear them hammering and prising wood below the decks of Sefton's abandoned vessel. She thought about what Jake had told her, and thought, too, that he had left orders for another, more thorough search for the gold or any other evidence. She nibbled a worried fingertip and turned to contemplate Sacramento City.

Front Street was crowded, the most packed with restless men that she had ever seen it. There was a palpable air of excitement. Men clustered in groups, moved on, joined other groups, all talking, talking. They stared at her with open speculation when she pushed her way through the throng to the theater. She could hear them talking, shouting. The murders and the verdict were all the conversation; they were still laying bets, for she heard them call the odds. The men were all hanging about waiting, she realized apprehensively, to see if Jake Dexter would stay away or come back. Apparently few had any idea of where the limits of Sacramento City ended or began; some called out that he would not be safe until he reached Monterey . . . and Monterey was a deal more than twelve hours' ride away, no matter how good the horse and urgent the ride.

The crowd hanging about the door of the theater was equally large and sensation-seeking. The jostling men recognized her and tried to stop her from reaching the door. She kicked at a few knees, used her sharp elbows, and then hammered on the door until Mr. King let her in.

He was red-faced and sweating, all of a pompous loud dither over the coming first performance. He was hearing Mrs. Marchant shrilly practice her lines. Royal was equally red-faced and in a foul temper as well. None of the preparations were going to plan, for Mrs. Marchant showed all the temperament of a prima donna already. Never had a day passed so slowly, and time passed so fast. Harriet found herself shivering every now and then, wracked with foreboding. When the head juryman walked in the door in the late afternoon it was as if she'd been expecting this all the time.

There was icy foreboding inside her. She straightened slowly to face him. He was wearing the same blue coat with brass buttons and was back to wearing the yellow scratch wig. Mr. King had let him in.

Harriet swallowed. Then, her voice deliberately steady, she said, "How can I help you?" She braced her breathing, ready for the worst.

Instead he said crossly, "Do this here theater belong to Cap'n Dexter?"

"What?" She frowned. "Why do you ask?"

"Wa-al, that brig out there, that brig *Hakluyt*, it do belong to him, don't it?"

Oh, dear God, she thought, had the shadows of Jake's past come here to make his present situation worse? She said curtly, "The brig is his. He owns the *Hakluyt*."

"But he ain't taken the vessel yet . . . and he's gone, it seems, so who has the papers?"

"Papers? What papers?"

"The ship's papers, ma'am," he bawled, as if she were deaf. "How else can we lawfully seize the brig?"

"*What*?"

"He heard the verdict, so he knows what he stands to lose. He were told to pack up his affairs within twenty-four hours and make himself scarce. Wa-al, he ain't packing up his affairs, no how, so he'll lose his brig, and that is certain. Now I want to know about the theater."

Harriet stared at him, refusing to credit what he had said for one long, furious moment. Then she snapped, "The theater is mine!"

"What?" His eyes popped. "But wimmenfolks can't own property like this, and married wimmenfolks particular!"

"I am not married!" she shouted. She was shaking with fury, never so angry in her life. "I'm a widow, sir, if that's any of your affair, and I signed for this theater, sir, with a signature that I assure you is legal! Ask Mr. King if you don't choose to believe me, and then you can offer your apologies, sir, but don't rely on them being accepted!"

The head juryman merely gobbled. Mr. King, to her augmented fury, dithered about and looked embarrassed. "Tell him that I was the one who hired you this theater, along with my brother's and my services!" she shouted, and Mr. King got more red-faced than ever.

"You did it under your stage-name, Miss Gray," he mumbled, and, "I accepted your signature only a-cause Cap'n Dexter were there as guarantor."

She snapped, "And did he have to countersign, Mr. King?" He shook his head, reluctantly. Both men seemed scandalized that she knew so much of these legal matters. Then at last, mumbling and grumbling, the old man went, and she flew out of the theater and shoved her way through the crowd to the brig.

Charlie was on board, looking harrassed. She didn't have time for preliminaries. She ordered, "Ready the brig for sailing downriver."

"*What?*"

"You heard me, Mr. Martin. If this brig is not quit clear of this place by the time the deadline is up, the posse and the jury will confiscate the vessel."

"But that ain't possible," he objected.

"I assure you it is!" she cried, and stamped her foot in frustration. "The head juryman has just been to see me; he tries, even, to claim the theater as confiscated property, for when the verdict said that Captain Dexter had to pack up his affairs and leave, the jury had all his possessions here in mind!"

"Tarnation," muttered Charlie. He hauled at his beard and looked unhappy. "I never thought on it like that," he confessed.

"None of us did, Mr. Martin!"

"And it ain't as easy as you think, Miss Gray. Getting ready to weigh anchor will take more'n one hour, more'n two."

Harriet stared at him, shaken. Then she whispered, "Oh, dear God." Had the head juryman deliberately delayed his call, to make certain that Jake would lose his brig? "Why?" she said desperately. "Why so long?"

Charlie did his best to tell her. The hours the men had spent on her theater, Harriet deduced at last, were hours they had not spent on keeping the brig in shipshape order. She shut her eyes as her mind whisked from possibility to eventuality to guess-work and devious scheme. Then she snapped, "Start now. Get the men together and do your best. I'll delay the deadline as long as I can."

Charlie's mouth was more agape than ever. "But how, Miss Gray?" he cried. She didn't wait to explain. Instead she ran pell-mell to the theater.

Mr. King, thank Providence, was still there. He was still awkward and inclined to hem and haw, however, and for some moments she thought desperately that he wouldn't pay attention. Then, when she threatened to resign her part, he did consent to lend an ear. "I took your signature as lawful only to humor your mood," he grumbled, and then declared that if she liked doing men's business so much, then he'd have to have a talk with her, on theater business matters. Then he looked scandalized when he heard what she asked. "Give away tickets to tonight's show free?" he cried. "But we ain't got no room, and it ain't good business! Why do you want to do something so plumb unwise sure bothers me, Miss Gray, and I sure don't know what your brother would say!"

Royal had nothing to say, for he was far too busy, and Harriet had no intention of telling Mr. King her very good reason for wanting the posse and the men of the jury safely installed in the theater while the *Hakluyt* men worked to get the brig under sail. "By this device," said she craftily, "word of Mrs. Marchant's undoubted talent will be spread as far as the upper Feather River!"

That clinched it. Mr. King grudgingly allowed her to order more benches squeezed into the auditorium and to give complimentary tickets to the men of the posse and the jury. "But we'll have that talk," he threatened.

"Tomorrow," said Harriet, crossing her fingers. She had no idea at all where she might be this time next day. Then she set off to give the tickets personally to each and every man; she didn't trust anyone else to do it. They were all in the taproom of Mr. King's partially built hotel, which made it easier than it might have been. The old man in the wig peevishly declared that it was a common device to avoid the apology that she owed him. Harriet agreed through clenched teeth, and then flew back to the theater.

Within an hour the auditorium was packed full. Harriet peeped through the curtain in an agony of suspense, and saw the posse and the jury take their places; none of them had turned down this chance of free entertainment. Mr. King was seated beneficently in the middle of his row of guests, as affable as if the idea had been his own. He was smoking a cigar and wearing a top hat. As Harriet watched the miner behind him knocked the hat off. She withdrew her head before the fight got properly started.

The whole crowd was restive, the atmosphere stifling: sweaty and rowdy and hot. Captain Jake Dexter had stayed away and had avoided his hanging, so all these men had been cheated of a spectacle. Now they demanded that the theater make up for this. There was an orchestra of five, hired at great expense by Mr. King, but their squeaking refrains could scarcely be heard, so loud was the commotion.

Was anyone left on the Embarcadero to watch Charlie and the *Hakluyt* men work desperately against time? Harriet fervently hoped not. Two hours, Charlie had said, at least two hours more. Harriet breathed slowly to still her trembling suspense, and listened to the impatient boots stamping on the floor planks as the audience, one and all, voiced their dissatisfaction with the delay.

Then, the curtain twitched. Harriet, as Malvina, took her place center stage. The curtain rose and billowed with the force of cheering and applauding. Then Jed, alias Royal, slouched in from the wings to join her, along with many improper suggestions from the pit.

> . . . *Malvina! Love!*
> *Fain would I place you in a loftier home! When first our flag*
> *Was reared in Mexico, that land of gold*
> *I touched on that wondrous coast, and there I must return*
> *To be made rich, with wealth untold, California gold!*

He recited his lines in a shout, and the whole audience, it seemed, went mad. The air was split and split again, with stamping, hollering, whistling. Surely, Harriet thought bemusedly, the bard himself had not received such rapturous acclaim. Then she saw the reason. Mrs. Marchant, as Malvina's grieving mother, had bounded prematurely onto the stage.

And the miners adored her. Here, without a doubt, was the Darling of her Admirers, the certain Rage of the Season. "Swamp it," said Royal, " 'tain't possible." But it was. Mrs. Marchant, visibly palpitating, curtsied like a cork in the ocean while every man stamped and roared. She kissed her hands, threw them out, and for quite five minutes it was impossible for the show to go on. Then, at last, she went, and the orchestra, sounding rather shaken, was able to start scraping again. Then, within four minutes, she was back.

"She's got fame all run to the brain," said Royal. He was highly disgusted; it was all part of the intemperate American character, he averred. Harriet did not mind in the slightest; the longer Mrs. Marchant delayed the progress of the play, the longer the *Hakluyt* men had to quit the Embarcadero. Harriet, as Malvina, and Royal, as Jed, were married, and Mrs. Marchant rushed about, threw herself into attitudes of alarm, wept noisily, had hysterics, all to ecstatic applause. Malvina and Jed set foot poetically on the deck of the ship that would bear them both to El Dorado, and still Mrs. Marchant insisted on hogging the stage. Thunder crashed, lightning flashed, sea splashed and waterspouts gushed, but still Mrs. Marchant ranted on.

> *Once more upon the land* [she cried]
> *O' er the appalling wilds of Panama*
> *That place of skulls, they took their pilgrim way!*

Then she fell to the floor, clasping Harriet about the knees, weeping, imploring her to repent and come home "a'fore 'tis too late, too late!" It was like some strange feverish nightmare. Never had a play progressed so slowly, never had time fled so fast.

Never had it taken Malvina so long to die, even in the most tedious rehearsals. And never had Harriet died in a part so perfunctorily. However, neither the miners nor Mrs. Marchant seemed to mind. Mrs. Marchant triumphantly took over most of the stage, and Harriet sneaked off through the wings, out the tiny back entrance, along the alley made by the fabric wall of the theater and the calico wall of the building next door, and to Front Street.

It was damp, and quiet; dark, and silent. In the distance dogs yapped. It was a sad and lonely noise, after the rowdy heat indoors. The river made no sound, flowing softly to the sea. Harriet's heart was in her mouth, and she stared at the dark, scared to blink unless she missed what was there.

Or not there. She heard an outbreak of stamping from the theater. She whirled and ran back to her position in the wings, ready to don a calico cover and hold a spermaceti candle to her chin, to act the entrancing specter. Even with the cloth over her head, the din the miners made was deafening. She felt alarm, the clappings became rhythmic, the stampings grew apace, Mrs. Marchant was bobbing and bowing, the miners all whistled, Harriet began to feel serious alarm for the building itself . . . and there came a series of creakings, and . . . *Thump!*

With an abrupt jolt the theater settled. The stage of a sudden was four inches higher than it had been before, but none of the audience seemed to care a whit. Mrs. Marchant didn't even seem to notice. She threw curtsies, and then with another *thump* an object fell on the stage.

It had been tossed by one of the audience. It was a purse; it was a wallet full of gold dust. It was immediately followed for four more of the same, and then all at once a hailstorm of nuggets. "My God," said Royal, and began to laugh. Then he said, "Harriet?"

She said nothing; she merely smiled wearily. She had arrived on the Embarcadero just in time.

Just in time to see the brig slip her cables and quietly steal off downriver.

Harriet slept in one of the boxlike single rooms of Mr. King's partially built hotel. Where Royal slept she had not a notion; in the theater, perhaps, she thought. Despite Mr. King's grand plans the hotel, like the theater, was mostly made of calico. Rats skittered about between the double layers of fabric behind her head all night, but Harriet nevertheless slept the stunned sleep of exhaustion.

She was awaked in the gray light of almost-dawn by a commotion in the street outside. Something was being delivered, she thought. She lay still, frowning. She recognized Mr. King's voice and Mrs. Marchant's shrill giggle. The other voices belonged to American men, one of them slightly familiar. When she heard them all go away she got up and dressed. Then she walked slowly along the calico corridor to the lobby.

The hotel despite its unfinished condition was full; the walls blew softly in and out to the tune of massed snoring. The lobby was also the billiard room and was empty of people. Then Harriet stopped short, brought to a frozen halt by the sight of the *thing* that had been delivered.

She said aloud, "Oh, dear God, who brought this?"

Mr. King came in from outside and beamed when he saw her. Mrs. Marchant was with him. They were wearing the same clothes they had worn the night before and did not look as if they had been to bed. They were both very bright-eyed and smelled most highly of champagne. Harriet scarcely looked at them; the most of her attention was on the thing before her. She said very carefully, "Where did . . . this come from?"

"Ah," said Mr. King, most affable. "A boat from the frigate *Savannah* delivered it; a Dr. Stirling bid me give it to you. 'Tis a coffin," said he helpfully.

"I know," said Harriet. The last time she had seen it the coffin had been propped in the pinnace, ready for the reception of Sefton's corpse.

" 'Tis yours, he said," said Mr. King. When he guffawed she could smell brandy as well as wine. Then, to Harriet's horror, he gripped the lid and began to haul. Harriet gasped, and Mrs. Marchant squealed, but he ignored them both. Instead he heaved. The lid was heavy, or perhaps screwed down, but then the metal began to creak . . .

"That Dr. Stirling," grunted he in conversational manner while his muscles and the metal creaked, "also bid me tell you 'tis a scandal—" and with a screech the lid jerked up, held in his powerful hands.

Harriet convulsively shut her eyes. Then she heard Mrs. Marchant giggle, so she opened them again. The coffin was empty. The dawn light bounced off its clean metal insides.

Harriet swallowed. Then she said in a miraculously steady voice, "What did he mean, *scandal*?"

"He said 'tis a scandal to have the bones of an unbaptized heathen Indian layin' in a grave what is supposed to be that of a prominent Philadelphia citizen. He said to tell you 'twas the wrong body, and that he was scandalized about it."

Wrong . . . wrong body. Time stopped still. Harriet stared at Mr. King, her entire body rigid. The wrong body. Not Sefton . . . and Mei-mei, in that grave, but not with Sefton. Mei-mei. Ah Wong, the first day here in Sacramento City, Ah Wong, shouting, beseeching, pleading with her to run away.

Ah Wong. *She had to find Ah Wong* . . . she had to find Ah Wong and clear Jake's name . . . she had to find Ah Wong, for she knew now who had killed Don Roberto. Then, as if from a great distance, she heard Mr. King's voice say, "That business."

"What?"

"You promised to talk. I've drawn up the paper, all I need is a price and your lawful signature."

Then he shoved a paper under her nose. Harriet stared at it. It was impossible to think. Then he rattled it irritably and shouted, "Name a price, Miss Gray, jest name it!"

So she did. She said the first figure that ran into her mind. Ah Wong, she thought fiercely, Ah Wong, he had to be still at the barracks.

Everything was beginning to make sense, dreadful sense. Then, bemusedly, Harriet found the paper under her nose again. Mr. King had written in the number; she had to be told several times where to sign her name. She didn't bother to read it; it was like watching some remote drama that had nothing to do with Harriet Gray. Then she heard Mr. King say jovially, "Wa-al, what you goin' to do with it?"

"I . . . I beg your pardon?"

"The coffin, Miss Gray, the coffin! Quite a thing," he remarked right merrily. "A coffin, all of your own, to keep in case of emergency, huh?"

Then he began to guffaw, slapping his thigh in time to his mirth. Harriet was shaking her head, trying to think. The situation had all the clarity and insanity of delirium. She said wildly, "You can have it."

"What?"

"Take the coffin, do. Consider it yours, sir."

"But what the tarnation would I do with the thing?"

"Install it upstairs, in your best bathroom; it'll be the first long bath in California, Mr. King!" Long enough for a man to stretch his bones, she thought, and winced. Mr. King was staring at the coffin, seeming most thoughtful, and Harriet looked at the door and walked away from him. She walked out of the room, out the door, out along Front Street. Front Street was about deserted, not quite roused by dawn yet. Mr. King did not follow her; no doubt he was contemplating his new possession. When Harriet got onto the path that led to the barracks past the fort she began to run. The most if not all of the coolies would be out of the barracks and busy in the various kitchens of Sacramento City; this was the best time possible to find Ah Wong, winkle him out, soothe his fears, reassure him, persuade him to testify to the men of the posse and the jury.

Still she ran. Her breathing was harsh in her chest, her throat sore and dry with her panting, and she had a sharp pain in her side. Nevertheless, she ran. Then she saw the men . . . the horses. They made a small cavalcade, coming slowly down the slope behind the barracks, coming in from the foothills. Her sight was blurred, but she could see them . . . one, two men on horseback, a man on a mule, an Indian on a third horse, leading a fourth horse by the rein.

Harriet ran stumblingly, beginning to weave from side to side. Then she recognized the men: Tib, Dan, Mr. Giles on his mule . . . the Indian. The fourth horse was carrying the body of a man, a man who lay across the saddle facedown. Arms and legs dangled; the man, unmistakably, was dead.

It had to be Jake. Harriet cried, "No . . . oh no." Still she ran. She ran past the high fence of the corral and saw the well and the bear in blurred glimpses, jerkily through her tears and the palings. Then she ran into the empty barracks and

screamed, "Ah Wong, Ah Wong, come out, Ah Wong, I know
you are here!"

The first big room of the barracks was empty, except for the
pine tables and the tiers of berths. She ran stumblingly and
knocked her hip against the first table, crying, "Ah
Wong . . . please . . ." She saw a man come toward her.
"Tell me, where is Ah Wong?" Her sight cleared, and she saw
the man properly.

It was Joaquin Murieta. She stopped, frozen, and stared at
him. He was holding a knife, a big knife. It had a shiny blade,
very sharp, but her throat was too frozen to scream. He
laughed . . . he *laughed*. The sound gave her the strength of
fury. She whirled, taking him by surprise, and ran into the next
big room, slammed the door and looked around wildly for a
table to wedge against it. She was breathing fast, the sound
filling her ears, panting too raggedly to call for Ah Wong.

And Frank Sefton walked through another door and into the
room.

Harriet stilled, utterly. Frank Sefton looked the same as
always. He was wearing a silk shirt and brown riding clothes;
he was carrying a whip. He had been out riding . . . riding.
She thought of the body on the fourth horse, and said numbly,
"Where is Ah Wong."

"Dead, my dear Harriet, several weeks dead."

She said, "Oh, dear God." Then, viciously, with loathing
inside her, she yelled, "You killed him—poor little Ah
Wong—*you killed him*."

"No, no, you killed him yourself, my dear. You killed him
when you came to Sacramento City. You killed them all, for
when you came I found that they had all lied to me. I had
ordered that you be killed, that your body be put into the bed
before the house was set afire, to give verisimilitude to the
other body beside yours, to fool everyone, my dear, that I was
dead . . . and they failed me. They lied! Ah Wong helped
you escape, dear Harriet, so *you* killed him, my dear."

She said with horror, "You're mad." His eyes were red, she
saw, bloodshot with eternal rage.

" 'Twas Ah Wong who was mad, dear Harriet. He helped
you escape, he cheated me, he lied to me, he killed his own
daughter so that I would never know that you still lived, and
put her body in your bed."

Mei-mei . . . Ah Wong's daughter? It was impossible, Ah
Wong had been only thirty-two years old. Mei-mei must have

been . . . how old? Sefton had enjoyed despoiling innocence, Harriet remembered, and she felt sick. She said bitterly,
"I thought you had insisted on giving me the shares in your
bank to leave me the scapegoat, as you did in New Zealand,
Frank. I was wrong. You gave me the exact worth of twenty
thousand to give you the pseudolegal means to steal the
Hakluyt gold. How you must have enjoyed that evil jest! Then
you took the gold and ran—or Don Roberto took the gold and
ran. Where is the gold now, Frank, in Mexico, all spent—or is
most of it stashed somewhere here?"

She stared at him, but he said nothing. The red eyes were
unblinking, as intent as the stare of a hunting lizard. Only his
hands moved, drawing out the thong of the whip, letting the
end drop, drawing it out again.

She said, "Then Don Roberto thought it was safe to return to
California; you'd had plenty of time to quit clear with your
share of the loot. But he was wrong. You were hidden here, in
these barracks, why? All these Chinese coolies, they sheltered
you, why? Did you bring all these coolies to California, Frank?
Why, I believe you did. But why did you stop here, why didn't
you leave?"

Then she remembered, the items clicking one by one into her
mind, making sense, making a pattern. "Captain Mervine—he
was here, searching every vessel for deserters and their gold.
He arrested your crew; what foul luck! What a scare it must
have put into you; what evil luck you had, you evil man.
Mervine stayed, and then I came, and you realized how your
fellow conspirators had lied to you. Poor Ah Wong, you killed
him, but you were helpless to do anything else . . . until
Joaquin Murieta arrived and Captain Mervine left. Such
frustration, such thwarted rage; no wonder your sanity broke!"

"It did not!" he screamed. It was as if a pent-up flood of bile
had been released. His whip lashed out, stinging her face. She
cried out and jumped back. He laughed when he saw her fear,
and cracked the lash again. The whip was long, thin, and
plaited, Californian style. He had no other weapon; the whip
was enough.

She kept on backing away from him, and Sefton walked
forward, one step at a time. Behind her were the winding stairs
that led to the balcony; behind him, the room with Joaquin
Murieta; and the door to the side through which he'd come in.
She was forced to retreat to the stairs, the flight of stairs that

corkscrewed within the corner bastion and then came up where the balcony overlooked the corral and the bear.

There, she would be trapped, but she could scream. She shrieked, projecting her voice to reach the man who waited in the other room, "Joaquin Murieta, listen to me; Joaquin Murieta, this man shot your kin, he followed them and shot them down like dogs! Listen to me, Joaquin Murieta, for I speak the truth!"

The whip cracked. Frank Sefton snarled, "Bitch." The end of the lash touched her shoulder in a fiery strand of clean sharp pain. She screamed again, "Listen, Joaquin Murieta!" and then she turned and ran, up and up the stairs, round and round in dizzying circles while Sefton advanced step by step, keeping pace with her frantic flight. Breath sobbed in her ears; she knew with ghastly clarity exactly what would happen, in nightmarish progression: her dizzy stumbling exit onto the balcony, tripping, falling, perhaps pushed, falling . . . the bear, the roar, the gnashing jaws, no mark or shot on her to tell the world that she had been murdered by Frank Sefton, who was innocent, had to be, for Frank Sefton was dead and buried.

She lurched out onto the balcony, sobbing, stumbling, sick with dizziness, lurched toward the rail, utterly helpless to stop her momentum—and Jake Dexter caught her in his arms.

She gasped. It was impossible, the impossible had happened. She shivered wildly; she touched him all over, Jake, her love, Jake, warm, tough, Jake, alive. She gasped, "Oh, dear God, I thought you were dead." Then, violently: "Sefton! Sefton is alive!"

"I know," said he gently, and Sefton ran out onto the balcony.

For an instant Harriet thought Sefton would topple, in the death he had planned for herself. But he stopped. He stopped in the doorway. There had been no danger of Frank Sefton toppling. He had merely come to see if a last push were necessary. His mouth was open a little, like a half-open rosebud. The red eyes glared. He stopped and looked at Jake.

He said in a loud demanding voice, "Harriet, my dear, who is this man?" She stared at him with a horror that was almost pitying, for he sounded so very insane. "He'll have to die, you know," he said in that awful polite hectoring voice. "You are overimpetuous, my dear Harriet. You cause too many deaths, for it must not be known that I am still alive! Everyone must believe that I am dead . . . or how else will I ever retrieve my gold? I'm dead, I say, I'm dead!"

"Then you shouldn't leave your cigarettos about so freely," Jake said grimly, "where men who know you can recognize your traces." Cigarettos? Harriet stared from one man to the other, bewildered, and then thought, yes, Mrs. Giles knew that Sefton affected the womanish habit. Mr. Giles was on the path below, looking up, still seated on his mule. It was like a tableau. Tib and Dan, on their horses, were farther up the path. The Indian was closer, and the body was on the ground, lying face up as if for identification. Harriet took one glance and then had to look away, swallowing sickness. The dead man was Davy, poor Davy, dead and gone and much decayed. Then she heard Joaquin Murieta scream, "Sefton!"

Her heart clenched. Then she looked. Joaquin Murieta stood on the path straddle-legged, near to the corpse, and he looked up at the balcony as he screamed. It was a shriek, the wild shriek of vendetta. The scream put chills up her neck, and she felt Jake's arm tighten.

Then she saw Sefton move to the rail and look down. He seemed unmoved, if indeed he could see what sane men could see. He said crossly, "Shut up, you fool, no one must suspect that I am not dead."

Instead Joaquin Murieta shouted. "This man is the black man, the one you told me shot my brothers; this black man has been dead a long time, Sefton; this black man died a long time, yes, in a gully not two miles from here. She was right, the gray filly, it was you, you who murdered my kin!"

Joaquin Murieta was shouting in Spanish. Sefton shouted in English, "I told you to shut your mouth!" Then he moved. Harriet flinched and felt Jake shift to shield her. However, Sefton merely whirled and ran angrily down the winding stairs. She could hear the furious clatter of his riding boots go round and round and then fade with distance. Then he came into sight, on the path below. He was slapping the air with his whip, irritably. He snapped, "I'll teach you to be quiet, Murieta." Then he was looking around and did not appear even to see Mr. Giles, Tib and Dan, the Indian. Harriet could see more men in the distance, coming from the fort, drawn by the commotion.

Sefton said in English. "You have to get me away from here. I will get the gold, and then we will go. It is well hidden; I hid it myself, in the night when my men had been arrested. I had to bring it up from the schooner alone, with naught but my

Chinese servant and a mule. Now all we have to do is shoot the bear. You must help me."

"Yes," said Joaquin. His voice was strange, and he still spoke in Spanish. "I will help you, yes . . . to leave." Then he stepped forward. He had the knife raised in his hand. Sefton frowned, and as Joaquin stepped closer he stepped back, and cracked the whip. He lashed it out with all his strength. Harriet heard the crackling sound, but the South American did not flinch. Instead he lifted a hand and snatched the end, and then, contemptuously, he flicked the whip out of Sefton's hand.

Then he threw it away. He said, "And now, you die." Then he grasped Sefton by the shoulder and pushed him down until he knelt in the dirt.

Harriet stood rigid, transfixed with horror. She saw the men in the distance point, heard them call out, and saw them run, but Tib and Dan and Mr. Giles seemed as immovable as the Indian. Jake stood as frozen as she; it was like some kind of ritual, too old and feudal to comprehend fully. It was impossible to move, and almost impossible to breathe.

Then Sefton began to wine with terror. *He groveled.* The sun was rising. The shaft of first light hit the blade of the knife as Joaquin Murieta held it poised. Sefton cried, "Spare me . . . spare me, help me, and the gold is all yours. All the others are dead, I made sure of that. They won't cheat again or take what is mine, 'tis well hidden, according to a puzzle, a puzzle in an old journal. No one could solve that puzzle save I, please . . ."

Joaquin Murieta waited, his attitude one of merciless scorn. The men from the fort were running up the path; Harriet recognized the men of the posse, the jurymen, and cried, "Oh, please, stop him!"

Instead, the men stopped only to stare. Sefton was silent. He looked about; she saw him look his last on the hills, the sky   and the knife plunged.

Jake said, "Oh, Christ." When the body slumped Joaquin put his boot on it, pressing it as a butcher presses the blood from a slaughtered sheep. Harriet shut her eyes, fighting sickness. Then she saw Joaquin Murieta take the horse that had carried Davy's body, setting his foot in the stirrup. The posse had begun to move again . . . and Jake stood beside her; she heard them call out his name. She shouted to Joaquin, "Tell them that Captain Dexter did not kill the alcalde!"

Joaquin stopped. He looked all around and then up. "He did

not," he said contemptuously. "And your husband, yes, was a coward."

He had spoken in English. Then he galloped away. The posse all stopped. No one tried to catch him.

Instead they took Jake and held another trial. It took ten minutes for the jury to declare that Joaquin Murieta, certainly, had killed Don Roberto. Had he? Harriet wondered . . . felt certain it had been Frank Sefton instead. But it did not matter, for Jake Dexter was acquitted. Then everyone walked to the corral where the bear had been held.

The bear was gone. Everyone had talked for weeks of shooting the bear, but when they actually looked like doing it the two mountainmen had come out of nowhere and taken the bear away. They walked into the corral and put a leash on the bear and led him out, just like that; it was another amazement.

Harriet held Jake's arm as she walked, luxuriating in the feel of him, his warmth, his scent, the way he strode, so strongly, the fact that he breathed, that they both of them lived. She said, "How long were you up on the balcony?"

"I'd only just arrived." He had gone by the second stair, via the long upper-story room. "We found the cigarettos near Davy's corpse, and I remembered that I'd seen the same evidence at the place where the murderer had shot the Murietas. Giles recognized them, and as soon as I realized that Sefton still lived, the place where he hid was obvious. Why else would Ah Wong have begged you to run away? I'd had this gut feeling all along that you were in danger; somehow I sensed that Sefton watched you."

She said, "Yes," and shivered. She thought of all the times she'd walked this path, always with an escort, for Jake had made sure of that. All those evenings she had sat at her window in the fort, and gazed at this very scene . . .

Jake stopped. She stopped too, and looked around. They were by the corral, now empty of bear. He said, "And you think you know where Sefton hid the gold?"

"I'm guessing. I'm guessing he was talking about old Rochester's book when he talked about the journal with the puzzle."

"What?" Then Jake laughed. "You think you've solved the puzzle?"

"Yes. I solved it a long time ago. While you were hunting for gold in Bedstead Gully, I was hunting for gold on Judas Island."

Everyone clustered around; she had an audience even Mrs. Marchant would have envied. She said, "The well."

"The . . . what?"

"The well. Remember the map, and the letters *L A S*? Under the *S*, there is a drawing of a bear. All the other animals were put there for distraction, to take attention away from the bear. And remember old Rochester's French . . . and his puns? The French for bear is *ours*, and if you add *ours* to *L A S* you get l-a-s-o-u-r-s, which is a pun for *la source*, the well."

"Jehovah," said Jake. Then he roared with laughter. "You think Sefton labored mightily to hide his gold, that he threw it down the well for safekeeping, and then two mountainmen wandered along and put a bear into the corral to keep the gold company?"

"Who can tell?" said Harriet, wondering. She hadn't thought of this most wry aspect of the business before. "Perhaps it was part of Sefton's awful luck, or perhaps he paid the men to put the bear in the corral."

It was impossible to prove . . . but easy to prove that the gold was in the well. A boy was lowered on a rope, and within two minutes a cry of *EUREKA-A-A!* echoed up the chimney. Then the boy came up, and so, in due course, did the gold. The brig arrived back at the Embarcadero just in time for the *Hakluyt* men to welcome rapturously their twenty thousand dollars worth of gold, still in parfleches just the way the Murietas had bagged it, marked with the names of the owners in dispute, just the way Don Roberto had marked them.

Oh-h-h! [sang Royal] *The gold, they say*
Is brighter than the day
And when 'tis mine, oh won't I shine,
And sing dull care away, oh!

"Do you think," said he, "that the well on Judas Island will yield such a rich abundance?"

Harriet smiled at Jake; she had thought about it often. "Why don't we go and see?" said she demurely.

"But what about your theater, madam?"

"Oh," she said, and was rather afraid she was blushing. "I sold it," she confessed. "On behalf of the *Hakluyt* Company."

"You . . . what?" cried Royal.

"I sold it. To Mr. King. He insisted. It was part of the bargain I made when I asked him for free tickets for the posse and the jury. Mrs. Marchant, you see," she said to Jake, "is the Rage of the Season, and no doubt about it. Mr. King is certain that she'll make his fortune, if only he owns the theater in which she performs."

"He could well be right," said Royal gloomily.

"Why," said Jake, "are you angry?"

"Never that, Captain, never! In fact," said Royal eloquently, "I am at last convinced that there is truly a divine Providence, for I have been saved from sharing the planks for a season at least with the most awful ham I have ever encountered." Then he said, "How much?" Harriet blinked, to find every man's eyes on her.

She looked around and was rather afraid that she was blushing, again. She said guiltily, "One hundred and ten thousand."

"What!" Then Jake roared, "You rogue, you beautiful rogue!"

"I think I could have got more, if I'd bargained, but I . . . didn't have the time to dicker."

"What next?" said Jake, and shook his head.

"Well, as a matter of fact . . ." said Royal, looking pensive. "I've been talking to a man, with the latest reports from New Zealand. Did you know," he said with animation, "that the colonists from New Zealand and New South Wales are all attention for this gold rush too? They are trying to come in their hundreds, and the authorities at San Francisco are all of a dither about it; they swear and declare that a colonial influx from those regions will corrupt California forever, and captains are making huge profits out of smuggling these unwanted aliens into the territory!"

"Jehovah," said Jake blankly. "You don't suggest we go in for such trade?"

"Good God, no! My scheme is much more exciting and profitable. In New Zealand," said Royal in conspiratorial tones, "there is a certain class of wealthy colonist who hankers after the ancient sport of deer hunting. They have got all together, to devise a wonderful reward, a rich reward indeed . . . to any men who manage to establish a breeding colony of deer in the forests of New Zealand . . ."

"And here we go again," said Jake.

ABOUT THE AUTHOR

Joan Druett is the prize-winning author of the non-fiction works *Exotic Intruders* and *Fulbright in New Zealand*. Her first novel, *Abigail*, also published by Bantam, drew on her expert knowledge of the old whaling days to tell the story of an extraordinary and captivating heroine.

A much-travelled New Zealander, she lives in Hamilton, a city in the North Island of that country. Her husband, Ron Druett, is a full-time marine artist whose works are permanently on display in the Maritime Gallery of Mystic Seaport, Connecticut. At present he is working on the illustrations for Joan's non-fiction account of the wives who went a-whaling, *Petticoat Whalers*.

Joan Druett has also edited the journals kept by one of the whaling women, Mary Brewster of Stonington, Connecticut, and is the author of a number of scholarly articles on the subject. She is a regular contributor to *Pacific Way*, the inflight magazine of Air New Zealand, and is presently at work on a third novel, *Night's Swift Dragons*, which is set in Boston, Marblehead, Salem and the South China Sea in the early nineteenth century.

THE UNFORGETTABLE NOVELS
by
CELESTE DE BLASIS
